CW00858376

Previous Publications by Arthur Byrd:

What the River Wants

CROSSING LAKE PONTCHARTRAIN

ARTHUR BYRD

CROSSING LAKE PONTCHARTRAIN

This is a work of fiction. All of the characters, names, incidents, organizations, and dialogue in this novel are either the products of the author's imagination or are used fictitiously.

iUniverse books may be ordered through booksellers or by contacting:

iUniverse
1663 Liberty Drive
Bloomington, IN 47403
www.iuniverse.com
844-349-9409

ISBN: 978-1-6632-4606-6 (sc)
ISBN: 978-1-6632-4608-0 (hc)
ISBN: 978-1-6632-4607-3 (e)

Library of Congress Control Number: 2022917889

Print information available on the last page.

iUniverse rev. date: 06/20/2023

For Pat and Davie

"Which of us has known his brother? Which of us has looked into his father's heart? Which of us has not remained forever prison-pent? Which of us is not forever a stranger and alone? . . .

O lost, and by the wind grieved, ghost, come back again."

Look Homeward, Angel
Thomas Wolfe

Acknowledgments

I want to thank my dear wife, Sally, for patiently enduring my reclusive work. Her brilliance and spiritual core inspire me every day. My best friend, and daily companion of choice.

Special gratitude to my editor, Avalon Radys, who helped me find a path through this wilderness of words. As well, much appreciation to David Goodman for insights about New Orleans and to James Lubas for yet another author photo.

And finally, to my departed parents, Rubye, and Arthur Jr., deep appreciation for providing me the youthful latitude to make mistakes and flounder with responsibility even before I was ready. Now that I'm a parent, I see now how difficult it is both to hold on and get out of the way all at the same time.

PART ONE

HATTIESBURG, MISSISSIPPI, 2013

"Every life is in many days, day after day. We walk through ourselves, meeting robbers, ghosts, giants, old men, young widows, brothers-in-love, but always meeting ourselves."

Ulysses
James Joyce

Chapter 1

Hours of silence hatched the noise of urgency. A pleasant Saturday watching baseball without my wife around would soon become a performance of pretense at her friend's party, where surely four years of my unemployment would be a reliable conversation starter.

With a swoop of my jacket, I slammed the door with accomplishment, but there it was, as always, the loose post at the end of the front porch. Three steps later, I leveled my best suburban karate kick, leaving the desultory pole dangling over the edge, clinging to the ceiling but without purpose. For my wifely status report, I had indeed addressed a home repair project.

The dry leaves of September reminded me of camping with Dad, back when he existed, and I so wanted to drift into those lost weekends. But searching through memory reruns had to wait as I was off to the christening of a nouveau riche mansion. My Saab dashboard clock glared 4:08, already an hour late. Janine would be mad, but I needed to pull into the Good Stuff convenience store for a Barq's root beer. The fifteen bucks she gave me for gas turned into eight dollars and a brisket panini, Ray Curry's smoker delicacies again too bewitching to resist.

A few back roads, then my last Newport before the long driveway up the highest hill within ten miles. Near the top, a switchback slowed me when a black poodle darted from behind a row of azaleas tucked into the steep drop-off. A skid saved his hide, but when I pushed the accelerator, my tires spun on the gravel surface. Car in neutral, drifting slowly backward, I punched into first gear, leaving the fake wood housing around the shifter cracked from front to back.

"Crap," I said, then spit my gum out the window and prayed for at least one good tread.

Up top at the far end of the circular drive, a BMW backed out, so I pulled into the slot, hoping the leaping concrete porpoises in the driveway fountain had camouflaged my entrance. The delusion melted as a perfect crowd gathered. Surely, I'd impressed the onlookers with my skillful driving, especially my six-foot-six host, Eric.

"Nice job there, Winstead; that last push to the peak is deadly, isn't it? Tell me, did you have to use oxygen, or did you just suck up the thin air? I bet you just sucked, right?" I stared into the distance, pretending not to hear, my trustworthy sarcasm apparently left at home.

From behind the porpoises, Janine flushed a pale smile, and before I could speak, she announced, "Larry has two good job prospects lined up, management jobs; isn't that great, Eric?" My God, if only I'd brought a cyanide tablet.

He looked at Janine as if she'd ordered a double laxative on the rocks and then almost seemed to acknowledge his rudeness, but instincts were stronger than civility.

"Well, well, that's good news, Larr; the little woman seems proud. And I didn't even know Taco Bonanza was hiring. Heck, with your driving skills, you got home delivery all to yourself."

This moment is why people should not carry hand grenades to parties because I'm fairly sure I would have hurled one at Thor. But the crowd parted as if someone had broken a bottle of red wine, then Eric seized me by the neck. "Only kidding there, sport. You know that."

The thought flashed to kick him where his primary brain sags, but Janine's bloodless expression insinuated restraint. Then she disappeared into the crowd. Talk about alone—even the gossipers had rushed for cover while Janine sought asylum in the ladies' room. Not even the dog wanted a sniff.

My lifelong skill at faking the truth had mysteriously disappeared, so to avoid the isolation of arrival, I plowed through the crowd, making loops through different rooms, trying to lose among the chandeliers and marble floors my trailing scent of sobriety. Washing my face helped, then I melded into the swarm of people guzzling tequila shots from a line of silver platters atop a white piano. At last, I didn't feel different, so I focused on my excellent new idea of how a roadkill skunk might end up floating in Eric's pool.

After an hour, Janine and I couldn't avoid each other any longer, and at the dessert station, we shared stares of survival. A language of wedded indifference carried us through cheesecake and strawberries, and as the sun burned down, we inched towards the car, skulking behind a Gatsby cluster all leaving together. Clara, Janine's old high school friend and hostess, was not fooled.

"Oh, Larry, hold up a moment, please. I want to thank you for coming. I realize you don't know many people here, but I appreciate your making the effort. We all adore Janine so; it's nice to see she has such a loving husband to support her." My eyes rolled back as the tequila continued pickling my brainstem, but resident charm seized control.

"No problem, Clar, enjoyed the hospitality. Your husband already made me feel quite special." Those words slipped from my mouth accidentally as I thought I was only talking to myself, but with rescuer's response, Janine intruded between her friend and me.

"Yes, about that," Clara said. "I heard Eric, and I want to apologize; he'd had a little too much margarita, I'm afraid. You understand he was only kidding. He's a super-kind person, and at the country club, he gives the caddies the biggest tips." Words seemed to fail her as she lost momentum in mid-thought, her eyes studying the loose stones of the driveway.

Unfortunately, my brain wasn't in full communication with my mouth, which in the absence of restraint, made a run for freedom. So, I sidestepped Janine's protection, then offered one last note of appreciation: "Sure, Clar, no problem. Maybe next Saturday I can lug his clubs around; you know, earn a few bucks myself. . ."

Janine jousted me towards the car, and I heard a blur of "thanks" and "see you soon" as I slid into the front passenger seat. The stuffy air almost made me gag before I cracked the window enough to catch a little breeze, but regretfully also to hear Janine's last words to Clara.

"Oh, it's Larry. He drinks too much. . ." I looked to see if Janine would offer me a glance. She did, a laser shot from emblazoned blue eyes, a would-be terminator unmasked in Hattiesburg. I'd only come to show her friends how I was changing my life, and yet something predictable had occurred. I rolled up the window, not wanting to hear my life anymore.

The thud of distant music hammered, and without warning, an image of my grandfather popped into my head. He'd dropped by the house on my sixteenth birthday to give me his old shotgun, and there in his left eye was a peering void I'd not seen before, a darkness that scared me, though I wasn't sure why. Two weeks later, he died without warning. Today, Janine's empty stare brought back that kindred knowledge of having looked through the pane shielding one life from another, encasing the secret dark matter of separateness. That glare penetrated me, searching for those unspoken things I'd meant to tell her but didn't, those withholdings I'd postponed without realizing.

The drive home quivered in the escapist blur of alcohol, but I'd glimpsed Janine's secret. Farms slipped past as dim forms, silhouettes languishing without sun, mildly aware of approaching winter; and through the Mississippi countryside, my wife and I traveled into the dusk of separated silence, alone, yet not.

Violence awaited me. Not puerile hitting or pushing—oh, if only. The lid to a long-sealed vault had shifted on the day's blunder, releasing within me a highly charged imbalance to merge with Janine's fury. Now, vintage stores of abandonment began surging upward, that hopelessness from my dad's unexplained disappearance two decades earlier mindlessly uncorked in the icy celebration of a failing marriage. And on the horizon, a dying star struggled to hold its heat.

Chapter 2

For the next few days, I lived in a walk-in freezer. Janine visited each night, then left in the morning as early as possible after sharing a few gutturals about "supermarket" or "credit card bill." Days passed with only an occasional call from my mom or that nice lady selling attic insulation, but mostly life consisted of my guitar, books, and the sound of ubiquitous nothing.

On Thursday morning, Janine announced she would attend another dance class after work. She'd been going on Tuesdays for a couple of months but got a price break for lessons twice a week. We couldn't afford the luxury since my job at Blockbuster ended so suddenly. But working as a paralegal for a shyster attorney, she deserved some reward; besides, I figured the house could heat up easier with her coming home later.

At least I didn't have to defend myself against the muffled wrath of a forty-year-old woman embarrassed in front of her high school friends. Instead, I drifted without wrestling pretense or rationalizing excuses that never got spoken. Oddly, her mother, Eleanor, became warmer toward me, though our past relationship had always been strained.

"No, Janine's not home right now. She usually gets back from dance around eight. Do you want her to call?"

"Dance class? I thought she went on Tuesdays."

"She does, but now she goes twice a week."

"Oh, I see. Funny, she didn't mention that. Well, I'll talk to her tomorrow. I wanted to invite you two to a barbecue lunch Saturday. Can you make it?"

"I guess so. I'll check with Janine. We're still getting over our last buffet."

It would have been the perfect time to make up a story and get out of the whole thing, but I didn't want anything to antagonize Janine. Eleanor annoyed me wanting to know every detail about our lives as if it mattered a twit if Janine took two dance classes a week or one, but those were the only words I'd spoken all day, and it felt good to hear a pleasant voice not trying to sell me something.

"Okay, Larry. Good night, love. Hope to see you. I always enjoy how funny you are."

The unexpected compliment quickened my heartrate, but I couldn't remember ever saying anything humorous to her. Over the years, Eleanor and I had endured our challenges, especially over her habit of drilling into meaningless personal information, but I eventually realized she does the same thing to everyone. But that comment, "Funny, she didn't mention that to me," unsettled me, though I wasn't sure why.

At seven-thirty, I thought to start dinner and have the house smell homey for Janine. Every day I tried to do something pleasant, even though she ignored the effort, but my theory was that with a little normality, time erodes memory. Perhaps not compatible with my planned new diet, I cooked biscuits and redeye gravy hoping the smell would melt a little of Janine's harshness. Before long, the place reminded me of Pete's Corner, the home cooking café where we used to eat family-style. I sure missed his banana pudding.

Biscuits done; a worry rippled up my neck. Janine had never been later than nine. Maybe the car broke down, so I called her cell—only voicemail. I was sure she'd forgotten to power up after class. Or had she told me she needed to stop by the store?

Fifteen minutes passed, then I heaped up a plate with three biscuits as a levee to make sure nothing leaked out. The cayenne peppers from the garden were about finished this season, so I'd picked a whole handful, and for the first time that day, I tried not to think.

An hour passed, and after peeking out the curtain for the thousandth time, I called Eleanor. No, she hadn't heard from Janine. I began pacing, peeking out every window, checking to see that the phone was on the hook, looking for a note that might have gotten covered up. Nothing.

6

I didn't even know the name of the dance studio, and minutes jogged arthritic laps.

Finally, the phone rang: an urgent message to vote yes on the middle school bond issue. Why couldn't they call in the daylight when I had time to chat? For the tenth time, I tried Janine's cell, but her mailbox was full.

At just after eleven, car lights glared through the den windows, and the old muffler rattled of weariness. My heart thudded, the blood swishing through the arteries in my neck sounded like rain. It was hard to control my emotions as rage wrestled with the realization that Janine was safe. Steady breathing, in and out—Janine's yoga tapes had taught me this, and I readied myself.

The door tweaked open as if she thought I might be asleep. I waited in the hallway with only the stove light dimly illuminating that part of the house.

"Oh, hey," she said. "Didn't see you standing there. Scared me." I didn't respond. "Good, I smell biscuits." Her friendly tone was effective, but my irascible self was in no mood to be pleasant.

"Yeah, four hours ago."

"Oh, about that, a couple of us got together after class, talking you know, and the time got by me. We stopped and had a drink and listened to some music."

"Drinks and music, huh," I said. "It didn't occur to you to give me a call? You didn't think I might be worried about that piece of junk car we drive?"

"Well, no," Janine rolled out her words as if calculating effect. "Really, I didn't think about it, and you didn't call. Besides, we took somebody else's car, so it was okay."

"I called twenty times. Who were you with?"

"Some people from class. Nobody you know." Then she turned her back to me.

"Well, maybe I should get to know them if you're going to stay out till midnight drinking without even bothering to let me know."

"It's not midnight; it's only eleven-thirty, and I'm tired. I'm going to take a shower and go to bed. We can talk in the morning."

"No. We're talking right now. I've been pacing around this house like a tiger in a shoebox. Good God, Janine, I was worried sick, and you act like it doesn't even matter."

"Larry, be reasonable. You can see I'm right here. There's no reason to worry."

"Something's not right. You did something, didn't you?"

"Of course not. I told you we had a glass of wine and talked, that's all." Her sideways glance reeked of a sneer.

"Who went with you?"

"People from the class, Kathy, Toni, and Bill."

"Whose car?"

"Well, I rode in Bill's, if that matters. Good grief, you sound like my mother."

"Oh, it was you and another man in his car, and you think I'm overreacting?"

"Well, you make it sound worse than it was. Bill is going through a divorce and needs somebody to talk to, that's all. I've got my own problems these days, so it seemed like we could support each other."

I stepped forward. "Have you ever been out to drinks or lunch or walks or anything else with this guy?"

"I'm tired of this inquisition and I'm going to bed," Janine said. "I don't need your paranoia. You can't stand that I had a little fun tonight while you sat here moping around like a has-been." The slamming bedroom door emptied the house. Only crickets outside breathed as they spread the word of a new ice age begun.

"I would have gone, too, if you'd asked me." Directed at the closed door, the words dribbled unheard and punctuated only by the cooling pop from the muffler groaning in the driveway.

Chapter 3

The following week, Janine committed to her oath of silence. She didn't even consider going to her mother's barbecue, and our marriage deflated into shrunken unwillingness. The first night, I slept on the couch, but then decided I wasn't at fault. The following night, I crawled into bed late. Janine hardly noticed, balled up like a squirrel on the end of an oak limb in winter.

Stumbling sleep led to an odd dream. I'd pulled into an oceanfront fish market, like the big one I'd seen in Seattle years earlier. Approaching a knife-sharpening shop, I realized I was carrying the cheap machete I'd bought a long time ago in Jamaica.

"How much to sharpen it?" I asked.

"Oh, about nine dollars."

"Could you fix the missing rivet in the handle?"

"Shore, no problem." The man stared at me with a funny grin, as if he'd thought of something clever but wasn't sure whether to say it, then he spoke up. "These flimsy knives are like husbands—sometimes they're easier to replace than fix."

Screaming blue jays erased the rest of the dream, then I slipped into the den to sit in the toilet-roll colored light. Janine had left a newspaper next to my coffee cup, a job ad circled. Subtle. Our local Walmart was remodeling and needed temp workers for restocking. My first reaction was embarrassment, but I decided to ride my bike over and apply.

Days blurred as I assembled metal shelving, punctuating each commute with motivational tapes blaring through my headphones. Yes, doing, not thinking, changes lives. Each trip, I pedaled faster.

Janine orbited in a separate solar system, rarely home. On Tuesday evening, I drug out my half-finished novel, "Depleted," now in its second decade of entropy. The stiff language reminded me of insurance paperwork. Transcribing the hand-written words into my computer, I deleted huge chunks even as my fingers dabbled bloats of hack science fiction overwriting.

After a puffy nine pages, I moved to my favorite thinking chair where Pabst often served as the backspace key on my life. There, 1992, Linda, the sophomore I dated who told me about the new creative writing institute the university was launching the following fall. She'd gushed about the professor from the Iowa Writer's Workshop, so I borrowed her dream of an MFA from Iowa, my preamble to writing the great American Gen X novel of indifference and rebellion.

Linda insisted my short stories oozed poetic rhythm, and I learned to crave the drip of her cherry lipstick after it first leaked down the back of my throat.

Da ring, da ring. The kitchen phone shattered my trance, though a new quote for vinyl siding did seem like a good idea.

Awkward roommate avoidance became protocol until a late October Sunday when new gravity emerged from the silence. The past two weekends, Janine and I staked out different home projects in different time zones—I even fixed the post that she thought the wind had blown loose. This weekend offered no agenda, and Saturday night I read Proust until midnight as prelude for sleeping until noon.

Just after daylight, my skin tingled, a fresh lime smell brimming from a bowl of drenched papaya next to my face. A warm washcloth recalled the smell of a tropical vacation. My achy toes stretched as firm fingers pressed stiffness towards the ceiling, then stroked the hidden places lost to shoes and too much bike riding.

A stream of hot breath drew across my stomach, then a head peeked from under the covers with Janine prostrate on top of me. I couldn't blink. Her lips brushed past mine in patrol while her body morphed into a garment perfectly designed to smother the cherry taste hiding in my throat. Two hours swirled, and we never left the bed.

Then, a picnic of toast and coffee among scattered sheets and my last indulgence, the *New York Times* Sunday paper where today I wanted to scan *The Book Review* for author biographies mentioning the Iowa Conference. Janine studied the crossword puzzle, her primitive hair camouflaging a guilty glance.

Pretending to nap, I rewound to that May morning in 1993, that last kiss before Linda got on the bus to Atlanta. "In September, we become real writers." Her last words now echoed as a dream I'd forgotten.

"I've missed you," Janine said. "These past weeks."

"I've been here on the other side of the bed." My sharpness surprised me.

"This distant feeling is not what I want, Larry, not at all. I can't be whole without you." Flicks of sunlight off the leaky windowsill signaled a warning. "I want to be honest," she said.

"All right. But first let me say something," I said. "I need you to forgive me."

Before I could collect the rest of my thought, she pounced. "It's okay. You drank too much, but I overreacted," she said.

"No, Janine, that's not it. I need to apologize for twenty years of lying."

"What?"

"That first time I met you in 1993. At Sissy's, remember? I didn't tell you the truth then. I'd been in love earlier. A girl from college. I told you about Dad disappearing but not about Linda."

"Don't be ridiculous. I couldn't care less about a college fling."

"No, it wasn't a fling; it was my dream. Linda and I wanted to go to the writer's program in Iowa."

"Iowa? What are you talking about?"

"When I met you that fall, Dad had disappeared; that's why I didn't go back to school right away. Then, you got pregnant."

"Oh my God. You never loved me?" she said.

"I did love you; I still love you. But my dream. . ."

"Jesus, Larry. Why are you telling me all this? Can't you see I have something I want to share with you, something important? And all you want to do is make this about you and your college girlfriend."

"No, I'm trying to apologize, to say that I let you down all these years."

Her snarl withdrew into a sexy wiggle. "That's perfect," she said.

11

"It means so much for us to save our marriage, and yet still be allowed to grow."

"I feel the same way," I said. "Why don't you go back to school, finish your psychology degree? That cheapskate lawyer will probably give you some tuition help, and I can do extra shifts at Walmart. . ."

"Hold up. That's a possibility, but not exactly what I'm talking about," she said. "Things are a little more complicated."

"I'm willing to do anything," I said.

"Exactly. Because you're so smart. I love that about you, your intuition, like you see things beyond words. And this is one of those times I need you to see beyond any judgment and simply listen to what my soul is saying."

"Okay."

"We can be closer than we've ever been," she said. "You fill a space in me that no one else can find, something practical, elemental, like nutrition for my soul."

"And I need that same sustenance from you," I said.

"Yes. But there's something else, so sit back and relax. Don't say anything, or form opinions, just listen." I sank into a brace of pillows. "Things have been hard for us these past few years, not only the financial stress but the strain on our relationship. We've drifted."

"Yeah, but. . ."

"No, let me speak and then you can talk. I promise I'll do nothing but listen. Anyway, it may be natural that the intimacy of a relationship fades over time as people identify each other's faults, but that essentialness between us has shifted, concreted almost, and isn't as pliable as it once was."

"Seemed pretty pliable this morning," I said.

"Well, yes, interestingly, we still have quite an intimate bond. That physical link always manifests, even when we're heading in different directions. But that's not what I'm talking about."

"You're pregnant, aren't you?"

"No. See, there's that practical thing I was talking about; it comes natural to you. But what I need isn't practicality, I need a relationship that goes to the depth of my being and releases the treasure locked away there. I need love like I don't even know how to express but can feel pulsing inside me."

Janine moved to my reading chair then released a slow undulation from her shoulders to her hips, an edgy wave collecting her.

"You want a divorce, don't you?"

"No, and yes," she said. "I don't want a divorce. In fact, I want us to be closer than we've ever been. But I need something else; I need Bill in my life, too. I need him just like I need you because he gives me what I struggle to get from you."

"Sex, you want more sex? Can't we buy a vibrator?" The thundercrack of my voice pushed closed the bedroom door as I realized I was standing.

"No, that isn't it. Bill offers an emotional vibrancy I've never experienced before; he touches my essential spirit. But I don't want to marry Bill. I want to stay married to you but spend two nights a week living with him."

Withering manhood puddled on the floor leaving me a zombie closing the window, the crank handle drizzling an unfriendly cold on my fingers. Janine slipped to the bed to cower in the blankets, a guilty beast holding sanctuary in a patchwork of quilt.

The brass knob of the bedroom door appeared in my hand, though I couldn't feel it, and a fleck of sun jumped from the windowsill in a suicide leap into the lightless room. "This is my fault," I said. "I failed you. I'm sorry. I'm changing; I want to change, and I'm willing to do anything to prove that to you. But I can't share you with another man."

"But you still don't get it," she said. "You're not changing. You're stuck. All that malarkey you told me when we met, those dreams of writing the next *Look Homeward, Angel*? Where's that guy? Asleep, that's where. Deal with reality—you're not a writer and your dad is never coming home. And guess what, neither am I." The bedroom door slammed so hard the top hinge popped loose leaving a swoon of failure blocking the hallway.

Chapter 4

Restocking shelves became mindless gratification while antlike memories of Janine crawled the grooves of my quietness, leaving me swatting away days of slinky negligees. My will power was as effective as deciding not to scratch an ant bite, and each night I wrote her handwritten letters of regret, catharsis, and self-disgust as if my unnoticed humiliation might win her back. I stacked love notes on her bed stand where that early draft of "Depleted" sat unread for a year. My other therapy was to bring every broken thing in the house to justice, starting with the broken bedroom door.

The twenty-minute bike ride to Walmart each morning became escape from the mental movies of Janine making coffee in her cutoff shorts with the rip in the back pocket. And pedaling became a ritual for spinning up apology monologues never to be spoken.

Biking to and from Walmart, I struggled to avoid memory. At the store, I tried never to talk and worked alone as people were happy to ignore me. November turned rainy and cold, and the evermore speedy bike ride struggled to keep me warm. Then, the weather brightened, and so did images of times when Janine respected me, when we were happy buying our house, when we first brought Tim home from the hospital to the bassinet that my father had made for me.

One day, laboring up the large hill a half mile from work, my legs began to cramp as I pushed ahead into a battleship-colored fog settled as a canopy over leafless oak limbs. I'd never paid much attention to these three red oaks, but glints of sun now revealed their fingers twiddling one another across a language of blank air.

The nearer I got, the more connected their reach appeared. Up close, light-starved grass languished under the interplay of limbs above. Maybe it was exhaustion, or perhaps the two root beers I'd had for breakfast, but I stopped to shake loose the pain seizing my right calf. All around, broken continents of the old sidewalk buckled, and I imagined the intertwined roots as the hidden balance supporting the canopy above. Pulling my fingers across the rough bark of the middle tree, I tried to tell it I wasn't an enemy.

Sparce grass reminded me of how I'd stunted my own life beneath a shade of broken thinking. Whining about Dad, about losing Linda and Iowa, and now driving Janine away had merely prevented hope from filtering down to the part of me still alive. My breathing became so rapid I got scared, but at the threshold of panic, a growl parted the fog, and two headlights appeared, a green tractor pulling a wagonload of dead corn stalks. As he passed, the farmer tipped his hat: "That sun is coming out, young fellow."

My Walmart shift ended with a half-gallon of black walnut ice cream in my backpack and me pedaling uphill. My main character, Vince, was about to become a Gen X slacker suckling MTV as he smokes dope and scorns Baby Boomer hypocrisy. I wanted to write him as a latchkey kid with too much freedom, his parents workaholics.

As I unlocked the front door, the phone rang. "I'm putting your father's birthday lasagna in the oven," Mom said, "so get yourself over here."

Before jumping on my bike to go enjoy Mom's low-calorie feast, I checked the mailbox and found a check for half the mortgage and a note: "Bill bought me a used Civic. You can have the Saab back. I think this spring we should sell the house and split the equity." Only then did I notice the Saab parked along the side of the house.

The drive to Mom's left me thinking how in a sane family, a birthday party would be ordinary, but in the Winstead clan, we tended to be a harmonic off normal.

"Hello, hon. I see you got your car back." On the kitchen table, a two-foot-long pan of pasta steamed. I suppressed the urge to jibe Mom about Dad coming home to eat. See, every sixth of November, Mom throws Dad a birthday party, each year expecting her husband to walk in from the fishing trip he took two decades ago, that July afternoon my dad surely disappeared right into the nothingness of an ordinary weekend. The whole event left everyone so twisted that even after the seven-year waiting period passed, Mom never could bring herself to collect the life insurance. Said it was bad luck. Crazy.

"Lordy, Mom. You know I'll only be able to eat half of this tonight," I said. She snorted a sip of iced tea. After all that heartache, seeing Mom laugh a little did more for my attitude than ten psychiatrists (or one pecan pie), but as I settled into our familiar ritual, a queasiness began to take root.

Somewhere in my eight-year college experience, I read this book called *Lord Jim*, about a young sailor who always imagines himself as heroic. One night during a bad storm, the captain deserts the ship and yells at Jim to save himself and jump into the lifeboat. The heroic moment Jim spent his whole life waiting for arrives, yet in confused panic, he abandons his first mate duties, a cargo of slaves below deck sentenced in a selfish moment.

My situation had been nowhere near as dramatic. Along with the rest of the family, I'd chipped in my part and sold the GTO Dad had rebuilt for me, then postponed my junior year of college. Together, we all saved Mom's house from the IRS, but now I wondered if I'd been strong enough for her back then, or strong enough for me. Losing Dad wasn't only about money. At twenty, it uprooted me from nascent maturity and left my parent's glorious expectations for my future starved by reality.

"You need to know something, Mom," I said. "You're the most loyal person I've ever known." My words blurted on their own, then she walked over to me, and cupped my face with warm, papery hands.

"And you're the best son the Lord could have given me." But I saw that wince on her face, that impulse to hide the truth; her heart had lost some of its volume that long-ago Saturday. Her doting on me and this ritual party were about trying to refill what had leaked out, and for a moment, I understood we hadn't lost faith in each other, even if we'd lost balance. "And by the way," she said, "it was Janine who quit on you. I know how you think, so don't you be taking on her mistake."

Chapter 5

The Tuesday morning before Thanksgiving, impromptu guitar strumming gave way to a ringing phone. "I'm furious with that girl," Eleanor said. "You really haven't seen her in two weeks?"

"Afraid not. She doesn't come around much since our big discussion."

"You mean the one where she announced she's totally out of her mind and wants two husbands?"

"Well, that's not exactly what she said, but yes, she wants a relationship with Bill the Home Wrecker and me. Seems she's a multitasker."

"That's pure crazy. She told me you had a big fight and needed time to cool off. It sounds like cooling off isn't what she has in mind." My clever response slipped into the quicksand of realized pain as Eleanor cleared her throat and I mimicked the sound of a vacuum tube. "You're dependable. My daughter could do a lot worse; maybe she already has. If she doesn't change her ways, she'll end up a Mata Hari and all alone with no home and an empty life." I had no idea who Mata Hari was, but I was sorry about her having no home.

"Maybe so," I said. "But she's only trying to figure her way out of this mess. Me too." In the gaps between judgments, I heard the dim wail of a failed mother. Probably Eleanor thought about my failure as a husband, but if she did, she didn't say, and the common link of shared rejection protected each of us from probing questions.

"This isn't your fault, and Janine knows that. She still loves you. I'm sure of it. Please don't give up on her." I don't remember hanging up the phone. Out the front door, sheets of banana-colored light helped glaze over the stale smell of unwashed dishes, so I walked. On the white fence by the mailbox, a male cardinal fidgeted, his head examining every detail around him. I think he recognized me.

My preening little buddy enjoyed the tiniest ripples in his ever so important existence, and his restlessness relaxed me. But the conversation with Eleanor scratched away at what I didn't trust about the life I'd been leading. I was tired of watching life, so I took my guitar out onto the porch intending to focus outward, away from the acquiescence of corrupted hope. The strumming soothed me; the air lifted, then it occurred to me that art can be a form of deflection, a thing to sift our world through. I wanted to make sound, to form rhythms without words or sticky links to all that should have been. And the *cheep* of my cheery friend urged me onward.

Leaves jumped with the sound, dancing to the drumbeat of yelping dogs down the street, and the day warmed. I don't know why, but I wanted to mimic the natural sounds around me: the harsh barks, the mockingbird's chorus. Words didn't seem that useful in the open air.

What an odd thumping rattled from the porch as two hearty maple twigs became drumsticks on the banister, then a nail chimed on a piece of copper pipe. At first, birds disappeared. The clanging not only bewildered them but probably raised their sense of danger as they understood what sounds typical and what sharpness offensive. But I'd broken the routine with offbeat disrespect. Out into the universe, unpolished clashes of metal, plastic, and wood signaled an alien world sparking to life.

I'd gotten too old for myself and needed to find that binding vibration I'd lost to hoarded regret. Porch noise seemed a start. Not noise really but flow helping me gather the uncluttered world around me, letting the easy breeze handle things, the chatter of leaves, and me finding me.

Drifting around the yard, unfamiliar patterns peeked at me. The hoe I'd forgotten to put away leaned against the garden fence, chatting with its neighbor about the changing season. Next to it, the cane fishing pole I'd taken over to the pond and caught bream with a few weeks back seemed to tell the story of the one bass I snagged that day and the thrill he gave as the long limber pole bent and stretched against the two-pounder. How surprised that fish looked when I put him back into the pond after the good fight; the moment reminded me of my chat with Eleanor.

My heavy flannel shirt warmed in the sun, and I stretched onto the grass with face buried in the blue above. I couldn't be sure how long I napped, but even through my thick shirt the cold ground prompted the leak in me to follow a dream, some river's pull. But before anything made sense, I heard a voice, a call I thought echoed from my sleep.

"Oh, Larry? Larry?" The sound slurred into a blurry figure sweeping around the corner of the house, a woman perhaps.

"Yeah. Right here." The suddenness of things made me tipsy as I clambered to my feet.

"Sorry, enjoying the sunshine. Must have dozed. Can I help you?"

"Why, Larry, you don't recognize me? It's Jean, Jean Batson."

"Oh, yeah, sorry, a little foggy from the bright light. Sure, how are you?" Truth is, I wouldn't have recognized her because she looked twenty years older than when I saw her five years earlier, her skin damaged and sagging, a fresh thirty pounds as unwelcome as fur.

"I know I look a little bad these days: too much California sun, and I'm afraid I like the wine out there, too. My divorce was pretty hard, and I kind of let myself go, I guess, but I've lost five pounds this past two weeks."

"That's great, Jean." The nap had clearly boosted my verbal abilities. "Your mom told me you were coming home. I can't wait to hear about the crazies out in California. Bet you got some good stories after all this time."

"Sure, but to tell you the truth, people are just as weird right here in south Mississippi. But listen, come with me—I've got a friend I want you to meet."

Now I remembered Mrs. B's story, Jean free and living the good life. But she didn't look like the good life; she looked like denial through the end of an uncorked wine bottle. Those teenage days flashed of her dreaming to become an artist, and me, well, of living in Key West writing stories, that crazy image I'd carried as a secret since that first little poem I scribbled and shared with her in eighth grade, *The Bright World.* Those childish words were the only ones I wrote down until tenth grade when a half-baked short story popped into my head. In our little treehouse become artist's salon, Randy used to play his guitar, and I would read hand-written scribbles about my characters of ruin. Then, the craziest thought tripped me: What would it sound like if I tapped an empty wine bottle with a ten-penny nail? Would it sound the same to both Jean and me?

"Here we go, Larry."

Turning the corner to the front porch, Jean rambled on about how she'd brought her mom the most amazing collection of South American coffees and how I'd have to come down and sample some. But before I could speak, a diaphanous flutter moved near the house. A white bird, perhaps—no, something trailing a figure near the porch. A nymph stepped from behind the dogwood blocking my view. She didn't look real. That clear skin reminded me of a ray of sun peeking through a leafy veneer, dappled gray eyes beneath black hair, a white scarf stark as a feather.

As if touching each blade of grass, seemingly everywhere at once, she appeared in front of me. No smile, her piercing gaze scanning my unlaced boots and wrinkled shirt, she looked right through me. Twiddling the pine stray in my hair, I wavered unmade in the sunlight as she listened to my self-scrutiny.

"May I present my dear friend Maya Vera from Argentina. She's one of my art teachers."

"Hello, Maya. Beautiful name—the mother of the Buddha?"

"Why, yes, how lovely that you know that. Most Americans associate Maya as Central American. In Hinduism, it's the material world, the world of illusion."

"Now, Maya," Jean said. "Larry doesn't care about all that; he's just a good old boy, probably thinks Maya is a flavor of ice cream down at Gray's parlor." Jean laughed, steering the conversation to more familiar ground, but her friend's searching gaze continued to pierce me. "I wanted to say hello and let you know we're in town."

"Sure thing," I said. "Glad you stopped by." But I couldn't take my eyes off Maya. "Would love to hear about Argentina, and maybe even the illusions of my current lifetime." The reference to the Hindu Wheel of Life dropped out of some unlocked storeroom in my head, a reference to reincarnation not yet trending in my Hattiesburg neighborhood. Maya yielded the tiniest of grins.

"Well, sorry," Jean said, "but we have to run now. Mom is waiting. Maybe we can catch lunch."

"Yeah, let me know, but I'm hosting the governor on Friday, so let's plan ahead." Then I turned back to Maya who hadn't moved a quiver. "Maya, glad you got the chance to meet me. Hope to see you again."

With a swish, she wrapped her scarf. "*Con mucho gusto, mi amigo*," she said, which I believed meant we'd have chili con queso later. The two women got into Jean's car, which made a U-turn in the driveway. Maya rolled down her window and leaned out with both arms folded across the opening. "I like to nap in the grass, too, Larry," she said.

Chapter 6

At nine-thirty Wednesday morning, the phone interrupted my morning nap. "Hello there, Mr. Sleep-in-the-Grass, this is Jean. Hope I'm not calling too early."

"No, course not. Just got back from my twelve-mile run," I said.

"Right," she said. "Listen, got a little favor to ask. Mom goes to the doctor this morning, so I told her I'd drive. We'll be gone a couple of hours, and I don't want poor Maya to sit around on such a beautiful day. I was wondering if you could entertain her while we're gone, if you're not busy with the governor, of course."

"Sure, Jean. I have a couple of bikes, and we can go for a ride if she'd like. Come on over when you're ready."

"What's say I drop Maya off at ten? We should be back by one."

"I'll air up the tires and get some sweet tea ready."

"Thanks, Larry. I appreciate this. Maya wants to know more about your writing, too; Mom told her you were working on a novel."

"Oh, we'll find something to talk about. Is she interested in squirrel hunting?"

I surveyed a puddle of dirty socks, then got to work organizing my bachelor home into a receiving salon. My sunglasses missing for a week appeared from the underworld, and the prospect of a strange woman visiting flushed a covey of overlooked home projects no one had prodded me to finish.

Soon, the place became presentable, but only barely, as I hadn't sprayed the kitchen counters for some time, and I'd noticed sugar ants lately. The doorbell rang. With a nudge, my missing belt scooted under the couch, and I plastered on a smile as if the cleverest thought had come to me.

Mrs. B's car pulled out of the driveway with Jean waving, and Maya stood with her back to me. Focusing on something funny to say, I walked right into the screen door. Maya pretended not to notice. "Morning. Come on in. Want some coffee?"

"No, thanks. Mrs. Batson is making pots of coffee like it'll be taxed if we don't drink it before Thursday, so I'm good. Ready to get moving?"

"*Vamos*, there, *senorita*."

Seconds later, the crunch of driveway gravel helped calm me as we pedaled, both of us more at ease with an occupying task. Over the side of my bike seat, my extra pounds drooped a semi-frozen glacier of flab as I noticed Maya's athletic posture. "Have you always lived around here?"

"Pretty much. My family home is down the road, but Janine and I bought our house after we got married. I've known Jean forever. We went to school together."

"It's lovely here. I like these rolling hills. Reminds me of Argentina."

"I'll get to South America someday. Jamaica is about as far south as I've been so far, but I have this feeling your country is really alive. So much of the United States is asleep, maybe even dead." *What? Can't you talk about soccer, or cows, or something?*

"No, that's not true," she said. "This land is alive. It cannot be killed even if we build destruction on it. The earth sees who we are and what we need. She is Mother willing to sacrifice herself." My little nap in the yard came back to me. How lonely the past few weeks had been but how comforting being outside felt. I pedaled faster, standing up so I wouldn't have to think.

"Where are we going?" she asked.

"Nowhere really. I thought we'd ride these country roads. It's nice today and we can catch the last of the fall colors."

"Is there somewhere special, near here? A place where you might go to hear God speak?" she asked.

People around here think of church when they talk about God, but it was apparent that Maya meant something different. The wind gusted through the leaves, reminding me I needed to respond.

"I do have one secret spot. My friends and I swam there as teenagers, but now I only go once in a while to think. It's maybe three miles, but we can go if you like."

"We must go. Lead."

I stepped up the pace while noticing a blur of oaks and beeches intertwined in a thinning canopy. I became a kid again, racing to a new adventure with my friends charging along as country boys daring the future. The colors streamed days of when we built treehouses and forts of raked pine straw and leaves, times the musty smell of autumn meant oiling up my twenty-gauge for hunting and playing "Smear" football at the abandoned lot next to Good Stuff.

Maya pedaled with no hands on the handlebar, clearly able to cruise twice this speed. Her dark hair streamlined in the breeze, she reminded me of a hawk, those sharp, angular eyes searching the distance ahead. How could such a simple moment be so necessary? And yet, I pedaled through lost time as if I were thirteen again, dreaming of The Falls ahead, but for the first time ever, I was bringing a woman with me.

Soon the road dipped and rose to the pull-off where we hid the bikes from view; my friends never liked cars knowing about this place, too invasive for boys and our secret talk about girls. Walking across the train trestle, Maya giggled the entire way, but she knew exactly how to place her head against the rail to listen for approaching danger. That was the thing about her, she blended into things without hesitation. A couple hundred yards later, the flat cliff above the river opened as if at the rim of a great canyon, the river still out of sight. Only the roar of rapids and waterfalls betrayed what lay beneath the rising fog. Maya crept forward, making no human sound.

The rim perched above a lower ledge that protruded out ten feet farther. This higher precipice we called "Randy's Launch" for my old friend who was the only one who would run and dive from here into the river gouge carved by the current. In the upstream shallows, autumn exposed hundreds of rocks piercing the waterline, sprinkling lichen grays in the bright light.

Downstream, five-foot cataracts roared, sounding like heavy machinery as dozens of smaller waterfalls flattened into rapids until they fell away. Looking upstream, then down toward the trestle, Maya hung her toes over this upper edge, then opened her arms to absorb this place. With deep breaths, she listened, allowing the river mist to settle on her face, her form barely moving in temptation of the dangerous drop. My neck hairs bristled, the November wind chilly here above the water, and yet Maya rested with arms open wide, relaxed, receiving.

At last, a tug pulled us down the river path she already knew, slipping on the loose gravel until we came to the lower ledge I'd dived from hundreds of times. She plunged both of her hands into the frigid current. "This water comes from deep in the earth. I can smell it. There are no mountains here for snow; the ground is its keeper." I couldn't form even a glimmer of response.

"See that big rock in the middle?" she asked. "I want to go to it. Come with me." And I followed, strangely with no jealousy for someone who effortlessly seized the familiarity of my secret world. A spirit darting over stone tops, she left me ploddingly human behind her speed, but I bobbled myself to the center of the river that held the boyhood wonder I'd forgotten.

We crawled up to the flat roof of Plateau rock where again she threw up her arms in reception of the enveloping fog; only this time, she turned to show me how to face upriver and accept its rush. Here, above the rapids, the sound quieted, but the launching shoots behind still rumbled in vibration, a complex machine of nature bathing the air in crystal vapor.

"This is the place I wanted to see," Maya said. "God lives here." So honest. I loved how she spoke things most people understood but couldn't relay into words, as if too embarrassed to utter ideas of truth. Goosebumps rose on my skin as the seasonal sun filtered through smoke-colored air. Maya moved close, looking almost fragile in the light. I thought she was ready to leave or maybe wanted to kiss me, her damp face chilled white and bloodless, eyes the color of the river rocks below.

"You've been wounded. I can see that," she said.

"It's the upcoming divorce," I said. "I've had a hard time adjusting."

"No, Larry, not the divorce, not the relationship, not the woman. Something has injured your soul."

As I shivered in the sunlight, I imagined my old friend Randy who had died five years earlier, there he stood beside me again as my dad waited aloof on the far shoreline. Maya knew, sensed the craggy caverns of my past I'd been afraid to explore. I wanted to tell her about Dad, about that rupture in my spirit, but I couldn't. "Yeah, losing my oldest friend to cancer has been rough. He and I sat on this rock a hundred times. It's like he's here."

"He is here. All your past is here, and you can allow its pain to wash away here." Without another sound, she turned to the path home. Those last syllables traveled in slow motion through my brain until I realized she was fifty feet ahead.

We cruised home in a trance. Maya said almost nothing while words fizzed inside me. Already, I dreaded her leaving Hattiesburg. I needed to tell her. With the bikes stored in the garage, Maya wrapped both hands around my arm as we walked to the front yard. I was becoming a teenager with a future again.

"Do you have another name besides Larry? Perhaps a first or middle name?" she asked.

"My middle name is Anthony, but no one calls me that."

"I see," she said. "Would you mind doing me a favor, perhaps?"

"Of course. What?"

"Would you allow me to call you by this name? Anthony is an artist, and he needs a friend." The words so alien left me trying to remember who Anthony was.

"Yeah, so how about Tony?" I asked.

"No, please. Only Anthony?" Before the scrambled egg of my brain was ready, Maya turned down the driveway to leave.

But wait. Will you go to the prom with me? My rusty old Saab seemed to frown at the fiction swamping my brain, while at the end of the driveway, the tick-tock of a swishing ponytail reeled me back to the day Linda got onto that bus, the last time the taste of cherry paralyzed me with hope.

Chapter 7

"This is the best pumpkin pie you've ever made," I said. "It's almost as good as that pecan pie I plan to re-sample later."

"Oh, Larry, you're so silly," Mom said. "You know they're both the best." Having Thanksgiving dinner together left Mom in a near squeal of joy, especially since I'd gotten a tentative job offer with a company called Genie Clean, a commercial janitorial business. Her sister, Dena, helped cheer the house, even if Uncle Ray had car trouble and might not make it. Days like this reminded me of Mom's dedication to family, and for a while, the pretense of normal didn't feel fake.

"Your mom says you landed this great job and have to go to New Orleans for training," Dena said.

"Not sure yet if it's a great job, but maybe I can get in on the ground floor of something new. Besides, who wouldn't like two weeks in New Orleans?"

Before Dena could say anything else, my cell rang. I stepped onto the porch, wanting Mr. Hardwick, the recruiter, to think I was available at any moment. "Larry, is that you?" A vague voice faltered.

"Yes. Who is this?"

"You don't know who this is? Has it been that long?" Janine asked.

"Oh, sorry. Didn't recognize the number. You sound different. Is something wrong?" I asked. A roller-coaster thrill pushed my voice into high register, but I remembered how to bluff.

"Sort of, it's complicated. Can I come over and see you?"

"Right now? No. I'm with Mom and her sister, and we're waiting on Uncle Ray. Besides, I figured you'd be at your mom's."

"I was. Long story. Can I drop by later? I need to talk to you."

"Guess so. Should be home around six."

Back inside, an all-female judiciary studied my deflation as I entered the ninety-degree den. "A friend needs something, dropping by later. Now, Dena, tell me about that karate class you're taking. . ." No one was fooled, but in our family, not asking or answering the right question is a defensive art form we all practice, so through the pies and lies, the coffee and deceit, we had our traditional gathering, never once allowing reality to spoil the moment.

Strolling around Mom's house, I could find barely any acknowledgment that Dad had ever lived there. She'd sanitized his presence, packed away most things he'd ever touched, even most of my things, like the solar system he'd helped me build for sixth grade science fair. His photographs had long since disappeared, and the only artifact I found that was purely him was the handrail down to a little root cellar where Mom stored potatoes and onions. Walking through those purged rooms felt like being in a museum freshly burglarized.

As I watched Mom pack up a box of leftovers, I wondered what strings of doubt floated in her quietness. There had to be something competing with her belief that Dad was on his way home, but her single-minded focus on me kept all hints secret.

Her stoic balance reminded me of what lay ahead that evening and how I must keep Janine on the other side of my private worries. Burying reminders of the past was the therapy Mom had adopted, and already I imagined throwing everything associated with Janine into a box for the Salvation Army. *But what did Eleanor say? "Don't give up on her."*

"Now, son, you take this food and you won't have to cook. I put in extra turkey and cranberry sauce."

"Okay. But I need to borrow your hand truck to save trips to the car."

"No problem. I'll help," she said.

My calorie trove loaded, I turned to give Mom a hug. "Good stuff, Mom."

"Now, I had some banana pudding left from yesterday," she said, "so I put that in an empty margarine container. Don't you mistake that for butter."

"No chance. My sugar antennae never loses contact with a pudding. But Mom, before I go, can I ask you something?" Her gaze fell to the ground reminding me of a little girl anticipating a scolding. "Why is everything of Dad's put away? I mean, like you don't want to remember him?" She turned sideways.

"You know that isn't true. I put his things away because I don't want my old brain forgetting the way he looked, how he walked. Pictures and things became a crutch making it too easy to forget." A spasm turned her toward the house.

"I love you, Mom." The words dissolved in the breeze but received a right hand raised above her head, though she didn't look back. And it occurred to me how tricky the truth can be.

Chapter 8

Taking a long way home, I stopped to buy milk though I knew there was plenty in the refrigerator. I aired up my tires and even went to the car wash to spend two dollars spraying the paint off my icy blue rust spots. The Saab looked worse after I finished, pockmarked with fresh injury.

My sleepy cave soon gave way to a warming wood stove and a cup of green tea. Occasional creaks in the oak floors and the relaxation of a roof rafter voiced the familiar, at least until rocks crunched in the driveway. I strained to listen without moving: the car door, light shoes on the porch, a timid knock.

For five seconds I couldn't respond, then there she stood opening the screen as I pulled at the heavy front door while realizing I'd forgotten to leave on the porch light. A dark specter, hair glistening in the weak streetlight, aquamarine earrings recontouring the story of our engagement trip to Jamaica. I stared at her black flat shoes, then made my way up to the miniskirt hem, low cut front, amber skin pristine in the muted light.

"Hope I'm not being a bother."

"No, just got home. Want some tea?"

"That would be lovely. I'll have that while I let this bottle of Bordeaux air out a bit." From her purse, she pulled a bottle of red wine.

"What? Well, okay, I guess. Yes, it sure needs to breathe." I sounded like a radio playing two channels at once, then practically leapt toward the kitchen trying to diagnose my sudden tongue fever. *Oh, where is that wine screwer thing?*

"You know," she said, "this past month has you looking a lot healthier. How much weight have you lost?"

"Not exactly sure. I've been riding my bike, and cooking for one person I don't eat so much. Usually eggs or cereal for dinner. But Mom covered a month's shortfall with her lunch today." Janine sank into the couch.

"Well, whatever you're doing, keep it up. You look fine."

Is she torturing me? Don't respond. The water began boiling. "Mom's doing well, by the way," I said.

"Yeah, meant to ask."

Janine moved to my favorite chair, surely knowing how that unnerves me, and there again, my shallow breath, her sexy torture, the disregard. But the drug of her presence couldn't quite extinguish the echoes of that final Sunday morning eruption.

I brought out the tea on a little serving tray I never used, then sat on the couch, feeling like a visitor in my prom date's house. On the end table behind her, the picture of her in that Jamaica bikini brightened in the firelight, and I wondered if the Salvation Army accepted vacation photos.

"Silly boy, you forgot to let the wine breathe." Her words, sultry and slow, she elongated each sound with extra breath. I still couldn't remember where the wine opener was, and before I realized, Janine stood directly in front of me. She signaled an innocent grin, then deftly slipped her left knee between my legs while bringing her right leg up to the couch, pinning me between her thighs. I struggled to remember how to operate my brain.

Leaning toward me in an aura of ghostly-white skin, she brushed the hair from my eyes, stroking my cheek with an unfired taser. Then, a leonine smirk tilted forward to share a wisp of Chanel No. 5. Closer, hair sloshing, she surveyed my attempt to hide behind my skin, then spoke: "You don't know how I've missed you. I really have. Like part of my soul has been wounded. Did you know that?"

"Well, no. I didn't. You left me for another man, so I didn't think you were wounded too badly." *What?* Then some lust override triggered my urge to drag Janine down to the couch and smother her with my surrender. But my chill tone had intrigued her and out came pouty lips before she dropped to her knees, our eyes now on the same plane.

Fingers rubbed my kneecaps, then thighs where her penetrating strength searched out my stiffness from too much pedaling. The moment delicious, my shoulders relaxed for the first time since she'd arrived.

Ding Dong.

Janine sprang to her feet while pulling back her hair. I wasn't sure if I'd had a brain aneurism, but I blundered my way to the front door. The porch still in darkness, a distant streetlight silhouetted a small, motionless figure facing the street.

"Maya? Is that you?"

"I'm sorry. It's a bad time—you have company. I didn't mean to intrude, but I leave in the morning, early, and wanted to say goodbye."

A sputtering word salad spilled into the dim porch light. "Oh, no, just an old friend—I mean—wife, really soon to be non-wife, that is, ex-wife, Janine." Maya took a half-step back.

"Oh. I see," she said.

"Please, come in."

"It's probably better if I say goodbye right here."

"It's okay. We're only having sex, I mean tea, hot tea. Would you like to join in? I mean have a cup. It's quite intoxicating."

"I can see that," Maya said. Her brow reminded me of Yoda as she clutched her purse. "Okay. Tea would be lovely. I'll only stay a moment."

If ever I'd felt more flabbergasted and utterly without intelligence, my brain had deleted all previous record. My eyes flitted in electronic ping pong as words couldn't keep pace with the data impressions firing in my brain. Without offering introductions, I took off for the kitchen.

"So, Maya, is it?" Janine asked. "How do you know my husband?" I banged the tea kettle loudly on the stove as Janine's ice bath greeting kicked on the furnace.

"Sorry," I said. "Just being clumsy. All is well. Show Maya the wine." *What?* My senses had so supercharged, all I wanted was to sprint to town and buy a pack of Newport.

"Oh, Anthony and I have only met this week. I'm Jean Batson's friend, from California."

"Did you say Anthony?" Janine asked. "I don't think anyone has ever called him that before."

"Such a beautiful name. Don't you think a new way of referring to oneself can sometimes change our expectations for the future?"

I glued my ear to the hallway opening to hear every syllable but careful to stay out of view. Could they hear my heartbeat overmatching the cheap battery clock ticking above the stove? My shoulders hunched up level with my ears. Oh, where was the rushing water of The Falls and that moment when Maya and I stood in the mist on top of Plateau rock?

"My, my, you do sound California. All this New Age and altered reality stuff. It must be the herb out there they sell like candy?"

"Actually, I'm from Argentina. I'm only in California studying psychology and teaching art. That's where I met Jean."

"Okay, here's the tea. I made another cup for you, too, Janine."

"What's this Anthony business, Larry? I'm not sure I understand," Janine said. The room filled with the territorial insinuation. Wanting to relieve the tension, I considered stabbing myself with that corkscrewer thing I'd finally found in the pantry.

"Oh, Maya is only having a little fun," I said. "We were talking the other day about pivotal moments leading to undiscovered possibilities, that kind of thing." The instant those last words fell into the arena, I knew tea had been a mistake.

"What kind of crap is this? She doesn't know you from fish stew. Who the hell is she to tell you who you are? If anybody knows you, it's me, and you're Larry, not Anthony. Simple, practical, Larry, the spineless clod I married."

Watching Janine ignite, Maya, calm as a set dinner table, cut her eyes toward me as if to say, "Observe, Anthony. Do not react." Then she sipped her tea, allowing Janine to boil over.

"I get the feeling something is going on here, that you two are up to no good. But I got news for you, Mayo. I'm not putting up with your California psychobabble while you try to steal my husband."

"Please, Janine, calm down," I said. "You don't even know what you're saying. I've only talked to Maya a couple times. Nothing is going on here."

Listening to my own words proved valuable. The stoic demeanor Maya held so easily reminded me she had revealed nothing about her personal circumstances and had maintained an almost clinical focus on me. The moment recalibrated with the oddest sense of freshness, and I enjoyed Janine becoming so thoroughly nonplussed.

"Please, Janine, do not overreact," Maya said. "You have absolutely nothing to worry about. I have no romantic interest in 'your husband.' In fact, I was under the impression you were filing for divorce. Anthony is my friend, and perhaps he needs support right now from someone who cares about him."

Maya took a long, delighted sip of tea and let her words search out the crevices of Janine's explosion chamber. Janine's brain failed to process quickly enough, and her face cringed as if she'd witnessed a car accident but hadn't yet classified the trauma. Never had I seen my wife unable to speak amid finely tuned fury.

"The life alteration you've chosen has affected Anthony profoundly. Perhaps you haven't considered that. . ."

Well, that was it. That was the match that lit the five-gallon jug of gasoline sitting beneath Janine, and she went berserk. "Why, you little con artist! That crap may fly with Larry but not with me, sister. I'm onto your game." Janine moved aggressively towards Maya at the same moment I intruded myself between them, but Maya never flinched. Curse words filled the room, red fingernails opening and closing violently, some reef creature lurking for California sashimi.

Between them, I tried nudging Janine towards the couch, but she bull-rammed at me instead. The sequence swept over me as an image I watched from the ceiling, Janine punch drunk and disoriented, Maya aloof and sober.

After what seemed an hour though probably only seconds, Maya stood, then opened the front door and with a half-smile said: "I'll be in touch. But don't forget, Anthony has a new friend."

Murder had been averted. Thank heaven the red wine only spectated because for the next hour Janine stormed the house searching for evidence. She yelled and cursed, cried, and moaned with a passion that exhausted me as I hid in my chair, cradling the frightened impulse to play my guitar. After trashing the house but finding no clue of my unfaithfulness, Janine rewarded me with a stinging slap while screaming what a lying infidel I'd always been. Then, peeling tires threw rocks across the porch.

Fading taillights and the bottle of unopened wine on the table rewound the shock. Had I met this incredible woman? Janine's "spineless clod" comment stung, but even that didn't penetrate like it would have a week earlier when I might have spoken the words myself. My old guitar pulled me into a place where I studied Maya's detachment, that complete belief she remained in control no matter the histrionic theater around her. That resolve was what I wanted for myself. And the overheated room nudged out the first line of my new song: "Now That's a Woman."

"You have absolutely nothing to worry about. I have no romantic interest in your husband." Sobering words, but I still didn't understand whether Maya intended them to deescalate Janine's anger or to inform me of true intention. Perhaps both. I decided a little rhyming and timing might be a more appropriate brain challenge and found the notebook I'd bought two days earlier. My new little song fragment logged into page one, the words lit up a distant outline of a nineteen-year-old college student with cherry-red lipstick and a voice rustling syllables of pure poetry.

PART TWO

"Others taunt me with having knelt at well-curbs
Always wrong to the light, so never seeing
Deeper down in the well than where the water
Gives me back in a shining surface picture
Me myself in the summer heaven, godlike,
Looking out of a wreath of fern and cloud puffs.
Once, when trying with chin against a well-curb,
I discerned, as I thought, beyond the picture,
Through the picture, a something white, uncertain,
Something more of the depths—and then I lost it.
Water came to rebuke the too clear water.
One drop fell from a fern, and lo, a ripple
Shook whatever it was lay there at bottom,
Blurred it, blotted it out. What was that whiteness?
Truth, A pebble of quartz? For once, then, something."

For Once, Then, Something
Robert Frost

Chapter 9

Mid-December busied on preparation to head south for training, my house now cleaner, clothes neater, and the Saab traded for a Toyota with only eighty-five thousand miles. Lately, images of crossword puzzles, sexy little dresses, and cutoff shorts tempted me with opioids of fantasy, but Janine continued to remain silent.

Since the tea party with Janine and Maya, I'd developed a new daily ritual. Afternoons I wrote poems and lyrics, then at night dredged through my college short stories in search of ideas to pump more excitement into "Depleted." Nothing fit. Before bed, I self-medicated with beer, frozen dinners, and Cheerios for dessert—the bachelor's food pyramid. I piddled with writing the required business plan outline for the upcoming training, but the effort was more of a yawn than a stretch. On occasion I enjoyed caviar and truffles, or maybe that was Ritz crackers and peanut butter, but the finale never varied from Pabst and Proust, possibly the most perfect sleep-inducing formula of the western world.

Two days before my trip to New Orleans, a package appeared on my front porch. My instinct was not to touch it, not to permit the demon of divorce papers entry into my home. But after a dozen porch laps, an ever-tightening spiral left me inches away from the case-of-beer-sized box that quite possibly contained a black hole. The only temptation was that perhaps it was something from Seattle where my son, Tim, had moved.

Back in the den I was still afraid to look at the return address but slipped my hand into bubble wrap to find blue sky and puffy clouds encased in a homemade picture frame. A painting was something I hadn't forecasted, but the scene drew me into its story rendered in three surrealistic segments. In the bottom right corner, only two lime slices but colored blue. I thought of margaritas. Placing the picture in my chair, I then began walking laps and studying the other two sections. The upper left was dotted with white clouds and little galaxies or what reminded me of those Van Gogh swirling stars. In the center, wavelike hills, or a river, cut a diagonal between the hint of sun at the top and those odd blue wedges at the bottom. Seconds later, I recognized the fruit slices to be bicycle wheels with no frame. No people. I picked up the box—too heavy. A second frame slipped out.

Twins, mirrored opposites, but the paintings told different stories. On the second one, the lime wedges were smaller, the cheery sky larger with more sun, but even more bizarre, those center hills were now speckled with colorful splotches resembling faces. I cheated a glance at the shipping label: *Maya Vera, California.*

From behind the couch, I grabbed the Maynard Dixon print, *Earth Knower*, which for five years had rested there framed yet unhung. That handsome Native American in the foreground, stoic among the mountains, his form wrapped in a serape mimicking the shape of hills. Maya must have seen the print here at Thanksgiving.

Digging inside, I found an envelope.

Anthony,

Merry Early Christmas.
    I call these two works: "Now" and "When." You figure it out.
    I'll be in New Orleans with my father the third week of January. His friend Javier owns a shop in the French Quarter, Gaucho Americano. Come.

— M.

At dawn, I crawled from the bed to go make coffee but miscalculated by not turning on any lights. I'd placed an old rug in the hallway, and in the dimness I tripped and took a dive onto the hardwood. Splat on the floor, my rapid breathing triggered the night's dream I'd lost after having increased medication to four beers. There, a man struggling up a steep hill with too much luggage, a hefty breeze from a valley below. A great ocean in the distance merges with the sky as backdrop when the man lurches forward, the wind ripping the smallest bag from his hand then yanking him to glide uphill on the gust. The sensation of flying lingered as a lightness.

Coffee brewing, ibuprofen and orange juice guzzled; I went back to the bedroom to study the strangeness now replacing Janine's wall mirror: Maya's paintings gaining color as half-opened blinds drizzled sunlight across the blue bicycle wheels. But as if awakened by a struck match, faces with tiny black dots for eyes stared back at me from between the spokes, ghosts seizing the sunlight in a yearn to be freed.

Wham. A magnolia branch outside slapped against the glass releasing a gold and shadowed strobe across my bedspread. The effect popped open a forgotten moment in my childhood, that birthday my grandmother gave me a book describing a teenaged Einstein sitting in a tree, pondering how the world would look if he were riding a light beam.

A low rumble threatened outside, or was it the future grumbling? And as I stretched across pillows to stare at the spokes, distant Iowa cornfields rustled in the flickering light, those lost open spaces once the teenage dream Linda and I shared of studying with real writers and discovering ourselves as artists. But that youthful harvest never happened, and as the mottled light across Maya's paintings faded to gray, I wondered if maybe, just maybe, I'd found my own lost light beam. For once, then, almost something.

Chapter 10

At last, my newly adopted Toyota welcomed my guitar, a thirty-year-old suitcase, and the ever-revising opening of "Depleted." A giddy notion that life may be finally grabbing a tread dropped me at Mom's for breakfast. Since Dad disappeared, I never go on any kind of trip without first going to see her. Maybe he'd forgotten to tell her he loved her that weekend he disappeared—I'm not sure—but she'd had plenty of moments that didn't happen. Me too.

A full buffet strained the legs of the kitchen table: grits and eggs, homemade biscuits and honey, ham (and bacon), and I wondered if Drew Brees was coming over. Mom always believed I was starving myself, though evidence clearly didn't support her theory. Since Janine left, I'd lost ten pounds with bicycling and a less voluminous diet, not the worst thing for my disposition, but I had plenty of reserves yet to be sacrificed to the cholesterol gods. But this day, I sported jokes and chocolate.

We ate, then relaxed over coffee before Mom began giving me the oddest stare, almost as if she didn't recognize me. At first, I pretended not to notice, but she persisted.

"Is everything okay?" I asked. She didn't answer, then after several seconds, slid around the table edge. I wasn't sure what to say, so in homage to Forrest Gump, I reached for another piece of chocolate. When she wrapped her arms around my shoulders, I recognized that misplaced strength of hers that couldn't find its way into words.

"I love you, son. I'm so proud of how you're rebuilding your life. Dad would be thrilled to see you going off to run that company of Genies." I couldn't help snickering as I put my arms around my mother who stood a head shorter, silver hair combed and perfect. She trembled as if a troubling wind passed through.

"I love you, too, Mom. Lost my way for a while, but I can see now."

"You were never lost, only searching. Your dad was that way. He sometimes got bored with fixing cars and needed time away to sort things out. That's why he bought that fish camp, for escape, and so he could bet the dogs in New Orleans. Do you remember that?" she asked. Her voice lifted as faded days wandered across her brown eyes.

"Not really," I said. "When we went to the camp, we only went to New Orleans a couple of time, only fished the Tickfaw River."

"He tried to keep it secret," Mom said, "but he liked to bet the dogs. I went with him a time or two, but it didn't mean anything to me and staying at that horrible fish camp was like sleeping in a dumpster. It always smelled like fried fish."

"Sure did but can't remember Dad loving anywhere more than that spot."

Mom walked toward the refrigerator, her steps hesitant. "Your daddy used to go to a place in New Orleans called Magazine Street," she said. "It's a long road with shops that sell just vases or glass, Hummel's, hub caps, you name it. Some of them only sell one thing like blue glass, and there may be five stores in a row doing the same. The craziest place I ever saw. When you're down there, maybe you could see if it's the same after Katrina. Maybe take a picture."

"Okay. Sounds interesting. I'll be at the edge of the Warehouse District, so hopefully it won't be too far away."

A blink returned Mom to her coffee and a deep contentment to sit alone in her little house, dreaming of days that ended before they were even born. Maybe that was what left me so confused because for twenty years Mom had simply cooked and waited while I only ate and waited, forgetting to restart my life. Mom and I needed change; she needed hope, and maybe I needed some untangled New Orleans' sunlight to rekindle the dormant parts of me.

Chapter 13

The first few days of training reminded me of the comradery I love about business. Monday and Tuesday, we reviewed policies, monthly reports, and success stories. Then on Wednesday, each of us paired with a classmate to organize a combined business plan for presentation a week later. My partner was Lyn Hyen, a thirty-something Vietnamese immigrant from Houston.

By six o'clock on Friday, Lyn and I had a first draft, so we decided to relax with a quick trip to Roy's for Friday night seafood and a cold beer. The huge engagement ring on Lyn's hand offered comfort in a way, like I didn't need to show off for her or obsess on my inadequacies. I also worked to keep Maya and Janine out of the moment.

"Roy, I been dreaming about oysters. What's cooking today?" I said as I met him at the counter.

"Still got my oyster happy hour, but ten minutes ago, I took forty pounds of shrimp out of the pot and they're cooling down in the back. Two whole bottles of Zatarain's Crab Boil, a bottle of cayenne pepper, and lots of lemons and goodies cooked in there, too. These babies are so spicy, they come with a fire extinguisher."

After a few raw oysters disappeared, a platter of boiled shrimp fogged my glasses. Mixed in were hunks of onion, celery, and lemon along with halved red potatoes and corn on the cob that had steeped in the shrimp boil. Yep, heaven had found its way to Roy's place as these things blistered my lips, and if ever a better-tasting potato has been served, I don't believe it. Lyn and I peeled shrimp, sucked the heads, and munched the spicy corn, all the while devouring potatoes dripping with melted butter.

Roy slid a couple fresh draughts in front of us about halfway through the feast. "I guess I can take your review as acceptable," he said.

Lyn and I broke out laughing as streams of hot liquid dripped from our elbows. It had been some time since I'd known such comradery, as if I belonged here at Roy's with people who'd known me forever. I began to see why Dad loved this town, this culture, and already I saw that making friends in New Orleans meant simply being open to life, the thing I hadn't avoided for such a long time. And my old friends Randy and Gus signaled to me from the edge of my thoughts.

A shot of grappa calmed the spicy tingle burning my mouth, then Lyn and I eased toward the door. Coming out of the kitchen, Roy boomed, "Now you tell your mama I said hello." Words choked in my throat; must have been the Zatarain's.

of a thin piece of wire. Each glass shape had a tiny hole near its head for attaching the stringer, the grouping an odd rainbow dangling as the only color on the sculpture. My breathing shallowed as I tiptoed in front of a companion sculpture to the boy's left.

A man and boy crafted in iron stared back me. Dad's Tickfaw fish camp swirled in my brain. A lamp behind me flickered highlighting a thin wire between the man and boy from which glass fish dangled. The father and son had caught their dinner but were displaying it for some unknown third person. The mother? Me? The perfect simplicity of it, the reflection of ordinary life, whisked me off to a hundred Saturday stringers burning my fingers with the weight of pure happiness.

"Touching, isn't it?" The words startled me as a tall African American woman of about thirty approached while adjusting her white framed glasses. "Welcome. My name is Shala. This piece is called *Saturday*. The one with the canoe is *Summer*. Mr. Perder made these pieces years ago but refuses to sell them, says they remind him of things he still hopes to find."

"That's odd isn't it, an artist with a studio not wanting to sell his works?"

"Not really. Many artists don't want to release their inspiration to others, or so Mr. Perder would say. The truth is, he does commission works for staircases, sculptures, furniture, that sort of thing—what he calls 'Daily Forms.' He's quite a fascinating man; I wish he were here so you could meet him."

"Too bad. I'd like to know the person who makes things like this."

"Mr. Perder can make anything. His hands are tools of the universe, and he can carve wood, mold metal, or blow glass. Did you notice the guitars along the upper wall here? He made each of them and plays them well."

To my left, a row of ten guitars hung up high, lovely pieces assembled from different woods, stained unusual colors, and filigreed with rich detail.

"When will Mr. Perder be in the shop?"

"Oh, I don't know. He's with his friend at the glass studio, working. I doubt he'll return today. Sometimes they go for many hours without stopping, once three days straight. He loves glass as much as metal and wood."

I didn't know why, but suddenly I became dizzy as if I needed more oxygen. I thought perhaps the light in the shop, the cold steely air, didn't sit properly with me, so I thanked Shala for her time and took a card which read, *Reid Perder: Times Remembered at Iron Arts.* Such an odd card—what did that mean? This man must be a character, and I hoped to meet him one day. Moments later, I tripped into the sunlight.

Dizzied by the brightness, I blundered down the sidewalk, bumping into a small child then stumbling off the curb. I needed shelter. Up the street, a neon blue cup of coffee in a large glass window offered refuge: an old café, probably around for decades, but it had a homey atmosphere with philodendron cuttings sitting in the windows.

"How about a piece of pie there, bub?" An ancient waitress, hair the color of Spanish moss, chewed gum and walked with a swagger that said she was the boss of this joint.

"What kind you got?"

"Pecan, lemon meringue, and oh yeah, Junior made a banana pudding this morning."

"Make it pudding and a black coffee. What's your name, hon?" I asked.

"Flo. My husband, Junior, and I own this place. He's the cook."

"I see. Listen, do you know Reid Perder's place up the street?"

"Sure. He was there before we bought this café. Makes stuff for rich folks uptown in the Garden District. A dear man, quiet."

"Yeah, interesting collection he has, but I didn't get to see it all. Need to go back for a second helping."

"You should. See if he still has *Blue Pearl.* Has a haunting feel to it."

Picking up *The Times-Picayune* from the counter, I was reminded that it now published only on Wednesdays, Fridays, and Sundays, a sad treatment for its Pulitzer Prize coverage of Katrina. Next to it were a couple of new publications sprung up to fill the daily void, but I was feeling a little old and wanted to hold on to the past, even if it didn't exist anymore. The calligraphy of the paper's name hinted I'd been in this café a thousand times, picked up this newspaper every morning to test the pulse of a river town flowing through me.

I pulled my gaze around the café: the Formica countertop, avocado green booths, even the black-and-white checkered floor tile all spoke a familiar language I wanted to hear. Not déjà vu, exactly, no—some faded memory of life I used to know, maybe an old smell like those pine straw caves we kids built in the fall after raking Mom's roof. That musty wet heaviness beginning its journey back into the soil. Gus and Randy, Jean, too, all of us crouched in the darkness, yearling wonders huddled against the otherness of growing up.

The seduction of strong coffee, a Pete Fountain tune drifting from the kitchen, this place must be a clubhouse for some, a spot Mr. Perder uses to be silent and conjure twists of glass and steel. And late morning swirled on thoughts of blue pearls, Saturdays, summers, and a peaceful soul smoothing steel around the footsteps of childhood. Can a town mold a person? I wasn't sure, but here the tyranny of grinding habits faded as these strangers and their places cracked against the shell of my hardened self.

"More coffee there, bub?"

"Yeah, thanks. And another pudding for sustenance. I'm trying to remember the things I've misplaced, and overlooking always makes me hungry."

Chapter 15

After an afternoon of PowerPoint, Lyn headed off to girls' night out, so I decided to put in more research on Roy's Cajun cooking.

"Okay, little fellow, I've decided you're drugging this food; something makes me want to crawl here every day."

"You caught me, Sherlock. It's called cayenne pepper. You hungry?"

"A smidge. I went on a banana pudding tour this morning. But I'm listening."

"Made a turnip root stew that is something else. Set over a little rice with a big hunk of jalapeno cornbread. You'll be Popeye in no time."

"Well, you ain't steered me wrong yet."

"Coming right up, boss."

"Hey Roy, you ever heard of Reid Perder, does ironwork?"

"Sure. Comes in here pretty regular; serious fellow, but I like him."

"I was in his place this morning. Interesting stuff, glass and iron, impressive guitars, too."

"Yeah, he can play a twelve-string guitar that'll bring you to tears. People think he's a little eccentric and won't sell stuff unless someone asks him to make it special for them. Can't see how he makes any money like that but seems to work for him."

With those words, a hot steaming bowl of turnips and small pieces of Lord knows what kind of meat appeared, along with two large slices of cornbread. Roy picked up a bottle of Tabasco sauce from the counter, removed the lid, and looked at me as if to get permission to douse the food. I nodded consent, then ten hearty splashes sent my heartrate into turbo mode.

"This is Nawlins, son. You got to pick up the pace up to keep step here." A moment later, Heaven blurred my eyes, and after ten minutes the plate-sized dish sat empty. At the other end of the bar, Roy watched me all but lick the bowl clean. "Was that up to your standards there, Yankee boy?"

"Yankee? Who you talking to? I live in south Mississippi. Heck, we're neighbors."

"North of here, my friend, north of here."

We both laughed, and I knew then that Roy liked me. He had a carefree way and loved to cook, which made a perfect friendship since I loved to eat. The growing roll on my stomach told me if I stayed in New Orleans much longer, I might need to be a little less friendly.

Chapter 16

The final days of training ended in an ambush. Before anyone presented business plans, the head of HR announced that as an experiment, all sections of our PowerPoint be swapped between partners. Turns out the exercise had been a charade because rather than evaluating business plan presentations, management focused instead on team-oriented behaviors (or the lack of) from classmates in the audience. Since Lyn and I didn't mumble or try to slip cheat-sheets to one another during the other presentations, we each received top rankings and a $2,500 bonus.

I barely remember checking out of the hotel, but a few minutes later walked into Gaucho Americano. The tinkling doorbell disturbed the pool of soft light inside, Manu Chao music smoothed silky sounds over lily pads of light. All around, a curated landscape of oils and watercolors, ocean sprays, and mountain ranges alternated in gemstones of color. Argentina. Cowboys with chaps riding wild horses, cattle on grass-filled plains, field workers harvesting never-ending crops, all suggested a Walt Whitman spirit from an unfamiliar country.

"Lovely, aren't they?" The soft voice from a distance sounded so comforting I continued staring at a surrealistic image of a horse face devouring the sky.

"Yes, the colors. . ." In mid-sentence, I stopped breathing when a slight woman stepped to my side, long black hair, black olive eyes, her dress aster blue.

"It is from a popular surrealistic school outside Buenos Aires," she said. "Realism of the past has given way to subtle images of our country now becoming mature in the global art community."

"Well, yes, I see that." I had no idea what she was talking about.

"Is there something in particular that interests you? I know many of these artists and am familiar with all the pieces here."

"Well, thank you, Montanita, is it? My Spanish is *malo*, but I think that's what your name tag says."

"Yes, it is. I'm from Argentina," she said.

"A friend from California told me about this shop," I said.

"Wonderful. We see many West Coast people here."

"Her dad sells things to this store. Maybe you know her—Maya Vera."

Montanita laughed. "Maya is my cousin; my father is her father's youngest brother."

"Well, pleased to meet you, Montanita. My name is Larry. I'm supposed to see Maya here in January, so I wanted to slip by and find the store before I return for training. Maya is coming with her father then."

"Oh yes, I know. We're all excited to see her as she is the most wonderful person. Here is one of her paintings." She pointed to an oil image of what looked to be the Golden Gate Bridge in San Francisco. But on one side it went directly into the mid-point of a mountain covered with snow and on the other side directly into what looked like a jungle with animals painted as fragmented images. I barely recognized anything.

"Have you seen Maya's work before?" she asked.

"A little. She did a pair of watercolors for me."

"Indeed. Then you are quite special, Señor Larry. Maya's work sells in many galleries in Argentina. But, as her friend, you know this already."

The data file on Maya flashed empty of detail. Meeting her father would be my first real glimpse into her private life. As my brain overheated, Montanita took control. "So, Larry, what can I show you?"

"How about a surprise for my mother? I won a cash award in class, and Mom has had a difficult time since losing my father years ago. Perhaps something to do with gardening, you know, roses, flowers, that sort of thing."

Her nod then led us to the back of the store past the silver and gold jewelry. Everywhere, showcases glowed with intricate works, but she walked to a corner where a three-foot-wide lighted glass case hung from the wall. Her long red fingernails lifted my face to exactly what I wanted.

In the case, a sculpture roughly eight inches tall hung from black velvet. Halogen lights highlighted a silver garden trellis with a thatched pattern of hand-rolled copper. The verdigris reminded me of the sundial in my grandmother's yard when I was a child, the one I broke with a baseball.

I studied the left side of the latticework covered in an intricate sprawl of a climbing pink rose interlaced with white-dotted blooms. On the right side, similarly sculpted sprays of yellow and white sprouted from a second rose vine. The two climbers mimicked each other with small and larger clusters woven into harmonic profusion sunning under the intense lights. Montanita stood motionless.

"This is stone, right?"

"Yes, Rhodochrosite, often called the national stone of Argentina."

"Impressive, but how in the world is this work done?"

"The stone forms as manganese and dissolves in groundwater combining with a carbonate material. The mixture drips from the ceilings of underground Argentine caves. You would know the formations as stalactites and stalagmites. This is why the artist can get longer pieces that contain such lovely, striated colors."

"I see. But are the flowers the same?"

"Yes. Being quite brittle, the stone is often used to make figurines or other carvings. This particular artist does much of that work. He saves the chipped pieces. Those fragments here have become bouquets of color."

"My mother will love this."

"Yes. In my country, Rhodochrosite is thought to help the owner release past worries and pain. The actual name of the stone means 'rose-colored' and many people believe it improves life as negativity about the past disappears from thought."

"This is perfect. But one question, do I hang it the way you do here? How would Mom display it?"

"With the hooks on the back, you certainly could, but the piece also has a base made of Argentine granite called 'Red Dragon.' Two holes have been drilled so that the two feet of the trellis fit perfectly into it; the granite is heavy enough to support the weight of the sculpture."

"I see. Okay, now for the moment of truth. How many organs do I have to sell to afford this?"

"The piece is priced at twelve hundred dollars, but since you're a friend of Maya's, I can offer you a twenty percent discount."

I needed to use some of this prize money to catch up on bills, but there was something here that touched my soul, and I knew I had to give it to Mom. That whole conversation before I left Hattiesburg—she needed freshness in her heart right now, a new thread to knit together the past and future. Maybe Rhodochrosite could help.

"This is exactly what I want, Montanita. Wrap it up, please. By the way, what's the piece called?"

"This artist, Arturo Estrella, always uses whimsical names for his work. He calls this piece, *Escaladores del Sol, Climbers of the Sun.*

Chapter 17

The weight of the granite base reminded me of the cinder blocks I'd helped Dad unload before he built his shop, but this stone in its own wooden box wasn't like anything Dad had ever handled. The trellis nestled perfectly into a silk-lined box while the base occupied a separate home, but I had one more errand before leaving New Orleans.

Having misplaced Vi's business card, I wanted to pick up another one, but in truth I wanted to brag about *Climbers* before heading north. Inside, next to the little table, Vi stood grinning. "I've been expecting you."

"Me? Heck, I didn't even know I was coming."

"I didn't say I knew; I said I was expecting you."

I needed to ponder those words but didn't have time as she ushered me over to a table in front of the open curtains. A teapot steeped next to two cups and a plate of cookies.

"I want you to try this tea," she said. "My friend sends it to me from Zimbabwe. They say it is a memory clarifier, you know, something to help us find importance among the debris of thought. Try some."

"Well, okay. I've got a few minutes. Mom will get a kick out of my coming here."

"Yes, I'm sure she will. She sounds like a woman full of understanding."

"For sure, but a little full of pain, too."

"I expect your gift should cheer her nicely." My eyes bugged out. She must have seen me in the store or on the street."

"You know about my gift, do you?"

"Oh, Larry, I know no such thing. I simply expected you to buy your mother a surprise. You seemed so close to her when we spoke."

"Maybe. But I get lost in my head sometimes and don't express how much I appreciate her."

"My, how sad. A good son who thinks of his mother and makes a sacrifice of the money you've earned, and yet still you won't allow yourself contentment."

"I'm a little off my game these days, sort of beat up by life." Vi didn't move or look up from the cream she stirred into her tea. "But I'm feeling stronger, even did great in class. Maybe I'm finding a part of me I like."

Vi lifted her eyes. "Larry, you have not yet found what you seek. You must keep searching."

"Now you see, Vi, I don't know what that means. This walking and searching stuff? Is it here or in Mississippi? Where is it?"

"Yes, it is." And with that statement, she lifted her hand to halt conversation. I peered into those inky orbs, wondering if she was tricking me. "Your search will soon end. But for now, tell me about your mother's gift."

I rambled about the granite base and silver trellis. Vi liked the part about Rhodochrosite having mystical properties.

"Thanks for being my friend today," I said. "I needed someone to talk to." I meant those words, but they sounded so strange being directed to a fortune teller, a near stranger.

"You've done well today," Vi said. "You've been kind to your mother and to yourself." Her pause allowed my mind to rest. "You're now on a journey to becoming what my daughter calls being 'fully incomplete.' This has to be." She then turned toward the door and I stepped outside into a yellow cream light.

Chapter 18

A fender bender snarled the entrance to I-10, so I drifted into a deep recalibration of the past two weeks until the *ka-plump* of highway expansion dividers seduced me to that place where the car drives itself. Malarkey, that's what Vi was up to, so I'd keep coming back to her red door. *"Fully incomplete, what does that even mean?"*

Before long, the exhausted fumes of the past two weeks faded. Janine was disappearing, too, but I missed her strength. Why had I never told her that? And to my left, those concrete pylons supporting the opposite span of bridge plunged into Lake Pontchartrain. I'd never noticed how they were tied together as a tripod bundle of legs, and off I drifted back to that copse of oak trees near Walmart, that light-starved grass straining under the umbra of those three oaks. I needed more light, and behind me, New Orleans glimmered of glass and steel.

The Slidell shoreline ran up under me as I realized I'd forgotten to ask Vi about Dad. Maybe my brain was so linked to a remembered past that never happened that I'd forgotten how to separate the real from the imagined, then the sound of the road changed pitch over the dry land.

Ninety minutes later, Hattiesburg conjured her own grip as the sizzle of Ray Curry's pork ribs exploded into a seductive cloud of temptation. That fresh hickory smell marked the buoy telling me I was home again, the place I'd forgotten to notice for too long.

Half a block later, a red light signaled. To the right, a country road ambled off to nowhere; to the left, one trailed home. All my life, I'd been on these country roads with no signs, no clarity to guide me to the right place, no big city or mountain range to give me reference. Most of my youth, I'd craved the guidance I was afraid to ask for while I waited for childhood mediocrity to ripen into the genius of adulthood.

That stunted step into manhood after Dad disappeared, that pit of confusion when "Depleted" sat on Janine's nightstand untouched for a year, now these pits of doubt littered the road home. All that smothered intimacy of our young marriage had been buried by indifference. She wasn't trying to hurt me, only showing who she thought I wasn't. But a tangled whisper had echoed through that book, clues about our young love and the lives we could lead together. She never found those scattered hints, and I never spoke the words out loud, and all those details became our fictional lives written as love notes never to be opened.

The traffic light to home turned green. Ahead, a string of newly planted telephone poles jutted up a hill looking like bicycle spokes unfurled from their circular loop. Behind me, Ray Curry's hickory-smoked goodness billowed. Ahead, those freshly set wooden markers set an unknown channel ahead, and the idea of a children's story lurched into my head, a family of blue people with black-dotted eyes set free by a farmer's tractor digging post holes under a blazing sun.

Chapter 19

The front door punctured the quiet, spilling cold air onto the sunny porch as the phone rang a final complaint. Soon, split oak in the wood-burning stove released me to gather the lost specter of Janine still roaming the house. That sexy black dress, the unopened wine, the surreal moment that never happened before Maya's knock. Why was it always physical with Janine? Why couldn't I remember who she really was?

Unpacking helped, but a strangeness lingered on the stale air. The couch had moved slightly from where I'd left it; even my shirts in the closet didn't hang right. Home had changed as if someone had deposited an unfamiliar presence, then left. Maybe Janine. But nothing was missing other than my imprint now become oddness. All through the rooms a tilt, cupboard glasses disheveled, Maya's paintings not quite level in the shaken pylons of home.

The phone screeched. "Well, well, you're home," Mom said. "Good trip?'

I sank into my chair. "The class was great—met some people I'll tell you about at Christmas."

"Fabulous. Can't wait. Listen, for Christmas I'm doing lunch around two, so come in the morning and you can help me stuff the turkey. I've got the tree up and it's beautiful. I wish your dad was here. Oh, I'm sorry. . ."

"Mom, it's okay. I wish he was, too. We'll sacrifice a lemon meringue pie in his honor."

"Yes, of course," she said. "Anyway, looking forward to hearing about all the genies and Magazine Street. Oops, gotta go, someone's knocking at the door. Come by tomorrow."

Typical. All Mom cared about was me and wishing Dad would appear. Hers was a peaceful life compared to mine, and I couldn't figure out whether I liked that better or not.

No word from Janine, but I still struggled to remember what we'd ever talked about that mattered. I don't think I even knew her philosophy of life, or whether she had creative dreams, who was her private self beyond negligees and red wine. The flickering of the fire helped reconstruct hints of serious life between us, the real sacrifice she'd made for me. But I'd stolen her dreams too, though I never asked what they were. Turns out, memory doesn't reveal much about unnoticed time.

Chapter 20

I didn't make it to Mom's until Christmas Eve, then dropped by unannounced to find her busy wrapping treats. When she wasn't looking, I hid her gift in the hall closet. The smell of cookies filled the house as Mom wrapped little packages for the paperboy and mailman. Not much, but she always made sure those who took care of her had a little something sweet for their holiday.

"Oh, you're here. Fabulous. I need you to stick your finger right there so I can tie this bow. I'm giving Teensa a new set of wooden spoons; she said her big one broke when she made gumbo while Jean was home. She's such a dear."

"Got it," I said. "By the way, the tree looks great, but I think it needs water."

"Now don't you be mean. That's the same artificial tree I've had for fifteen years. When it wears out, I'll get a new one, but it's got a few more Jesus birthdays to go." We kidded each other, enjoying the relief of my having a job and not hiding the stress of necessity. Mom never asked about Janine and usually managed to overlook her own disappointments so that they seemed always absent. Funny how being around Mom tamed my tendency to overthink.

"I forgot to tell you, I found this great astrologer woman, a clairvoyant I think she called herself. Here's her card. She was interesting. Said I'd win a million dollars and would become mayor of Hattiesburg."

"Oh, that's wonderful. You'll be such a good mayor."

"No, Mom. I'm joking. She told me stuff like there's a big void in my life and if I'll keep walking, I can plug it. Sounded more like a Dr.

Scholl's promo, but I think you'd like Vi. She didn't seem like too big a crook."

"You're too judgmental," Mom said. "I've met fortune-tellers over the years that gave me good advice. One told me I'd own a tree that would never need watering." We both howled. It was so great to see Mom lighthearted, like she'd been when I was a kid and she bowled in a league and stood out as the star of the rose garden club.

"Is there anyone you'd like to bring along tomorrow?" Mom asked. "A friend from work perhaps? I sure liked that Maya girl. I wish she was around."

"No, Mom. Let's keep it simple. Maya is in California, but I'll be seeing her and her dad in New Orleans when I go back to training in January."

"Now, now, isn't this interesting? My little boy has his sights on someone. You can't fool me, Larry Winstead. I see that twinkle."

"Stop it. Now I know why your eyes are brown—you're full of it." Then we settled into mugs of hot chocolate.

"I want to talk to you about something," Mom said. "I may be crazy, but lately I've had someone call and hang up without saying a word. Probably some shy salesperson, but it never happened before a couple weeks ago."

"Only a slow computer call, I'm sure. Could you see a phone number?"

"No, comes in as private. The other thing is that I came home from church last week and the back door was unlocked. I'm sure I bolted it as I never go out without checking. I think maybe someone went through my bureau drawer, too, and on that secretariat where I keep my bills, some papers had been scattered. Am I nuts?"

I struggled not to show concern and took out my pocketknife, pretending to trim something off my thumbnail. "Could be you're going a little looney, Mom." I said as I gave her a wink. "But it's got nothing to do with someone reading your mail. Heck, a while back, I had the same idea until I remembered I'd been looking for an old envelope with pictures in it and must have tossed things myself. That's all it is, well, unless maybe you're a double agent and the Russians have cracked your cover."

Mom slapped my shoulder. "Now, stop that. I'm being serious, but I guess I'm a silly old woman, that's all." She opened the refrigerator while a long sip of cocoa helped me hide a sudden chill—I'd had a call like Mom's that same morning, maybe from Janine, but to Mom's house, too?

PART THREE

"True life, life at last discovered and illuminated, the only life therefore really lived, that life is literature."

Marcel Proust

Chapter 21

"Hey, Tim? It's Dad,"

"What's up, Pop?"

"Checking to see if you got that speeding ticket worked out. Sorry, I was a little lean and couldn't send the two hundred bucks."

"It's all good. My boss lent me the cash. I'm learning a lot from Florida—he's even teaching me some artwork. Working in this body shop has been a good move."

"Glad to hear that."

"Yeah, he's helping me stay on track, and a couple other fellows, too. His motto is, 'skills change lives, not words.'"

"But I won this cash award in my training class, so I really can send you some money."

"No, I'm good. Staying in the back room at the shop is super cheap." The line went quiet a couple of seconds. "So, does Mom ever mention me?"

"We don't talk a lot. She has a new boyfriend, you know." The words sounded like something I'd read in the newspaper.

"Gosh, I hate to hear that. It seems so final. I know she gave up on me, but I can't believe she gave up on you, too."

"Yeah, well, she filed for divorce and is living with another man. But it's okay. I'm playing my guitar, even hacking away at my novel again."

"That's good, Pop. Keep it up. You're still young. Florida, now he's old but spry as a kitten," Tim said. "Listen, if things don't work out right, why don't you think about moving to Seattle? Lots of musicians and writers out here. You could grow your hair long and write books."

"Yep, call me Mississippi Twain," I said. "But I'll stick it out in the south. I'd never leave here as long as Mom is alone." Those words stabbed me. I hoped they didn't embarrass Tim. "Anyway, good to talk to you. Send me your new address so I can write."

"Dad. I'm sorry I left Hattiesburg. Kind of had to. Maybe I can come home for Christmas next year, if Mom agrees to a ceasefire."

"You know Grandma would love that." Tears swelled so quickly I didn't know how to process what I'd detected in Tim's voice. He'd move to Seattle after an ugly blowup when he got busted for smoking pot and one of his friends turned out to be a dealer. Janine went full-blown Mount St. Helens. "And Tim, I'm sorry if I've let you down, not just the money. I missed a lot of things. . ." And words stopped forming as I realized lost time can't be restored with a single phone call.

Chapter 22

Christmas morning led to coffee on the front porch under a blue dome. The company had sent a basket of chocolates, little bottles of infused cooking oils, and other goodies, so my haul of presents was sure to beat last year's Wrangler jeans Mom had given me. I didn't care—I never do about such things—but the wasabi powder in the basket sparked an image of broiled flounder like I'd seen that Contessa lady on television cook up.

I hadn't bothered with a Christmas tree, the image of decorating alone proved a little too cheery for my holiday mood. Mom said she would come over and string lights, but I never called her back.

My old buddies had gotten together for Secret Santa poker on Friday night, but I made up a story about work and didn't go, even though I missed yakking with Gus who always makes me laugh. Up the street, lawn decorations and plastic reindeer announced neighborhood pride. My house looked closed for the season.

But lights soon dangled off the porch railing—coming home later in the dark would be a lot cheerier, more like someone still lives here. The image stoked me, so out came boxes of decoration, my stocking soon hung next to Tim's into which I stuffed Hungarian hot paprika and rosemary-garlic oil from the gift basket. The zillion lights hanging from the eaves reminded me of that cool beach bar Janine and I discovered in Negril.

Soon, forgotten fossils peeked from musty cardboard boxes, on top were Tim's papier-mâché star he made in second grade and that glass hot-air balloon ornament I gave Janine our first Christmas in this house. All that locked-away life had been waiting to release crumpled time, and the smell of old pinecones took me back to days I wished I could find inside that box. After an hour, the place looked like a Macy's store window, balls dangling, lights twinkling, while Elvis played the room. Around ten the phone rang, a full pot of coffee sent me long-jumping.

"Anthony? It's Maya. Merry Christmas."

"Well, Ms. Santa Claus herself."

"That's me," she said. "Checking to see if my elves are busy making Christmas down there in Mississippi." There again, she showcased her ability to peer through space at the unboxing I'd apparently done just for her to notice.

"Funny you say that. I just decorated, and this place looks like a Clark Griswold fantasy."

"I had a sense you'd be busy making things beautiful. It is your nature."

"Maybe, but my nature is really to drink beer and watch baseball." I paused to admire what an idiot I sounded like. "Headed over to Mom's in a while to give her that rose trellis."

"How special for her. You tell her I said Merry Christmas and to stuff her son with all those pies I know she's making."

"Will do. . . So, you in California?"

"I am. Having a little fiesta with friends this afternoon, but I wanted to catch you before you got away for the day. Anyway, still hoping to see you after New Year's."

"Definitely. Already got the training materials and a hotel reservation for the twelfth of January. We spend time out in the field this trip. Should be interesting."

"That's great. I'll let you know firm details, but Dad hopes to arrive on the eighteenth and stay a couple days. I'm not exactly sure. But one more thing, I'll be bringing a girlfriend with me, Lily. Is that okay?" she asked.

"Of course. It's your party, your father for heaven's sake. Is she from Argentina?"

"No, San Diego. You'll love her. She's quite beautiful."

"All right. Two gorgeous babes in New Orleans, real Anthony-style."

"Oh, you're such a talker. You always make me laugh. Have a wonderful Christmas."

"You, too. I guess in California you guys must feast on steamed avocados and stuffed celery, huh? Sounds delicious but gassy."

"Not. You old crow, we're having a beefsteak with grilled vegetables, so how do you like that?"

"That's great. Make a mushroom kabob for me, and don't forget, beet juice makes a snappy chaser." I started to bounce the instant the phone settled into its cradle. Maybe, just maybe, I'd finally found a woman to talk to who wasn't divorcing me or over the age of seventy.

Chapter 23

I arrived at Mom's with two bottles of Moet and a dry sherry. This Christmas would be a holiday to remember—or maybe to forget.

Platters of raw oysters soon covered the table, along with chilled champagne. Mom had to tell us again that Dad always ate oysters on Christmas Day because he believed it brought him good luck. I ignored the temptation to point out the obvious and instead dove into a bowl of steaming gumbo packed with crab claws. When the doorbell rang, Mom broke into a sprint to greet Mrs. Batson.

"Oh Larry, I talked to my daughter this morning, and she said that in January Maya will be seeing you in New Orleans."

My mom's sister had driven over from Meridian and seized the gossip. "Oh, really there, Mr. Keep-Your-Mouth-Shut. Tell me about this Maya person and why you're meeting her in the sin capital of the south?" Aunt Dena said.

"Nothing to it. Her dad is going to be in town, and she wants to introduce me. She's even bringing some girlfriend of hers."

Now, Mom sniffed the pack instinct. "So, Mr. Playboy. You're going to meet her father?" Pretending not to already know this juicy slice of gossip, Mom gave Mrs. Batson a conspiratorial grin. Seems I wasn't the only one enjoying the champagne.

"Don't be ridiculous," I said. "Heck, I don't even know if Maya has a boyfriend. She never said, and I never asked." A crimson flush covered Mrs. Batson's face. Something was up, and she suddenly needed more horseradish for her oyster.

"Do you know something I don't, Mrs. B.?" I winked at her. "About a boyfriend maybe?"

"I'm sorry, but Maya's business is her own, and I don't feel comfortable discussing her personal life. If you didn't care to ask when she was here, then it certainly isn't my place to intrude now." A clever stall, but Mrs. B. couldn't wait to say something and only wanted to see me grovel.

"Be that way. I don't care," I said. "Heck, living out in California, I wouldn't be surprised if she was one of those fruits and nuts San Francisco is so famous for."

My attempt at humor came off crude, but two things happened. Mom huffed, "Now that's enough of that rude talk, Larry. We won't have that in my house." Mrs. Batson, however, almost choked and had to sip water to regain control. She could only blame the spicy horseradish.

"Are you okay, Mrs. B.? They say that not speaking the truth can choke a person on a raw oyster. Old Buddhist saying." Mrs. Batson dropped a serious eye towards me. Aunt Dena leaned forward. Mom leaned back.

"As I said, a person's private affairs are none of my concern, but Maya does seem to have an unusually close interest in some person I'm not familiar with. I think the name was Lily."

My brain sputtered then lurched back to my call with Maya: "She's quite beautiful." A shade fell across my mind as I struggled to picture Lily.

A touch on my shoulder interrupted my disorientation. "It's okay, son." Mom kissed the top of my head, and a pod of kindly bystanders huddled around the spasm of me.

"I'm sorry," Mrs. B. said. "I assumed you knew about Maya, especially since Jean announced she was gay." And the thread of time snapped once again until finally my eyes fell upon a blue ribbon. A small box with a ticking inside. Mom poured me a glass of sherry.

"This sherry is delicious," Mom said, her face distorting as if she were sipping lighter fluid. Hours passed in that unzipped thirty seconds, then I discovered a black leather band and a platinum colored watch strapped to my arm.

"And thank you for bringing this delicious wine. . ." All Mom needed was a match to get the fire-eating contest roaring, but the meal continued with me in cognitive absentia. Turkey carnage. I stared at candied yams and wondered if I'd already eaten them. Pecan pie diverted the chaos as Mom placed her hand on mine, but the bottom wall of my will had ruptured on the word: Lily.

Now I saw why Maya had been so reserved that day with Jean and also with the delicate news that Lily would join her in New Orleans. Blind again, always blind. And yet, there sat Mom, damaged by Dad's escape into time, and me, self-involved as I searched for my reality-denial software. "Sorry, Mom, a little off my game from that champagne and sherry. This healthy lifestyle has weakened my drinking stamina. I need more practice."

"You're so crazy," Mom said. "You're just tired from traveling and winning that big prize." And there was the Winstead brilliance, Mom's ability to veneer the truth with an instant manipulation of context. Protecting me was her instinct, but her technique was pure family learning—diversion. And just as I was crowning her the Duchess of Deception, she allowed truth back into the moment: "But Maya is a fine girl, and I do like her."

Simplify and move on. It's how Mom learned to defend herself from the debilitation of thought. And a little masking of truth to lessen the pain of life couldn't be too wrong, could it?

"Ladies," I said, "I have a surprise. Something Mom loves but will never age, fade, or disappoint." Stepping into the front closet where I'd hidden her gift, I retrieved the two boxes.

Mom touched the heavy base one first, but I pointed her to the other package. Her hands seemed frail, spotted with age marks, bony from the darkness she never wanted to consider. Tentative, fearful almost, she stalled before the pink wrapping. I whispered in her ear: "Mom, it's a new bowling ball and shoes." Her face sequenced belief, trepidation, and I'm sure a regret that I'd spent my money.

Her sister moved closer, and Mrs. B. pulled out her camera. Then polished mahogany emerged. When Mom flipped up the latch, pinks and greens and copper-thatched silver flooded the room like an exploding party favor. The baby blue silk casing highlighted the delicate, almost candied appearance of the carvings. Damp eyes lifted across the table, and Mom became a young girl on Christmas day, her friends nestling close, her hope for the future in full bloom.

"My God, it's stunning. What is it?" Dena said with syllables dribbling.

Rhodochrosite, a stone from Argentina. From caves there, hand-carved." I didn't mention spiritual value or powers to allay painful memories; the little card inside would explain that. Words too light for the task, I let Mrs. B. and her trusty camera work the moment, bright flashes helping synchronize disrupted synapses in my brain, the healing powers of the stone already at work.

Chapter 24

Coffee and dessert allowed me a moment to breathe. For rebooting my cheerful disposition, Mom used her most powerful tool: pecan pie with whipped cream. Two hours later I opened the car trunk to tuck in my latest leftover harvest. There under a plastic bag, the flashlight I'd looked for the past two days, its glass face now cracked, and off into my fifth-grade field trip to Jackson I drifted back to that museum with the painting of a lighthouse darkened by a burned-out beacon. Reaching for one last hug, I saw on Mom's face a tinge of embarrassment betraying her stilted smile, my pain again infused as hers.

I don't remember driving but only the strobe of Christmas lights on empty streets. A block from home old Mr. Herrod piddled with his door wreath, the man whose wife died of a brain tumor leaving him all alone. And as I turned off my cheery porch lights, the darkness reminded me it was time to pack away memories I'd never owned.

A half hour later, the wood-burning stove relaxed me as green tea steeped on the counter. My old guitar rested next to me as the friend I needed, and boastful colored lights down the hallway urged me to a snooze on the couch. But a tap at the door left darkness from the porch leaking inside and a specter silhouetted by a streetlight.

"Thought you might be asleep." The familiar voice dripped tiredness, then a red scarf floated into the light.

"Come on in," I said. "This wind is chilly."

Janine draped her coat on a chair, and soon we sipped tea as I plucked a few notes of a George Strait tune. Eyes dulled against the firelight. Makeup hinted a tangled sadness. "Mom said to tell you hello," she said. "Even sent this Reba CD, *Duets*." Eleanor could be clever when it comes to subtlety with a hammer."

"Funny thing," I said. "Your mom's sure been nice to me lately. Should have run you off years ago." A recoil sent Janine hiding in couch pillows. "I may have been wrong all these years about Eleanor not liking me," I said.

"As much as I want to say, 'I told you so,' I won't," Janine said. "It's the opposite with me. She's so judgmental. Looks like we've switched places." She stared at the burning wood.

"Hey," I said. "A friend left me a bottle of Bordeaux. We could celebrate our first Christmas out of jail." My danger-monitoring software had malfunctioned.

"Sure, but only if I can take off these darn shoes."

"Were you at Eleanor's by yourself?" I asked.

"Yeah. Mom doesn't like Bill coming over, so he went to his brother's."

"Is everything okay?" I asked. "You seem a little down, and let's face it, we're sitting here in our old house together on Christmas night." She looked at me, mussed hair making her look older.

"Things are okay. Nothing is perfect. . .Bill has a girlfriend, Connie."

For the second time that day, a jolt from the outer universe reminded me that Hattiesburg, too, was part of the Thoreau-filled world of quiet desperation. My instinct toward sympathy triggered a warning signal.

"Does he want her to move in with the two of you?" I asked.

"Yeah. Thinks we could be one happy family."

"Family, is it?" I strummed my guitar a few times to shake loose a sudden rise of temper. Janine gulped a second glass of wine, a slight tremble faltering through her right hand.

"It's okay," she said. "In a way, she's like a sister. It's all confusing. When this mess started, I thought I needed his soulful touch and your loyalty. Now I don't have either."

I'd fallen into the perilous moment of Janine's wine-soaked vulnerability next to a sentimental fire. I considered taking down the Christmas decorations.

"Do you love that Maya girl?" Janine asked. "She's so beautiful. I almost fell in love with her myself, and I was mad at her." I laughed even as I noticed the spill of a tear across a black smudge.

"Maya is more than a friend, but I'm not ready for a relationship." I knew I was misrepresenting the news, but I needed all my defenses.

"Will you see her in New Orleans?"

I stood to put my guitar away, needing to hide my scorched complexion. "Yeah, in a couple weeks, her and another woman, Lily." I didn't mean for these words to sound coy, but the illusion of strength didn't disappoint me. "They're coming in from California."

"Are you going to be with both of them? You know, together?" Janine's misinterpretation knitted together some of the unraveling in my brain, but I liked her unforced error.

"We'll be together in the French Quarter. Not sure of the details yet." Enough said. All true. Janine emptied her glass with two big swallows, then discarded her fuchsia silk scarf, her face now sunburnt.

"You're a dog, you know that? I try to get you to experiment with our relationship and here you end up shacking up with two women in New Orleans like you're some kind of playboy." Her words slurred, but the humor in her voice magnetized me.

"Now wait a minute, girlie girl. You wanted to have two men, remember? It was never about my having two women. Let's keep the facts straight. And besides, I never said anything about shacking up." I knew a non-aggressive move would entice Janine. She never could hold her wine.

"Yes, it has nothing to do with that licentious beast you carry hidden inside that Clark Kent world of yours." Janine's drift into what I call 'James Joyce mode' was familiar, though usually I was the stream-of-consciousness drifter, not her. She stood up, bent forward, then shook her hair as if drying it in the sun like that Robert Frost poem. Can men be terrified of flirting women?

"I need to wash my face," she said. "You've gotten me a little drunk. I'll be right back."

I'd gotten her drunk? I guess technically I'd suggested the wine, but I'd only had one glass and she had three. Is it my fault she drinks too much?

A loud noise moved outside, and through the curtain I saw a yellow Cadillac convertible drive by with Christmas carols pounding from large speakers sitting on the trunk. In the car, a half dozen young people, happy, alive, laughing, and singing through the landscape of a fading holiday. I remembered days driving Hardy Street Boulevard with my friends, yelling at one another as familiar cars passed or as people planned quarter-mile drag races out at River Road. Those days were gone, youth now yielded to hot tea in the vessel of middle age.

The sound turned the corner leaving darkness to wrestle the house lights. I pivoted back to the warm room to find Janine standing ten feet from me in nothing but white bikini panties and a skimpy French bra, pale as a snow creature.

"Ready for your Christmas present?" she asked.

I pretended to be stunned, even unwilling, but Janine pushed me down onto the couch, crawling up over me with angles and arms I couldn't calculate, some winter predator with tongue tasting the air around my face before burrowing into my chest. The intoxicating smell of White Shoulders perfume paralyzed me until she shoved the taste of her lips onto mine and smothered me in that soft, powdery feel of supple skin I still dream about. And into a distant land of familiarity, I wandered yet again.

Chapter 25

Two more days before returning to New Orleans, and mid-January blues began grooving an impression that our Genie office was a part-time business in a full-time lease.

Saturday afternoon, I headed to Mom's for dinner after fortifying myself with a Barq's root beer from Good Stuff. While unlocking my car and trying not to spill a bag of hot popcorn, I twitched my head toward a fleck of pink ripping into the parking lot, Sissy Schrock's black Hummer with pink rims.

"I don't believe it: Larry Winstead in the flesh. I asked Gus about you yesterday."

"New job keeps me busy, plus writing, War and Peace, Part II."

"A comedy, right?" She stepped closer. "We miss you, Larry. The divorce doesn't mean you have to let your friends go. Gus is upset you never return his calls."

"I know, sorry. But you were Janine's friend, and I didn't want to make you uneasy."

"That's ridiculous." She wrapped her arm inside mine and urged a walk down the sidewalk. "I watched my sister withdraw after her divorce," Sissy said. "She told me her old friends could only see her through a prism of the past. Now she lives in Atlanta and has become something of a total stranger."

"That's too bad. But I'm okay."

Two kids counting their change walked out of the store. I so wanted to go with them. My only instinct was to tell Sissy I was late for an appointment. There again I prompted that irritated look I often notice on faces around me, but instead of retreating, she leaned close to my car window. "Come shoot pool with us. I'm pretty good these days." She then offered a hip-high wave.

The mile and a half to Mom's helped fill the car with misplaced memories: laughing around Kirby's pinball machine, hitting golf balls in Mitchell's cow pasture, even tipping over that old tractor at Lee's. Unlike thoughts about Dad, these memories hadn't fossilized as scars. And the smell of popcorn reminded me of college when Linda and I used to cook Jiffy Pop and drink strawberry wine.

January sun filtered through the naked trees, and the prospect of drinking beer anywhere other than my couch nudged a little freshnessinto my brain. I needed unentangled air. Then, opening Mom's front door, I stepped into the smell of childhood, pecan fudge. I hoped I'd have the energy to nibble a piece. All those times gathering nuts in my grandmother's grove brought back a yesterday I didn't regret or have to autopsy. Granny Irma used to tell me how smart I was, how I'd be someone important one day, so she'd better bake fudge for me before I turned into a big shot and drifted away from her kitchen. Her voice still lingered in the smell of chocolate.

Mom had taken down and stored her Christmas decor, the little fake tree once again hidden in some closet. She couldn't stand decorations staying up too long. One year by dusk on Christmas day, she had everything stored away. I complained then, so now each year she patiently waits until December 26 to file away the trimmings she so methodically coordinates before the holiday. Studying her ritual was a little sad really, too much like watching a practice burial of the things we hold on to and that one day after the moment of living passes will be forsaken as someone else's junk.

"I'm here," I said. The words clattered down the hallway, and that familiar family whistle I'd heard all my life bounced back, the one that could grab my attention at baseball practice above the noise of dozens of kids. She'd taught it to me just as her dad had taught her, and even now I believed I could hear that family call from miles away if needed, that sound saying, "I'm here. Come."

While heading to the kitchen, new things caught my eye. *Climbers of the Sun* rested on the right side of the fireplace mantle, lovely against the white wall. Having replaced my grandmother's Hummel collection, the stone vines now reached upward toward the oil painting of Granny Irma's homestead, Mom's childhood home.

The Wedgewood saucer and stand on the left side of the mantle had also been cleared away, and now, something different balanced the weighty stone climbers off to the opposite side. I recognized the relic from days I'd forgotten, a gift my dad gave Mom on their anniversary when I couldn't have been over six or seven: a dramatic sprawl of ten metal gladiolas he'd made in his shop. Mom loved this flower and years ago grew them in a cutting bed opposite her roses. Now framed in white, this fossilized artifact catalogued a season when the Winstead family had thrived on the wholeness of uncluttered time.

Onto thin steel rods used as long gladiola stems, Dad had affixed flower petals made of sheet metal from his shop where he worked on cars for money but on little sculptures for fun, things he gave to Mom, things he created during brief paroles from the shackles of necessity. He'd shown me how he'd made the flowers using an old trailer hitch mounted to an anvil, jagged sheet metal carefully pounded into concave gladiola petals of different sizes and slightly irregular shapes. After all that, he welded each little leaf and flower petal onto the steel backbone to create each long, full flower stalk. It was genius, I'd thought then, as the flowers at the bottom opened fully, narrower in the middle and rounding to mere buds at the very top. The bouquet unfurled now as a rainbow of memory.

The vase holding the flowers he'd thrown on Uncle Ray's pottery wheel; peeking inside I found still there the bounty of pennies used to anchor the tall shafts. Dad had joked how he was a rich man worth a thousand pennies. The change jar from his dresser that long-ago day provided the weight to secure his gift, but I was sure he'd had no idea what a thousand pennies were worth.

Maybe Dad and I weren't that different. A sensitive man trapped in an insensitive reality, he'd been an artist of sorts, and here was proof. Metalworker, fisherman, husband, all Dad, and those little gifts he'd made were windows into his soul, glimpses beyond the pecuniary fence enclosing him in a world needing repair.

"Well, come into the kitchen," Mom said. "I need a little help. Are you daydreaming in there?"

I shook my head to break the spell, the climbers and penny vase now a perfectly wedded equilibrium across the chasm of the mantle. Here was Mom's touch, a brilliant composition of past and present, multidimensional with her parents and old family home presiding over the legacy of her husband's tenderness and her own natural love of flowers. Mom's private world was subtle with creative design, and as the room stretched itself open, it revealed parts of both my parents I wanted to cherish.

"Well, I guess if you're not going to bring my coffee in here, I'll have to walk all the way to the kitchen and get it myself." I knew Mom would be shaking her head.

"What is the matter with you? Can't you see I need you to lift that pot of chocolate? I guess you don't want any fudge when I'm done?" Her beaming face cemented the Norman Rockwell moment, her cooking a favorite family treat in a kitchen filled with splattered bowls. Mom so beautiful in her apron, hair in a bun, and as soon as she put the last pan in the oven, I put my arms around her to give her my best hug.

"Mom, you're okay. I think I'll keep you." Her face blushed the color of that pink climber now searching out the old homestead. We sat down to an hour of pure escape where she related the day Dad had given her the gladiolas and how granny had the best green thumb in the world and even grew artichokes. I hadn't realized those bizarre shapes were the cradle for unopened flower blossoms.

"I kind of remember a big cutting garden you grew, didn't you?" I asked.

Her response required a long sip of coffee. "Yes, that house you were born in had such good soil. When I used to hang clothes on the line, in one direction I could see my rose bed, coming back the other direction, my beautiful gladiolas." Her voice wavered. Then she turned to me with a serious look. "It's good to see you happy, Larry."

"Yeah. Working hard. Been digging into my novel, too. Changed things up. That whole alien stealing the elements from our atmosphere idea turned out to be cartoonish." My voice ran out of strength, though I refueled with extra pecan fudge.

"I'm sure all that deep thinking is exhausting." She hesitated, then made a slight downturn with her lips. "You know, son, you're not always going to be alone."

"I know. Just adjusting to Janine being gone."

"Yes. And I guess that Lily person threw you a curveball, too?" I'm pretty sure my face flashed burnt sienna.

The seconds ahead scared me. "Guess so. But there was never anything with Maya, only daydreams." Mom walked over to me, then kissed my forehead like she used to before I went off to first grade.

"You're a good man, a decent man with a kind soul. One day, you're going to write something important, words to help move people away from their pain." With those words, all her priming of my youth rinsed over me as healing cleanse, how smart I was, how capable. But Mom didn't allow me to dawdle and pulled me straight ahead into her thought. "Thomas had a notion you'd be a writer. He marveled at how you could string words together. See, he saw creativity in you as the thing he couldn't allow himself in his own life, but I'm not sure he ever understood that himself; that's why those gladiolas are so important."

Before I could take up the thought, she interrupted. "Maybe for now, why not put your emotion into this story you're writing, make it as human as you can. And maybe don't fret so much about women for a while."

Some gentle vortex turned me to the past, then to the present, and then to the past again on a rotation of understanding and doubt.

"When Thomas went missing," Mom said, "you tried to find your own life by solving his disappearance, pouring yourself into something that wasn't to be. That didn't work. Now, losing Janine is the same, but your life isn't inside that twisting search either."

Mom sat down. We let the finches scrambling at the birdfeeder fill the blank of sound. But a pale image blinked inside my head. An image of a man I didn't recognize. But he stood at the door of a steely future world and spoke his name to me. "Raja." The word came from nowhere, meant nothing, but his voice thumped a heartbeat of someone I needed to write into life.

"Larry . . . Larry, are you napping?"

"No, Mom. I'm awake. But I need to ask you something."

"Okay. Do I need to sit down first?"

"No. I only want to know how you do it, how you keep Dad in your mind but still manage to live such a contented life. I can't do that. He's like an eclipse blocking out the light from me, and I can't see." My words sent Mom into a trembling.

"You got it wrong, son. Thomas eclipses everything for me, too. But I don't turn that darkness inward; I find more light—that light is you." My first instinct was not to react, not to embarrass her, the same way I'd avoided too many unsaid truths with Janine, but this time, I walked over behind her, kissed the top of her head, then wrapped my arms around our shared darkness.

"I know it hurts, Mom, not knowing. And I've been wrong teasing you about Dad's birthday parties. I'm sorry for that."

"It's okay, son. You just didn't see. I have it easier because Jesus lights the way for me. Maybe writing that deep book can help light the way for you, too."

PART FOUR

"Life is like a public performance of the violin, in which
you must learn the instrument as you go along."

Room with a View
E.M. Forster

Chapter 26

Getting out of town took more preparation than I'd thought, and on Sunday I realized I hadn't picked up my dress pants from the cleaners. Losing my couture sent me into a tizzy until I realized that every city has a Walmart. I worried about not being around to help respond to the request for a proposal we'd received from a large chemical company, but corporate didn't seem to mind.

Boring radio and Mom's chicken-fried steak soon melted into the drone of my car heater laboring to replicate the scorch of August, and on a cloudy January Sunday, hypnotic white lines thrummed a rewind of my life. Dad never bought anything new, preferring to let Mom enjoy a new Sunday dress and me new school clothes when arms and legs grew too long. His self-indulgence was to make surprises for people, things not for pay but for satisfaction. I'd never really appreciated that before, or the bond my parents had. They never talked about love openly, and the canceled project of their marriage seemed now to frame the strength of their differences.

"I put that vase out because it reminded me of my yard," Mom had said. "Those zinnias, the glads, and sweet-smelling lilies were the Lord's paintbrush." She still carried that yard among the hanging laundry from three decades ago. Where I'd been searching out loss, she'd found sunlight and blossoms sprouting in the past. No pain of practicality, no hint that pulling weeds or hustling me off to school every day had ever been a bother. She had that Zen thing, that core not needing to boast or prove someone wrong.

Yesterday, watching her dip fudge in her coffee, metal flowers over her shoulder down the hallway, I saw how she never falters the way I do, doesn't need to levitate above practicality so she can see deeper into the well of life's mystery. But now I'd seen that soft center of hope she protects tucked away in her heart. She'd grasped without hesitation the aesthetic of the mantle, her creativity so subtle I'd never perceived how hers is a world of organic expression, of appreciation for ease rather than an urge to control. A lovely meal, a beautiful flower bed, a happy child lost in his pursuit of growing up—these had always been the artifacts of her procreant will, and she needed no acknowledgment for what she had brought into the world. Or did she? Did either of my parents?

"Larry, now I want you to take this envelope to that Viola lady. You give it to her and then tell me what she says when you come home."

How crazy, sending a letter to a clairvoyant she'd never met, someone she hoped could solve puzzles the rest of us couldn't penetrate, but that was Mom. Where Dad and I calculated, she relied on the intuitive, the predictability of routine rarified by the mystical. And I remembered joking with Dad about Mom working at her crystal ball every time she'd go for a fortune-teller reading. Embarrassed now by how dismissive my attitude had been, I wanted to drive faster, to speed through ingrate memories and deliver that envelope to Vi.

Soon the Slidell sign slipped past as the I-10 bridge waited ahead. Mom heard these echoes of Dad, too, yet I'd never appreciated how her spiritual essence kept her so centered. She always grasped the core of life while Dad and I got confused by its edges, and the thud of expansion dividers punctuated the radical disruption my missing dad left behind, that chasm of uncertainty still stranding me between youth and adulthood.

I couldn't quite recall the words from the card describing the powers of Rhodochrosite. But Mom didn't need words. She tuned to the natural world while Dad tended toward the mechanical, and I glimpsed how the blended elements of Mom and Dad coalesced as me, but not the complete me, I had to fill in those pieces.

The elevated span of I-10 lifted me above a thin fog. Ahead, glass and steel bathed in the sunlight. *An urban reef.* I liked that phrase, a lyric maybe, and off to my right, a distant flash reflected from the glass cabin of a huge crane working the shoreline, the operator like me perched above the world below. Was he content to lift and move things all day long? Was he really? And as I flew along at sixty miles an hour, the world whizzed by as if it all knew where it was headed, and why. Maybe one day I would, too. Soon I'd have to come down from the clouds, and maybe even grow up. But first I needed a little refueling.

Chapter 27

Rambling streets, almost four o'clock, I recalled okra and tomatoes on the Sunday menu at Roy's. A half-hour later and without a single wrong turn, my Toyota slipped into one of the few open spaces in the parking lot. An odd time to be busy, but a BMW pulled out, leaving a spot behind a concrete light pole. Off to my left, Roy waved his arms and bellowed next to a huge smoker chained to a white pickup truck. Unnoticed, I disappeared into the café where a lone waitress wiped down the counter.

"Come on in here, good looking. I need some company," she said, clad in a black uniform and white apron reminding me of a French maid's outfit, but I quickly filed that thought in the Janine archives. Her small frame moved with precision as she paused to re-pin a bun of black hair. My body paralyzed as her perfect teeth and exactly the right amount of eye makeup fired a stun gun that left me tripping into an umbrella stand by the door.

"What the heck has Roy got going on out there?" I wanted her to know I wasn't a first timer, though apparently, I was just learning to walk.

"Oh, that's Sam Liverett's shindig. Sold his tool business and having a little party. Roy cooked a pig, and they been whooping it up since noon. What can I get you, young fellow?" Sitting down at the counter, I got a good look at this woman. She was maybe forty, petite but with defined muscles in her arms.

"Draft beer sounds good."

She slid over a mug of Abita. "So, you been here to Roy's before?"

"Yeah. I'm Larry Winstead. Live up in Hattiesburg but come down for training once in a while. Can't resist Roy's cayenne cocaine."

"Pleased to know you, Larry. I'm Roy's sister, Emma." Her firm handshake reminded me to suck in my gut.

"What you got on the stove tonight, Emma?"

"A big pot of okra and tomatoes, and I've been making biscuits. Roy had some pulled pork left from yesterday and threw it over in the stew. You'll want seconds."

"Sold. Bring me another cold one and some of that okra ambrosia of which you speak," I said. My twang hinted of Gomer Pyle doing Shakespeare, so I tapped the show-off brakes.

"You got it, Mississippi."

Through the front door, Roy's voice bull horned through the empty café. "I thought that was you sneaking in here," Roy said. "What's the matter, your mama run you off?"

I could tell that Roy had been entertaining, heavily. The four other men he'd walked in with cast a quick look, then headed for a booth. I gave a little wave. Sasquatch with sauce on his chin stomped toward me.

"Stand up." In half a second, he grabbed me and squeezed me so hard my eyes hurt. "Good to see you there, little fellow." From the corner of my eye, Emma drew another beer as my six-foot frame became Lilliputian.

"How long you in town?" I wondered if Roy remembered my name.

"Couple weeks, more training." I grabbed the frosty mug as Emma slid it over.

"Hey, sis, did you meet Larry? He's a foreigner. From up north around Hattiesburg, somewhere." His huge right arm winched my neck.

"Yeah, we met. Said he could smell your cooking as soon as he crossed Lake Pontchartrain." She wiped the already spotless counter.

"This boy can eat, let me tell you," Roy said. "You should see what he did to that pile of boiled shrimp I served him." He turned to me. "You need to come on Saturday if you can; I'm doing something special for my friends." One of the four men in the booth trudged over to the counter to buy cigarettes.

"Reid, come here a sec. This is my friend from Mississippi, Larry Winstead. This here is Reid Perder, owns Iron Arts."

I stood to shake Mr. Perder's hand. "An honor to meet you, sir," I said. The strength in his grip cleared my mind. Not a large man, less than six feet, but his upper body neatly filled his shirt. Sagging gray hair, frosty blue eyes, his stare had a cold center to it.

"Call me Reid, son, everyone does." He punched Roy on the shoulder to show familiarity. "You know my shop?"

"I was down here for training before Christmas and stumbled in to look around. Impressive stuff. My dad used to be a body man, made all kind of things with metal, even some art. Used to say there is nothing more alive than a piece of sheet metal waiting to be born."

Funny, but until that moment I'd forgotten that old saying and how Dad loved to opine about metal having a soul. Mr. Perder offered a kindly look, a reverence for a fellow metal worker, I figured. I saw him as a successful businessman, someone who could make things people needed and things they only wanted to look at, so he felt familiar in a distant way.

"I see," Mr. Perder said. "Well, thank you for the compliment. Does your dad still work with the hard stuff?" The words sucked the blood from my face and all I could remember was that thin fog swallowing Lake Pontchartrain.

"Dad? No. He doesn't. I mean, he died. Ah, been gone a long time." My throat went dry, and Reid morphed into the color of a half-ripe strawberry.

"Oh, I'm sorry—didn't mean to pry. I'm an old fud, too used to metal that don't get offended. Please accept my apology."

"No, Mr. Perder, it's okay. Dad's been gone twenty years, but yesterday my mom pulled out some gladiolas he'd made from rebar and sheet metal and painted up a long time ago. The memory is a little fresh right now." Roy and Emma hung back rigid as portraits.

"I understand, son. I lost a daughter a long time ago. Some kind of fever and she died. Still can't go through a single Easter without thinking of her when she was five, running through the yard in her new dress, looking for painted eggs. Don't think that image will die until I do."

The moment flooded with unexpectedness, a human-to-human contact unusual between strangers and one as rare as a total eclipse for me. I could nearly touch the pain in those faded eyes. This man was probably seventy-five but still virile, a man's man. And yet, I knew there was a sensitive heart there. I'd seen his craftsmanship, but there was more to him than that. I wondered if Reid had been an artist before his daughter died, had he always known he needed to create beauty to be happy? Mr. Perder glanced over to his friends in the booth.

"I better get over to those reprobates before my coffee gets cold. It's Ray's celebration, and I'm afraid I might have to play taxi tonight." Mr. Perder winked, but we both had seen something. "If you're in town a while, drop by the shop. I'll show you around myself."

"I'd love that. Last time I didn't get to see everything. When will you be there?"

"Oh, I'm in and out during the week, but next Saturday morning I'll be there. Come on by, then maybe we'll slip over and see what Roy's cooking up for lunch."

Chapter 28

After another bowl of heaven and two biscuits, I could hardly find room for that sixth beer, but I managed, then coffee and goodbyes aplenty sent me on my way. Futzing with my keys, I noticed Emma slipping out the café side door to sneak a cigarette. I pretended to throw something into the garbage can so I could have a quick word.

"Those things will kill you, I've heard," I said.

"So will getting older, but I'm doing that, too." The half-darkness hid those bright teeth. I walked closer.

"Where's your hotel?"

"A few blocks."

"What are you getting trained on? Brain surgery?"

"Yeah, that's it. I'm a brain surgeon driving this new Bentley."

She leaned back against a storage area wall, then took a long puff like she was Lauren Bacall.

"No, I'm a manager for Genie Clean. They do office building cleaning at night. I'm opening a new branch in Hattiesburg." My ears overheated as in a handful of weeks I'd gone from feeling like this job had rescued me to instant humiliation about working in the fast-paced janitorial industry.

"Hey Larr, guess what. I'm a forty-year-old going to school and waiting tables. You don't have to be proud for my sake. Heck, you're opening a branch office. Somebody thinks a lot of you."

"You're right. Four years of unemployment and a stint at being a substitute English teacher might have left me a little jaded. Let's start over, okay?"

"Not necessary," she said, then took a long draw. "Roy tells me your mother thinks you're a prince." Her smile signaled Roy had enjoyed a little fun at my expense, but clearly this woman had spunk.

"You're in school, huh?" I asked. "What are you studying?"

"Look, Larry, no need to get chummy. I've got an eleven-year-old at home, and my loser husband took off with some hussy selling cocaine dreams. Trying to teach my daughter how to write paragraphs is my top priority, so don't waste your time on me."

I guess it was my day to depress people; that's what I got for trying to be likable.

"No, Emma, you got me wrong. I'm just chatting. Don't know anyone down here. Didn't mean to insinuate. . ."

She rubbed out her cigarette and threw the butt in the garbage. "Sorry. Didn't mean to be so hard," she said. "I'm learning to be a yoga instructor. Roy's helping me pay for the certification. Says he'll take classes when I'm legit." We both erupted in laughter.

"Can you imagine Roy doing Sun Salutation?" I said. "Better give him ten feet on all sides or you'll be a hot grounder to the shortstop. So, why'd you decide on yoga?"

"I like the discipline, the whole physical rhythm of movement. And the mysticism helps me stay calm, forget about the broken world." As if a shadow clouded her spirit, she retreated into some mental hiding place, and for a moment I was sure we already knew one another.

"Are you teaching your daughter yoga?"

"Yeah, sure. But she likes to play with dolls, cats, mud pies, most anything. She's a real kid, not one of these robot warriors parents like building these days.

"That's good," I said. "Most kids I see act like adult understudies."

"You're right," she said. "We Gen X'ers are raising some real brats, almost as bad as we used to be." Her chuckle pulled me a micron closer.

"Funny you say that. I was thinking the other day how over-praised I'd been and how it made me a tad unrealistic as an adult." *What! You idiot.* I prayed she wouldn't laugh, then studied her structured mind classifying me, trying to figure out if I was an imposture.

"It's easier to be unrealistic, just not helpful," she said. Her vulnerability hinted that there might be chemistry with this woman, but then she turned to go back inside.

"Unrealistic is my trademark. I don't even know if I'm a nice guy; my ex-wife doesn't think so." The words landed on a placid pool of skepticism.

"Divorce does that," she said. "Yoga teaches how progress uses setback. . ."

"Hey, Em, Roy is looking for you," a voice announced through the door.

"Sorry," I said. "Didn't mean get you in trouble with the boss man."

"Nah, all the cooking is done. It's okay. But listen, if you'd like to do a swap for a home-cooked meal, I'm in the market for a good paragraph tutor."

Chapter 29

A few unintended circles at last landed me in the hotel parking lot. Maybe New Orleans was just like Hattiesburg, familiar, only with more streets and strangers, but the food was way better and connecting to people didn't seem as hard.

On television, nothing but static, no channels, so I took my time unpacking. The chat with Emma kept replaying, and I wondered if I could trust my instinct. Maybe Mom was right and fretting about women wasn't a great hobby right now.

A spider the size of a dime ran up the wall behind the television, froze himself on a little spot where molding paint had chipped. I was sure he studied me, and I had the lunatic idea that he looked lonely. On my laptop, "Depleted" opened like an out-of-date magazine, but I began to type with mindless boredom. In bold center-spaced letters, "New Washington," the hometown of that new Raja character that had popped into my head. Ideas spewed onto the page of a futuristic urban culture devastated by an environmental catastrophe yet technologically advanced with artificial intelligence controlling everything, no work.

A dystopian all-inclusive resort. The absurdity of the whimsical thought reminded me to lighten the tone.

After two hours, I turned off the muted snow on television that had kept me company, but the button I pushed opened a fresh new world, Bette Davis. I held the clicker as if a talisman I might use in this strange new land, then realized I'd simply hit the wrong button earlier. The wrong button, the wrong thought, the difference in right and wrong muddled. And Raja listened.

The neon billboard across the street spilled egg yolk across my faded beige wall, then my spider friend froze. I wondered if he thought the bright yellow was the sun coming out.

Chapter 30

Monday and Tuesday, I focused on doing. Each morning in the gym at six, I walked an hour on the treadmill. Uneventful but satisfying, the steady trampling loosened my mind. During the first workout Raja lost his parents in a terrorist bombing; the second morning, nerve damage from that same bombing left slight paralysis on his six-year-old's face, I debated how significant to make the injury.

Out the hotel window, New Orleans winced from her own scars of economic thievery and environmental damage, and I imagined this great river depositing heartland silt as it built the protective wetlands around the city. Urban overdevelopment and climate change had now narrowed the river's work area leaving the city vulnerable to ocean storms, the same way the debris of my own thought silted over what was at the core of me. Raja needed more of a life. His story couldn't be only about a vault-sealed life; he needed to become the friend I could help.

Every spare moment I wrote. On neighborhood walks, I studied the syncopation of devastation and renewal. Wine bottles and indigents alternated with new building construction and road repair, the scuzzy tide ring of a drowned past slowly being scraped away. An abandoned corner grocery oozed the pox of economic ruin as shady characters wandered across the street. Behind shattered windows, murmurs of lost voices, tribes now fled from the rot of dreams. And I pushed into the onrush of working people getting off a bus to lumber home with grocery bags shrunken as deflated balloons.

Looping back to my hotel, I passed a church that had flooded, restored now with a new white steeple after Katrina slapped the old one onto the sidewalk. The old spire now leaned upside down between two oaks, the pointy end a giant pencil point stabbed into the ground. And from the splintered hole at the top, Bishop's Weed trailed in a twine of purple mingling with yellow pansies as if sprinkles on a huge ice cream cone.

Strolling before dark on the third day, I found that abandoned pharmacy where I'd seen the vagrant with his Saints beach towel; he'd upgraded to a cardboard refrigerator box. Behind him in a cave of moldy sheetrock, a thin voice trickled. His friend? No, something different, and in that fleck of sound I imagined an automated drug dispensary near Raja's apartment, a talking box allowing and denying but no longer requiring the presence of humans.

On a different street home, an entire bulldozed block opened onto a sea of yellow machinery lording over piles of rock and debris. Next to a flattened plastic trumpet, a restaurant menu diddled in the breeze, fluttering its summary of the founding of New Orleans. A 1788 fire burned the whole city, then again before the 1803 Louisiana Purchase. This town refused to break. Something indominable thrived here, a vital thing holding up the world and suckling creative will in the grooved canyons of a dangerous struggle.

Each day at my computer, New Washington gelled into form. Human value equaled the mere consumption of goods, and I struggled to locate artistic hope there. My own belief that working only for money wastes human life conflicted with Raja's fantasy of winning the job lottery where maintaining personal fitness and the metered consumption of goods earned chances for treasured part-time employment. Raja and I wrestled, then, I labored to do six push-ups in sympathetic support.

Back in Genie-land, I showed up late for class; a quick lie about a broken alarm clock solved the problem. Days trudged. The second week would be spent with an actual cleaning crew and their management. Maybe humans would work there.

Emma said to meet Thursday at the Audubon Zoo to be followed by paragraph tutoring and dinner at her house. Whenever the guys in the class got together for happy hour shots or a game of pool, I made the effort to join them. Hearing stupid talk about cars and football helped ease my disinterest.

Each day in class, I stoked myself by greeting everyone individually. The previous class had set a personal standard to be upheld. But the more I listened to discussion of policy and the more I affected friendliness, the more discouraged I became. I sank. I wanted to tell Gus I'd come to poker night, and even call Janine to confess how I missed her, but instead I walked city streets, then returned to search for my spider friend.

Before meeting Emma on Thursday afternoon, I picked up a note at the front desk:

Larry, can't meet at the zoo today. Nicole is sick. Sorry.

Em

"Oh good, you got my message. Listen, Nicole has a fever and isn't a very good paragraph pupil at the moment. Can we reschedule?"

"No problem. We'll figure it out later. Hope you don't get sick, too. I know a good pharmacy."

"No, I'm fine. Roy already picked up the prescription."

"I guess being a single parent is tough, huh?"

"Yeah. Seems like I never have enough money. If something isn't on sale, I don't buy it, and even then, I go for off-brand. But my family helps out, especially Roy. When I get down on myself, I try to think about this little human treasure living in my house with me. My job is to be that person she trusts."

"How spiritual."

"Well, I wouldn't call myself the Dalai Lama, but love rewards duty. Material things will disappear in any old life storm; a mother's bond won't."

Chapter 31

Thursday I couldn't take any more genie-speak, so rather than joining the group at the sports bar across the street, I jumped into my car. I wanted to ask Vi about that Jazz Station photo and maybe get out of my head for a minute. I wasn't sure if she'd be there at six.

A tinkling bell introduced tinsel and holiday lights left up too long. *The Jazz Station* had been moved closer to the front window where lamplight revealed the scene as an old railroad car with a picture of ham and eggs in the window. The rear of the attached building was much larger than I'd realized.

"Look what the river done drug up: some Mississippi mud come to see old Vi." That exaggerated accent shot into me like a sedative. "Listen," she said, "I made some special tea my Indian friend gave me for Christmas. Have a sip with me. Cheer you up."

"Sure thing, Vi. I need a little pluck up after this week's training." My chipper lilt tried to hide discontent, but no tricking this woman.

"You don't fool me. This training has nothing to do with why you're here."

"You're right; I'm here to deliver the mail. Mom sent you this letter." She accepted the pastel blue envelope without hesitation, then grabbed my right wrist.

"Tell me, now. What's in this letter your mother wants?"

"Huh? I don't know. She didn't say." I became the child explaining why he'd nibbled the plate of cookies.

"Really? Do you think your mom wants some kind of answer? A

message you could take back to her?" I heard a clock ticking beyond the beaded curtain.

"Guess so. Why don't you read it?"

"I am reading it. I'm reading it clearly. Here is something unusual, something personal. You didn't even discuss this with her, did you? You put it in your pocket like a grocery list, right?" She pulled me to the table.

"Tell me, did you study lots of details at training this week? The company's focus, maybe have some conversations about how you and your classmates form a community of sorts?"

My head wagged. "I guess. We're studying the business."

"I see," she said. "So, you can fill your mind up with facts about profits and reasons for this form or that form, but the person closest to you in your life, the person never wavering at your side, you can't even ask one question about a letter you're delivering to a stranger and the response you're supposed to bring back."

All I could think was how meaningless my entire career experience had become this week and that I'd probably not understood any of my recent talks with Mom. Again, I halted before a stern teacher, but a teacher who cared. Her eyes scanned me as if using machine vision to catalog broken parts.

"I know what's in this letter," she said. "And if you were listening to your mother, really trying to help her the way she helps you, then you'd know what's in it, too." With that, she got up and left the room, then the tea kettle in the back began to whistle.

After Vi returned with the tea, she stirred sugar into hers while peering into me without speaking.

"My dad disappeared a long time ago. I think she wants to know if he's alive."

"And what about you? Do you want to know about your daddy, too?"

"It's all I've thought about my whole adult life."

"I see. And while you weren't ever thinking about yourself, did you ever think about your mom?"

"Well, yeah. I mean, I dropped out of my college writing program to help Mom." Vi allowed me to cinch myself into a familiar knot, then she changed tactics.

"Son, did you know that at one time there was over ten thousand Africans a day sold as slaves in New Orleans? Biggest flesh market in this country."

"Huh? No, but what does that mean?"

"In New Orleans, whole families sold as a lot, didn't break families apart like they did in Atlanta and Richmond. New Orleans kept generations living together even if they was trapped as slaves." She sipped her tea.

"I guess that's good." I said. "Can't say many good things about slavery, but I reckon being together was better than busting everyone up. Especially for kids." Words trundled out of my head like gravel falling out of a slow-moving dump truck.

"This town been burnt to the ground and flooded a dozen times." Vi said. "Most places would have given up on this spot. But not here. This river pumps in life, pulls in folks who been robbed and looking to rob, or dream, or build, and everything in between. And here we all gets stirred into one big pot of hardship stew."

"So you think I haven't been pulling together with Mom?"

"All I'm saying is maybe you need to keep your eyes open for the roses starting to bloom. They see spring coming." Vi, cryptic as always, sent me off to the climbers resting on Mom's mantle, toward her family homestead and all those clotheslines in her past when she wasn't alone.

A bell tinkled and a man in a black beret walked through the vestibule. "Bonjour, Armand," Vi said, then chatted with him in a lovely French accent. Minutes later, my car drove itself through the drizzle while Vi's last words continued tumbling in my head: "Come see me Thursday. I'll make jambalaya. Now, you go look for them roses; they God's children, just like you."

Chapter 32

I made a call while having morning coffee. "Hey there, what's for breakfast?" I asked.

"My Goodness," Mom said. "Is this long distance? Is everything okay?"

"Everything is fine. Learning a lot. Gone to Roy's a couple times, and yesterday I saw Vi."

"Well, listen to you, going to the fortune-teller. Did she give you any news?"

"I only dropped in for a minute, but I'm going back Thursday for dinner. I gave her your note."

"What did she say?"

"She asked me what was in the note."

"She didn't open it?" In Mom's world, things strung together in simple connections without a lot of quantum confusion. She didn't invite chaos.

"Mom, I want to tell you I'm sorry I haven't been listening to you like I should."

"Don't be ridiculous. I wouldn't have you waste time on a silly old woman like me for anything. It makes me happy to see you absorbed in your own life."

Clear as a coach's pep talk, her words revealed how easily Mom's humility distracted me. "That's sweet, Mom, but it's wrong. I need to stop being so self-centered. I know it's not clear yet, but I'm learning to pay attention better to the people around me."

Mom snickered as she spoke: "Have you been drinking? I want to make sure you're okay."

I couldn't win, not over the phone at least. "I knew that quart of tequila was enough, but there I had to go and drink a second one." Mom didn't speak. "I haven't been drinking," I said. "But I have been figuring out some things, and I want you to know we're going to be okay, you and me."

"I know, son. I've always known we'll be okay because you're the most caring son a mother could want."

Chapter 33

I woke at five and wrote until finally bouncing down the stairs on my way to Iron Arts. On the way, I stopped and bought a dozen donuts—it occurred to me that anyone working on a Saturday wouldn't mind a little treat. Ten minutes later, I stared at a sculpture over the front door of Iron Arts that hadn't been there on my first visit—a spray of copper roses drooping an elegant Gulf of Mexico green two feet down on either side of the studio entrance.

No one moved inside Iron Arts. Scanning the room I noticed an empty slot at the center of the grouping of guitars, then a cluster of floor lamps sprang to life.

"Good morning, sir. My name is Trevor. How may I help you today?" A handsome young man about twenty-five and dressed in black appeared from the shadows, his skin the color of fall pine straw, his accent British.

"Hi there. My name is Larry Winstead, here to see Mr. Perder. I believe he's expecting me."

"Certainly. I'll tell him you're here."

"Please, Trevor, take these and share them with whomever is here. I hope someone has a sweet tooth."

"This is New Orleans, my friend; sugar is our oxygen. In the meantime, may I offer you coffee, or perhaps a donut?" After a declining nod, I walked over to the *Summer* and *Saturday* sculptures. I wondered if Mr. Perder had a son.

A moment later, Trevor walked past carrying a wipe cloth. "Did you notice these staircases?" he asked. "Form and functionality are the soul of Reid's work." He smiled, then walked away.

Stepping into an adjoining room framed by large boat sails stretched out as walls, I found smaller objects on low tables, blown glass light fixtures, a child sculpture holding a parasol, each piece a gentle warmth in hard material. Squeaky floorboards introduced Mr. Perder approaching with a distant look in 'his eye, wiping his hands on a red cloth.

"Larry, so good of you to come." He patted my shoulder after first crushing my beer-drinking hand.

"I want to thank you, Mr. Perder, for allowing me to look around this morning." I waved my other hand like Vanna White hoping I could loosen the beartrap, and a crazy thought hit me that a fish hooked on a line must feel the same helplessness.

"Don't be silly. You're welcome anytime, especially when you bring Miss Rubye's donuts." He chuckled, then ushered me toward the rear of the building.

"Mr. Perder, when I was here before, the lady told me *Summer* and *Saturday* weren't for sale. What's the story with them?"

He glanced at the two pieces. "I must confess my fondness isn't what keeps them in the shop. See, they aren't mine exactly. A few years back, I had this fellow working for me, called himself Mobile Max." He searched his shirt pocket for a pack of gum. "Anyway, Max worked here five or six years, then disappeared one day. Never came back. Didn't even pick up his final pay."

"So, he made these?" I asked.

"Sort of. He started the work before he skipped out. Left both unfinished." Mr. Perder began walking away as if an old habit prevented completing the thought. "Odd duck Max was, liked that raw energy of beginning something but wasn't too good a finisher. Always figured it was a commitment thing, and I'm sure there's a woman or two out there who could tell stories about odd old Max."

I imagined clandestine affairs and a life without roots. "Which piece did he start first?"

"The boy in the canoe. He'd done the whole thing except for smoothing out the boy's shape. I added the fish stringer, felt like I needed to stamp a little of me on the idea."

"You both made it, huh?"

"I guess so, but it was his inspiration. On this other one, he did the boy and a rough form of the man. Told me he wanted to use slices of cut stone as the fish between them, so after he left, I smoothed things out and added the fish."

"Cool. You're the glass guy," I said.

"Yeah, but Max is the one who got me making art pieces again. Mostly commercial work before that. He made things that sold pretty well, so I started adding some glass touches. That's why I won't sell these two. An homage to a fellow struggler, I guess."

His puzzled look struck me as admiration for this other artist, the respect of a craftsman, and maybe a lost friendship. I wanted Mr. Perder to talk about that collaboration, but he cut off my rising questions as he walked away. I had the impression he wanted not to think about that Max fellow, but he'd piqued my curiosity.

A large storage room opened to materials piled high all around: metal, welding supplies, and equipment I'd never seen before, but across the room, a trove hid in the dust.

"This one took me two years." A marble pedestal supported a stone and glass sculpture almost three feet high and half that in width. A flowing wisteria vine draped over a trellis—the North American cousin to *Climbers of the Sun*, I wanted to blurt out, but didn't.

"This is all in copper. See how I rounded the leaves, nine hundred of them, then welded them all to the undercarriage. Sat outside for six months weathering this green patina while I worked in my friend's glass studio to make these amethyst flower clusters. Could have grown a real vine in the same time. *Early June,* I call it.

"Why isn't it out front?"

"Was out there until Thanksgiving. Sold it to an investment banker in New York City to put in the four-story Manhattan apartment he's renovating."

"How much did you sell it for? If you don't mind my asking?"

"Well, I never divulge what clients pay for things, but he bought this one and another piece called, *Blue Pearl*. Took that one to his Hampton's summer house. But to answer your question, a fellow could drive a nice German car for what they cost." Mr. Perder seemed unbothered having to give up his creations.

"Do you mind my asking a personal question, as an artist, I mean?" I asked.

"I suppose not."

"I'm a writer and play the guitar a little. When I write something, it becomes a piece of me I never want to give up. One day I'd love to publish a great novel, but if I did, I'd always still have a copy. I noticed one of your guitars out front is gone; is that a loss for you?" Mr. Perder glanced toward the front of the store, his eyes settling on the shadow of staircases.

"The answer isn't so simple. For years I drifted as a struggling artist, but the better I got, the less I wanted to sell my creations. That's when I got the idea to do commercial work, daily forms people could use. I still made aesthetic pieces, but my pride always urged me to store them in the garage. Selfish, I suppose. Then one day I lost someone I loved." His forehead flushed lilac pink.

"I'm sorry. Didn't mean to pry," I said.

He stared as if carving through my soul. "Realized then things are only objects that can't love me back. Sold most everything." With a slight tremor, he felt his shirt pocket for a cigarette. "Pretty soon, some fellow who'd bought a couple of my pieces offered me a job as a foreman in this place, all commercial stuff then. Ended up buying the business when he retired." He snickered. "See, son, I'm still only a starving artist at heart."

He rubbed out the cigarette. I tried not to breathe. "After I took over, I did commission art pieces, but only for friends. Wanted to know where my babies got off to." He glanced up at the high window.

"A few years later, this Max fellow came along. Wouldn't talk about his past, but I understood he'd done the opposite of me. He started as a metalworker, but deep inside needed to be an artist. The practical world crushed him, never had time or energy to find his differentness." I worried a little about how pale Reid had become.

"Don't know what happened in his past, but by the time I met Max, he'd chucked it all. Only really wanted to make art pieces. Heck, I had a hard time getting him to work at all let alone finish commercial projects, but he'd give me about twenty percent of his mindshare for making functional stuff, and I took half the profit on his art creations made on company time. Seemed like a fair trade, and it was about all I'd get. Weird really, but watching old Max bring metal to life helped patch a hole inside me."

Mr. Perder caught himself, I think realizing his thoughts were being spoken out loud. The moment filled me with exactly what I'd wanted to hear—how artists think. "Mr. Perder, did Max mind selling his work?" I asked.

"Larry, call me Reid, please. But, no, Max never looked back. For him, the creative urge, the craftsmanship, that's all he wanted. When something was done, he was finished. Heck, look at those two marvels out front. He walked away from them like a dried-out sandwich. I'm the one who won't sell, hoping one day he'll come back and claim them, but I know he won't...he never will."

What a strange concept, being able to sell your creations without sentimentalism. I wondered why Max would never mention his past— some prison term, perhaps, where he learned to be hard but also to shape things, or a brutal childhood where he struggled to survive before his soul had time to sweeten with life. My writer juices pumped, and an interesting idea came to life that maybe this Max fellow could be a character to write about, maybe help me find my own secrets of torn life. Instantly I imagined Max losing his wife and kids in a tragic fire that altered the course of his future.

My daydream left Reid walking away as a door inside him had closed. "Here's something else I want you to see."

On a round slab of marble, a coliseum shaped scene divided into two semicircular regions. In the center, a chunk of solid clear glass had been shaped to resemble a child, a girl with long hair and a dress, but impressionistic in a smooth finished glass with no edges. Surrounding her figure, protrusions of twisted metal interleaved with shorter jagged glass pieces, each separate, ranged from two to six inches high. The pointed metal and glass resembled tongues of fire, reddish blue and yellow, five deep around the girl.

Directly in front of the child, a gap in the flames revealed a similar glass figure, a man, his arms straight in a lifting motion toward the girl. I knew it was Jesus.

"This piece is called *Fever*," he said. I couldn't speak. Before me was the most personal artwork I'd ever experienced. Reid stared into the abyss of the sculpture showing no expression.

"Your daughter?" No response for several seconds.

"I did mention that to you, didn't I?" He offered no other information. My heart drummed too loudly to concentrate while Reid walked away then pulled back a large curtain hanging from the ceiling. A rush of lights, then visions appeared.

Dozens of glass forms floated in suspension from nearly invisible wires, a school of fish, colorful, translucent pieces swimming through the air. At the front of the school, an adult cluster led a score of smaller fishes huddling close. The adults ranged from a foot to two feet in length, all made the same. The effect reminded me of fourth of July fireworks.

The entire collection formed the shape of a panfish, such as a tropical butterfly fish or sheepshead so common in the gulf. But individually, each specimen was trout shaped, long and slender, made of a thin metal cage forming an exoskeleton and filled with stacks of glass, some green, some blue, some thin, some thicker. Uneven layers produced the imbricated effect of fish scales.

The federation dazzled in the oscillating floor light. Against a sandy-hued canvas above the cluster, the effect teased the idea me of snorkeling, of floating into an ocean of life-filled air. From an unlit area off to my right, a similar display of fish mounted to a wall sprang to life with the flip of a switch.

"Speckled trout," Reid said. "I first made these individual displays, then had the idea of suspending a grouping as a mobile and letting the rotating light create the sense of movement. I call it *Family Time*."

I gawked in silence as the light went dark. "Okay, all this talk about fish is making me hungry. Let's go see what Roy is cooking up. My treat," he said.

I followed Reid to the front door with each step chipping away at the idea art can clarify pain, and maybe heal it. Creativity didn't have to be impractical or aesthetically pure; it could be mere function, and simple. And old Max came to mind, that injured artist searching out yearning among the dark corridors of all that should have been.

Reid almost spoke, then pulled back, and I knew this little tour had connected him to familiar old roots. He'd gotten to visit a missing friend's work and linger in the memory of his lost daughter, but this practical man had also reached into the fallowness of me. A stirring, a loosening of some seasonal hardness stayed too long, then that New Orleans vibrancy probed for the part of me that might still be real.

Settling into my warm car, I strained to hear again the words from inside Iron Arts, those voices of strangers I'd never met. Reid's ancient beige pickup, 1962 Chevy I think it was, ripped to life on the grumble of a worn-out muffler, and he crept out of the parking lot as if content with nowhere to go. Behind me, the splay of draped copper rested over the doorway, that metallic kinsman of Mom's *Climbers* a hundred miles to the north. Mom and Reid shared that kinship of tender souls snipping away at cuttings in the garden of unselfishness, a place they shared as they waited for me. And I wondered if Vi could see the roses I'd found.

Chapter 34

At the edge of Roy's parking lot, a gentle creature stood over a cinder block fire pit billowing smoke. He glanced up to see Reid's truck, but I'm not sure he recognized my Toyota. Soon a crowd gathered around the smoky Saturday hearth.

"Yep, sonny boy," Roy said, "you're in for some fine smoked oysters today, and I'm barbecuing a mess of shrimp just to fill in the gaps. If that don't stuff your gullet, I got sixty dozen Oysters Bienville made up inside that will melt in your mouth quicker than Belgian chocolate. Aunt Maggie's recipe, best one ever."

On the grill, a large mound warmed off to the side, something already cooked and wrapped in foil. After Roy stirred the oak coals with his long hickory stick, he pushed the mystery dish over to the cool side of the hot grate. "Thought you might be a little hungry after your tour of Reid's museum, so I fixed a little appetizer to snack on while the coals cool down for the oysters. It's my world-famous sausage and onions in homemade barbecue sauce, my Uncle Dave's favorite camping food. Can't tell you how many times we came back from setting trotlines to find Aunt Maggie dishing out sausage and onions next to a hunk of French bread."

A glint flashed in Roy's eye, but he quickly busied himself opening the aluminum foil delicacy. Inside was a mass of dark barbecue with melted onions and sliced pieces of Andouille sausage so rich and spicy that not even a cold Abita could stall the scald. He scooped a ladle into a paper bowl for each of us. Hot as primordial lava, the crunchy outside of the sausage nestled into luscious, sweet onions as a marriage of true equals. I loved thinking how this giant of a man had the sensitivity to weave together the subtle details of cooking and yet never give a hint that it took skill or effort. His artful touch bonded our little party tribe around this modern cave fire where the only thing that mattered was being present.

The afternoon diffused into a semi-mosh pit of laughing and beer-sloshed jokes. Other people came, and Roy treated them all as his brothers and sisters, the same way he made me feel, and before long, the congregation of the family Roy roared.

Mountains of oysters steamed under wet burlap. Much of the crowd brought their own yellow or black rubber gloves and took the hot delicacies off the grate, slurping them right out of the shells. Roy squeezed fresh lemon juice and minced parsley over the whole gaping cluster and also set out bottles of Tabasco and bowls of wicked spicy horseradish. Such a feast I'd never seen as we sucked the heads of barbecued shrimp then doused the sweetness with lemony bubbling oysters bolstered by cold beer.

Around four, we'd demolished everything outside, so Roy directed everyone inside to sample the Bienville cooking in the oven, delicacies served in oyster shells crammed with simmering garlic, chopped mushrooms, shrimp, and parmesan cheese. Sumptuous, each platter served with toasted garlic bread and roasted red potatoes came out on special dishes slotted to hold the hot oyster shells, twelve at a time. As Em picked up the empty platter in front of me, I realized it was the first time I'd seen her all day. "Hello there, mama's boy," she said.

"I was wondering if you were working." Emma winked at me then headed into the kitchen. I followed. "Need any help?" I asked.

"Sure do, but unfortunately you can't be back here as the health department has some picky rules. It's okay though—I got it under control." Her hands, eyes, and ears operated as if guided by separate microprocessors. The smell of simmering garlic set off an intoxicating urge to tell Emma how I liked talking to her. Two helpers scurried about barely noticing my presence as Emma put six dozen more Bienville servings in the oven and set a timer.

"I'll get out of the way, but I wanted to know if your daughter is better."

"Thanks, that's sweet. She's still weak, but I'm hoping she can go back to school Monday."

"That's good news. Listen, do you want to try again for dinner? Maybe take you girls out for pasta and pizza. *Do yoga instructors even eat pasta?* A frown rejected my idea.

"Wednesday might work, but why don't you come over? Remember, this is a tutoring trade, and besides I want to keep Nicole inside at night." Her big smile inflated me. "You do like tofu, right?" Her words struck me as a foreign language.

"Sure, love tofu. It's in season now, right?" Mountain Dew squirted from her nose, then I'm sure without any conscious intent she touched my hand.

"Yep, I'll pluck it right off my tofu tree." I decided to shut up rather than risk spoiling this wisp of intimacy. "Okay, so you're not a big tofu person, but have you ever tried it?"

"Once. Had it stuffed with deer sausage. Scrumptious." She popped me playfully with her dish towel as it occurred to me that I didn't know if tofu was animal or chemical."

"Good. Then I'll open your eyes to something healthy. Come over at six and we'll have a glass of wine. Here's my address, the duplex above Roy and his wife."

"By the way, it's good to see you," I said.

"Yeah, glad you made it. I taught a yoga class this morning and almost took the afternoon off, but Roy needed the help, and I need the money." Her eyes trailed away as if embarrassed, then she cut those blue beacons at me just as Roy barged into the kitchen.

"There you are. Reid's looking for you," Roy said.

"Get on out of here," Emma said to me. "And listen, take it a little easy, okay? That's a fast crowd out there; they've had practice." I gave her a confident grin, then two minutes later ordered a double tequila on the rocks.

Chapter 35

Sunday trudged along with my never leaving the hotel room. The throbbing behind my eyes chimed with periodic lurches in my stomach, and the idea of speaking stirred suicidal ambition. At noon I nibbled cereal. I'd never had such a reaction to oysters before. Who knew? Around four-thirty, the phone rang. I prayed it wasn't the police as I couldn't remember how Saturday night ended.

"Hello, it's Maya." Her chipper voice triggered my gag reflex.

"Oh, hi." Even those words took a year off my life.

"Are you okay, Anthony?" The screeching jukebox at Roy's still reverberated beneath the erratic effort of coordinating ears and voice as my six functioning brain cells baulked before the vast conversation desert I now had to crawl across.

"Had a little accident yesterday. Got hit by a tequila truck loaded with oysters."

"You don't sound well."

"Only brain dead, but that's normal."

"Oh, I get it, a tequila truck. Funny. Anyway, I can call back tomorrow."

"No, I'm sorry. How are you?" I turned up the volume on my fakery infuser enough that I could pretend to be alive. "When will you be in Louisiana?"

"On Friday. Hope you're still around." I was scheduled to check out of the hotel midday Friday. Before Lily appeared, I would have done anything Maya wanted, but now our relationship felt tilted. I wanted to say I couldn't stay, but I'd walked out on enough friendships these past few years.

"I can hang around if you like. I don't mind." There I went again, saying exactly the opposite of what I wanted—or had I?

"I hate to ask you to do that, but I would like to see you and have you meet my father. Would it be too much trouble? Our plane doesn't get in until nine at night, so Friday evening might be too uncertain. We could meet for lunch on Saturday." At least now I understood the situation. Frankly, I would have agreed to perm my hair just to get off the phone.

"Sure, that's fine," I said. "Where should we go?"

"I'll email you details. Sorry about imposing." She sounded uncomfortable, but the shifting sludge in my stomach made it okay.

Chapter 36

Monday morning the phone woke me. "Mr. Winstead, this is the hotel manager, Mr. Loveland. I'm calling to inform you that your car in the parking lot was vandalized last night. We'd like you to come down and take a look, please." The announcement distracted me from my exhaustion, and ten minutes later I inspected where two jars of red spaghetti sauce had been broken and smeared over the front and driver's side of my car. "We apologize and, of course, will clean up the entire mess."

My brain still hadn't regained full power after the Saturday night lobotomy, but I managed a response. "I think it looks better." My words seemed to puzzle the manager. A drastic absence of nutrients in my body filled me with a giddy stupidity I rather liked, the cumulative goodness of the previous month's healthy behavior now only another dream deferred. Back in my room, oatmeal and two cups of coffee convinced me the spaghetti fiasco was real. Then I began to panic as not only could I not remember how my car and I had gotten home from Roy's feast, but I could recall almost nothing after my chat with Emma in the kitchen. Perhaps this healthy Larry business wasn't working out so well. I even questioned whether in an alcoholic hallucination I'd splattered the Ragu myself.

Images wandered through my head as homeless nomads: dancing with some black-haired woman with large breasts, talking a second time to Emma and realizing she wasn't listening. Kaleidoscopic fragments shifted Saturday night's bravado into the embarrassment of Monday's recall, as Sunday disappeared from memory mostly unnoticed. Sipping a protein shake, I still struggled to recall anything whole.

The last complete context available was my first conversation with

Emma. After that, I became a victim of the tequila terrorist attack, but not enough synapses had shown up for duty even to consider giving Emma a call to apologize for the things I couldn't remember. That fun-filled September barbecue at Eric's came to mind, Janine's soul-killing stare after I embarrassed her. And off in a distant cellblock, Raja observed, his world of hyper-order oddly appealing. *Where's that spider? I hope he's poisonous.*

The orientation and crew assignment didn't begin until four, and parts of my personality were still missing. But a MacGyver instinct guided me, and soon I remembered my name but considered calling myself Anthony as a reality blocker. This first night in the field we were to be janitors, the second night to shadow a crew supervisor. On Wednesday afternoon, I would meet with the District Operations Director to pass along my feedback. Maybe emptying office trash cans would give my life meaning.

Flipping through the training binder, after ten minutes I fell asleep. Two hours later my IQ had doubled, well on its way to the low eighties. "New Washington" had atrophied untouched for days now.

Fragments from the past two days struggled to cohere, the tour of Reid's shop, those ideas that I was a creative person frustrated with pedestrian life. And from the charred ashes of my kamikaze character came a flash of recognition that I still had to face Emma. I worried all that alcohol had dissolved my ability to dodge the truth.

The praline texture of the ceiling lit up as shadows and craters from a distant planetary landscape, while I lay on the bed staring at a frail spider web drooping from the ceiling light. A mosquito twitched helpless among the wispy threads; he was a victim, unlike me as both predator and prey in my own trapped life. I grabbed the phone.

"Hello, Emma, this is Larry." A century passed.

"So?"

"Listen, I wanted to apologize. I know I got a little rowdy Saturday. Can't remember exactly what happened, but I'm sure I must have offended you." With no real conviction, even I hated my insincerity.

"Forget it. I've known lots of guys like you." Ouch.

"Emma, please. I feel horrible. I want you to know that." Weak, weaker, weakest.

"Good. You deserve a two-day hangover."

"Yes, but that's not what I mean. I acted like a teenaged fool. I don't even know why."

"I don't care," she said. "Your life is clearly about escape—that's how you define fun. And apologizing for something you can't remember; how does that work?"

"Look," I said, "I won't bother you ever again, I promise. But can we have a cup of coffee, then go our separate ways?" Even I didn't understand what I was asking.

"What's the point?" she asked.

"Because maybe I sensed something between us, but I messed it up. I want to take responsibility for what I did."

"You can do that on the phone," she said. "Here, let me help. You're so awfully sorry you slept with that woman in the parking lot, right? Look, I don't care who you fork or spoon. You're a jerk and a defective man-child, so leave me alone."

A thud punctured my ear drum. My hangover revived on fresh stimuli, and I tried to remember the parking lot. Sherlock Holmes, I was not. I grabbed my keys. Emma's address was still in my wallet, though all my money was gone.

The car had been cleaned up for my fated mission. Ten minutes later, a two-story house appeared with side steps to the second floor. I knocked hesitantly three times until a prison guard glared through the top pane of three glass rectangles. The deadbolt cracked.

"What are you doing here? I didn't invite you. If I call Roy up from downstairs, your career as a serial jackass is over." Finally, I was awake.

"Five minutes, please? I'll say my piece and get out." Her stare petrified my words before an eye twitch hinted that she was calculating the fastest way to get away from me.

"Five minutes," she said. "But I'm waiting for a call and need to be inside. You're leaving after you tell your lie."

Her modest house was a home. In each window, stained glass lit red bird images and seagulls in patterns. Oriental carpets dressed up the hardwood floors and Tiffany lamps and candles hummed a soft yellow light. The place reminded me of a temple, and of Vi.

"Four minutes. You're not a very fast liar," she said.

Her scorn drained my confidence into puddles dripping into sunlit pools on the carpet. "I'll go. This was a mistake. I'm sorry," I said. As I walked toward the door, I remembered the day Janine left me, her scorn, my obsequious need to hold on to her and how final the desertion after the bedroom door broke it's hinge. But this mess with Emma was my fault alone. I stepped outside. The cold wind slapped me, then I shuffled down the steps straining to hear Em's voice call after me. Nothing, only wind moaning across the stinky beer bottle of my empty mind.

As I backed out of the driveway, my cell rang. "Okay, three minutes. You talk, then you leave." Up the steps I hurried into the rising wind of a singing tea kettle. I prayed Vi wasn't watching my tour-de-force performance on her psychic network.

"Sit down. Tea? I don't have any alcohol." Ouch.

"Yes, please." I was glad she left the room so I could steady myself. On a bookcase next to me were pictures of a child and other people, surely her daughter, Mom, and Dad. Most of the volumes I'd never heard of but a couple I recognized, *Siddhartha* and *The Upanishads*. Before I could scan the entire shelf, Emma brought in a tray.

"Is Nicole any better?"

"Two minutes."

"Okay, good to know. As you've seen, I like to take things in shots." Crazily the joke worked, and her face cracked.

"Yes, you do. But this tea is hot; you might reconsider your preferred behavior." Subtle. I had to admire the control.

"That's one of the reasons I'm here. You see, I've been going through some kind of life change these past few months—maybe even years—and I know you don't believe it, but I think I'm figuring things out."

"Fascinating. But it's none of my business. I don't care who you are or who you were. You're a stranger, a narcissist who at middle age seems committed to remaining a teenager. My life doesn't have room for people who confuse apology with behavior." Check and mate.

"Look, I'm not trying to get you to understand me or fix me or pity me. I'm saying I'm working on my life and thought I saw something in you that reached that better place in me I want to hold on to."

"One minute."

"Emma, my dad disappeared without a trace twenty years ago; nobody knows what happened. His boat showed up near Lake Pontchartrain, but no corpse, no note. I always thought somehow I was to blame. Like maybe he wasn't dead but left home because of me. Since then, I've just focused on screwing up my life."

She scrunched her nose. "Sounds like you need a therapist, not a girlfriend."

"You're right." I swigged the cooling tea, then stood. "Time's up. Thanks for letting me humiliate myself. I suppose all this change stuff is only another delusion." Nothing, no nibble at the mystical bait. I closed the front door behind me.

"Act different. There's a change." Through the glass pane, she stared from a thousand miles away, and then a stinging gust pinched my ear lobes. For an hour I drove aimlessly, then stopped at a used bookstore I'd passed a couple times. I liked the name: *Read This*. The crowded shelves overflowed with mostly contemporary novels, but back in the dustiest corner I found a nook of random serious things: history books, a Bertrand Russell philosophy survey I'd once read, and scattered science books. On the bottom shelf, a faded green cloth stood out: *The Bhagavad Gita*.

In the deserted park across the street, I plopped onto a bench and watched the leaves dance, the day now distinctly colder. As I flipped pages, the writing became too complicated. I knew this was the mystical stuff Emma studied, and she probably even understood how this arcane instruction applied to her world, but I didn't. These days I no longer went to church, no longer prayed, maybe only thought about nature as godlike because I enjoyed being outside. Only the cold steel bench reminded me I was alive and creating my own pain.

In the book's front matter, someone had written an inscription: "For your search." I wondered what that meant; was it scholarly or some life message? Had a man or a woman written it? There were only the initials "TW," my dad's own initials inside a dusty volume no one wanted.

I pulled out my ink pen: "I've begun. LW." With my own little imprint inside the traveling volume, I headed out to deposit the book into Emma's oversized mailbox used to collect magazines and junk mail from annoying strangers.

Chapter 37

Emma's electroshock therapy crackled while I drove back to the hotel. Maybe Mom had been right about recalibrating my emotional investments in women. Pulling into my regular parking spot at the hotel, I noticed a hippie-looking guy behind the wheel of a green Volkswagen van at the back of the lot. Floppy hat and shaggy hair suggested he might be an undercover cop on a stakeout. I hoped I hadn't intruded on some parking lot drug deal, then the van squealed away.

A nap produced a dose of oblivion, then at four, I met Leon and Ortiz. These two workers explained how cleaning the five-story building would proceed. We each had specific wiping, vacuuming, and dumping duties outlined in a checklist with estimated times to accomplish each task. None of us could go to another floor without all three making the move together. The mindless work served the right purpose as I concentrated on efficiency rather than insanity, and by the end of the shift all three of us bantered like old school chums.

Those guys worked hard and were happy. They had wives and kids depending on them and both wanted me to know how proud they were of their families, but I struggled to keep myself present. The first couple of hours I faked small talk with them while I wondered if they thought I was an empty suit masquerading in coveralls.

I was slow to catch on, but after a couple of hours the pattern grooved. At ten at night, we had lunch. Ortiz and Leon both talked about church and how their kids loved school; Leon's daughter wanted to go to Tulane to become an accountant, his son an astronomer. These guys centered themselves around other people. They didn't fret that someone had spilled a pot of coffee in the break room and hadn't wiped down the cabinets or had left party streamers all over one of the cubicles.

After our shift, we crawled into the panel truck to return to the dispatch garage. Ortiz brought along pralines his wife had made, so we all pepped up on the sugar. He insisted I ride shotgun as he slipped into the second-row seating. Looking back on that night, it felt as if Ortiz knew I was missing something and wanted Leon to help me find it before it was too late.

"How'd you like the work tonight?" Leon asked. He knew I'd be writing a report.

"Better than I thought. Enjoyed the serenity of the building where people had been all day, like strange echoes floating in the air. Of course, you two guys were a pain in the derriere, but the work was good."

"You got that right. Me and my Dominican brother here, we some grumpy cats for sure." Leon's friendliness reminded me of high school when Randy, Gus, and I did everything together as a pack and when joking with each other bonded us as a tribe.

"So did you grow up in New Orleans?" I asked, expecting a one-word response, but Leon wanted to chat.

"My mom was a Chinese immigrant from Canada, but I was born in New Orleans. My dad died when I was fourteen, and I been working ever since."

"That's rough. But you had your mom, right?"

"Yeah, Mom worked washing clothes, cleaning houses. Most anything. She had two boys and weren't nothing she wouldn't do to keep us clean and in school, at least for a while."

"So, you finished high school here?"

"No, got my GED, then a bookkeeper friend of Mom's helped me learn some stuff. I've always been good with numbers. Wanted to work at NASA till my dad died. But Mom never blinked and kept pushing me and my brother to make good."

"My dad disappeared too," I said. "But we don't know what happened to him, never came home from fishing one day. My mom was strong, too." I stopped short of self-pity, keenly aware that for no reason I'd made the conversation about me. Leon glanced as if gauging my authenticity.

"Moms be like that." Leon said, then went quiet, but his jaw twitched like he had something more to say.

"How'd you handle things when your dad died?" I asked. "I'm writing a novel about a kid who lost his parents in an explosion, so maybe you can give me a little insight." Leon twisted his head like an insect had stung him, but still he said nothing. Seems I'd gotten pretty good at spoiling other peoples' day. Three traffic lights later, muffled words interrupted the streetlights whizzing past outside.

"Mom used to have this saying: Chop Wood, Carry Water. She always said it like it made sense. But I couldn't listen then, only thought how tough life was, what a bum rap I got not being raised rich, or white. I built up a poison in me telling me how wrong it was for my mama to be scrubbing white folks' clothes for money."

Leon slipped behind the hum of the purring heater. A couple of traffic lights later, I couldn't sit still any longer. "Is Chop Wood, Carry Water a riddle?"

Leon twitched. "Made no sense to me either, but every day Mom kept saying it was the secret to a happy life." An ambulance passed us with lights and siren punctuating the mantra of the heater. "Tell me something. Are you a happy man?" Leon asked, his silky voice relaxing me into rising heat.

"Not really. Getting divorced, and this week got drunk and the girl I like, well, she told me to leave her alone. I guess my batting average on satisfaction is in a slump right now. How about you? Are you happy?" I glanced in the back at Ortiz snoozing against a box of yellow towels.

"Sure. I'm a very happy man. Thanks for asking." He offered nothing more. Those big hands on the steering wheel had control of his life though as we passed a bright construction light, a two-inch scar on his neck reminded me that everyone has a past.

"Are you happy because of Chop Wood, Carry Water?" I asked. He flipped me a surprised look, like a parent when a baby says its first word.

"You got it. See, Mama told me that life breaks down when you only think about what you can get out of it, like, what's in it for me kind of thinking. She says life can't be full if you only fill it with yourself."

"I've been running on empty for a long time," I said, thinking my quip would make Leon smile. He only turned down the heater.

"You want to hear a little story?" Leon asked. I nodded. "When I was thirteen, I had a bicycle paper route. But I liked football and baseball, so sometimes I'd deliver a little late, or maybe skip a few old folks I knew would be asleep by dark. The *Times-Picayune* gave my route to another kid. I got mad and wrecked my bike on purpose, broke the front wheel. After I got home that day, Moona, that's my mom, she done knew what I did."

"I bet she scorched your butt," I said.

"You'd think. But she sat me down, held my hand so I couldn't squirm away, then whopped me with something I didn't see coming. 'Son, the only way to a good life is to do things as best you can, even the little things, especially the unpleasant things, because somebody somewhere is always counting on you.'"

"Don't know if I really get her point," I said. "I mean a couple of folks getting their paper late doesn't sound too awful."

"You sound like me. So, I started to argue with her. But here's the weird part. The minute I backtalked her, she drug me into the bathroom and handed me my toothbrush."

"Huh? What the heck does that mean?"

"Pretty much what I said too. But Mom weren't done. 'Son, this is the most important tool you'll ever own; use it like a surgeon handles a scalpel because I am counting on you to take care of yourself, especially when I'm not around." I couldn't help thinking of Emma, her disappointment'.

Leon's words reverberated as the van glided into the dispatch lot, then he gave me a little pat on the shoulder before opening his driver's side door. I sat for a few seconds, digesting our conversation while considering how deliberate he'd been all night, how clear-minded. Leon's story recalled Reid, that first night we met when he mentioned his daughter's death, that memory almost too personal for a stranger. This town's voice was speaking to me in whispers about life everyone seemed to understand except me.

I slammed the van door and walked over to Leon. He poured a hot cup of coffee from a red thermos, then flashed perfect teeth luminary against the dark morning, a feature of his I hadn't noticed all night. My hand instinctively reached out to shake goodbye just as Ortiz walked by after punching his timecard.

"Hey, Larry, you got to meet our very own Dalai Lama tonight. Cool stuff, huh?" Then he turned away with a friendly half wave. Leon pounced on the comment.

"Ortiz likes to call hisself that." Nice misdirection, but it was clear Leon was uncomfortable with the compliment and had moved it gently away as if it were a hot ember that might burn if held too long. Leon's humble joke unfroze the tension, then he crushed the bones in my hand. "You take care of yourself, my friend." And he turned to walk toward the steel building.

"Wait up, Leon. Think maybe I could hear some more of your mom's stories sometime? Maybe grab a beer one day?" The desperation I heard in my own voice shattered that reserved distance I'd measured between us all night.

"I don't drink no more." His gruff tone surprised both of us, then he added, "But do you like shrimp and grits?"

"Sure. You know a good place?"

"Yeah. My house. Lorraine is working two shifts at the hospital, so my mom is watching the kids right now. She's cooking grits."

Chapter 38

Following Leon's car through a blur of traffic lights, all I kept hearing in my head was the hum of fading voices from that empty building. After parking, I realized his Treme neighborhood was only a couple of blocks from Vi's red door. A small church lighted the corner where we found a couple of spaces. Down the street, tightly packed houses reflected the soft light from the mostly broken streetlamps, every house sharing a different color of red or green or yellow mostly flaking from humidity and flood. This city still frightened me, especially in this too-still morning, so I trailed closely behind Leon. He stopped to hand a dollar to a pencil-thin woman dressed in tattered purple, and I heard her faint, "Bless you."

"Mom's expecting us," Leon said. "But looks like Lorraine ran off without her pocketbook, so I need to run it over to Touro right quick. That'll give you and Mom a chance to chat." The news stole my voice.

"Now don't dawdle, Leon, and get me a stick of unsalted butter, too," Moona said, then she showed me to the worn lounger. A cup of coffee helped calm me. "So how long you known Leon?"

"Only tonight. He was showing me the job." Another sip of liquid asphalt nudged me into a lucid scan of the room. A trombone case rested in a corner, bookshelves on two walls.

"Have you been to New Orleans before?" Moona rocked comfortable in her chair. I tried to make out family pictures on top of the bookcase to my right, two boys with what looked to be an identical replica of Leon, had to be his father.

"Oh sure, but first time here since Katrina. Things have changed."

"You better believe it. My house in the ninth ward burned in the water when a transformer exploded. Most folks skedaddled for higher ground."

"How come you didn't leave?" I asked.

"Go where? All I ever had is right here, my boys and me, since Woodrow died."

"Leon told me about his dad, about Chop Wood, Carry Water, anyway." I slurped a gallon of coffee.

Moona paused her rocking. "Leon was a fretful child. Could have been a athlete, smart, started reading when he was four. Even wrote poetry, and the first time he picked up a trombone, music came to him like song to a mockingbird. I knew early on he was a special soul."

"Wrote poetry? I'm a bit of a writer myself when I get out of my own way." My fake laugh didn't faze her.

"Oh, Leon got in his own way all right. When he was in ninth grade, right before his dad passed, he wrote a essay about this Langston Hugh's poem, *Dream Deferred*. Won a school contest for it and toward the end, he added a little poem of his own. I copied it down and still carry it with me." Her eyes drifted toward the kitchen.

"I'd like to hear it, I mean, if that's okay." I had a sense she needed to step back into the past. "Holding on to our kid's childhood is special, isn't it? This past Christmas, I pulled out the old ornaments my son made in grade school."

"Yes, we need to keep hold of what's been lived," I said. She reached into her purse to produce a piece of notebook paper tucked into the recesses of her wallet. As I held it, the frail creases marked the thousand times it must have been folded and unfolded. Moona offered the yellowed page as if a cherished piece of artwork, but I asked her to read it to me instead.

> *Move to the light*
> *Trapped in its fight with time,*
>
> *And know:*
>
> *That the brightness behind my eyes*
> *Shines from a life divine.*

> L. Simms.

"That's beautiful. Thank you, Moona."

She refolded the ancient scroll with care. "Weren't long after that, Woodrow died out on the oil rigs and that shining light in Leon went dark. He got mean, started drinking, drugs. Never mentioned working for NASA again."

"But he's so calm now, Buddhist-like almost." She stood to pour us another Community coffee.

"For a long time, he was confused. Blamed his dad for drinking too much and ruining his health. Woodrow used to play trumpet all over, with some big names, too. But he didn't know how to check his drinking, so by the time he went out to the oil rigs to cook, he was already in more trouble than we knew."

"I lost my dad when I was twenty. I kind of chucked my plans, too."

"Yeah, Leon was a mess, wanted to wreck his whole life just like he did that time when he tore up his bicycle and lost his paper route."

"He told me that story. Said that's when you talked about how brushing his teeth was the most important thing he could learn."

Moona slapped her knee with a friendly yelp. "That tooth brushing lesson worked pretty good until his dad died, but then trouble fogged everything. Smart boy though. It was a good while later when one day he just straightened himself out. Quit messing up, got a job in the grocery store, even tutored neighborhood kids at math. I don't really know what switched him back onto the right path."

"Maybe he saw the future."

"I guess so. By then it was just the two of us. His older brother, Lavon, had joined the Army. But one night Leon came home in a foul mood, had been in some kind of fight. I went into his room and sat in this very chair, where I used to feed him his bottle when he was a baby. He was all huffy and didn't want to listen, never did back then, but I told him I had a light in me, the light of Jesus, and that light couldn't shine unless it got reflected back to me." She started rocking again.

"So how did he react?"

"Grumpy. Never said nothing. But that very next night after he'd been playing football, he came and kissed the top of my head right before I went to sleep.

"'I see that light, Mama.' That's all he said."

The front door opened with Leon carrying a brown paper sack. "Salted, right?" Showing Moona his full smile, Leon pulled the unsalted butter out of the bag. She exited to the kitchen while Leon took me out onto the porch to listen to the jazz still playing two blocks over.

"They'll go till daylight," he said.

"I see you play trombone, huh?"

"A little. Used to play over on Frenchman's Street all the time, The Spotted Cat, clubs like that. Even played with Trombone Shorty, same as my dad did. That was back when I did bookkeeping in the daytime."

"How long have you worked for Genie Clean?"

"Six months. Hoping to get a day slot one day, then I can play a little music again. But Moona and me still go second-lining once in a while. She got the same parasol she used at my dad's funeral, and I get to rip a few bars on my horn." Leon looked down at the floor as if he'd lost his thought.

"Biscuits are hot. Let's eat."

The next hour I journeyed through a sea of shrimp and grits, spicy to the max. The first half hour required serious pace management, then a little conversation reminded me that the meal wasn't a speed-eating competition.

"Have you always lived in Hattiesburg?" Moona asked.

"Yep. The same house a lot of my life, then Dad disappeared."

"Oh yeah, you did mention that. How did he pass?"

"I don't know," I said. Wrinkles gathered along Moona's forehead. "I mean, he went fishing and never came home. I think he got washed out into Pontchartrain, but Mom still thinks he'll come walking in the front door any day now." Leon and his mom passed an informed glance.

"Why is she so sure of that?" Leon asked.

"I don't know, never thought about it that way. Mom has this intuitive nature about stuff. She's convinced that believing in something can make it happen." I would have given a thousand dollars for a cold Pabst.

"And what do you think happened?" Moona asked. I began searching my tool chest for a good excuse to call it a night.

"I'm not sure. I never believed Dad would leave without a word, so in my mind, he had to be dead."

"I guess Moona and I were a little better off," Leon said. "At least we knew my dad wasn't coming home. Not knowing for sure had to be tough."

"Still is. Mom throws Dad a birthday party every November. Don't know why that irritates me so much."

"More coffee?" Moona asked. I shook my head no.

"I guess your mom decided her role was to stay ready for him," Moona said. "Sometimes, any decision beats being stuck." I had the feeling Moona could hear me thinking.

"Guess so," I said, then cleaned up my last speck of butter and hot sauce.

"But listen, I got a question for you two," I said, my full-blown redirection software now activated. "Looks like New Orleans is making a comeback after Katrina tried to kill everybody and the bankers fleeced the system. Don't you reckon?" My diversion was as skillful as Gomer Pyle giving a Kennedy Center lecture, but at least I expected to hear lots of opinion. They simply stared at their plates as if my question had been spoken in a foreign language.

"Things are okay. The city is fixing up the French Quarter just fine; it didn't flood. Looks like Disneyland over there," Moona said. "But my house in the lower ninth is still a pile of burned trash. Most of us poor folks got deserted. Thank heaven for Leon." Her seriousness reminded me I was tourist looking at this town through rose-colored ignorance, not to mention a lens of whiteness.

"This whole place flooded," Leon said. "Still ain't much good happening here. They trying to tear down the Catholic girl's school to build a hotel. Seems white tourists in the French Quarter need another place to stay, no matter that school been a community center for two decades."

"I'm sorry. I didn't mean to upset either of you. I should keep my mouth shut about what I don't understand." The words rippled from an uncommon moment of clarity as a glimpse of a clue came to me that life for Moona and Leon was far different from what tourists like me encountered. Their life here was real, while mine was a theme-park ride I could get off of and go home.

"It's okay, son," Moona said. "Don't get us wrong, we don't resent tourists the way some folks might. We know they bring money and jobs

145

and that the French Quarter is a heartbeat for the city, but all of them people bring problems, too. Sex business. Alcoholics and such."

Leon leaned forward with about as much tension as I'd seen him exhibit all night. "Most of New Orleans has always been poor black folks, goes back to slavery," Leon said. "After Katrina, anybody with any money skedaddled out of here, leaving us have-nots like that fancy aquarium after the hurricane, no oxygen to breathe. Now we got rich folks buying up all this cheap property, and them folks that left for Houston and Atlanta, they can't afford to move back here no more."

"That's pretty bleak. But you're still here," I said. "And what about that 'silicon bayou' stuff I read about? That ought to bring jobs and people back?"

"How we going to be high tech when we got no skills here, no schools to train folks? A bunch of tourists or part-time property owners don't care about that stuff. They don't want no taxes to educate black kids." Leon leaned back as if angry, so Moona picked up the tag-team topic, but with a skillful re-direction.

"They's some good things happening. That Cowen fellow from Tulane runs something called the Bring Back New Orleans Commission. Now there's a white man trying to help out. New Jersey boy, got this Institute that requires all these Tulane smart-folks to do public service, and now we building the best school system in the country." Moona spoke with an obvious pride. But Leon hadn't given up his earlier protestation.

"So here we go again with the city doubling down on French Quarter privilege, just like when they bulldozed my granddaddy's home off St. Charles to put in that Canal Street entrance to I-10. But they didn't cut down no three-hundred-year-old live oaks in the Garden District, did they?"

The phone rang and it was Lorraine reminding Leon that Lucy and young Woodrow had dentist appointments. I realized I was completely ignorant of the cultural crosscurrents changing life well beyond Katrina's waters.

I needed some air, so I walked out onto the porch. The sun wasn't up yet but the eastern sky was shifting from violet to burgundy, and I could see down the street better now. Creole townhouses and cottages, a thin forest of skinny poles holding up second story balconies and real gas light posts lined the street but were mostly extinguished from neglect. *French Quarter privilege.*

I sat in an old rocker and allowed the back and forth to loosen up my mind. *White privilege. Tourists with picture-painted glasses.*

"Nice out here, huh?" Leon asked, then sat in the rocker next to me. "Sorry about tonight. Me and Mom got a little heavy-handed."

"No. You see what's really going on." My words lost power as I realized I had no status here. My new friend rocked in quiet deliberation. "Leon, you don't know me from fish stew, but I'm a big pile of mess, and I'm sorry if I talked out of turn tonight. Can't figure things too good lately, but I got a sense that New Orleans might be some kind of doorway for me."

"What you so messed up about, white boy?" he asked, his jab reminding me I'd never faced true hardship simply because I'd been born poor or with a different shade of skin.

"You mean other than everything?" I said. "But it isn't just divorce and all those tangles about my dad being gone. I'm seeing now that a long time ago I gave up on my dream to write books about my generation. And frankly, though I need this job, I don't like to work. That messed up enough for you?"

"And you think New Orleans got answers?"

"I don't know. The people here maybe."

"You still got a dream of being a writer?"

I snorted as if he'd made a joke, then realized he was staring me in the eye. "I think so. But now I don't want to write about revolution but about life having meaning, how pain can lead to something better. Got this Raja character kind of channeling my brokenness." I didn't know how to finish the thought.

"Sounds promising. Tell me something: does this Raja have a drinking problem? I mean, you said you got drunk and upset this new girl you like."

"You're not some kind of religious freak, are you?" I asked.

"No. But I've seen the blur of cocaine and alcohol. Alcoholics Anonymous saved me," Leon said. "See this scar? A junkie jumped me on the way home from playing a gig in the French Quarter. I was stoned and it was four in the morning. I beat him half to dead until another junkie cut me. I'd of bled out if a wino hadn't stole my phone and called an ambulance."

"Yeah, but I'm not that bad. Don't do drugs." Leon rocked faster.

"Good. But tell me, do you sometimes drink a little more than you planned, or maybe get a craving?"

I must've been thinking too loud. "Yeah, but everybody does. I'm on the edge sometimes, but I'm trying to be careful." I stared down the street at a burning gas light with a cracked glass leaking hints of violet.

"I bet you are trying," Leon said. "But if you ever decide your relationship with alcohol is too tricky, I run a AA meeting down at that New Life church where you parked. You can come anytime, even tell your story if you like." The softness of his words left me with a warm blanket feel, the opposite of Janine's old Taser jolts.

"I appreciate the offer," I said as Leon leaned back in his chair, his demeanor clearly familiar with my little genre of denial. Time for misdirection. "Hey, you think this might be the beginning of one of those beautiful friendships like Bogart and Claude Rains?" He looked at me sideways, sans the humor I expected.

"Could be. War makes for buddies."

Something about Leon's presence stabilized me, gave me the nudge of courage I'd lost, but I wasn't exactly sure what he meant by war.

"One of these days, I'm going to call you," I said. "So, write down your number for me; I left my phone in the car." He went to get a pen, and when he stepped back onto the porch, I barged further into the unfamiliarity between us.

"Before I go, I want to ask you about something your mom told me." He sat down, twiddling a small piece of yellow paper between his fingers. "She said after your dad died, you just straightened up one day. She didn't even know why. I keep waiting for one of those clear moments in my life, but it never comes. Do you mind telling me what changed you? I mean, if isn't too personal." He turned to face me.

"Mom and me was having problems, mostly because of me. I was mad at everything because I missed school and my dad, missed the idea of having a future. But Mom, she kept right on telling me how Jesus was helping us, but that it was also my job to help myself."

"Sounds like my mom." My little chuckle didn't break his focus.

"One day I came inside and Moona was in the dining room dusting the sideboard. She kept a few pieces of china she'd picked up over the years at flea markets. None of it matched. She didn't hear me, so I stood watching her. She picked up each one of those serving plates and cups, all different patterns, and polished each one like it was going to serve the governor that night. I saw her concentrate on every tiny piece, the napkin ring, the gold rim, the saucer, and she never got in a hurry, never tried to rush the job along. Sure looked boring, but she took the time to do her job right just because it needed to be that way." Leon paused, and I saw a tear.

"It's okay, Leon. Don't worry about it," I said.

"It ain't that, Larry. I'm remembering how for so long I never listened good to Mom, never put together that all that brushing my teeth and doing things right stuff really meant something. But that afternoon, seeing Mom like she was in some temple doing the Lord's work, my mind opened, and I understood what she'd always meant with her Chop Wood, Carry Water business."

"Satori," I said. He cricked his neck with a frown. "Buddhist term, means enlightenment, seeing the true nature of who you are."

"Sure enough," Leon said, "I saw then that to find the God in us we got to be alive right now, this second, totally alive. No thinking about ourselves, just doing things the very best we know how, no hold back, no hurry to be done. I saw God in my mama that day. Yep, sure as sunrise Jesus was wiping down cups and saucers in that dusty afternoon." A persimmon-orange sun peeked between burned out streetlights, and there again was that big Leon smile.

"Well, I better get going before I have to start paying you rent," I said. "Besides, you're on dentist duty." A bone realigning handshake sent me walking. "Tell Moona my mama would approve of her shrimp and grits." I gave a little wave but never turned to face Leon.

"Hey, Larry. You want me to walk with you?" I began shaking my head no, then I saw a group of rowdies gathering across from where my car was parked.

"Yeah, sure. Since we're work buddies and all." We began a slow stroll. "Thanks again for inviting me. I really like your mom."

"Anytime. You a good listener. Folks are coming back to New Orleans now. See some hope. Asians, Europeans, all the colors in the rainbow. Ain't no fire or flood can run folks off this spot on the river." It occurred to me that maybe Leon also had a touch of James Joyce mode still inside.

"Broke down don't mean broke for good." My words fell lifeless on the sidewalk.

"Good folks be sticking together here at New Church, fighting that war with ourselves. Maybe you'll come be a soldier too one of these days."

"Could be. But first you got to riddle me one more thing. You're a smart man, music talent, good family, so why did you take this job working nights with the Genies?"

"Easy. I get tuition reimbursement after a year. Gonna get me a business degree at Xavier." Leon's jawline stiffened as he straightened up his back and walked ahead like a steel crane inching toward a work site. Turning his head slightly, he left me with my own satori of sorts: "See, white boy, folks like me, we don't get to start out as district manager on the first day."

Chapter 39

Darkness and dawn met as men stepped onto porches with lunch pails and women clutched purses against the morning chill. The Lucky Day bar went dark while an old man at Horn-Dog Bob's music club pulled down steel shutters. All along the tight blocks, bright colors juxtaposed trash in gutters with stray cats ripping into black bags placed on curbs as buoys in the tide of a new workday.

Hungarian and Vietnamese cafés dotted a neighborhood pockmarked by unfinished renovations, and I pulled over to the Bien Pharmacy to pick up some razor blades. The bell above the door clanked and a balding Asian man behind the counter tipped his Saints cap. I'd expected this would be a Latino business but a sign on the wall corrected me: *Thanh's Vietnamese Egg Coffee $2.*

The place was a mancave of Saints memorabilia from super bowl 2010, even a signed eight-by-ten-inch photograph of Drew Brees.

"Are you Mr. Thanh?" I asked.

He noticed my glance at his sign and with a friendly chuckle responded, "No. That's my wife. I only work for her."

"Is her coffee good?"

"Dessert in a cup." His beautiful accent sounded like music. As he stepped into a back room, I studied the football collectables and disaster photos on the wall behind the counter. There, that span of I-10 connecting to Canal street, the place Leon had described as a copse of live oaks shading his grandfather's homestead now stood swamped with thousands of people stranded on a concrete island above Katrina's flood. Homemade signs pleaded for water, and in a photo apparently taken from a helicopter, throngs of people in the distance looked like seashells on a forgotten beach. A child held cardboard with crayon lettering: *We're not dead.*

Oddly, across the top of the picture display, masses of Mardi Gras beads hung in the colors of a rainbow. I placed a pack of blades on the counter. "You're a Saints fan, huh?" I wanted to ask this fiftyish-year-old man if he was in any of those pictures, but I didn't know if I should. He deserved the humanity of a question, but I wasn't sure what was right, or worse, what was wrong, and I imagined myself watching from that picture-taking helicopter.

"Drew Brees top saint." He chuckled at his obviously standard joke. "You live in French Quarter?" he asked.

"No. Visiting friends." The sun pierced the plate glass window to my right.

"But I was wondering if there's a good place to eat around here, dinner maybe."

"Oh, yes. You in the heart of food. Istvan, across street, Hungarian. It's how fish cooked in the modern day." I was taken by his neighborhood pride. At that moment, the front door opened, and Mr. Bien greeted in fluent French a woman he clearly knew as he complimented her new glasses. She blushed as she touched the black frames, then they joked in waves of unfamiliar sound.

I slipped outside without notice, the bright sunshine leaving me wondering whether I could survive here with my glaring otherness.

Back at the hotel, the parking lot of half-filled spaces reminded me of a used car lot. It seemed a strange time to be coming home so early, especially sober, but my new parking spot closer to the hotel entrance waited with only a discarded Popeye's Chicken bag as a marker. I popped open the trunk to grab my things, and as I slammed it shut, a disheveled man appeared from the passenger side of my car. "What do you want?" I asked, backing away.

"Relax, sir, only want to bum a cigarette." A slight man dressed in camouflage fatigues; his mud-colored ponytail almost made him look like a woman. He stepped forward trying to hide the hitch in his right leg.

"Don't have any," I said. "Get away from me."

"Please, mister, I'm only a veteran hoping you could spare a dollar.

Haven't eaten today." He stared at the ground. I wondered if he knew it was morning.

Remembering I'd stuffed in my pocket the change from the drugstore, I pulled out a five and some coins. "Here, get yourself breakfast."

"Thanks. And you best be careful around here. People might be watching, maybe having some bad thoughts," he said.

"Why do you say that? Do you know something about my car being vandalized?"

"No, sir. Only passing through from Baton Rouge. Don't know nothing about this car." His voice didn't sound right, too pleasant, almost like he was laughing underneath his words. *Whoosh*. Through the hotel door came a man carrying a briefcase, and in that second, my vagrant slipped to the edge of the building and disappeared leaving behind only a wisp of his beer-tinged sweat.

Chapter 40

By Tuesday, my weekend hangover had vanished, but I knew I'd better skip any more oysters for a while. At four in the afternoon, I met a supervisor, Chub Phillips, who wore a watch with a timer and constantly set little goals for us to walk somewhere, review something, or take a break during which he seemed to figure square roots in his secret mind. Time spent with him was a night course in statistics.

"So, you seem to enjoy the precision of numbers," I said.

"Yes. How long something takes and how long it should take. I calculate facility size and function and can model service time to within a ten percent margin of error. No deadbeats in my crews," he said. Chub's hyper practicality painted over the purity of Moona's spiritual lesson to young Leon. Chub was a sergeant without a military. For over an hour, he shared the intricacies of vacuuming efficiency, cleaning solvents, and the necessity of prescribing time increments. My soul corroded when I heard people must be motivated by task-defined numbers or they would be unproductive. Then, the revelation.

"You think I'm boring, don't you?" Chub asked.

"No, it's not that. Maybe a little more analytical than me. I'm a word guy." He rose while wiping his wire-rimmed eyeglasses, then sat on the corner of his desk looking down at me slumped in a faux leather chair.

"Numbers are the skeleton of life. Everything can be measured; it's the only way you can determine change." I suppose my head nodded slightly because he leaned in. "But life isn't only a skeleton. See, numbers are poetry to me. But I can't spend all my time there, too addictive. That's why I paint on Sundays."

"You paint? Like Habitat for Humanity?"

"I paint scenes down at the zoo or sometimes the river." Chub bloomed a crimson pink.

"Really? How long you been painting?" I had an image of some mechanical paint-by-number collision in color.

"Started five years ago. After my wife left me." He paused, his left hand in a minor tremor. While other guys were watching the Saints and drinking beer, old Chub was off painting sunsets and bluebirds. I know it's wrong, but I couldn't imagine him finding that part of his soul he didn't have to calibrate.

"Do you have anything I could look at?" I asked.

A slight movement of his head indicated no, then he turned and opened his credenza, pulling out two paintings, each the size of a manila folder. One was a rainbow over the river with a paddleboat passing in the foreground. The other, I struggled to process. A rear-facing silhouette of a man and woman holding hands while walking down a grassy path, a distinct sunset ahead of them. The man in dark clothes, the woman in a lemony drop-waist dress. But the fascinating thing was the impressionistic flow trailing behind the woman as a shimmering wave disturbance unsettling the air as she passed, ripples of a personal image in the language of Renoir.

"My God. This is spectacular."

"Only the other side of the equation," Chub said, before putting the paintings away.

"What do you mean?" I asked.

He twitched his head right to left, looked at his watch, then spoke while staring at papers on his desk. "Life has an algorithm. Bodily functions, work, recreation, all represent variables. But survival isn't living; it's only existing. That's why I paint." He stopped in mid-sentence, then turtled back inside himself.

"I agree," I said, "creativity allows. . ." He raised his hand stop me.

"I must get back to work," he said. Perfunctory words, mechanical tone, the zap of manufactured precision had returned the world to order. Outside his office, the hallway blurred in evaporating images of an artist lost inside a vast calculator. A torn, *"Go Saints"* sticker peeled loose from Chub's door. *Chub, are you just a good old boy?*

155

Outside the glass foyer, a yellow moon throbbed inside a thin red trim. I thought of Hal in the movie *2001: A Space Odyssey*. Chub would understand what caused the moon's red lining, but I wondered what night looked like in the sludgy air of New Washington. Raja's world over-engineered by people like Chub leaving generalists like Raja and me peering at life from the outside.

Chub perceived detail where I saw vistas, but maybe art is the merge of both views. And on the sidewalk, a lost name badge: Thea Moran. I knew Thea as the Greek goddess of light. It hit me the name formed an anagram of "heat." *Yes, Thea, Thea Vitale would become Raja's lover.*

Chapter 41

My Wednesday afternoon work session was canceled as the manager had to race to the hospital to welcome his first child making his big entrance a month early, so I sat in my room browsing the Internet. Turns out, Chop Wood, Carry Water is a Zen Buddhist proverb about what we do before enlightenment, and then also afterward. The phrase left me wondering if I was always supposed to do things without judgment, like when Leon and Ortiz hadn't gotten angry at the party mess left in that cubicle. Those guys hadn't shown resentment the way I had, but that didn't mean they hadn't experienced it. They knew I would be writing a report and that I was management, and perhaps more problematic, I was white.

My whiteness created a different reality for me, one a lot less focused on caution. The cleaning business was becoming less charming, but what scared me most was the realization that I was craving tequila. I tried meditating like I'd seen in those Internet videos, but all it did was hurt my knees, and my mind kept obsessing on Thanh's egg coffee. I needed distraction.

While searching for my spider friend, something Emma had said lit up on the blank wall of my mind: "Act different." Those words lobbed at me through her front door jolted my fingers into motion.

"Hey, it's Larry."

"You hungry again?" Leon asked.

"Yeah, actually, but I'm calling to see if you got a New Life thing happening today. My work session got cancelled." The volume control on my stupidity infuser had stopped functioning, and I laughed for no reason.

"Starts in forty-five minutes. There's a sign outside the choir room door."

I don't remember driving to the church but only thinking about what to do if I got called on to speak. *Do I have to say I'm an alcoholic?*

Someone had brought hot donuts, and immediately I liked this group of six men and three women sharing a New Orleans Yat in their muffled conversation.

"Welcome, Larry. We don't have a speaker today, and since you're the only first-timer, I'll offer you a chance to speak first if you like. We support each other here. No pressure."

Every instinct urged me to decline as I figured Leon ambushed me because he was afraid I'd leave if he waited, but I walked to the podium, then Leon sobered me with a handshake. I surveyed the group, older men, and women under forty. A gentleman wearing a fedora with a blue feather gave me a wink and the jolt of connection almost launched me into the fake opening I'd concocted, but something about the earnest look on a pregnant Asian young woman wearing two different kind of shoes stopped me. She deserved some truth.

"My name is Larry Winstead, though some people call me Anthony. Twenty years ago, my dad went fishing one summer day and never came home. My mom kept right on going, but me, I tripped on the step from teenager to adulthood." I lunged at a water bottle.

"To help Mom pay off the IRS, I dropped out of my college writing program and went to work at Blockbuster in the daytime and the Rebel theater at night, but my dad's shoes proved too big to fill, and I needed a few drinks to help keep my courage up." Car horns blared outside as some fender bender excited the traffic. I finished the bottle of water.

"Got a girl pregnant and pretty much quit writing." The young girl in the front row rubbed her belly. "These days, my son is on the west coast and my wife moved in with a marriage thief, so my best friends Jose Cuervo and Mr. Pabst mostly keep me company. But they're getting a little hard to manage." A siren outside flustered the room.

The man with the fedora spoke up: "Take it slow, son; we got plenty of donuts and time."

"I mentioned some folks call me Anthony. Only one person really, she thinks there's an artist inside me that needs a new friend." The fedora nodded. "I been punishing my mom for believing Dad will come home someday. Don't know why I do that. Guess it distracts me from how much I dislike myself." A heave overwhelmed my own words, and I started backing away from the podium.

Leon met me halfway. Tepid applause dripped as whispers. *I wasn't ready. I messed it up.* Leon stepped to the lectern.

"Thank you, Larry. Everyone here has lost something or made a mess of things. But we're all here because we've found something. We found each other. And we've found a higher power that might be able to help you, too."

Chapter 42

On Thursday morning, a four-hour review of our week concreted the capillaries in my brain until my only pulsing thought was of dinner at Vi's. At four, I parked at the zoo so I could stretch my legs. All the thoughtful categorizing and naming of animals by the Audubon staff left me scanning faces for Chub. No wonder he liked to paint here in the hyper-regulation of these natural looking scenes. All around, parents and children meandered as they spent money, societal order functioning as a stylized regimen encasing our forgotten lives and urging us not to notice.

An older woman painted the naturalized home the monkeys pretended to accept. I snuck a glance at her artful hints of flowers and food and almost gagged when considering the symbolism of my pecuniary shackles chaining me to garbage cans that must be counted. Before the industrial revolution, people grew their food or hunted it; now we'd substituted money for nature, and my soul withered at the thought of a bank vault symbolizing a teeming modern forest. *Do they sell beer here?*

A gorilla stared at me. Had depriving him of the chance to find his own food destroyed his connection to the deep nature of his species? His boredom looked like an injury. That open-air yet caged life hinted of Raja's ennui, his entitled survival suffocating his wildness.

A Tennessee Williams quote ripped through my head: "Man is by instinct a lover, a hunter, a fighter, and none of those instincts are given much play at the warehouse." *Maybe a swim in the alligator pit?*

Over by the giraffe habitat, a dark-haired child stepped up and down off a curb while yanking at her mother's coat—Nicole and Emma.

They hadn't seen me. Fight or flight, my instinct was to hide in the underbrush of avoidance, but without giving myself time to decide, I brazened into hostile territory.

"You know those are man-eaters, don't you? I wouldn't get too close." My words reached ahead announcing my approach. Emma frosted me with a stare.

"No, they aren't, Mommy. Giraffes eat leaves." The little girl's correction seemed so perfect, so organized. "Now if you were a caterpillar on a leaf up in that tree, then you'd be in danger. Right, Mommy?"

What a lovely compromise, so focused on the immediate. Seeing the little girl hold her mother's hand reminded me how experience creates a hazy film through which we struggle to view the real world, Plato's world of shadows cast on the cave wall.

"Didn't mean to bother you, only to say hello and meet this lovely person with you. Your sister, I presume?"

Nicole immediately got the joke. "He's funny, Mommy."

"Yes, he's quite the joker." Her sarcasm reminded me that I was alive but also that simple choices carry significance, especially for single parents. Emma didn't have the luxury of squandering time the way I did.

"Well, it was nice to meet you, Nicole. Don't forget to check out the alligator pit. It's scary."

"How do you know my name?" Nicole asked. "And what's your name?" I realized I'd been so abrupt I sailed past the civilities.

"I apologize, young lady. My name is Larry. I know your uncle Roy, and of course, your mom. She told me your name. Only wanted to say hi and caution you about the giraffe danger." Nicole fidgeted, and I inserted a mental cork.

"Yes, Nicole, Larry is a friend of Roy's. He likes to party at the café." Cold.

"Okay, I hear the Crescent train coming. I best run. See you girls around." I turned away but heard Nicole speak:

"Mommy, that train doesn't come here. He said the Crescent was coming."

"He's only having fun. He's not serious." I kept walking, then stopped at a kiosk to buy popcorn. As the young man gave me change, a hand touched my shoulder.

"I apologize, Larry. I was rude," Emma said. "That's the wrong behavior to teach my daughter." A few feet away Nicole was buying an ice cream cone, giving us a brief moment of privacy.

"It's okay."

"Hard to believe," Emma said, "but you're almost nice when you're real."

I couldn't quite understand what to do with this statement, but I had an idea. "Emma, I'm trying to pull myself together. Still have some chopping and carrying to take care of. . ." I ran out of words.

"Oh really, Zen Buddhism?" Now I was in trouble.

"Spent a little time at a bookstore looking over some things." My position strengthened but only slightly.

"Oh yeah. I forgot to say thanks for the book you left. You should have kept it since you're a student."

"Student? I'm a foggy lamp hoping the sun will come out." I wasn't even sure what that meant. She softened more.

"Look, can I ask a question?" Emma said, staring at the ground. "If I wanted to start over with you, would you promise it would only be as friends, nothing but friends? I need slow."

"I need slow, too," I said. "It's my high-performance speed." She didn't react. "But I'm tired of pretending. I want to figure out the real me."

Those last words were supposed to remain in my thoughts. Maybe this woman had a stabilizing effect, or maybe I was finally gestating as an adult. She walked towards Nicole who had chocolate ice cream dripping down her dress, her head cocked as she studied the helium balloons above a vendor stand.

"Do you go home tomorrow?" Emma asked.

"Supposed to but on Saturday I'm having lunch with a friend and her dad, so not sure."

"Well, tofu season did open last week. Plus, I'm still looking for a good paragraph tutor." Her light tone spread salve over the skin-peeling narrative of the past few days as we watched a little boy staring at the sky, his red balloon wafting away on a breeze. I wondered if the boy realized the symbolism of his life slipping past unnoticed, of the regret thoughtless moments can leave on the tick of time. So much depends upon a red balloon.

Chapter 43

Mother-daughter glances twirled in my head as I idled in accident-slowed traffic. They lived in a private hive I could only observe. But Mom and I had our own hive, though ours was filled with more doubt. Then, the too-hot car heater lulled me back to idle days when Linda's voice brimmed with poetry, those moments of sound and touch and taste inside the bud of youth.

Standing at Vi's door, I wondered if she ever felt lonely, then beyond a doorway of hanging beads a radio moaned while books lazed on dusty countertops. *Winning* by Jack Welch was the only title I caught—odd.

"Have a seat. Wine or vodka?" To my right a courtyard opened onto red bougainvillea, yet we sat in the kitchen cramp.

"Wine, please." Around the room, paintings lined the walls, primitives mostly of a women looking at the ocean, a mother and daughter picking flowers, and a giant navy-blue chasm falling off into darkness with occasional bright lights dotting the sides of a shrinking hole to nowhere.

"Did you paint these?"

"Some of them. My daughter did that portrait of me, but it looks more like my grandmother back in Indonesia." A red wine appeared.

"Here's to your search," she said, then scanned my face.

"Vi, you keep talking about this journey, but I still don't get it. Maybe it's only the quest we all follow in life, like a river looking for the ocean even when it doesn't know what an ocean is." Vi said nothing. "I've had a pretty tough week. Not so good with people. Drank too much and offended this woman I like. Even forgot to tell Mr. Perder thanks for showing me his studio." Vi sipped her wine. "Need me a little Vi time right now." I figured leaving out the AA meeting might simplify the conversation.

"Are you talking about Reid Perder's shop?" She skipped over my self-pity to sort out a fact instead.

"Yeah, you know him? Talented fellow."

"He made a staircase for a woman I knew years ago over in the Garden District. Mr. Perder built this beautiful iron thing and had a little seat installed on it with a motor so Mrs. Tate could get up and down the stairs on her own." The words fell as if Vi had nothing else to say, so I sat back hoping she'd get back to my question about the journey.

"Before we eat, I need to tell you something," she said. "A couple days ago, I called your mother in Mississippi."

"Oh really?"

"In that letter you gave me, she asked me to. We've talked twice now."

"Chummy."

Vi stepped to a chest of drawers where she'd placed the wine bottle, then poured each of us a refill. "Your mom wants to know where your daddy is." The low rumble of my monologue at the New Life church thudded like a lone tuba.

"How would she expect you to know about Dad?"

"I know you think I'm a charlatan," Vi said, "but your mother is more trusting. You think you know things. Maybe you think you're in control. But you ain't. Nobody is—no white man, no politician, no golf-playing CEO."

"I didn't mean to offend you—"

She held up her hand. "You said what you meant. That's a good thing. Most times you say what you don't believe." Vi leaned forward, her onyx pendant absorbing the light. "Your mother has a secret. Did you know that?"

My throat tightened, so I slurped to hide myself. "No, I didn't. But I do know she has a crazy birthday party for Dad every year."

"Maybe your haughty attitude is why she don't tell you things." Vi leaned back, as if a patient scientist watching me frog boil in slow realization. "See how short-tempered you got with me? How you made fun of Ina's birthday party? All because you still mad at your daddy? Maybe mad at yourself, too."

"What difference does it make? He left us. He's dead. Even if he did come back, I wouldn't love him."

"Now, that's what I'm talking about," Vi said. "You ain't saying what you mean or understanding what you believe. You miss your daddy, but you think he stopped loving you. This is why it's hard for you to love yourself; it's what makes you mean." She stood, then moved a glass figurine on the dresser to the other side beneath a painting of an old boat abandoned on a muddy bank.

"Did you ever think maybe he can't get back? Maybe it's for your own good he don't come home? You've filled yourself with all this judgment, and you don't even know what you judging."

The skin around my nose stretched tight around a sharp pain drilling into the back of my nostrils.

"Your mama got something to say," she said.

"I don't know any secret," I said. Vi sprung to her feet as if twenty years old.

"You stubborn child. Your mother been protecting you. More than a husband, she wants her son's daddy back; she sees what it done to you. And what you been doing this whole time? Trading her goodness for your arrogance? You need to shut up and listen to your mama."

Vi, stepped close to me, her dark eyes a flint in the wine light. "I don't know what your mama's secret is either, but I do know you still searching for your daddy. You been walking ahead even when your mind was doodling behind." As she cupped her hands around my jaws, the wrinkles of her forehead stretched into deep rivers.

"Son, you been disrupted. Your future went one way, but your hope went another. You been unraveling ever since." Then she turned and sat. "They's one more thing. Every day your mama has been with you is a day she might have been gone. You see, the Lord can take us whenever he wants. You ever think about who you'd be if Ina had been swept away to go help Jesus?"

"No. Yes, I mean. . ."

"You're not a selfish child," Vi said. "You a good son. But you learned bad habits that needs to be let go. You act like somebody owes you something. Nobody owes you nothing. All this loneliness you got, you creating that yourself."

"But. . ." And I forgot what I wanted to say.

"Your daddy may not be alive," Vi said, "but you still looking for him and denying it at the same time. Best let go of that struggle and get on with sharing your mama's hope."

"You think this is why I gave up on being a writer?"

"Did you give up on being a writer? You sure ain't talked about it much."

"Yeah, after Dad disappeared, I quit my writing program."

"Just shut your mouth. I ain't listening to no whining. You was a coward then, weren't you? Didn't think you could cut it, so you used the pain of your Daddy leaving to give up on your dream. Maybe to give up on living. Maybe you can write, maybe you can't. But I do know you afraid."

She pointed to the painting off in the corner, the one with the dark chasm leading down into a vortex dotted with receding lights marking the way. "See that picture? It's called *Desperation*. A friend of mine painted it after his wife left him and took his son away to Haiti. Disappeared into nothing. Nearly killed poor Jude. But he painted this and gave it to me a long time ago. Said he'd been in a well of darkness and that I'd helped him find enough light to climb back up out of that hole."

She offered nothing else, but I stared into those dotted splotches of white. I'd seen the painting wrong; it wasn't a picture of going into the well but of finding the lighted handholds to get out. Vi levitated in a quietness that reminded me of Maya standing on that cliff in November, the roaring current down below. I'd stepped into my own riptide in 1993, flipped myself upside down so that everything up looked wrong to me.

Vi's silhouette hovered before the dusk-colored courtyard behind her, and I swear I heard the rush of the falls back in Hattiesburg, that cold water Maya dipped her hands into before christening me as Anthony that afternoon.

"Vi, I got a little secret of my own, something I'm just now figuring out. Yesterday, I went to an AA meeting over at the New Life church." Vi looked at me with the placid stare of a Rembrandt portrait, then dropped her eyes to my empty wine glass.

"Is that Leon Simms's meeting you went to?"

"You know him?"

"I do. Knew his daddy, Woodrow, and been second-lining with Moona for forty years."

"Moona ever tell you her Leon story about Chop Wood, Carry Water?" I asked.

"You mean about when Leon tore up his bike on purpose? Who do you think bought him his new wheels?" Vi pointed to the chest of drawers. "Why don't you light that candle there for us? We need some light, don't you think? So we can both see what we ain't been seeing."

Chapter 44

Friday morning, we received our management rankings. My lowest performance was for enthusiasm, seems my faked interest in building maintenance lacked sincerity. But instead of obsessing on my score, I headed to Iron Arts.

Reid had added something to the roses above the entrance. The leaves still held that copper patina, but he'd painted the vining flowers a dogwood white, the trailing spray now wrapping the door in permanent springtime. Inside, Shala stepped from behind a muslin wall.

"Hello there. Nice to see you again. I was about to pour myself some tea. Would you care for a cup?" Her cheery voice made me wish I'd brought donuts.

"No, thanks. I wanted to check out these glass fish that Mr. Perder showed me on Saturday."

"Of course." And she flipped on the sun. In the distance a door opened.

"I thought that sounded like you. How are you, Larry?" Reid shoved his bone cruncher over my hand, this time giving me a less punishing welcome.

"Fine, thank you. Listen, I want to apologize for getting a little out of control last weekend." His craggy face turned pink. "And thanks for the meal at Roy's," I said.

"You don't need to apologize to me, but you picked up the tab. I ought to be thanking you for being the big spender that night, though I tried to pay. You did make lots of new friends—close friends—before I took you home." He checked his words as he glanced at Shala standing next to us. I wanted to swim with the fishes.

"Anyway, I was thinking I'd pick out one of these glass beauties."

"Fine idea. These with the slabs of clear green inside the frame are the most affordable; those up at the top have a leaded crystal. This yearling trout is two hundred dollars. But I'll knock off a hundred since you paid for the feast at Roy's."

"Oh, no. My treat to Roy's fiesta was as a friend. This purchase is as a customer, and I insist you charge me what anyone else would pay." He frowned but didn't argue. Then I realized I was demanding maximum cost.

"Well, if that's what you want," Reid said. His slight embarrassment inspired me.

"You're a real artist," I said. "You deserve what you earn here." The words sounded like a drunken brother-in-law's toast at a wedding, so I decided not to mention how I wished my dad could see his collection. Though my sentiment was genuine, I couldn't help noticing how phony I must have sounded, and the words draped over the moment like an oversized costume.

"Thank you for that," he said. "I work hard—all my team does, and we're proud of what we do. So, my friend, you've got yourself a deal, though you drive a mighty hard bargain." And his firm voice hinted outside the words that he respected I'd tried to be generous, his vacant blue eyes playful for a moment. This was a man not driven by avarice, the kind of man I think my dad might have been in a different life. I wondered what a long-term friendship with Reid would look like, how much he would allow anyone to see his essence.

Chapter 45

An hour before going to Emma's for dinner, I found a little café filled with sunflower-colored light, then soon cradled a hot mug. Voices from the past few days gathered around the steaming coffee now become a little campfire holding close the fresh stories of a fading week.

The waitress broke my trance with a refill before wiping down the next table, her fuchsia blouse reminding me of an azalea luffing in the breeze. She rearranged flowers in a small, beveled vase, refreshing their moment while wiping clean crystal edges, her attentiveness invisible to the entire world except me.

Above the terracotta roofline a warm breeze stirred, heat from the tiles lifting away the heavy air while nudging me toward that fissure within me I could never get beyond. Had my father simply become some Odysseus wandering but never arriving? Did he sit in a lonesome café thinking of Mom and me?

I slouched before the final glints of sun pinged the clever cut of light-splitting crystal shaped by fingers long since withdrawn. And there, a tiny rainbow summoned me into its brilliant resistance of the fading day beckoning beyond the courtyard, beyond the box of life, outside the thought-filled walls so comfortably set in time. And to comfort my squall of thought, oak leaves lurched into the breeze around me. I so wished I could have seen that street of mighty trees where Leon's father had been raised, that boulevard of dream-filled houses groomed now into groves of concrete.

From the serving station, a shriek of shattering glass rushed my table just as a wayward leaf sailed onto the chair next to me. Its frilled edge reached up to the light, perhaps out to the red oaks fretting seasonal change along the sidewalk at New Life church. Family trust steadied Leon's life: his loss hadn't become the entrapment I'd allowed mine to be, and I imagined Moona might say that uncertainty casts a suffocating shade.

Beneath the chair opposite me, a wary sparrow gathered crumbs, its little head vibrating as practical machinery. What mind lived in that busy dime-sized brain? Was there thought of love, or the fading day, a memory of his mother, or his first flight? His world functioned without the torture of wonder, impervious to doubt. And as the rainbow crawled back into its crystal womb and the nearly bare oak limbs around the café swayed in the breeze, I imagined that trees feel sadness when leaves give up on summer.

Chapter 46

"I'm not sure I'd call myself the paragraph man, but I told your mom I'd share something my grandmother taught me a long time ago," I said.

"Your grandmother knew how to write paragraphs?" Nicole asked.

"Yep, used to etch symbols onto the cave walls."

"Huh?" Nicole said.

"Never mind. My mom's Mom taught English for thirty years at Petal High School. She showed me how a paragraph gets built just like a house. First, put in the floor. Next, put up the walls, and then finally, add a pointy topped roof. Simple as that."

"Maybe you're not the paragraph man," Nicole said.

"I don't disagree," I said. "But let's say you want to write about how great your mom is. The sentence that starts the paragraph is the floor. For example, 'My mom shows me love every single day.' Next, you need to add walls, like, 'she keeps my clothes washed, she makes me breakfast and dinner every day, and she takes me to the doctor when I'm sick.' Make sense?"

"So, I can only have three walls?"

"Good question. You can have as many walls as you want; you can even take each one of those walls and make a separate paragraph out of it," I said.

"What about the roof? What's that?"

"After you get the walls put up, the roof goes on top. The roof to the sky shows your reader how to spot other ideas you might use in your next paragraph. For example, how's this for a roof? 'My mom will always be my best friend because she wants me to be happy.' The next paragraph could then be about how she helps you be happy."

The next twenty minutes wandered through tales of Nicole's dance lessons, her cat, and pictures her mom asked her to draw. The paragraph idea took us off into the unexplored universe between us. Emma's wink showed me my work had been successful.

"I can play the drums," Nicole said. "My cousin has a drum set and Mom takes me over there sometimes. She won't let me get my own drums. I don't know why."

"Maybe when you're a little older, but you have to be a good girl first." Sparkling dialogue that Nicole discounted.

"I don't think so, Mr. Winstead. Mommy says I shouldn't act a certain way just to get rewards. I should do things because they are right."

"Okay, class is over," Emma said, realizing I required tethering back to the mothership. "Why don't you go take a quick bath? Dinner is almost ready. Then we'll show Mr. Winstead your drawings." Nicole held up two pictures she'd done that afternoon, a field of flowers and another of an elephant, then disappeared into the rear of the house.

"She's a smart thing. You've done a nice job."

"Thanks. Nicole has always been a good child. Came out that way. Do you have children?"

"Tim works in Seattle. We talk every couple of weeks. One day I'm going to surprise him with a visit."

"What are you waiting on?" she asked.

"Unemployment cut down on my coast-to-coast travel, but after I save a little money, I'm going to do it." My energy flagged, but Emma pushed further.

"This new job should help out. Tim misses you, I bet." I hadn't thought so much about Tim missing me, and again Emma rotated my thinking. Watching her stir the wok, her hair pinned in a ball atop her head, I pretended to relax in the homey kitchen released for the moment from worries about unnoticed life, especially Mom's unshared secret.

"Em, can I ask you something?" She nodded. "Nicole said something interesting about not doing things for reward but doing them because they're the right thing to do. Struck me as curious."

Emma shuffled a bowl then dropped more vegetables into the stir-fry, even doing that with easy grace, and I glimpsed that artistic immediacy Renoir (and Chub) captured in color as they feathered the blur of change with paint.

"Oh, that's nothing," she said. "An idea I picked up from a meditation instructor. She told me when we think of the end goal too much, we substitute illusion for being alive." I must have frowned, and Emma turned back to the stove.

"Please, don't stop," I said. "I can't say I get what you're saying, but I'm listening." She stirred as if digging for answers. I wanted to relieve the tension. "I met this guy Leon a few days ago. He talked about focusing on things as they happen, being fully aware of right now. What Nicole said sounded the same."

"Your Leon seems at peace."

"I suppose. He has a gentle way about him, like things didn't ruffle him." She offered no response, but a doubtful look told me she wondered if I was playing head games. "One day when he was a kid, Leon came up behind his mom while she was polishing the mismatch of china their poor family owned. She took each piece carefully and gave it full attention; Leon said this was part of some philosophy his mom called Chop Wood, Carry Water.'" Emma spun around.

"Ah, that's where you got that from. It's a well-known Zen Buddhist saying. The Buddha said that before we achieve enlightenment, we must chop wood and carry water, and after enlightenment, we must chop wood and carry water."

"So, chopping and carrying don't have anything to do with becoming enlightened?" I asked. She grunted as if I'd told a knock-knock joke.

"How western of you—we must do A to achieve B, right?" I stared back, trying not to agree or disagree as I wasn't sure which answer was correct. She took her time removing three glasses from the shelf, then poured iced tea.

"An old instructor helped me with a proverb," she said. "It's like standing on a hillside pointing at the moon and confusing the finger with the moon. That's what thinking is: life in planning mode, regurgitating the past, plotting the future, all while ignoring the present." She shifted weight to her left leg. "Life is the tiny detail of now, the polishing of silver, the pouring of tea, the chopping and carrying in our lives."

More confused than enlightened, I nodded to show I was still listening. Then without warning, Nicole sprang into the kitchen. "Mommy, the twins got their new puppy! Can I go see him, please, please?" Her face shone like a full moon, and I was reminded how children live in the universal presence of now. Emma cut her eyes to see if I'd noticed.

"Dinner is almost ready. I hate to make Mr. Winstead wait."

"Oh, don't worry about me," I said. "A good tofu can simmer for a while, makes it tender." My smile stepped on the punch line, but Nicole laughed, leaving an inaudible bee hum in the room.

"Okay, run downstairs, but only ten minutes." Emma turned off the stir-fry. "Come with me," she said. We passed through the den into a separate room with no furniture, only a wooden floor and yoga mats. A crime scene might have been cheerier.

"I'm going to give you something to carry back to Hattiesburg. Lie down on your back. Place your palms up beside you, ankles together." She turned on some eastern style music, not too loud, and I did as instructed. "Close your eyes. Feel the floor pressing up into little places of tension in your body. Let irritation melt away." As Em spoke short phrases then paused, I began to gather an image of a gentle, lapping surf.

"Relax the muscles controlling your jaw, the strongest muscles in your body. Welcome the strength of gravity. Reee-laaax." The music sped faster. "Slowly slide your arms up above your head. Let your fingers and toes stretch your spine and place oxygen between your vertebrae. Reee-laaax." She taught me how to breathe through my nose, pushing out my stomach first, then how to point fresh breath to areas of my body asking to be noticed: feet, hips, back, and neck, each location receiving patient attention in sequence.

"Do you feel pain?" My hips were tense as I wasn't used to lying on the floor. I nodded my head yes. "Don't try to control the pain—allow it, then relax the parts of your body around the sensation. Permit escaping stress to un-crowd the muscles." Then a five-second pause. "The waves

175

on Lake Pontchartrain are crashing all those miles away. Can you hear them? That's the sound of the world breathing."

A screen door slammed, the child's doorbell, but though I heard the sound, I didn't move. A snowflake landing, Em touched my shoulder, no words, only the ceiling fan wafting my forehead, a tingle in my hips. My jaw relaxed as she leaned toward me, careful not to insinuate but to collect my attention.

"We are never separate. Only minds think we must be."

Chapter 47

Little Nicole, happy from her puppy visit, bubbled about how fuzzy it was and how it tripped when it walked. Emma encouraged her daughter to eat, but each time the effort was lost to another zooming puppy story. I'd forgotten how children changed a home, how their animated presence repels the demons of loneliness.

"I'm done. Can I go watch TV? Please?" Nicole asked. Then the three of us cleared the table.

"Hope she wasn't too excited at dinner."

"I'd forgotten what nuclear furnaces kids are. Nicole is a mature child."

"I suppose, but I encourage her to be a little girl. I want her to fall in love with toys and play with friends. She can get serious later. Too many kids chew through childhood like it's a mediocre appetizer."

"Now see, that's what I'm talking about, that thing Nicole said earlier, doing things because they're right not because of the reward. You two speak an alien language."

"She listens to me, and I listen to her. She teaches me more than I do her, not so much in words, but with actions. Children are clear, you know, right and wrong, like and dislike; they are happy or sad. It's adults who muddy things up with pretense."

"I know. I tend to camouflage my true self like it isn't good enough." Uneasy, I realized I'd spoken words I should have only thought. Emma took a long calm breath.

"Sensitive people try to please others," Emma said. "The problem is, we often invest energy into manipulating the truth rather than becoming the person we truly are. Perhaps it's time to consider that you're not broken."

The steel point of my car key jabbed at my leg, and I glanced at the door. "But what if I am broken?"

"You're not." She paused and I wasn't sure if I was supposed to disagree. "When we help others, we discover our spirituality, and yet culture teaches us to scheme for power. Your calculating behavior is what sustains your sense of separation."

"I'm scheming for power?"

"We all are. The mind is the source of suffering because selfishness defends the ego," she said. I so badly wanted a beer.

"Is that why you meditate, to trick the mind?" I asked.

"Yes. To quiet the ego's yammering for attention. When we allow silence, we hear the tones of eternity."

Slack jawed, I must have looked like Jethro Bodine at the Louvre. She saw. "But what a blabbermouth I am," she said. "I'm sorry. Let's have coffee." The dull pupil had again frustrated the teacher.

"Please don't apologize. Look, I'm a functional guy, meat and potatoes kind of life, semi-bright, though I kid myself. What you teach is interesting—I just don't understand i." As the words left my mouth, I knew my cowardly deflection had failed.

"Of course, you're right," she said. "I'm so sorry. I took you for a thinker, perhaps an artist, someone examining life beneath the surface, maybe even a poet. I, too, had forgotten you are a dull boy with eyes searching for a woman's blouse and shapely jeans, a brute looking for parking-lot love. . ."

"Hey, wait a minute. You can't talk to me like that."

"Why not? It's the way you talk to yourself, isn't it? You want to see yourself as that flannel shirt guy with a fishing rod in hand, mind emptied of vexing notions about love and intimacy, right? You want to see yourself as a failure, a victim misunderstood? Am I close?"

"What? I don't know what you're talking about. I'm not trying to be dumb or brilliant, just to figure my way ahead."

She stared at the veneer she'd ripped open, and I imagined my costumed personality unravelling. But she was right. I'd ensured my own failure and yet held everyone else accountable. She moved closer.

"You don't remember that night at Roy's when you got so drunk and screwed that stranger in the parking lot, but that night you were quoting poetry, E.E. Cummings, and you were speaking of the sculptures you'd seen at Iron Arts in the most elegant, attuned language I've ever heard a man use. That night all the real Larry came out to play: the debaucher, the poet, the artist, the lyricist, the drunkard, the friend, the enemy, and the self-sabotaging tyrant. I saw them all. You were completely out of your head, but the thing you weren't that night was practical or fake.

With such sketchy recall, I would have believed I wore a bikini and pole danced on a police car. "You sure that was me?"

"I'm not trying to play dominatrix; I'm only saying maybe it's time to wake up. You're acting out some persona you adopted and now hold on to like a child's favorite blanket." She paused. I stared at an unraveling olive-colored stitch in one of her oriental carpets, a fray perhaps the cat had chewed, a flaw revealed in the soft light.

"Inside you are different potential selves bobbing beneath the surface of an ocean called Larry. Each waits to become the emergent whitecap of you."

Em pulled a book from the shelf. "Let me read you one sentence. It's by Alan Watts: 'We do not 'come into' this world; we come out of it, as leaves from a tree. As the ocean 'waves,' the universe 'peoples.' Every individual is an expression of the whole realm of nature, a unique action of the total universe.'"

I hung on every word, until the sound of her voice faded. "A friend of mine, Maya, told me I have a wounded artist inside me. She calls him Anthony, my middle name. Says he needs a friend."

"I like it. But does Anthony have to be blind drunk to come out and play?"

"I don't know. For sure my writing is better when I'm not drinking, but my mind is freer when I am. I'm not sure who is the real me."

"Did you get any counseling after your dad disappeared?"

"No. Mom said I should. But I wanted to show her how tough I was."

"Being injured and giving up on yourself doesn't make you tough."

"True, but I tried to find out what happened to Dad. Had this image of being the hero. But nothing ever happened, except I stopped trying."

"Have you ever gone to an AA meeting? I mean to talk to other people who also might have experienced some kind of trauma?"

"Not until yesterday. I went to see Leon. But I wasn't ready."

"Yes, you were. You went. That took courage."

"I'm sorry, Em. Didn't mean to gush all this. Let's talk about you for a while."

"Next time, okay? Right now, I need to ask a favor." She scooted an inch closer. "Would you please stop putting yourself down? You're not weak, or inept, or stupid. You've been hurt and now it's time to heal." She wrapped both hands around mine. "And let's get this straight—from here on, Anthony has a second new friend."

"Okay. But I have a question. What's your middle name?" I asked.

"I'm Emma Gianna Landrieux. I don't use my ex-husband's name, Gilpen."

"Well, Gianna, meet Anthony; he's learning how to meditate in New Orleans."

Chapter 48

Droplets meander above a yawning ocean steely in the pre-dawn light. No defining reference of self, only rises and gentle glides as flatness heaves and relaxes. A rose-tinted eyeball peers from the east releasing tiny crests to their morning dance. And from an endless carpet of ripples, human forms rise to pierce the morning air as beings.

Turning onto my side, a cold breeze fans my face, then fluttering orange curtains reveal the hotel air conditioner as Em's voice still echoed in my head: "Pain is how the mind resists change. Accept. Release its grip. Life advances not as war, but as peace."

Doo-do, doo-do.

"Hope I'm not waking you," Emma said.

"Of course not. Thinking about a swim."

"How nice," she said. "I wanted to tell you how much I enjoyed last night. Sorry to keep you up so late."

"No, I was the doubtful guest who wouldn't leave. Got bored around eight but stayed just to torture you." Quietness. "I'm kidding. Didn't get bored until eight-thirty." Playful boundaries hinted familiarity, releasing the stress of romance.

"Look, I know you've got your luncheon, but maybe come by later and have dinner. Nicole isn't home tonight. You could even stay in her room and skip the hotel."

"Okay. Don't know what to expect from today, so the timing might be a little iffy, but I'll call later when I see how things are going?"

"Fine. Roy and Julia are coming over at seven and bringing a red wine venison roast, tender as tofu. You can come any time though."

The end of our chat left me dazed until outside I discovered a flat tire on the driver's side. I popped the trunk.

"Looks like a problem." From the other side of the car the stringy-haired guy I'd given breakfast money spoke in a soft voice, his US Army shirt stained with what might have been red clay. "I can change it for you?"

"Okay. Yeah. That would be good." He jacked up the car while I pretended to check the other tires. "Have my share of trouble in this parking lot. Lucky for me the US Army is here to help. Coincidence, huh?"

"Guess so," he said. "New Orleans got lots of problems for strangers. You ain't seen no trouble yet. Stick around long enough, you will."

Chapter 49

I drove over the Industrial Canal by mistake. That veteran had needed a safe memory to help forget something, or somebody, and I wished I'd asked about his service. But the cool morning brightened on Saturday routines with couples pushing strollers and a man juggling balls in the sun. All of us in motion in the same place, aware of each other at a distance, or maybe not. I wondered if it mattered. I'd seen this documentary on television about quantum mechanics and how fields of probability around us produce changes by the mere act of being watched, the observer effect. And the notion came to me that self-scrutiny of my own thoughts may be re-mapping my potential future.

Almost every light turned green, no frustrated traffic, no honking horns, only the universe and me as buzzing electrons in search of a time to shift orbit and release energy the way that television program described. Were other people thinking the same things? Could my thoughts activate fresh ideas in their heads? Maybe this is how a zeitgeist works, or how love transcends distance?

Gaucho Americano reached forward to me, her grand windows staring as if eyeballs over the sign's elegant calligraphy scrolled onto white porcelain. Inside, the rich, earthy smell of leather lingered in the dimly lit room overflowing with treasure. Through a curtain, Maya burst toward me as if I'd returned from war.

"Oh, my heavens! You are beautiful," she said. "You've lost weight." Essential Maya.

"It's my new beer diet. I'm quite dedicated." She wrapped her arms around me. I'd forgotten how diminutive she was, and yet powerful.

"Let me look at you, turn around," she said. "This is a new jacket. I can tell you bought it to impress me." The woman was clairvoyant as I had bought it for no other purpose. "You look manly in leather."

"Hey, I look manly in everything." But before I could finish my joke, the curtain parted and in walked Montanita followed by a woman in a wheelchair. Maya scooted toward them.

"You know my cousin, I believe, and this is my partner, Lily."

My brain departed on a flight to Fiji. The lovely blond-haired woman extended her hand.

"Pleased to meet you, Anthony. Maya speaks of you frequently, and I must say I'm a bit jealous." A rosy flush of her cheeks left me wondering if there wasn't a smidgen of truth in her confession.

"Well, I must say I've had a pang of jealousy about you as well." With that I hugged Maya with my right arm while realizing I'd actually said what I meant. The moment tilted toward awkward, so I tried to reduce the tension. "Actually, Maya, I haven't told you yet but I've met a new friend here in New Orleans. A yoga instructor."

"My heart is broken," Maya said, continuing the charade by holding the back of her left hand up to her forehead before pinching my cheek. "I knew the real Anthony would find his way." And with that, she gave Lily a kiss, and I finally greeted Montanita.

"And hello again, Montanita. I'm not sure you remember me."

"Of course, I do. You purchased the magnificent 'Escaladores' for your mother. How could I forget? But I'm sorry, I misunderstood your name to be Larry.

"Yes, I was Larry at that time. But I've upgraded to a new personality model." We all laughed, and Montanita offered a puzzled gesture toward the smell of coffee where everyone pulled up chairs around a large country table. Maya, so beautiful in an eggshell blue dress that flowed as she walked then fluttered as she paused. Her infatuation with Lily was apparent, and with telling eye flashes, they shared a private energy so different from that stoic first impression I'd gathered back at Thanksgiving.

"So, Anthony," Lily said, "I understand you are the star student in class. Any big trophies this trip?" This lady knew more than I'd realized.

"Nope. More passive this session."

"Why is that?" Maya asked.

"Conditions weren't the same as this training was in the field with workers and managers. Becoming part of the team was the point, not being a standout."

"Interesting," Lily said. "Smart, allowing people to perform roles rather than merely assess them. I imagine you now have a deeper awareness of the environment." Lily surely sensed my insincerity.

"Sure, an appreciation of the people, too. I got to see the management hierarchy as well as the guys who empty the garbage cans at night. Before this role training, I identified more with the managers, but now, maybe more with the guys working in the buildings because while the managers look at spreadsheets and measure productivity, the workers have more fun."

"I don't understand," Maya said.

"Working with the cleaning guys, I got to know them, to understand their world, even to listen to their philosophy of life. Heck, I met this guy Leon who was a regular Dalai Lama, told me all about how he learned the secret of life watching his mother polish mismatched pieces of china. When I worked with the number's guys—the managers, that is—they never got their nose out of spreadsheets; I could have spent eight hours with a computer and had the same dose of humanity." Imagining Chub sitting on his desk talking about his painting reminded me I was back to my old habits of not saying what I truly meant. Lily noticed my glitch.

"Maybe the managers have learned to withhold themselves better, not play the personal card too quickly," Lily said. "Perhaps they were in role and wanted to be perceived as in control rather than open."

"That's exactly it," I said. "The cleaning guys engaged me as Larry, or I guess it's Anthony today. The managers didn't care who I was. To them I was a function, an entity. I'm tired of being treated like a symbol and viewing other people that same way. I want to know people, to understand their lives, not just their facades." My voice had risen, the room warmed.

"I told you he was a poet," Maya said.

"Yes, indeed, the trapped artist wrestling a controlling mind," Lily said, eye lashes drilling holes through me as she spoke. It occurred to me that an entire conversation in unspoken form was occurring among the four of us, each of us reading invisible waves of connection, bundles of awareness operating on undetected frequencies wielding shared influence. I broke off the staring contest with Lily, her blue eyeshadow too overpowering.

"Yep, a controlling mind, but my friend Emma is teaching me that I can step back from my ego's selfish demands." I wasn't quite sure where these words came from, but I had a notion that Em could hear me.

"You're obviously studying yoga," Lily said. "I was a devotee myself, before my car accident. I still meditate, but it's quite lovely to hear your fresh enthusiasm."

"I don't know anything," I said. "But Emma is helping me find a little of my truth, that's all." The three women stared, and I visualized oxygen flowing into the vacuum between my ears. I wished it was happy hour.

"Each of us battles the blindness our ego imposes, the pain it generates. You're smart to let yoga help," Lily said.

In a moment of syllabic panic, I proposed a toast. "From illusion to truth." With a sigh of relief, everyone clinked coffee cups. But before anyone could speak, the doorbell tinkled and Montanita walked upfront. A minute later, she returned to retrieve Maya for commentary on a painting. Lily and I now had a private moment.

"I hear you're doing graduate work?" I asked. *Brilliant. More ego talk.*

"Not at present. I've taken a break."

"Sorry, if you don't want to talk about it. . ."

"It's okay. In my undergraduate work I became interested in the effects of media on individual attitude and how subconscious perception might be measured en masse, but by the time I finished my senior thesis, my window of opportunity had closed. Now, I'm struggling to reframe those ideas."

"Emma talks about how the mind uses perceived pain to support its authority. Maybe that's what media and government do, too?"

"Perhaps." Her eyes twitched side to side. "Years ago, I rushed myself into thinking how special technologies might be put into phones and countertops so that when people touched these things, store clerks or doctors could get instant stress readings or monitor a person's reaction over the phone. I moved too slowly and now this approach is perhaps out of date."

"Too bad, it sounds cool. I'd love to be able to look at my phone and tell if the person I'm talking to is stressing over my words. The phone company, or makeup counter manufacturer, could aggregate all that data as marketing info—"

"My, you are the businessman, aren't you? You instantly saw practical application where I was more focused on analyzing cultural themes." Her voice faded. "Now I'm trying to connect my thinking to the coming dominance of artificial intelligence and machine learning. I want to build economic models focused on when machines are your therapist, surgeon, firefighter, and novelist, when robots write their own software and the role of AI is no longer human augmentation but rather the gateway to unleashed universal human creativity. In that world, individual responsibility will predicate on consuming things rather than making them."

"Won't someone need to build and maintain all those robots?"

"Yes. But machines will design, build, and maintain themselves and their deep learning capability will far exceed human capability in every field of learning. Personal innovation and design will likely be more for art rather than capitalism."

"Bleak," I said. *Is Lily depressed?*

"My point is economics, not prediction. I've begun drawing up incentive models for sustaining mass consumption, like paying people to maintain health and educational fitness. Perhaps more free time will inspire a renaissance of art and creativity."

Before I could respond, Maya walked back into the room, her presence lifting the thick air of thought. And my mind jumped to what a future dystopian society would look like where lotteries dole out highly prized part-time jobs and everyone must be educated.

Chapter 50

After coffee, Maya toured me through the goods her dad had shipped from Argentina and Peru, the fine leather filling the room with a supple aroma. I found one beautifully worked vest that looked old from the distressed finish but was brand new.

"You'd look great in that, Anthony. The color sets off your brown eyes."

"Maybe, but I think it also sets off my beer gut. A fine vest like this deserves some young caballero with a thousand-dollar pair of boots and a new Stetson."

"Well, sir, we have those items to choose from as well." Lily had gone to change clothes, so after her quip, Maya took a moment to be serious. "If you don't mind my asking, are you still seeing Janine? I remember she was visiting your house in November." Rare diffidence leaked into her voice.

"No, don't see her much these days. She'd probably like to, but I need something without so many tangles to it." Janine's Christmas present came to mind.

"I see. And this Emma, she doesn't have so many tangles?"

"We only met on this trip, but both of us just need a good friendship."

Maya walked over to me. "You deserve someone who sees your genuine self."

In the corner of the room, light through a high window reflected off a tiny portrait of a young soldier tipping his dashing red hat. I envied the painting's precision, how the artist plucked subtlety from life's over-packed volume of detail always drowning me. The rapier at the young man's side triggered a thought of that funky Mobile Max fellow who touched steel and made it breathe. What could Iron Arts and Reid teach me? Everywhere, stories, unique lives, an inspiring blur so heavy I wanted to sit on a bench and soak up the blue skies of New Orleans.

"Time to go, Anthony."

Chapter 51

Maya's dad was waiting at his friend's house uptown in the Garden District. I decided driving my own car might offer me a more manageable exit, and the ride gave me a chance to digest the ideas Lily had shared. Radio noise blurred, then I stood in the foyer of a white Queen Anne Victorian home wrapped by a covered porch.

Javier, the old friend of Maya's father, greeted us warmly, hugging Maya as he walked to his car in a rush toward some last-minute errand. People. Cranberry and cobalt light through stained-glass windows. A stream of sensation left me mildly nauseous before a hand touched my arm, guiding me to the end of the porch.

"You look like you need some fresh air, my friend," Maya's father said.

"Thanks. I think I do. Maybe had a little too much coffee."

"Yes, I understand. Sometimes too much domesticity weakens a man's focus; we are inferior to words, you see." I nodded, not sure if his comment was a joke. Six feet tall, rugged cowboy face closely shaven, he stared into me with artic cold eyes. "I'm Maya's father, Alfredo. She tells me that you are a deep feeling person. Perhaps an odd thing to say about a man, don't you think? What does my daughter mean by that?"

The question caught me off guard, but realizing I wasn't yet alert, Señor Vera busied himself with a cigar cutter, then offered me a smoke. At last, my mind caught up. "Ahh, yes. Maya does have a curious artistic notion about me." The rest of my thought vanished.

"My daughter has always shown awareness beyond her years." The hard lines of his face relaxed me into a distraction that his blondish hair made him look like Robert Redford.

Cushioned chairs and a gently moving porch fan slowed down time. From a bottle on a small table, Alfredo poured two glasses of sherry. "I will not pry into your life if you choose," he said. "I, too, am a man who values his private thoughts. But Maya asked me to speak with you about your inclinations as a writer, so if you don't mind, I'd like to understand more about your art." Blue eyes flashed beneath his wrinkled brow, trophies of a prosperous life.

"There isn't much to know. Average American, no real success, no creative accomplishment of significance." Alfredo puffed a smoky donut ring reminding me of a life preserver. My words did not touch him. "Enough said, Senor Vera, so tell me about life in South America."

"Please, Anthony, call me Alfredo. You are a friend of my family now." We clinked our sherry glasses, and he unfurled a stare as focused as magnified light.

"When I was a young man, I thought I had something important in me," he said. "An idea of destiny. My father had taught me well, shown me life on a large Argentine ranch and how to run it, and I benefited from the finest tutors. I remember when I was nine, one of them took a small watercolor I'd painted of horses grazing on a gently sloping foothill, and he presented it to my father with the declaration that this was the work of genius." He drew on his cigar as if visiting that lost moment while I relaxed into his story, relieved he was speaking about himself.

"I remember being proud and embarrassed when my father called me in to discuss the work. I still feel that moment he kissed the top of my head, looked me in the eyes as he held my shoulders and told me that a great man lived within my life and that it was my duty to find that man and to free him." Alfredo thumped his ash. At first hesitant to speak, I realized he wanted me to respond.

"A touching story," I said. "I can see how such a lesson at an impressionable age would influence a boy's thoughts about his potential." And as my perfunctory response joined the sound of our two chairs rocking in slow motion, a misplaced memory appeared: 'You got a feel for words, son. Like nobody I know. You could write books one of these days.' I'd forgotten my dad's words from that afternoon I became a teenager.

"I see pain in your face, Anthony. Now please know that Maya told me your father disappeared years ago, so forgive my being so personal."

"Yes, I lost my father, but I was grown then. It shouldn't have affected me so profoundly." Such a pretentious lie, but Alfredo ignored the diversion.

"I see. And so, now my question to you. Did your father ever speak to you of the greatness inside you?"

My heel tapped the floor. Sucking at the sherry glass, I then bit too hard on the cigar leaving a piece of tobacco burning my tongue.

"Well, my dad wasn't a man of many words. But he loved me, protected me from the messiness of life. Told me I'd have an easier time than he did if I used my mind rather than my hands."

Alfredo twirled his cigar. "I see. Very American, isn't it? The idea that a softer life should be the goal for each generation."

"I suppose," I said. "I'm not sure. Most people want to make life less demanding for their children, give them better opportunities."

Alfredo sat back. "This is true," he said. "But as parents, we often forget that denying our children the hardship of work produces weak character, a person whose confidence fails to be tempered by challenge."

His words trickled through me as insight now freed from a locked place I'd learned to ignore. Motionless, showing me he was fully present but not a threat, he allowed me to explore my reaction without pressuring me to speak.

"My dad shielded me from the work of his metal and paint. He wanted me to excel with my mind. But I see now what neither of us realized then." Alfredo leaned toward me. "I never got to share my dad's work world, only times fishing and hunting. Maybe mine was only half a boyhood."

"Yes, my boy. You see deeply. You see exactly. This bond between a boy and his father, this connection is where character awakens." But rather than letting me dwell, Alfredo shifted. "And so, do you also see this artist in you that Maya speaks of?"

"Not really. I can bang out a tune on my guitar, but I'm no performer.

As for writing, I've published a couple of short stories, but only in po-dunk magazines." If I were a mirror, it would have been blank.

"Anthony, it sounds like my daughter could be incorrect." He raised his cigar for a patient draw. "You have this artist's sensibility, I believe the word is, but perhaps you prefer to think on the world rather than create the world. Is this not true?"

"Well, no, I like to create things, but I haven't had much success—"

He cut me off. "What success have you sought? You've let your friends read your writings, yes? And they ignored them—or worse—in their superior judgment, they found mistakes but rarely took the effort to point out the things they liked? Am I close? Did your manuscript sit on some trusted person's table for weeks untouched? Maybe they found grammatical errors and repeated words." His machine gun paused for reloading.

I wanted to disappear, then grunted, "No. My grammar was good. They wanted a fairytale ending."

"Yes, indeed. A happy ending, as of course, reality demands. And did your father also require this happy ending?"

"He told me I had a gift with words. But I never showed him my writing." And there at last, I'd answered Alfredo's question with the truth I'd avoided, the realization I hadn't shared my dream with Dad. Maybe I'd abandoned him before he left us.

"So, tell me, that day your father told you of your gift with words, did you perhaps note his greatness as well?" Not critical or superior, but rather as the teacher realizing his pupil has at last grasped the meaning of some difficult concept, Alfredo allowed me time to rewind the deleted juncture from that conversation in dad's garage surrounded by real-world carcasses of broken cars. With a touch on my shoulder, Alfredo pulled me back to the moment, then raised his glass: "To the artists among us."

Chapter 52

Javier's car squealed into the driveway as Maya waved to her father to come speak with an old friend, Dr. Perdomo. I sat alone on the porch searching the countless times I'd admired my dad's talent and yet could never remember telling him so.

The sound of clinking bottles from Javier's front seat shifted to tango music wafting from the side yard. Images of matadors and brave bulls yielded to Maya tussling me onto the patio to stomp a few toes. Immersed in snapping fingers and syncopated movement, I tilted Maya to the seductive music while an echo of long-ago salsa lessons with Janine flashed an unwelcome intrusion.

"So, how do you like my father?" Maya asked as the music ended and we walked toward the tent. Free-flowing sangria had tempted me to doom, and without warning, my words slurred into gluey chunks sticking to the roof of my mouth. *Drunk again?* I hadn't even realized.

I wasn't sure I could respond to Maya's question. "Your dad's direct on the cigar." *What?* My southern accent had thickened into an ill-formed slurry of stupidity. I pretended to choke on a sip of water.

"Oh, yeah. Dad loves good cigars; you're in expert hands with that stuff—a good argument, too, so feel free to push back when he opines. He expects people to stand up to him and loves to goad an overreaction."

"For sure."

"Dad is a respected artist in Argentina and perhaps could have been world famous if he had desired. His childhood teachers wanted him to study in Paris, but he refused. My grandmother insisted that he not be forced. He does not like to discuss this choice as it may now be his one regret."

"He still paint?" Another bottle of water helped unthicken my tongue.

"Not like he could. Dad's collection got Javier started with Gaucho Americano. He gave Javier twenty paintings on consignment to attract other artists while building a reputation as a New Orleans' art dealer. The name of the shop was a surrealist painting of a red bull charging from South America, his jaws wrapped around the middle part of the United States while a matador jabbed at him with a dollar bill in the shape of a sword. Javier loved that painting, so Dad gave it to him as a gift to sell for startup money."

"Javier sold it?" Guzzling helped cool my rise of panic as Maya deliberately carried the bulk of conversation between us.

"Yes, in retrospect I think he regrets giving up the painting, but at the time Javier had no other option. He comes from humble roots. His father worked on my grandfather's ranch, the one my dad inherited. As boys, Javier and Dad rode horses together and hunted; that's where their lifelong friendship began. Javier is more of an uncle to me, and I often introduce him to friends as *mi tio*." *Who is tio? Did I miss that?* Maya drifted into a private world while watching Alfredo approach.

"Maya," Alfredo said, "I'm afraid you will have to rescue poor Lily. Dr. Lu is pontificating about how psychologists are nothing more than dog trainers, and I think she was searching her handbag for a weapon. Perhaps the sangria has been a bit too liberating for the good doctor."

With the intensity of a terminator, Maya targeted Lily's entanglement. I wanted her same certainty of purpose in my life, some moment of clarity when I didn't have to unwind the needless complexities I create. And the tango finished to a swell of clapping hands.

"I'd hoped for a quieter forum with you today," Alfredo said. "But Javier cannot resist a good fiesta when Maya comes to town. One day, I shall have him tell you his story; it is one of duty to the family." He lit a cigarette-sized cigar, unhurried, but his mind had not yet left his old friend. "Yes, Javier remembers well our dear Argentina." I expected another conversation, but Alfredo began to walk away, following home unspoken trails to his past. I touched his arm.

"I wanted to thank you for offering me a father's perspective today." He turned to stare me down.

"Anthony, do you believe in your art enough to withstand public indifference?"

"I don't know," I said. "I'm not sure."

"I thought so. Perhaps you should focus on creating what pleases you. Don't show people, don't ask their opinion. Create, but do not discuss creating. If you do not love your work, do not share it."

Chapter 53

"This Emma sounds delightful," Lily said. "Perhaps Maya and I could meet her later this afternoon?"

"Oh, not today. She's busy. With her daughter. Nicole is sick." I don't know why I panicked, but the deflection was the only instinct I could find. Maya meeting Emma could have been a coming together of my world, and I knew that's what I wanted, but habit spoke before my mind could catch up.

Lily excused herself to the lady's room, and I stretched out under a live oak limb dipping almost to the ground. I needed a good exit plan that wouldn't appear abrupt. Tiny oak leaves stretched above me in a sea of dots offering no reference to up or down, then, off to the side, something gray under the draped tablecloth next to the grill. I lifted the corner to find the barbecue table was an upside-down boat, its underside now used as a work surface. But underneath where I'd assumed sawhorses supported the boat, two sets of human feet stood planted in the grass, as if two kids held the upside-down boat on their hidden shoulders.

Javier watched as I touched their unlaced iron tennis shoes, bare ankles, and knees. Sure enough, lower leg sections were welded to the flat surface above, two boys toting a skiff down some childhood path, a sculpture masquerading as a table. "It's called *Boy's Work*."

"Cool. Did you make it?"

"No. Bought it from the old man who sold me this house; he said something about a Markey or Manuel building it custom, but he was ancient and couldn't remember. Said his son had bought it before he died in Iraq."

Javier then went inside to bring out more steaks for the grill, so I drifted back to the live oak. A minute later someone touched me on the shoulder.

"Why are you sitting here alone?" Montanita asked. "Such an interesting man should attract many female friends."

No brilliant syllables came to my rescue. She dazzled in the afternoon light with her chiffon blouse in pale pink, and though still mildly anesthetized, I sighed at her joke. "Waiting on Lily to come back. Besides, I have been approached by a captivating female." She blushed, my rendition of Owen Wilson doing Cary Grant apparently useful.

"Well, yes, I suppose," Montanita said, then sat on a concrete bench. The youthful quality of her bouncy personality reminded me of the singer Shakira with her quirky smile.

"Were you born in the US?" I asked.

"In Baton Rouge, then moved to New Orleans after Gaucho Americano became successful."

"Do you like it here?"

"New Orleans is exciting. I live in Marigny in a run-down Creole cottage, but I love it because I hear music from Frenchman's street. Yesterday I was looking at a rotten post on the porch eaten out by termites, and I found a yellow pansy growing out of the wet wood. Don't know how it got there." Her face reminded me of a shy teenager, and I was sure I'd glimpsed Montanita the poet.

Before I could comment, Alfredo brought Javier and Maria over to sit with us. Soon, we said our goodbyes. Maria insisted I come to visit them the next time I was in New Orleans, and Javier proclaimed that we'd go speckled trout fishing as soon as the spring run started. He joked we could turn the barbecue table upside down and paddle out into the Gulf as boys again.

A few moments with Maya and Lily sent me heading downtown, streetlights now semaphores guiding me the tourist. I'd drank too much again, embarrassed myself by slurring words to Maya, but at least the party ended without complete James Joyce incoherency. Little things, I guess. I had to be more thankful, the way Montanita was when she found that pansy growing from her porch post. Flipping open my phone, I almost called Leon, then cruising past a neon-lit bar named Terminator, I missed Janine.

Chapter 54

A quick call to Emma changed our plan. She had the date wrong for Roy's deer roast, so she'd decided instead to have a friend put new brake shoes on her car. My task was to pick her up.

A block from where I was to meet Emma, I realized the address was Flo's Diner with its blinking coffee cup beacon. Three cups of espresso before leaving the party had double-stepped my heartrate, so I practiced deep breathing then parked between two pick-up trucks. The bouquet of daisies I'd picked up at a gas station drooped as I approached the diner door.

I took one last deep breath before the café door flew open and out ran a man wearing a sparrow-colored fishing hat with a long flap covering his neck. His filthy green raincoat reminded me of pond scum. In his arms he clutched half a dozen women's purses.

"Thief, thief! Stop him." From inside the diner, Flo's voice shrieked like a police whistle.

"No, Earl, no!" Then, a projectile plunged through the door, Emma.

The man changed direction, scurrying toward the vacant lot to his right. He hadn't noticed me until I took three quick steps and with my best suburban sidekick blindsided him on his left hip. He spun like a summer sprinkler, launching purses into the sky while my head Hindenburg-landed onto the ground.

Whack. I suspected a ripping artery in my brain before realizing Emma had clobbered the purse snatcher with an umbrella. He regained his footing, but she mounted his back in a game of ride-the-horsey. *Crack.* An elbow to the nose deposited her into a hedgerow of boxwoods, then with a skulking limp, the thief rounded the corner into the darkness. Human yellow jackets streamed from the café.

"What the hell?" I said, laboring to my feet.

"Earl, my deadbeat husband," Emma said while wiping blood from her nose.

Flo grabbed my arm. "Settle down, daisy boy. He's been on the run for two years. We thought he was dead." Police, noise, statements, confusion. I caught Emma's eye several times, but the swarm protected her.

"You might need this," Flo said, and she put a banana pudding in front of me. "Listen. He's a cretin. Meth head."

"I don't get it. Stealing purses?"

"He didn't know Emma was here because Junior is working on her car. Earl hit this place because he knows we have a monthly woman's club where we talk about art and stuff."

"Huh?" I said, my skilled repartee now restored.

"You know she's an artist, right? A good one."

"Guess so. Saw a watercolor at her house. She never said much."

"She don't paint no more."

"Why's that?" I asked.

"Look. That Karate Kid move you did shows me you're an okay guy, so I'm going to show you something." Flo opened a double door to a back room I hadn't even noticed. When she turned on the lights, the first thing I saw was a handmade sign pronouncing this room as, *The Local Louvre*. A couple dozen paintings hung in rows reminiscent of Mr. Bien's photo gallery. "Junior met Emma in a painting class years ago. Now, we try and help the locals sell a piece or two."

"Sell any of Emma's?" I asked.

"Two. There's only one left." Behind us hung a foot-square painting, abstract. In the center, a blank cube shape. In each corner of the canvas, similar shapes radiated a spectrum of color toward the center. "Em calls this one, *Prism of Friends*."

I stepped a couple of yards back as if studying a Monet, calibrating the overlapping color frequencies. *Prism of Friends*, huh?"

Pink Floyd came to mind, but more so that little shard of crystal from the vase in that sidewalk café. Maybe life was beginning to take on color for me again, and the gray days of Hattiesburg dirtied as a fog of lost time.

"Why did Em stop painting?"

"That's a story she'll have to tell you herself. But hear me now, not over pasta."

Chapter 55

An hour later, we pulled into Emma's driveway. Roy ripped in behind us. "You okay?" he asked.

"Yeah," Emma said. "That fool elbowed me in the nose, but we got the purses back."

"I heard. When I get my hands on that little squirrel. . ." Roy said, his voice trailing off as Emma wrapped her arms around her brother.

"Please. Let the police handle it."

"Earl better hope they do. I already warned him once." Roy took a step back, the big muscle in his jaw pulsing. I wanted to tell him to relax and breathe but didn't want to risk being skinned myself. He finally noticed me standing on the other side of the car. "I heard what you did there, Mississippi. I owe you."

Then he turned to Emma. "You still got your Smith & Wesson?"

"Yeah," she said, shuffling from one leg to the other.

"If Earl comes around this house, shoot him. Dead. Don't talk to him—shoot him. I'll take care of the rest," Roy said.

Roy's wife, Julia, came outside and hugged Em, then we went upstairs for hot tea. Breathing in the green tea steam, I wondered what wormhole had opened here.

"Sorry about today," Emma said. "But before I could respond, she raised her hand. "Tonight, let's go back to being normal, okay? Nicole is at my cousin's house, and I made a chicken Caesar salad. Let's be friends again and not talk about our real lives." My head was a pump handle, but nothing flowed. "Start by telling me about your lunch today with your California babes."

I couldn't remember if I'd gone. "Oh, yeah," I said. "Got to play horseshoes. And Maya's dad is a cross between George Clooney and Ernest Hemingway. He said I might want to keep my writings private for now and not get all tensed up with approval and rejection. Oh, sorry. Forgot, no reality tonight."

"It's okay. Just no Earl talk."

I knew she needed distraction. "But I kind of agree with her dad's thinking."

"Tricky, though," Emma said. "People like to express enthusiasm. Human nature is to be social."

"My social side has issues."

"Yeah, but understanding our craving for approval is important," she said. "How the ego obsesses after perceived failure." Her glance signaled she hadn't said what she wanted.

"Got to watch out for the old ego," I said. "But maybe hiding is good. Don't want to be comfortable with negative feedback, right?"

"It's not negative feedback that drives withdrawal; it's unmet expectation," she said.

Unmet expectation sounded like the anthem describing my life, and I wanted to wrap my arms around Em. But the look on my face must have confused her.

"There I go preaching again," she said. "Still in pedagogical mode from the seminar I taught this morning." She released the edge of a little laugh.

"You're not preaching, you're sharing. And thanks for that. But how about we share a little of that strawberry pie over there, then we find ourselves a clueless movie."

"Oh, thank you. I can't think anymore today," she said. The next few hours passed as an unplanned vacation with *My Cousin Vinny*. All that New York accent and two helpings of strawberry heaven distracted me and only a couple of times did I wonder where Em kept her pistol.

Chapter 56

"Are you hungry?" Emma asked, walking into the den where peeking from under a homemade quilt I stared up at a cranberry aperitif collection lit in the morning sun.

"Tofu and grits are my favorite, but that coffee smells good." A banana hue washed through the kitchen window.

"Yesterday must seem bizarre?" she said.

"Not really, I'm used to breaking up robberies. We learn that in Genie school."

Emma relaxed into her pink housecoat as we plopped at the kitchen table. "Earl left me four years ago. Drugs. Then an old girlfriend rescued him from the drudgery of marriage. I tried to divorce him, but he disappeared before the papers could be served."

"You haven't seen him in four years?" I asked.

"Not exactly. Two years ago, he showed up out of the blue." Her spine straightened.

"I heard Roy say he'd warned Earl. Was that the time?"

"Yeah." She seemed to fade into the yellow light, then slow-marched into words. "That Monday, Roy had a filling come loose, so I covered the café for him. All was quiet until a noise out front turned into Freddie Kruger barging into the kitchen. I threw a ten-pound bag of rice at him that exploded like confetti, then two seconds later he trapped me between those two worktables."

"'Well, if it ain't my pretty little bride cooking up something for her husband. How about a kiss there, honey?'" He backed me up to the wall where his forearm pinned me to the smell of stale beer." Her coffee cup wavered as she took a sip. "He saw me look at the meat cleaver on the table, so he grabbed my hair and slammed my head onto the stainless steel. 'I need money,' he said.

"His face was the color of urine, and I was sure he was going to kill me, but the kitchen door swung open. Earl tried to jump the table, but Roy snagged him then picked up the cleaver. *Wham*. A chunk of dishwater slimy hair fell on the floor." Em buried her head in folded arms.

"It's okay. You don't have to talk about it."

"No. I do. I have to get that smell out of my head," she said.

Roy said, 'Now Earl, listen good to what I'm saying. I don't like you. My sister don't like you, and you ain't welcome here for any reason.'

"Then, a squeal leaked as Roy drug the cleaver across Earl's filthy forehead, leaving an inch-long red ribbon. I didn't even try to breathe."

'These are the last words I'm ever speaking to you: if you ever come inside seeing distance of my sister again, I'll cut the top of your empty head off and piss in your skull till your eyes turn school-bus yellow. Then, my crab traps got themselves some fresh bait.' Those words launched a backhand that sent Earl's slobber to the far wall before Roy drug him to the back door and pitched him to the ground like a bucket of mop water."

"Did Earl go to the cops?"

"No. He had half dozen outstanding warrants. Besides, Sherriff Thigpen has been my brother's fishing buddy for twenty years. Roy put out the word that if anybody saw Earl in New Orleans to let him know. Around here, that's kind of like the FBI posting your eight-by-ten in the post office."

I slid my chair close and touched her hand, careful not to insinuate. "You're not alone, Em."

Chapter 57

From the bottom of the stairs, Roy announced shrimp and grits. Moments later, Julia treated me like a brother while the twins toddled around as if permanently charged robots. But I couldn't get Earl out of my head. After a two thousand calorie breakfast, Em and I decided to go for a waddle.

"Something has been bothering me about yesterday," I said. "Last night I woke up thinking I recognized Earl from somewhere."

"Spent any time in the Orleans Parish jailhouse? His man cave."

"Nope, but the way he hobbled off looked familiar. I guess my Tae Kwan Do training as an eight-year-old was too expert for him." I paused for a laugh, but Em hung on every word, not realizing I was kidding.

"You'd remember Earl. He's a mix of thoughtful and demonic. Pain killers let that monster loose and meth murdered the good man I married, the one who used to surprise me with new paints or mow a sick neighbor's yard. The only thing left of him now is flat ruin."

"Flat. Yeah, that's it. The guy who changed my flat tire had that same kind of limp. Was Earl a veteran—in the Army maybe?"

"No. Crooked spine so the military had no interest."

"I see, but the guy who changed my tire said he was a vet. Coincidence maybe, but I didn't get a good look at Earl yesterday."

"Forget it. Earl hasn't been a good guy for a long time, especially enough to help out a Yankee boy like you. Now, if you said that vet highjacked your car, then Earl would be your usual suspect."

PART FIVE

"The poet was right when he spoke of the 'mysterious threads' which are broken by life. But the truth, even more, is that life is perpetually weaving fresh threads which link one individual and one event to another, and that these threads are crossed and re-crossed, doubled and redoubled to thicken the web, so that between any slightest point of our past and all the others a rich network of memories gives us an almost infinite variety of communicating paths to choose from. At every moment of our lives we are surrounded by things and people which once were endowed with a rich emotional significance that they no longer possess."

In Search of Lost Time
Marcel Proust

Chapter 58

Up the highway, Hattiesburg nestled into the smell of pine trees. New Orleans had been sticky—not the humid air, but the compacted threads of a city world wrapping themselves around me. That crazy Vi, mysterious Reid, and even Earl, heck I'd never been robbed in Mississippi where the only stickiness I was familiar with was spilled beer. But the notion that a genuine connection with Em continued to teeter, and most of all, I prayed things wouldn't fall apart.

A yellow note on my front door twiddled in the breeze, Janine saying to call her. All those buoyant words Vi had used, and Alfredo's honesty, now oozed through my head. Yet all around me, the once youthful brightness of Hattiesburg continued to dim into a familiar puddle of blah.

The chill of hardwood inside left a smell of absence. Where were those bright pink and green houses on Leon's street? *Where's the noise?* New Orleans had music and accent but here only the dead television that burned out the night before I left. I needed evidence I'd ever been alive in this house, so out onto the porch I drifted hoping to find a pansy sprouting from some rotten post.

On my desk, a printed draft of my novel languished out of step with electron Raja eager inside my computer. Then, Lily's world led me back to my out-of-date alien plot in "Depleted," its unbreathable air perhaps now a available thread to New Washington. Nuclear fallout, or better yet, an unexplained virus spewed from an under-ocean fissure.

Rebalancing the atmosphere could be a project where Raja volunteers, where he might meet Thea Vitale, the new resident who fails to notice his old facial injury. New Washington without aliens, only alienation. And even my old chair seemed the wrong color.

Chapter 59

"It's about time you called. You do know it's Wednesday, right?" Mom asked.

"Sorry, had to meet with the governor. Special assignment."

"You're such a nut." The rest of the conversation saturated me with the pedestrian details of her simple life, her words bouncing off me like water onto WD-40. And everything irritated me, the size of my desk, the clock ticking, and after only a day back in the office, I called in sick. I needed rest.

I couldn't remember anything Mom and I discussed. Not even Proust could help me sleep while half-finished home projects left me anxious about the wrong paint or nails too large. Back to 2059 I drifted to explore the upside-down economics of future work. Two hours in my chair generated machines designing everything, fixing everything, fighting fires and crime, and anticipating disasters, while citizens focused only on how to spend mandatory government stipends and how best to promote personal wellness as they collected degrees and certifications.

Glancing at my dead television made me want to escape the anesthetizing effects of Raja's techno-world, so I went for a walk through the crunch of dull green grass. January air returned me to Emma's yoga lesson, but now those wave-linked breaths fretted me rather than left me calm. *What did Einstein say?* "Creativity is the residue of time wasted." I needed to untangle myself from too much thinking. I called Mom.

"Hi, darling," she said. "Spoiling me with two calls in one week. What's up?"

"I've been wanting some homemade vegetable soup," I said. "So how about coming over Saturday afternoon for cornbread and a bowl of goody?"

"Wonderful. I'll bring banana pudding."

"I figure we'll eat, then watch a movie. How about twelve thirty? I know you want to be home before dark."

"Oh, Larry, you're so good. I wish everyone was like you."

What would that world be if everyone was like me? Raja knows.

Two minutes later the phone rang. "Okay, so do you want to watch Cary Grant or Clint Eastwood?" I asked as I answered.

"Excuse me, Anthony, is that you? It's Maya."

"Oh, sorry. Thought you were Mom. We just hung up. Anyway, how goes it?"

"Fine." The jerky dialogue reminded me of the first time I rode a horse at YMCA camp. I leaned back.

"So, how is everything?" I asked. Ah, yes, dazzling.

"Fine, Anthony, I'm fine, Lily is fine, Dad is fine. We're all just fine." I liked the sarcasm.

"Well, that's really fine," I said. When I broke out laughing, she did too.

"Seriously, I'm surprised to hear from you so soon. I've been thinking about you and want to send a thank-you note for the party."

"How sweet. I'll look forward to receiving that and will pass it along to Javier. Anyway, my dad wanted me to tell you how much he enjoyed meeting you. Said you were refreshingly humble. That's not his impression of many Americans, I'm afraid."

"Why, thanks," I said. "I think of myself as half-witted. Makes it easier to meet expectations." Silence. "Your dad was refreshingly direct, but not condescending. Intimidating in a good way."

"Yes, Papi can be challenging. If he doesn't like you, he's even worse. As a teenager, he spent time with his uncle in Seville where he loved bullfighting. I think he sometimes sees social interchange as a bullfight, a place to stab people until they give up. In your case, he liked you and used the cape rather than the sword."

"I'm sure you had something to do with that because he knew all about me.

"Perhaps I did prep him a bit, but what he liked was how you showed respect without trying to impress him as being macho. He said it was like you'd lost something which had made your soul cautious."

"Well, my mind has been missing lately," I said.

"Lily said she enjoyed talking to you, too. Said you grasped things quickly." I let the comment pass. "And one more thing," Maya said.

"What's that?"

"She has this friend, Robert Pippen, in Seattle. A teacher who runs a writers' workshop. He's conducting a seminar this April. Lily thought you might be interested in attending."

"Oh. How long is the workshop? Is there a website?" I wanted to show interest, but also to keep my reaction in check. I'd participated in uneventful writing workshops before, plus the restart on my book hadn't even crossed the hundred-page mark. *But in Seattle I could go see Tim.*

"I'll have Lily send you the details. Not sure if she's planning on attending." That tidbit caught my attention. "Don't know if I told you, but she's a bit of an author. I mean not only scholarly articles, she's written many of those, but she's a decent fiction writer. Met Pip back in college."

"That girl is a Greek goddess," I said.

"Yes, my muse, maybe she can offer Anthony a little light, too."

Chapter 60

Saturday morning at dawn, I inhaled a pot of espresso before making a "Hello, Mom," banner out of butcher paper. She deserved a celebration, and though I wanted to find out about the secret she'd mentioned to Vi, I vowed not to ask. When she was ready, Mom would open up. By noon, with *An Affair to Remember* queued, the smell of soup soothed that raw layer in me I couldn't quite heal these days. I thought about writing but didn't want dystopian Raja-land contaminating my mood, so instead, spicy hummus and baby carrots became my meditation, until the phone interrupted.

"Hey, good looking, what you doing?" Janine asked. At first, I thought it was a wrong number.

"Making soup. Playing chef for Mom today."

"That's nice. Tell her hi. I love how you're so good to your mom."

"Thanks," I said. "You're good to your parents, too. Who says we don't have anything in common?" I didn't mean to be snarky.

"Yeah, I guess," she said. "But we have more than that in common. We still have Tim, remember? Plus, a memory or two of us together."

"True. Didn't mean to sound shrill, only chatting. Have you talked to Tim lately?" I asked. Guess my habit of trying to put Janine on the defensive hadn't completely faded.

"Oh, not exactly," she said. "It's been a while. Got a Christmas card but didn't . . . Ugh. . ."

"You mean you didn't send him one or call?" Post-divorce reflex. I pictured a bullfight.

"Now don't start. He's the one who left Hattiesburg. He . . ."

"Please, stop right there. I've heard this story, so let's start over. What can I do for you, Janine?"

"Well, I only wanted to say hi and ask about your training. When did you get home?"

"You mean, you wanted to be nosey. What you want to know is did I see Maya? Right?"

What was I thinking? Janine went psycho. Blabbering. Denying. I put the phone on speaker and whipped an egg with milk to get the cornbread rising.

"Larry, Larry, are you still there?"

"Yep, right here. Making cornbread."

The cooking distraction worked. "Sorry," she said. "I get it. You're busy, but sure wish I could have a piece of that hot stuff." I didn't answer but considered hiding under the sink. "Okay, look," she said. "I found something of yours in some old boxes and wanted to drop it off later if that's all right. Some old coins."

"No rush. Leave them inside the screen on the back porch anytime."

"Oh, I see. Well, anyway," she said. "Be sure to tell your mom hello for me. And when you bite into that cornbread, think of me."

A hundred quips came to mind, but I restrained. "Sure thing. Butter go. Catch you later." The click of the phone back in its cradle thudded a solitary note, like the clang of a jailhouse door reaffirming what's walled in and walled out. But Janine was only hiding loneliness inside her friendly shell, maybe trying to tell me she needed a friend. *I didn't have to be so hard.* A month earlier, I'd craved her touch, could smell her shampoo, yet now I'd treated her like an irritating neighbor. A gust mouthed at the window, voices almost, threads to something I couldn't see yet, hopefully something other than the past delivering fresh regret.

"Yew-hoo. Banana pudding delivery."

Chapter 61

The afternoon drifted on updates about Mrs. Batson's leaky roof and other special reports, but Mom's presence helped dilute the ripples from Janine's call. After two bowls of banana pudding and a nap with Cary Grant in my ear, I awoke to credits scrolling across my new television and Mom knitting a sweater.

"Man, that was a great movie," I said.

"Yeah? If you enjoyed it so much, how come you're not crying?"

"Oh, I was hoping for the Romeo and Juliet double-suicide ending." She slapped my leg playfully as she stood to gather her things; the sun would set in only two hours.

"No reason to rush, hang around and we'll see what the pharmaceutical companies are selling on the boob tube." I wanted to probe her about the mystery Vi planted in my head, but Mom's happy mood shifted my curiosity into neutral.

"I'd love to stay, but I washed a load of clothes before I left and need to get them in the dryer." Always a plan. "One thing though," she said. "You never told me about your visit with Vi."

"All good. She's mysterious but likable." Mom's face reddened.

"That Vi is a special lady," she said. "Can't wait to meet her one day." Mom paused as if unsure how to proceed. "Vi agrees with me that your father is still alive."

I flipped off the television. "Well, okay," I said. "But seriously, she's a stranger telling a vague story." Mom winced. I stopped short, realizing I might have slipped back into divorce mode.

"Do you remember when I told you I thought someone had come into the house?" Mom said. "How things on my desk got a little messed?"

"Yeah," I said. "You do have a cat, right?"

"Son, I haven't been completely honest with you," she continued. "And something has been worrying me." She placed her purse on the chair. "But you have to promise you'll never tell anyone."

Now I was awake. "Okay," I said. "Let's take this slow. We're in this together, so let's have the truth—are you a bank robber?"

"How did you know?" she said, her face now a shade of cantaloupe. "A year after your dad's disappearance, I got a note in the mailbox." She paused to fumble a memory. "Anyway, the envelope had twenty-five hundred dollars inside."

My conversation with Vi hadn't forecasted this twist. "I see. What did the note say?" She pulled an ancient piece of paper from her pocketbook, and I had a flash of Moona unfolding Leon's childhood poem.

Mrs. Winstead,

This $2,500 is from an interested party wishing to remain anonymous. You will receive this sum on approximately six-month intervals providing you never say anything to anyone, including your son, and that this arrangement is never discovered by anyone else.

The giver chooses not to be identified. Should the nature of this transaction ever be revealed, all future grants will be terminated.

"Mom? Were there any other payments?"

"Yes. Exactly as the note indicated, but there was never anything else written, only cash in a blank envelope left in my mailbox."

"Do you have any idea who's doing this?" I asked. "Could it be the guy who lost all dad's money on that investment?"

"I thought that, too, but he died five years ago, and the money kept coming. Now you see why I always celebrate your dad's birthday. I believe he's alive."

"Mom, listen to me. I don't think you should get your hopes up. Dad has been gone a long time. If he was coming back, he'd have made it here by now. This is probably some friend who wants to help but knows how proud you are."

"I know," she said. "For a while, I thought it was you doing it. But when you lost your job, the money didn't stop."

Her words hit me like a right hook to the jaw, but I blustered ahead pretending I hadn't noticed: "So, did Vi have any insight?" I asked.

"I didn't tell her about the money, but she does sense your father's spirit. Said he can't come to me yet."

"Did you mention to Vi about someone going through your desk?"

"No, I didn't. Only told her that something I couldn't quite understand was bothering me," Mom said. "Vi told me I was sensing your dad's loneliness."

"Let's stick to the facts, okay? Over the years how much money have you gotten from this benefactor?"

"About a hundred thousand dollars; the past three years the cash has been at least three thousand dollars each time."

"What? Have you been able to save any of it? I mean, I know how tough it's been."

"I have it all hidden in the house."

"Mom, you can't do that. If someone is poking around, maybe that's what they're looking for. Maybe they know you haven't spent it or put it in the bank."

"I'm afraid to put it in the bank. I can't justify where it came from. It might cause problems."

"You haven't done anything wrong, only accepted an anonymous gift. You never cashed in the life insurance like I wanted you to. You have nothing to be afraid of."

"I can't take that chance," she said. "I know in my soul it's from Thomas. I had a dream that I confessed to you; that's why I know it's time now to be truthful."

Tears pooled on her thin makeup, then over another pot of coffee, we unearthed a dozen vignettes of Dad's lost past until we both deflated in exhaustion. Watching her walk to the car, I realized her complexity, and what a good liar she was. For years she'd fended off my belligerence with a mask of simplicity, carrying the weight of this secret in hopes of finding the thing she knew had left my future so upside down. A pulsing in my fingers itched to call Leon, Em, even my old friend, Gus, and tell them I might have been wrong about Dad. Instead, I defaulted to a medicinal bowl of banana pudding.

Chapter 62

Em helped keep me sane with our nearly daily calls, and I planned to visit the following Saturday, but Mom's money revelation seasoned my thoughts with a fresh uncertainty. Maybe all Vi's walking and searching advice hadn't been about New Orleans after all, and the key to my future was hiding right here in Hattiesburg.

The next day, Mom showed me her desk and what had been moved, how her address book had gotten put on the left side when she always kept it on the right, how the box of cards and letters on top of the secretariat had been scrambled. It all appeared trivial, as if the cat had chased a bug into the box, but Mom believed she was the object of some clandestine operation involving Dad.

I thought back to how sure I'd been that my house had been browsed, back before Janine admitted she'd been there snooping. She'd fumbled my question, then admitted she was searching for her passport—no, it was her social security card. But someone could have come in after Janine.

All the semiannual envelopes Mom had collected didn't reveal much, nothing more than blank paper with a date and noted amount, like an entry into a payment log, completely impersonal. That's why I didn't think it was Dad, too devoid of intimacy. These transactions looked like a bookkeeper registering a bill payment more than a missing husband trying to help his family. Maybe someone was double-crossing Dad, handling his payments for him but now looking to steal back the money. I had no idea what I was supposed to believe.

In late February, before I was to go to Emma's the next day, the phone rang. Maya and Lily joking tended to brighten my dreary work week of three lost proposal deals. There simply wasn't enough corporate work in Hattiesburg, and the local firms with good old boy relationships weren't about to let some out-of-town firm poach from their backyard. I didn't even care.

"Glad to hear you're still hard at work on your novel," Maya said. "You'll be rewarded someday. Oh, Lil wants to ask you something."

"Did you get a chance to look at the website? Pip is a gifted teacher who knows how to shape ideas into structure. I hope you give him a chance."

"Gosh, Lily, I'd love to but that would take all my vacation time, and besides, I can't afford it. I'm still in debt mode."

They had me on speakerphone, and Maya was ready for my objection. "That's a weak excuse. If you trust your talent, you will find a way."

"Maybe, but I've been pretending I have a writing talent. Nobody cares about my stuff. For once, I'm trying to live my actual life and be practical." It wasn't a lie, but it wasn't the truth either.

"Incorrect. You're quitting because you don't have anyone begging you to keep going. Your problem isn't talent, it's attitude." Ouch. The prosecution rested and I wanted to hide from irate justice. At last, Lily intervened.

"Anthony. I understand. You need confirmation. That's okay—you will learn not to rely on this crutch, but you will not get there unless you move to own your art."

My silence dredged old conversations where Janine framed me as Mr. Practical, and the stress of unresolved memory triggered a craving for nicotine.

"If I could get you a free ride at least to Seattle," Maya said, "do you think you could manage to attend the workshop?"

"I don't know. What do you mean?"

"My father has to be in New Orleans for an auction right before the workshop date, then he heads to Seattle for a big trade show. Maybe he could give you a lift out there on his private plane. Besides, he wants to talk more with you." Maya already knew I would be taking this adventure, and I felt like the USS Enterprise seized by a Romulan tractor beam.

"I would like to see my son in Seattle."

"But Dad only has one condition—he wants to read your book before you get on the plane."

Chapter 63

"Mom, I know this sounds looney, but I need to borrow money to go see Tim."

"What? Is he in trouble?"

"Everything is fine. Truth is, there's a special writing workshop out there, some fellow Maya and Lily know. They think he can help me. But I also want to see Tim."

"Can you get time off work? You don't want anyone thinking you're a slacker."

"Yeah, thought about that, but this seminar could be pivotal. Can't explain it."

Mom moved toward me as a half-grin seeped through initial concern. "I figured one day you'd ask me for help. Thought it would be when you didn't have a job, but you never did, and I didn't want to embarrass you by offering." She turned to get fresh coffee while I thought of all the hardship I'd gone through, riding a bicycle to and from Walmart, letting Janine's friends snipe at my manhood, and all this time I only had to ask for help but didn't know I could.

"I don't know much about fancy writing," she said. "The Bible and Billy Graham are about all I know as good literature, but one thing is for sure—you're a decent man, a good person who's been roughed up a little by life. Maybe you've had to step back and chew on a little humility, but you have a Christian soul." My grin gave her a chance to reload the ambrosia gun. If there's a story in you wanting to get out, then set it free because one day you're going to write something important, words that will help people move away from their pain in life. I know you will."

Mom cut to the root of things quicker than a television preacher to his 800-number. She didn't see me as practical or brilliant, only decent, but that would be Mom seeing part of herself in me.

"And to think I only expected a kiss on the cheek before you go off to New Orleans," Mom said. "Here I am about to become a benefactor to a world-famous author. Lordy Mercy, I wish your daddy was here."

"Before you start planning the Larry Winstead Memorial Library," I said, "let's remember, I'm going to a writing workshop, not accepting the Nobel Prize for literature. That may take a couple more ticks on the clock."

Mom pinched my cheek. "That's okay. I can wait."

Chapter 64

Late February made for a cool, cloudy drive to New Orleans, and crossing over Pontchartrain at ten o'clock I realized Em was in class until noon. I decided to pay Vi a little visit to deliver the twenty dollars from Mom for being so nice on the phone.

A half-hour later, the red door opened into a different space from the one I had last seen. She had removed all the heavy draperies, and the windows stood naked in the sunlight. In the brightness, The Jazz Station looked to be a larger building than I'd realized. Vi appeared wearing a red bandana and yellow rubber gloves.

"Look what the crow dropped off. Good Gracious, Larry, get yourself over here and let me take a look. My, you must have lost twenty pounds." She grabbed my shoulders, shoving me into her bosom.

"More like gained ten," I said. "Looks like I caught you giving the place a winter cleaning."

"In New Orleans, it's always spring. Besides, around Mardi Gras time I like to polish up these dingy windows. A lady I know done me two stained-glass pieces to hang in this morning light. Don't seem right to put beautiful colors behind blindness you can't see through, does it? Kind of like what the Lord must think looking at how ignorant people act in this beautiful world he gave us." My philosophical everywoman. Yes, it was good to be back with Vi.

"I reckon you're kind of like a piece of stained glass for Mom and me. You shine a little color on our lives."

"Yes, indeed, that's exactly how life works. We all put these colored lenses on, then think what we see is real. Sometimes we call these lenses

225

hatred, sometimes greed. That's why I need this stained glass up here, to remind me that we see what we choose to see."

I pulled Vi close and gave her another big hug. "You're a pearl," I said. "A real, bottom of the ocean, hidden on the urban reef treasure, and I've missed you."

Vi slapped me on the arm with the dishtowel in her hand. "You a big pile of bull droppings, Larry Winstead. You hear me? I know when my leg's being pulled." With a jaunty step, she waved me to a side table. "Look here at these," she said.

On the table lay two stained glass pieces, one depicting the broken-out frequencies of light split by a raindrop, and the other a scene of a simple house with what looked to be rain falling all around but which turned out to be drops of yellow sunlight falling from a blue sky. I'd never seen such impressionistic hanging glass, each the size of a cookie sheet, the first one portrayed in landscape and the house in portrait.

"Oh my. Who did these?"

"A lady from the bayou. People call her a witch doctor because she lives next to a graveyard. Knows her voodoo, too, but she's mostly an artist living without colored glasses. She can see life, and she can see death."

"I'd like to meet her sometime, maybe have her make me a gris-gris for this outlaw I ran into at Flo's diner."

"That can never happen. She hasn't left her house in twenty years, and as for myself, I don't truck with evil spirits. Only a few people speak with this lady and only when she calls for them. She is a woman you do not offend."

"So how do you know her?"

"She's my sister."

"Really? What's her name?"

"I do not wish to speak of this anymore. She has cursed anyone who uses her name, and I've already said too much."

"Sorry, didn't mean to pry." The coldness in Vi's eye left me with that otherness feeling I sometimes get, as if I'm watching my life but not from the inside. I dug in my pocket. "Mom sent this twenty dollars to thank you for being so kind on the phone. Said you were patient."

"Tell her thank you," Vi said. "Your mother is a dear. She was quite open with me, and I liked her from the first moment." It seemed more was going on here than I understood, but I'd gotten the message that not everything should be spoken.

"My teapot is boiling. Care for some? It's Moringa from the Dominican Republic. Gives you energy and can help you lose weight."

Only now did I hear the whistle from the back. "Well, let's have some, and maybe test out that Moringa power."

Soon we were clinking cups and enjoying the chocolate cream treasures I'd picked up at Miss Rubye's, news dribbling between us as if I'd dropped by to check on my favorite aunt. Vi, almost too calm, nestled into a quietness.

"Is there anything I should know about your conversation with my Mom?" I asked, hoping to trigger Vi into reacting. Zero chance. She slurped her tea while staring right through me.

"Has your mom mentioned any strange things, unexplained happenings, perhaps?" Very deft, that Vi.

"She told me about the envelopes, if that's what you mean." My stare into her dark eyes prompted a grin as if I'd made a shrewd chess move.

"It's about time. Even cold honey will pour if you wait long enough." Vi held the porcelain teapot over my cup, then eased herself back into the chair.

"Who do you think that money comes from?" I asked.

"What money?" *Dang. Mom said she hadn't told Vi.* "You don't know, do you? Mom's been getting money anonymously for years." The moment these words escaped, I realized why Mom had never told me. To console myself, I tested another donut.

"I can believe that," Vi said. "But it ain't my place to do your work. Somebody's trying to tell you something. Don't you find that intriguing?"

"Course I do. I think Dad must have left some investment or something with instructions to keep it all quiet, so the IRS wouldn't get their sticky paws on it."

"That's your theory? Is that what your mama thinks?"

"Not sure," I said. "Mom wants to believe he's still alive. Always has." My eyes twitched toward the stained glass, then I felt Vi listening to the blood cells flowing through my brain.

"You right. Your mama does believe your daddy is alive, but it

227

bothers her that you don't. She lets you say your dumb stuff and don't try to make you feel bad. See, she's listening with her soul; you listening through rose-colored denial."

Vi walked to a screen door to stare into the courtyard off the kitchen, a hummingbird feeder blurred in a frenzy.

"You ain't understanding yet. You too cynical. Your daddy disappearing upended you, left the colors of your soul behind a filter. You gray inside, suspicious, even a little mean, especially to yourself. A spirit is talking. I hear it. But the sounds ain't words yet."

"So, I need to listen to some whispering specter?" Vi grabbed a folded newspaper and swatted it down on the table, leaving the hairs on my neck standing like rows of corn.

"I'm going to tell you something you need to know," Vi said. "People look at each other asking, 'Who are you?' They look at themselves asking the same question. That's what you do. You always trying to find out who you is. But the question you should be asking is what happened to you. See, that's what makes you who you is. What happened is your daddy disappeared. Then, inside your head, you tried to lose yourself."

"But I tried to find out what happened to Dad. Even hired a private investigator till I ran out of money. I don't know what else to do."

Vi's hand touched my shoulder, light as a shadow. "Son, you don't have to be what happened to you; you just have to start there. Since you can't find your daddy just yet, why don't you go find yourself instead? It ain't right you both stay lost."

Chapter 65

For an hour I walked streets with Vi's down-home drawl sloshing the Mississippi mud in me. A man about my age passed wearing boots with untied laces and all over again I remembered that day Mom accidentally showed me who I was, and who I wasn't.

"Son, it's been two weeks now. What are we going to do?" Mom had asked, still in her pajamas at noon as days of waiting for news about Dad's disappearance had wrung out the sturdiness of her being. "You need to be the man of the family for a while." Her voice then trailed into a thinness of hope. Until that instant, I'd remained chipper, defiantly believing this aberration of reality was only temporary, but her pleading grin informed me I had to do something, though I had no idea what.

The volume of me draining away, I'd turned toward the coffee pot, but through the back door, a sunny breeze slowed me. And there they were, Dad's work boots. Muddy with paint-soaked Bondo dust, laces frayed, scuffed brown, each shoe now sprawled to the size of a canyon. *I have to drop out of school to help Mom.* But the image of those boots also began filling me again, and when I picked them up, a rattle clicked inside the right one, two little steel men Dad had shaped out of two-inch bolts, still crude, unfinished.

A few minutes later, the whine of my tires snapped me back to the present as I crossed an unfamiliar canal then stopped at the same intersection where I'd turned the wrong way a half-hour earlier. All these years of stopping and starting, wrong turns, all those half-formed plans and hollowed-out dreams now dallied behind me as I headed toward a line of old telephone poles along a freshly paved road. I had no idea where the road led, but the gleam of black asphalt shimmered a ghostly mirage of that road up from Ray Curry's place. And a notion came to me that maybe I wasn't so much lost as confused, so I kept driving.

Maybe no answer could be found, maybe what happened to Dad was an endpoint without an ending, nothing to be done except listen to those dented sounds of teenage me stumbling through my life. At a traffic light, a hawk-screech of scorched tires smoldered under a taxi, the driver's silent scorn mimicking Emma's scowl that day through the glass panes of her front door. And I stared at him as if it wasn't my place to get out of his way.

Cafés and houses, stores and shops, languishing currents drifting past, then my phone beeped, "Go to Roy's." *I wonder what Mom did with those boots?* Then a mild nausea rose as I remembered getting drunk one night and throwing those two sculpted bolts into the pond by my house, so I wouldn't have to look at them and feel so lost.

"Well, lookie here, mama's boy." Behind the counter with a white dish towel in hand, Roy looked like a giant trapped in servitude. A minute later, my feet dangled in the air as he swooped me into a bear hug, an overgrown child shaking me with the force of his joy. "Em said you'd be showing up. You hungry?" The chalkboard special read *Speckled Half Shell—$5.* I wasn't sure what that was.

"It's a fried oyster po'boy with a grilled fillet of speckled trout laid on fresh French bread. You ain't never had one?" He seemed mystified at my ignorance.

"No sir, but I'm a seeker of the unknown, so let's have it." Roy's huge hand squeezed my shoulder until my blood pressure doubled. Seeing Roy was about as close to brotherly camaraderie as I'd known for years now, and his grip seemed to fence out the image of work boots.

"Dang Roy, quiet for a Saturday. Where is everybody?"

"They'll be around later. We had a big to-do down the road last night, one of them charity things to raise money for the community center Katrina ruined. Got a turkey shoot next week, not killing a bird but just seeing who's the best shot."

"You shooting, Roy?"

"Cataracts about spoiled my shooting days, but Emma will."

"Emma? With all her yoga and tofu stuff?"

"That's where you'd be mistaken. Emma is meditation and incense today, but she grew up checking trotlines and skinning squirrels for supper. Let loose that temper of hers, and you'll understand right quick she can take care of herself."

"I ran into that beast once." Just then the bell over the door tinkled while tight dark yoga pants and a snug white top stepped inside riding a light beam. A ponytail pinned me to my stool.

"Hey, sis." Roy hugged her as if today's visit were a rare occasion. "Your Yankee friend is here. Said he can't get a decent meal north of Slidell."

"Well, give him a bowl of that crawfish étouffée you made yesterday." Before she finished the thought, she wrapped her arms around me in a big hug, and I lifted her from the floor. She pecked me on the cheek, relieving me to sit. This was family without all the romantic complexity that cluttered up a man getting to know a woman. I remembered again the rules Emma had set out—friends, just good friends. *Maybe Janine and I forgot to take this step.*

"What you eating there, sis?"

"Nothing. Still sweating from class, but I'd take a seltzer."

Seconds later, we buzzed on conversation about my drive, then how Nicole loved science. I didn't even see Roy bring her drink, and my po'boy appeared so magically my nose discovered it before my eyes did. Emma and I flipped right back to the closeness we'd shared the last trip, and though Earl crept across the room where I'd hidden remembered work boots, I kept that door closed to protect this fragile moment. And with each little touch on my arm, the insignificant contact of our knees as my bar stool turned, subtleties alerted me to a new vocabulary developing between Em and me, threads of energy still too tiny to fill a syllable.

Chapter 66

The afternoon lazed as we strolled the grounds at Tulane University. Pulling her close against the chill happened so naturally it took a few seconds to notice. In another hour, Nicole would return from drum practice, so for a moment, we left our worries outside a street café where coffees cozied us up around little campfires of chicory and roasted beans.

"You seem more relaxed," Emma said. "Last trip you got pretty tangled up. Maybe your California girls confused you."

"No, not confused—tempted."

"Hmm," she said.

"I told you about that writing workshop out west. I'm tempted to go meet Lily's friend." I stopped to gauge her reaction, having only shared with Em a single short story.

"What is it you think you'll find there?" she asked.

"Good question. Something maybe I can't see from here. I've been thinking about what you said the last trip," I said. "Stuff like doing things not for the result but because they're right. It helps me understand what I want, not so much what I'm afraid of doing."

"What are you afraid of, Larry? You have a good job. You're pretty secure, right?"

"True. But the more I accumulate, the more meaningless it becomes. It's nothing but stuff. I'm afraid of living a life with no purpose." No response. "If I fell dead, all people would have to remember me by would be stuff: couches, dishes, a house that needs to be painted and sold." I wondered if Emma could hear me thinking. She lifted my hand, those blue beams scooping into my brain.

"I'm listening, but you've gone to that spot where no one can find you," she said. "Are you afraid I'll understand?" Both my feet tapped a march.

"I don't know why I act like I do," I said. "Something in me can't open, so I only show people what they want to see, and most times I don't even realize what I want."

Emma put her other hand on top of mine. "It's okay," she said. "Everyone does that."

Then, magic. Emma leaned over and kissed the back of my hand. "Inside you is a trove of something you've been hiding, a thing clamoring to be set free."

"You mean my writing?" Emma studied two sparrows feasting on a dropped piece of egg sandwich while I forced my feet to be quiet.

"Possibly," she said. I'd expected her to talk about my writing, and the winter sun cast a lamppost shadow over her face.

"Larry?" Her voice reminding the student to leave the dreamy playground outside and come into the classroom. "When you mentioned that if you died all people would have to remember you by would be your stuff, did you mean that?"

"Guess so. Not really. People have memories of me, too. . ." Emma squeezed my hand, forcing attention to where our bodies touched. She slid closer.

"Gratitude. The love of your own life. That's what's inside you aching to be released." She allowed me to empty unformed words. "In your litany of 'stuff,' you failed to mention another gratitude. . ." She stopped speaking, then leaned back in her chair.

I panicked, scrambling to think of what I'd forgotten to list. Was it Christ? Marriage? Maybe good health? I poured all my energy into keeping my emotions hidden.

"You know what I'm talking about," she said, and the Mississippi mud in me squished beneath her stare.

"Black walnut ice cream?" I said. Her scoff helped.

"My dear friend, the important thing in your life to be grateful for is your son, Tim, the trustee of your time on this planet, the electron of you split off as a new bundle of life. Don't you see? He is your very own

DNA containing all your parenting, your love and talents, everything you've created."

My head ached. The genetic connection made sense, but her depth of understanding zoomed above my capability, at least while sober. Maybe she was too deep for me, and yet in that instant I realized that Tim's presence had begun slipping away the same way Dad's had, and even Gus and Randy.

Em bobbed her head in and out of the buttery light behind a sycamore branch while an old image flickered of that slide show projector Janine bought our first Christmas. *Cachunk, cachunk.* And there Tim's first pony ride, his crash into the azalea bush when we took the training wheels off his bike. But Tim wasn't gone, only drifting from the gravity of me, and I wanted to hand him that green glass fish that had sat on the rear floorboard of my car for two weeks before I finally took it into the house, Reid's artwork I'd treated like myself.

A cellphone signaled to pick up Nicole. We would meet at the duplex in half an hour. And there, among the ripples of Em's fading presence, particles of light sketched an image for me of Chub's disappeared wife, that painted echo she'd left behind.

On the way to my car, I passed an artist hunched over his easel, dabbing craggy touches of an elderly man with a handlebar mustache. That painter didn't seem to need validation, didn't care if anyone noticed. He, the observer and the observed, only created. And the elderly man bloomed on the canvas.

At Em's house, we relaxed with hot tea. Roy had canceled dinner after the waitress at the café called in sick, so with Nicole having pizza downstairs with the twins, Em and I settled into the suddenness of a quiet moment.

"I know you're sensitive about your writing," Emma said. "That's why sometimes I'm afraid to ask about it. But I loved your short story, *Pieces of the Sea.*"

"Thanks," I said. "But if you don't mind, I'd rather talk about the novel I'm working on. Talking helps me see structure." My selfishness surprised even me.

"So, you don't have this big plan in your head?" Em asked. "How do you know what to write?" she asked.

"I have an impression of what I want but resist rushing at it; I let fragments float where they want. In bed, before sleep or when I first wake up, threads connect with words I've already written, or snippets of dialogue, or maybe a new scene forming in my head." Emma sipped her tea, then snuggled into couch cushions.

"Lots of these wiggling pieces fall away unused," I said. "But some self-organize around what I've seen or heard that day. It's almost like I'm a pass-through, an observer activated by some remote event. . . I'm not making any sense."

"But you are," she said. "For you, the creative process organizes impressions your mind is forever collecting. Observations self-generate a framework you sense but haven't yet grasped completely . . ."

"Yeah, that's it," I said. "Do you do this, too?" Her phrasing sounded clinical, like a surgical procedure instead of a creative blending, but she understood.

"I don't do that," she said. "I'm not so much a word person painting with syllables. I tend to be more physical. For me, it's how my body moves that excites creativity and finds connection. Words don't capture subtlety for me; they usually sound too blunt, like doors walling off understanding."

"You're not a word person, huh? You talk like a poet."

"Oh, don't pay me any attention. I ramble," she said. But she didn't mean it. That half-smile and perky elongation of her spine signaled she, too, yearned to be acknowledged but resisted the attention. "Half the time," she said, "I get in the middle of a thought and words get so hollow that my voice loses its will." Her shoulders slumped a thousandth of a millimeter.

She knew. I was positive she'd spotted this same lapse of confidence in me. Or maybe she was showing me how she fakes life, too. "Do you really do that?" I asked. "Feel like your words are thin watercolor struggling to paint an oil richness?"

"Yes, that's it," she said. "Sometimes a poem comes to me, or a song lyric, but I don't pull them up to the surface. They get stranded." Her face tightened while a fragile wave slipped from her body.

The next hour I shared my awkward hands, how they never understand machinery or moving parts, how they felt whole only when I gardened in the dirt or puttered on a keyboard or guitar. Emma revealed her intimidation of math, how numbers reversed for her, how she always worked backward to the rules and the ensuing confusion made her want to run away. Tentacles of vulnerability floated through each of us as if the atoms of our bodies expanded space, and new gravity continued to form in the unfilled regions between words we didn't need to speak.

"Em, how does it feel to be the center of the world to Nicole? I mean, without Earl around to help carry the load."

"It's wonderful. But I try not to think that way. I don't want Nicole believing anyone is the center of the world. Playing the performer in the spotlight on stage is the wrong frame of reference for a child. All that attention distorts their sense of self, makes it too easy for kids to become little ego monsters." Her fluid tone, so comfortable when she talked about Nicole, jolted to a stop. "I try to keep myself out of that spotlight, too."

"Not sure I get it."

"Love is what I want her filled with, not self, or me. My mom taught me that children need only two things: love and boundaries. That's what gives them a sense of competency and what leads them to good choices."

After cheese and apples, then garlicky shrimp and squash, the rest of the evening filled with looking at photo albums. Around ten, Emma began a gentle quizzing about New Washington. It had been a long time since I'd spoken with such enthusiasm without being blind drunk, but with a gentle tracing of the boundary between me and my fictional world, Em led me to where I didn't have to worry.

"Raja's world needs softening," she said. "Maybe Thea could inspire his hidden artistic yearning. Have her invite him over for coffee and see what happens."

"Yeah. How about Thea going to Raja's house for dinner?" I asked. "Then have her recite lines of poetry, something to prod his creative inspiration."

"Like what?"

"Oh, anything, Whitman's *Out of the Cradle Endlessly Rocking* would be perfect since that marked his poetic awakening. But that's too long." Emma said nothing.

"I have it," I said. "William Blake's *Auguries of Innocence.* Only the opening lines."

"Don't know it," she said.

"Yes, you do. Very common. Here you go," I said.

> "To see a World in a Grain of Sand
> And a Heaven in a Wild Flower
> Hold Infinity in the palm of your hand
> And Eternity in an hour"

"I have heard that," she said. "Maybe Thea connects Raja to an undiscovered yearn to paint?"

By two o'clock in the morning, we were both drained. She slid over close to brush the hair from my eyes. Terror. Inches from me, my rough fingers sanded her snowy skin scraping an ivory neckline. A knee, a pearly dress unveiling milk-colored thighs and a blue hint of panties unassuming as a prism in the shadows.

Chapter 67

Cream-colored skin behind a window, her face buried in a book of love stories, a woman twirls a ringlet. Toward her a man on the roof of an opposite building dodges solar arrays and clothes airing in the yellow breeze. He hurls himself into the ten-story gulf with an arrow-like aim toward the woman's window two stories below. Her lips quiver. The window opening seals into a solid wall of brick.

"Wake up, sleepy bones. It's ten o'clock," Nicole said as she drummed my chest. "Mom's making pancakes." Nicole's grape-jelly smile reminded me where I was.

"Come in here. Coffee is ready. Here you go, papa bear," Emma said. "Enjoy your winter's sleep?" There, those eyes behind the sealed window.

"Am I still dreaming?"

"We all live in a dream." She handed me the mug. "Especially when we stay up talking till three." I remembered baby blue.

"Yeah. Raja doesn't sleep much," I said.

"I see that," she said. "This morning I've been mulling over what it is about Raja's world that troubles me. No one working, part-time jobs as a lottery prize, I don't think I like it."

"Still searching out the right tone," I said. "Readers have to make a leap. Maybe I need more narrative about technology eliminating human labor. Does that make sense?"

"Yeah, the way vinegar makes sense as a cocktail," she said. "Most people think cheap foreign labor stealing our jobs is the problem. You're describing a view of mandated consumption, not scarcity. That's disorienting."

"Good. I want to disrupt perception."

"Last night I loved your idea about the psychological damage left by the death of Raja's parents," Em said. "But the theme of social conformance to earn chances in a job lottery feels too business-like. An artistic angle will make Raja's story more engaging. Readers crave emerging life not business theory."

She nailed what had been bugging me. Last night we'd talked about a world of intimate discovery and love, but this morning my hundred and eighteen pages oozed of bleakness.

"For me, a story needs emotion. Sex and violence are baby food for adults, so feed us. Maybe you want to give Raja some bad traits?" she said. "Make him human. Has he stolen something or planned a scheme to cheat people? Give him something a reader can hate, then let that conflict become creative growth."

She was smarter than me, and the comparison left me wooden. *What does she mean with this bad boy idea?* Maybe I'd been unpredictable and that intrigued her. Unlikeable yet sympathetic, essential Raja.

The door to the den flew open with Nicole begging to go watch Sunday morning cartoons. Emma and I retreated to organic strawberries. No makeup, hair a little wild, that healthy sheen to her skin, the morning revealed a realistic Emma unimpressed with herself.

"I've been thinking about Raja being emotionally damaged from his facial injury," I said, "but hadn't thought about using bad boy traits. Maybe he could mislead Thea. Perhaps Raja isn't capable of love but is obsessed only with winning the job lottery."

Raising her hand for me to stop, she stood up. "Please. Breathe. Too desolate. As a woman, I wouldn't advise taking that path. It starts to feel like a video game. Besides, isn't it the cliché of most men to focus on their one true love—work—the only thing that fulfills them. Maybe take a renaissance approach where excess leisure time in this overly-controlled world spawns an artistic spirit. In a culture where AI can generate creativity, allow New Washington to flower as non-engineered human imagination, an organic creativity you can reward with your lottery points." This woman saw eternity in a grain of sand.

She pressed me for an hour, challenging my assumptions, urging me to build a realistic portrait of Raja as a man rather than as a caricature.

The lingering taste of sticky sweet cherry from twenty years ago dripped down the back of my throat, the taste now tangy strawberry.

Em moved to the window to adjust one of her prisms, and a tiny rainbow appeared on the opposite wall. She cared about this creative venture of mine, and her words presented a Socratic challenge forcing me to remain present. This manuscript wouldn't sit unopened on her nightstand.

Around four, she walked me to my car while flipping a worry stone between her fingers. I prayed our having sex hadn't changed things. She leaned into the rolled-down car window. "You should go to the Seattle workshop," she said. "You need feedback from people who know about writing, not like me." Her voice trailed off. I put my hand on hers.

"You're right. I'm going to check out the details and go see Tim." The squeeze of her hand told me she didn't want me to leave. But I needed quiet.

"But Em, you're wrong. Workshop people may help me, but you already have. You may be the most clear-thinking person I've ever met." A strand of hair fell over her eyes, then she leaned through the car window piercing the invisible pane between us as if she'd opened a window shade.

"I hope last night doesn't change things for you," she said. "It did for me."

Chapter 68

The drive to Hattiesburg left me craving my guitar. With all the windows rolled down, I began to blurt random lyrics into the howling wind. My new handheld voice recorder captured one almost inaudible new line: "The window to me is you," but most of the recording sounded like a butt-dial from a ZZ Top concert.

Blenhh, blenhh. Five miles from Hattiesburg, a dump truck shoved me to the lined edge of the highway, the driver giving me the finger. I had driven miles without noticing, not exactly sure what I had done to offend Massey's Fill Dirt until I noticed the speedometer pegged at thirty miles per hour. Though the day had warmed, my heater pumped to the rhythm of white lines disappearing under the car, and again road noise released me back to my stupor. For too long I'd been committed to my dissatisfaction. Maybe it was okay not to know everything, not to deny the fault line Dad had fissured through me, but it wasn't okay to be the person always pushing myself down. I almost turned around and headed south.

Over the next few days, I worked myself into distracted exhaustion. Each morning at five a pot of espresso, then down the shaft of my past I wandered to gather fragments of what had shaped me into this forty-year-old contortion. And Raja collected tidbits of the person he would become.

Each day I gathered: a word, a streak of sunlight, the peccadillo of a stranger's twitch, a memory from first grade. Then, while lying in bed at night, bundles of detail began to self-organize. Most of the daily volume dissipated, failing to connect with narrative channels competing as grooves of story, and mornings became a gathering of sprouted potential.

In bed night or morning, I studied the popped nail hole on the ceiling above the headboard; the hint of steel acted like an antenna for receiving Em's presence. Each day the same routine, brief some mornings, lengthy others, crude some days requiring effort to refine, and yet perfectly crafted sentences other days. Up with the songbirds at daylight and into a trance of habit something like strolling into calm sunlight, I imagined myself chatting with Em as we surveyed green shoots of story emerging in a space all our own.

Behind the coldness and light of the real world, Raja and Thea roamed the unborn land, searching for parts of me they could use. Raja tried on practiced falsity, finding his special talent for costumed personality so easily drawn from the closet of my pretense couture. Thea discovered cynicism and the ability to be certain of things uncertain. And each day reading my written words aloud revealed to me what needed to be written next. The truth hid in unrefined sentences yearning to be worked and shaped, that unborn potential only the sound and rhythm of language could set free.

Chapter 69

Mid-March struggled into brighter days with chartreuse tufts bursting from Army-green pine needles. Emma had wanted me to come down for Mardi Gras, but I decided not to lose my mind, so she finally visited Hattiesburg the first week of spring. Saturday, we talked about how yoga influenced her philosophy and how her father had given her a watercolor paint set when she was ten. For a month, I'd not sent Em any writing updates, but at two in the morning, midway into a bottle of Cuervo blanco, I read her some new passages.

The next day, our late-night literary discussion languished in the haze of yet another alcohol wreckage. Emma woke up giddy over the writing updates while I struggled to find the light switch in the bathroom. At ten, we enjoyed a second pot of coffee and the cartoons from the *New Yorker* in the previous day's mail.

"You still look green," she said.

"I feel okay." A solid lie to anchor the morning.

"Do you remember what we talked about last night?"

"Some of it."

"I don't think you do," she said. "But remember, I'm a sounding board in this creative process. All that effusion you spread around last night, that's what you have to hold on to, then someday those sparks will become Raja and Thea."

My brain on slow rewind searched for the episode Emma remembered. "Look, I'm an idiot," I said. "I know I ran off at the mouth. James Joyce mode Janine used to call my incoherency. Haven't been drinking enough lately; my tolerance is low. I'll practice." The familiar joke aborted.

"Yes, you drank too much, and I do want to talk to you about that." Her pause stopped my breathing. "But first I want to tell you something: you were brilliant last night. Sometimes I got lost in the skipping around of ideas, but I saw your imagination at work. You molted out of Larry-mode for sure, but that Anthony guy, that guy that fuses real-life detail with the fictional world, that guy sees truth." She paused. I tried to remember who Anthony was.

"I'm sorry. You're trying to make me feel better, but last night I'm sure I mostly blabbered."

"Hmm," she said. "I accept your apology. You definitely weren't listening too well, but you circled in a creative flight that took me on a high-altitude adventure. Heck, I'm standing on the ground watching you ride balloons in this world you're creating."

"I don't think so. See, when we talked in New Orleans, you saw nuances in my writing that I'd missed. I'm only a factory worker in this process; every day I take things off the conveyor belt then package them onto the keyboard. I'm not sure its creativity at all. You're the one who sees future Raja."

"You're starting to sound like Mr. Joyce again," she said. "Besides, what you're saying is nothing but malarkey. Last night was all about the forming of unformed things, and you weren't some powerless factory worker. You were research and development, marketing, and the board of directors all collaborating on this thing in your head."

"See, that's exactly what I mean," I said. "You listen to my chaos and see order. I need that."

"Maybe I help guide a little, or polish, but you're the word artist." I almost tried to prove her wrong. "But listen, my dear friend, I need to tell you that your drinking can destroy this thing you're discovering. I adore your brilliance, but you're in jeopardy, and it's time for new choices."

Her eyes anesthetized me with the realization that this entire morning had been focused on me, exactly the opposite of what I'd planned. Em moved two steps closer, devilish slide of her feet, willowy negligee fluttering, and I knew how a deer on the highway feels before impact. Putting her left knee between my legs, she untied a string, revealing a baby blue bra and tissue-thin bikini panties the color of a summer sky.

The world fell away into an explosion of clothing and a blue sensual ocean. Her supple body spread itself over me, protecting the moment from my wandering mind, and I heard wave caps far away on Lake Pontchartrain.

An hour later, the late morning sun spotlighted Maya's two paintings and my mouth lurched into gear without my brain realizing. "Nicole showed me a painting of a little house with a creek running alongside. You painted that, right?" Emma continued resting on her right side, facing away from me. I touched her to see if she'd fallen back asleep. "You awake?" A kiss on her neck produced a slight quiver. After a few seconds, she rolled onto her back.

"It's the house she was a baby in, and that little creek became her playground for mud pies and crawfish fights." Her words unsentimental, the way someone speaks about a dead person no longer familiar, left me stranded.

"You never talk about your painting," I said. "Do you still try?" She rolled onto her side again, facing away.

"Do you want me to drop this? I only want to understand."

Again, she faced the ceiling. "It's okay," she said. "Those days are done. Nicole and I miss that home, but Earl destroyed that world."

"What happened?" This time she shifted onto her left side to face me as she snuggled a pillow like a favorite doll.

"My ex-husband is a psycho. Meth destroyed his brain." Cracking her neck with a head tilt, Em wandered into a forgotten land. A minute passed. "On the back of that house was a Florida room where I painted watercolors, all windows and light. Then, after a few art lessons, I began playing with oils. That's how I met Junior and Flo. At first, Earl encouraged me, before the accident leaving him a green-eyed demon." She got out of bed.

"Is that why you don't live there anymore? Because he fell apart?"

"He disappeared long before that, came home high one day while I was in class, crazy about something. I think that morning I'd burned his toast, I don't even remember. Anyway, he took a dirty paintbrush and a jar of spaghetti sauce, then slathered every painting on that porch, suffocated them all in red." A long sigh emptied her whole body, then I wrapped myself around her heaving shoulders. "I swore I'd never paint again. I only did that house because Nicole begged me."

"Isn't that what Earl wanted you to do? Give up?"

"He wanted to destroy my soul along with his."

"Em? I see how Earl hurt you. But you're still here. Someone once told me that people want to understand what life means as if it's a finite thing. But we can't. We're moving points absorbing influences that shift who we are, sometimes forever."

She turned her head away. I could see she held her breath, then she disappeared into the sound of a running shower.

Maya's painted mountains intensified after I raised the blinds, and I hoped the blue people would appear. Emma's struggle differed from the journey Maya had painted for me. Earl tried to destroy Em's creativity because he was envious; I'd walked away from mine to prove I was a victim. We'd each made choices. She had her protective covering, too. I saw that now, and I remembered that dream of the man climbing the hillside when the wind blew his suitcase up the slope. Maybe Em and I both had tried to carry what couldn't be held.

Pulling off my T-shirt, I smelled the stench of booze seeping from my skin, the smell triggering a picture of Earl stinking of stale beer that day he'd assaulted Em in Roy's kitchen. And the blue people stared at me.

Chapter 70

After breakfast, we took a half-mile walk over to a patch of woods sanctuary for me since childhood. As kids, we built a treehouse around the staircase limbs of a huge birch tree, but only a few knife-etched initials remained now as vestiges of a simpler time where those upper branches hosted debates about girls and baseball high above the practical lessons of adults.

"See this limb," I said. "We'd come down that staircase of branches, then inch out on this big limb we called the elevator. The farther out you slide, the lower to the ground it takes you. Club knowledge." Emma immediately began climbing.

"Hey wait. I need to talk to you about something," I said. She hopped down. "I didn't tell you this earlier because at the time I didn't think it was important. But that night when I went swamp-slurping crazy at Roy's oyster roast, something happened."

"You mean when the tequila gauge in New Orleans dropped to empty?"

"Yeah. But this is no time to brag. Seriously, I don't know who drove my car home that night, but they parked it towards the back of the hotel lot. Anyway, didn't move around too much Sunday, but Monday morning the manager told me it had been vandalized."

"Don't look at me," Emma said. "You were a jerk, but I didn't blame your car."

"One suspect eliminated. But I think I know who did it. See, while we were out inspecting the damage, I saw this banged up Volkswagen van take off as soon as I walked over to my car."

"So what?

"Em, the vandal smashed two quarts of red pasta sauce onto my car. I think the spaghetti terrorist may have been Earl watching me and cooking up a grudge."

Even the breeze paused to listen. Her plaster-white skin cemented, then she soaked my shirt. The thinness of our relationship revealed how unprepared I was for genuine intimacy, how Em's too generous deference to my writing might only have been her technique for pushing attention away from her own self-doubt.

"Maybe you shouldn't come back to New Orleans for a while. Until Earl is caught, anyway," she said.

"Don't think so," I said. "That little snort hole isn't in control. He's a junkie, but you have a Smith and Wesson and I have a .38. Besides, Roy needs bait for his crab traps."

Chapter 71

After a long walk, we huddled on the porch around a pot of tea. "Earl is my issue. I can't let you get involved." She zipped her jacket.

"Okay. I'll send you the bill for the scratches spaghetti boy carved into my car." She took off my Braves cap, then stuffed her hair underneath.

"Is this a problem for us? I can't tell," she said.

"No. Only a distraction," I said. "Heck, now we have a shared story that doesn't end with a tequila truck." She held her tea with both hands as if praying.

"Earl broke his hip in a motorcycle crash. Never walked right after that. Pills caused him to lose his construction job. That's when the wrong people came back into his life and he gave up on himself." Her body slumped, and she stepped to the edge of the porch where I'd fixed the broken post.

"Listen," I said, "he tried to take away the piece that makes you whole, but you're still an artist inside, one that needs a friend."

"You think so, Mr. Joyce," she said, then strutted a high-chinned glide toward me. Then we left Earl outside on the porch alone.

Two hours later the fading Sunday sent Emma south again and me sitting in the twilight rewinding weekend conversations. But by midnight, my fingers ached as Raja struggled to imagine love.

Earl's stench tried to pierce my bubble, then the ceiling fan began squeaking a friction that took me back to that old oscillating fan in Tim's nursery, those steel blades squawking each time the green motor reversed course. Janine still had hope back when Tim's red boots were his daily brand, back when memories weren't land mines. And now that green back-and-forth chunking unfolded a distant whimper, that meagre sound Tim delivered when I first held him.

But Raja can hear only the groan of his past, the thrumming of life that never happened. But he's more than simply what happened to him. And through Tim's baby wrinkles fading into a grating breezy sound, Raja discovers the glint of new life that will transform his future, a daughter.

The following day drowned in perfunctory contracts and shifting schedules, the office noise drumbeats without music. Just over a month until the Seattle conference, Maya called.

"Yeah, I'm finishing my first whole draft now." A glance at the mirror in the den confirmed it was me speaking, but I hadn't written in days.

"That's good news. Do you have a title yet?"

"Same one, *New Washington*. I decided *Depleted* was too cheerful."

"I like that. Cultural science fiction, right?" Lily asked.

"Kind of. It's a psycho-sociological story about people competing for jobs through government lotteries." My yawn required an extra breath. "But there's a love twist."

"Thank heaven," Maya said. "A world where people dream of work sounds like Silicon Valley."

"So, am I going to see 'Workless Washington' before the conference?" Lily asked.

"Maybe. Still editing."

"My father is eager to see if your writing voice matches your personality," Maya said. "Have you sent him the masterpiece yet?"

"No. Waiting on the Nobel committee to approve."

"His insight might be useful." Those words sent a shiver through me as I imagined Alfredo with a red pen shaped as a sword.

"Yeah, feedback can be ventilating."

"Don't worry," Maya said. "Think of criticism as material for your Nobel speech."

Chapter 72

At last, the manuscript had a postmark to Seattle. I'd welded on some hoopla about Raja falling in love with Thea's gift for music, but I hated it and knew it would be revised away. Imposing a deadline had stifled Raja's patient coalescing, his shift too stark now. And my morning rework of sentences failed to reveal truth but instead only hesitation. It troubled me that I couldn't quite hold on to the idea of an artistic renaissance in such a deadened culture, and in a conflicted way, I looked forward to the workshop.

A note from Mr. Pippen confirmed manuscript receipt, and his friendly nudge prompted me to send copies to Alfredo, Emma, and Maya. How different now from that year spent waiting for Janine to read the first draft of "Depleted," but I still wasn't sure my writing skill had improved.

March passed with Emma helping me plot Thea's relationship with Raja while I composted every daily experience in search of reusable detail. April brought nice weather, then a few days before Easter, I called to see if Mom wanted to go to Maxine's Fish Camp for fried catfish. Naturally, she'd already eaten at four o'clock, but she did offer a surprise.

"Listen, hon, for Easter I'm cooking a late lunch. I've got a surprise for you." The phone went quiet as if she'd gone to the refrigerator. "I wish you'd come with me to church."

"Mom, here's the thing. Going to church only on Easter is inconsistent. I'm focusing more on being predictable, so I'll let other sinners perform; they're more motivated."

"You're so bad. You know Reverend Polk will ask me where you are. What am I going to tell him?"

"Tell him I'm involved in a special project and that I should finish in about forty years."

"I don't know what I'm going to do with you. Anyway, come around two. I'm baking a ham. You'll have leftovers."

"No hint about this surprise?" I asked. "Maybe a new car or a first edition Faulkner novel? I can't wait to see how much you spent on me."

"Oh, the money will be well spent. You'll see." These days I didn't need anything, but I sorted every practicality from a new fishing rod to tires for my car.

Late Sunday morning, I made a batch of double chocolate fudge and freshened up the dozen red roses I'd ordered. Man can't live by ham alone. Pulling into Mom's driveway, I looked for hints. No car, so no one was visiting, no new bicycle tucked away in the garage. Mom had strategized for maximum effect. I slipped around the back to catch her off guard, and when I tapped on the storm door, she jumped for a high rebound.

"A little help here, please," I said.

"Always glad to assist a gentleman bearing gifts." She kissed my cheek then gave me that familiar pat on the shoulder while unburdening me of fudge and flowers. Her garnet necklace and earrings twinkled to match her spirited step at having her son home for another Sunday meal.

When I was a kid, Mom made sure Easter was packed with goodies, but she always added something special: a new watch, a compass, and one year an 1865 Liberty Seated dime for my coin collection. She knew that the combination of consistency and newness kept a child content and a grown man returning to a mother's kitchen.

"Okay, so you've had me guessing for three days now, but I don't see a new Mercedes in the driveway, so I've ruled that out. I'm still banking on the new yacht though. Is it down on the coast?"

"Shucks, you guessed it. And I went to all the trouble to buy the Queen Mary just for you." She gave me that pinch on the cheek.

"Well, then, what's the surprise?"

"You're a little boy, aren't you? All instant gratification and no patience. I'm in no hurry to reveal my secret, but I suppose I could do you one favor. Why don't you turn around and look behind you?"

I wheeled a one-eighty to a shock standing in the doorway. "Good Lord, what in the world are you doing here?"

Vi hugged my neck, then patted my cheek. "Your mother invited me for a nice Easter ham. How could I say no to that?" For the next hour, we laughed and kidded one another in a camaraderie of blood and bond. Soon, the table sagged under the spread of dishes.

At four, we settled into coffee and fudge, plus Mom's pecan pie. This new high fructose diet wasn't too bad. Then the grandma cabal went to work. "Vi and I have gotten to be pretty good friends these past few weeks," Mom said. "We write to each other and talk on the phone regularly, so I decided to meet her face-to-face."

"Yeah, you two have a lot in common—me," I said, then sipped the Community Coffee Vi had brought. "Tell me, Vi, what do you think of Mom's little home here?"

"I sense the love you and your mother share. And I also sense your father's presence. His spirit is strong."

My immediate reaction was to engage a debate, but I checked the impulse. "All right, I'll bite. Tell me, Vi, is Dad still alive?" I hadn't planned to be so assertive, but dessert sugars and high-test caffeine induced bravery. Silence, then Vi passed an eyelash semaphore to Mom.

"We can't know that for sure, Larry," Vi said. "Besides, deciding if your father is alive is business for you and Ina, not me."

"You're right, Vi." I turned to see Mom pull her hands up close to her chin as if she wanted to pray but hadn't realized the notion yet, probably afraid of what boorishness I might utter. "Maybe if we all think about Dad making it home this Easter Sunday, then we can help him find his way back," I said. Mom fidgeted a placement of her coffee cup from the right side of her dessert plate to the left. Her nervous glance struck me as dread. Behind her, in a shaded corner, the little plaster mold that had hung in that quiet spot for decades reflected the dining room brightness:

> *Behave as if you believe,*
> *Then, one day*
> *Soon,*
> *You will believe.*

253

My grandmother had made that little cast and given it to Mom somewhere in the ancient past. I'd thought it was some religious hocus pocus until this moment when I was almost sure I heard Dad's grinder at work in the garage.

"We should talk about something else," Mom said.

"It's okay, Mom. I meant what I said. I do hope Dad comes walking in with a mess of fish for supper." My fake-sounding words shellacked the room with skepticism. The cabal measured my sincerity, and as I stirred my coffee, the twiddle of steel against porcelain cued Vi to action.

"I wouldn't mind seeing your daddy stroll in myself, especially with a mess of blue cats." Vi said, her cheerful tone vented the strain in the room. Mom's jaw fluttered, her gaze magnetized toward coffee drops spilled in her saucer.

I slid my chair a few inches closer to Mom. "I need to say something to you." Her hands seized the frail cup. "I was wrong all these years to give you such a hard time. You believe in Dad. My doubt was all about me. I'm sorry. You deserved better." Both Mom and Vi froze without breathing, then Mom walked around behind me to place her hands on my shoulders.

"Don't say that. You are what I deserve. It's just that you thought your dad abandoned you. The whole thing confused me, too, except in my heart I knew whatever reason Thomas was gone, it wasn't because he didn't love us." I couldn't see Mom's face, but I heard it seize, and then I wrapped her in my tightest hug.

"You two doing good," Vi said. "Thomas is feeling this love, I'm sure of it." Vi ended her sermonette by hugging Mom and me while secretly pinching my arm. Normal tried to seep back into the day, but Vi used that Mississippi mud twang she'd avoided all through this luncheon to keep me focused on Mom. And there it was again, New Orleans pulling against distance all the way up to Hattiesburg where Mom had forgotten how to speak, and I was remembering how to listen.

S.I. Hayakawa once wrote about language being a kind of clothing we wear, something appropriate to each situation. I studied Vi's performance of nuance as she swapped accent costumes in this impromptu theater of Viola Veo. But hardness came to rebuke the too clear truth, and a shade of doubt crawled over Vi's caramel-colored brightness, and an errant thought escaped from inside my head. *Who is Vi really? Is she hiding something?*

And with Mom and Vi chirping about the rose climbers on the mantle and the bouquet on the table, their effervescence collided into my swell of otherness. I was both an insider and an outsider today. Was that what happened to Dad? Did he find himself in some undertow of some otherness dragging him from our family bubble? And as if an eclipse passing at last, an old familiarity brightened, an almost tangible sensation, not a sound or voice really, but more a beam of belief, some human gravity from a place I couldn't see but could almost touch.

Chapter 73

"Hey, I wanted to thank you for the nice lunch yesterday," I said when Mom answered the phone.

"You're welcome. Vi is such a treat, isn't she?"

"Yeah, Mom, she is, but maybe you should be a little careful with her. This money tree you have hidden could tempt her."

"Shut your mouth, Larry. I'm sick of all this wicked judgment."

"What?" I wasn't sure what I'd actually said.

"Vi is no con," Mom said. "This whole clairvoyant thing of hers is a hobby, a way to meet people and have a little fun with the tourists."

"I don't know about that," I said. "She needed the money you and I gave her."

"You think so?" Mom said. "Maybe she took the money because it opened you up to her, made you feel superior. You're pretty easy to manipulate sometimes. Maybe she was doing it for your own good."

"Don't think so. I'm pretty sure she's all about cash," I said, knowing I didn't believe my own words.

"Now you listen to me," Mom said. "You're wrong. Vi has money. She's even a little bit rich. She had a career as a singer in New Orleans. Sang at a place called The Jazz Station. Became one of the owners when she came up with the idea to attach a railroad car to the front of the club and serve all-night breakfast."

"Didn't know that," I said.

"Of course, you didn't, just like you didn't know she graduated with a business degree from Xavier and even made that studio of hers into a Christian bookstore for her daughter. After Vivian became a missionary,

Vi got lonely, then hung out that clairvoyant sign so she could tease in a few tourists for the fun of it."

Of all the phone calls I'd ever had with Mom, this one stood as my finest achievement of ignorant arrogance.

The following morning, I considered hurling myself from the two-foot porch into the ooze-sucking mud, but the mailman saved me from the plunge when he delivered a letter from Maya. She and Lily offered literary observations, those two brilliant minds detailing such succinct insights as, "Good characterization of Thea" and "Raja sounds depressed." *Do they really see me as eggshell?*

From New Orleans, Emma continued to shape Thea as a sunnier parallel to Raja. The evening after Easter, Em asked a favor. "Remember the Tequila Saturday at Roy's? You kept quoting an E.E. Cummings poem. The only line I can remember is, 'Not even the rain has such small hands.' Do you remember?"

"That night's a trifle fuzzy—had that bad reaction to oysters, if you remember." That was the first joke I'd cracked in a week, and my smile hurt the corners of my mouth. "I wrote a paper about that poem. The poem is called: "Somewhere I have never traveled."

"Yeah, that's the one."

"The poet Randall Jarrell called Cummings a 'moonshiner of language.' You got to love a guy like that."

Em skipped over my pontification. "The poem kept talking about flowers and fingers opening and closing and that's what the woman did for the guy speaking, right? Can you remember the last stanza now that you're sober.

"No, but I'm looking at it online," I said, then read the words aloud from the screen:

> (i do not know what it is about you that closes
> and opens;only something in me understands
> the voice of your eyes is deeper than all roses)
> nobody, not even the rain, has such small hands

"Yeah. This is what Thea has to do for Raja. Open him with the voice of her eyes. Love is the catalyst for his life, not the trauma of a childhood injury. He isn't what happened to him."

257

PART SIX

"What is the meaning of life? That was all—a simple question; one that tended to close in on one with years. The great revelation had never come. The great revelation never did come. Instead there were little daily miracles, illuminations, matches struck unexpectedly in the dark."

To the Lighthouse
Virginia Woolf

Chapter 74

Two days later I called Mom for the first time since my phone call debacle about Vi. "So, can you still take me to Pine Belt on Sunday? You know that airport is always deserted, so it'll only take a minute," I said.

"Of course." Her curt response prompted me to guzzle my cooled coffee.

"Mom, I really am sorry about that Vi stuff I said. . ." But fate intervened when Marge told me I had another call waiting, but before Mom hung up, she asked me to come early for Sunday breakfast.

After work, I stopped to buy a bottle of tequila blanco. A bad idea, but I needed liberation from service contracts and a disappointed mother. I even thought about calling Gus and going to Friday night poker, but instead brain pickling started at 5:15.

A frozen dinner prefaced tequila shots with a six-pack of Pabst as dessert. Em would be concerned, Leon, too; Janine would taser me. I decided not to care. Bruce Springsteen's "Tunnel of Love" got me to dancing with myself in a delayed one-man Mardi Gras, and one last shot of tequila pushed me into my chair to listen ten times in a row to "Brothers in Arms" by Dire Straits.

Janine had given me this album years ago. The song is a story told by a dead man still linked to his fellow soldiers by unbreakable comradery, but a noise from outside pulled me to stare at a streetlight until my head mushed against the window. An hour later, I awoke on the floor with a broken curtain rod in my hand and the smell of black peppered scrambled eggs in my head. On the Tickfaw, this was dad's favorite breakfast I had awakened to dozens of times.

Smells good, Dad. But I wasn't at the fish camp, and Dad hadn't come home. But he heard me. Somehow I know he did. Even if he was dead.

Chapter 75

Sunday morning at seven, I pulled into Mom's driveway. She would be my limo to the local airport. A plate of hot biscuits and an omelet on the table relieved the lingering tension from our festered skirmish over Vi. I hardly remember eating, then the grumble of her twenty-year-old muffler reminded me to be nervous about the firing squad in the sky.

The idea of my flying on a private jet filled Mom with caffeinated worry: "Does this Alfredo change the oil in his plane like he should?"

"Yep, rotates the tires, too," I said. Mom blew her nose into the talisman hanky she crushed.

"Mom, I can't leave without saying again how sorry I am about what I said. Vi is your friend, our friend, and I wasn't fair to her." The great speech I'd conjured dissolved into the morning chill reluctant to lift away.

"I know, son. But you were trying to protect me, so let's forget it. I know who you really are." I wanted to hug her as my soul needed touching, but I didn't want to get her all flustered before I left for a week. After passing through security, I turned to see Mom talking to an elderly woman as she pointed to the private jet sitting on the tarmac. Her animation told me Mom was reloading the ambrosia infuser.

The interior of the Gulfstream boasted macaroni-colored leather seats and maroon carpeting. Through a large oval window, the outside world became fictional, a painting hanging in the cool morning where Mom continued to chat in the distance behind a horizon of glass. After a perfunctory greeting, Alfredo disappeared into the cockpit while I inspected my surroundings, relieved I could relax before feigning nonchalance. Sipping coffee, I wondered if Mom was telling that tiny gray-haired lady I was a genie.

When we lifted off into the air, I became a kid again. Down below, my friend Lee's Three Oaks farm slipped past as I welcomed fruit and cheese, then a mimosa. Alfredo sorted some papers as my foot banged a sequel to the *1812 Overture*.

"So, you like this little bird, do you?" he asked.

"It's not my ten-year-old Toyota, but it'll do. My first private ride. 'Alfredo Air' isn't too bad." He closed his leather bag.

"Not my plane. It's part of a jet sharing program that sizes the aircraft we need for each trip." It occurred to me this flight must be blindingly expensive, but I knew not to ask. Alfredo saw my eyes darting towards my computer bag and read my mind.

"How about we take your picture?" he said, then suggested another mimosa. Ah yes, 10:00 a.m. happy hour at forty thousand feet. The Beverly Hillbillies would be proud.

"I enjoyed your story, especially the revisions," Alfredo said. "I have a professor friend who talks about technological displacement and how we must scrap the American educational system to prepare. Must be a zeitgeist these days."

"Well, yes. I've read articles, but after I lost my job years ago, I realized I had no real skills. Writing helped."

"Interesting. May I offer comments on your book?" I braced for impact. "You still have language smoothing to do, but the plot has implicit drama. The one structural point I would make is to question why, as a government worker, Thea isn't allowed to marry. That limitation detracts from your macroeconomic theme. Business is the culture in your story, not government." He finished his mimosa.

"You're right," I said. "Too much like Orwell, my editor says." I hoped Em could hear me.

"Your latest changes improved the structure. Raja is damaged by the trauma of his childhood, and his inability to connect emotionally comes through as psychological, not cultural. This is where you hit the idea perfectly. Thea is the product of the culture—objective, intense, and yet it is her sensitivity to art, to poetry, that transforms Raja into a human being who can love. The twists of intuition and calculation are effective." Wow, he did paint with words.

"Thea and Raja's emotional connection represents the heart of the book," I said. "Their sterilized culture. . ." Alfredo held up his hand to stop me.

"Wait, my friend. What you are thinking may be true, but do not speak it yet; the tension between these characters is fragile. Let your heart and head debate in private. Art is the output of happenings beneath our awareness." Alfredo checked himself as if he realized the mimosa had overruled his judgment, and I wondered if attending the seminar would be a mistake.

"I'm a little curious about something," I said. He glanced sideways at me, the grinning cat listening to the bird sing. "Maya tells me you no longer paint. May I ask why?"

"Well, that's not entirely true. I still dabble, but not like when I was younger. In those days, I wanted to be a great artist and never doubted I would be. But the color of passion diluted with time."

"Too bad, you're so alert."

"Yes, yes, the voice of young genius studying kinship for his quest." He stared at me a few seconds without speaking. "Anthony, art begins with self-gratification and ends with generosity as we learn not to be the self of the universe . . ." He paused, perhaps treading before his own James Joyce wormhole. I said nothing.

"As a young man, my art brought me pride, even fame, but it left me a laborer churning with brushes, until one day I had nothing left to proclaim." He turned to look across the aisle out the other side of the plane. "Attachment obscures spirituality. One must learn there is no intrinsic reality of the material world. Rather than the possession of things, love is the ultimate human quest."

Even after he stopped speaking, I heard the rush of his words.

"So, you didn't want to be redundant in your painting?" I asked.

"We must Chop Wood, Carry Water before we can find what we seek," he said. "My art no longer completed me, the way marriage can dull passion if one isn't mindful." Moona's far-away teacups tinkled. Here before me sat a wealthy, talented artist, and yet he'd shown me the imperfection of his failed inspiration. Why?

"But, Alfredo, this love, this connection to the eternal, is this possible between a man and woman?" I think Janine was listening.

"One must find his life not in accumulation but in the discovery of duty. The worth of our being reaches beyond lust or greed. Our duty on this earth is to our godlike essence."

"Alfredo, are you Hindu or a Buddhist?"

He laughed. "No, neither. I think it was Einstein who, when being interviewed for a professorship at the University of Prague, was asked what religion he claimed, and he answered, 'Mosaic.' I'm of that religion. I'm also of the religion of a woman's love." His voice faded, the moment overripened. His blue eyes wandered.

"And your religion, Anthony?" I hadn't anticipated the question.

"If I had to pick, it would be Pantheism. I suppose I'm with Spinoza and Einstein in seeing God manifested as nature around us."

"Yes," he said. "Man is both the matter and consciousness of the universe. We cannot understand the true essence of life, so we are seduced by the tangible even as we ponder the ineffable presence of God."

The attendant interrupted to bring a tray for lunch. I had thought we'd discuss my book further, but it seemed Alfredo thought analysis premature. Instead, he'd been teaching me. Maya seemed so much more familiar now. We each settled into solitude, then, after sandwiches, I dozed off. Seemingly moments later, the pilot announced we were about to land. Alfredo leaned toward me.

"Spinoza postulated that if you throw a rock through the air and then ask it while still in flight if it has free will, the insistence would be 'yes,' though the stone knows not why it flies or from where it comes," he said. A pause let me catch up to the words. "Perhaps your book could wrestle this idea." Alfredo grinned at my paralysis.

"The past few years," Alfredo said, "Anna and I have opened our ranch to a gathering of creative minds. Each summer in Argentina, we invite a variety of artists and intellectuals to spend a month during which we share ideas, and my guests can work in peace. I would like you to come next February and join us. Your stay will cost you nothing. We will eat fine steaks and smoke cigars, then drink the best red wine in South America. You will see that some rocks fly closer to Heaven."

Chapter 76

Maya and Lily chattered as they entered the cabin. "Oh my," Lily said. Her wide eyes hinted this private ride was a treat for her, too. Maya hugged her dad, then he went to speak with the pilot. "Now, tell me about this fascinating yoga woman in New Orleans."

"We're more friends than anything. But she's smart and spiritual, clear in a way that focuses the gibberish I get lost in." Lily and Maya synched a glance. "Your dad helped me think about structure for my novel, but Emma represents the emotional wellspring for Thea." Alfredo's return allowed me to reroute the conversation. "But what have you two been up to?"

Maya effused about the exhibit she'd organized for three new artists. Normally so reserved, she lifted into enthusiasm. Here was the little girl, Maya, the joyful child at her father's side, excited by this trip. "Lil, tell Anthony about your article."

"He doesn't care about that. Only something I'll be working on with one of my former teachers."

"Well," I said, "I, too, am in literary collaboration—my mailman is reviewing my manuscript for the popular journal, *Neither Rain nor Sleet*. Even I was shocked at this inane comment, but Lily relaxed into a soft glance at Maya. I wondered if Lil had been a timid child.

"So, Anthony, you must be thrilled to see your son?" Maya said.

"Yes. Been over two years. Hope he isn't fat and bald."

"I doubt that; Janine didn't seem a bit bald or fat to me." Everyone laughed while settling into leather thrones.

"It's hard to imagine not seeing Tim for such a long time," I said.

"How often do you talk?" Maya asked.

"At least once a month. We write letters, too."

"How nice," Maya said. "People don't write anymore; they're beginning to tweet now like insects."

"All the more reason for art," Alfredo said. "Humans need creative expression to clarify life. In techno-culture, the need for art will be even more paramount."

"You're right, Dad. This Great Recession has poisoned culture with greed. Maybe artists like Anthony are harbingers of a new creative epoch."

"Yes," Lily said. "New blades of grass perhaps, our Whitman of the south proclaiming revitalization." Lily blushed pink.

"Lily is correct," Alfredo said." The revival of the individual matters, as young Anthony demonstrates."

"But Dad, you've always been a patron of free expression," Maya said, her adoration blossoming into an openness my family would hide.

"Thank you, darling. And with this timely introduction, allow me to make an announcement. I have invited Anthony to Tucumán next February. I hope he will be able to join us. Also—and no one knows this—I've been working for the past year on a collection of new paintings I will present at our festival." Maya shrieked, throwing her arms around her father's neck, kissing him as if a baby first discovering ice cream.

As Maya moved to embrace Lily, the droning engine took me to the familiar *ker-plopping* of my car over Lake Pontchartrain. Out my window, I gazed at clouds and fog beyond ice crystals splayed on the window, and the shapes flickered in the light like new bicycle spokes.

Maya chirped the news. I don't think she even considered that I might not be able to attend the South American gathering. In her world, a job could never negate personal fulfillment. I wondered if I believed the same.

Maya flitted as a honeybee investigating each of us with aggressive curiosity. Alfredo adored watching her. She had ways of lifting worry, reframing difficulty, and though I was nervous about the days ahead, the cocoon of the cabin offered peace at forty thousand feet.

Lily, too, receded into observing her partner gather the room. Was that rational mind extricating data bytes from the invisible waves around us? She floated on aloofness, distant yet approachable, and I imagined her secrets. Had she been more the scientist than the artist before the accident? That aura of discontent from when we first met now signaled that Lily knows where fear hides.

"Anthony, are you awake?" Maya asked.

"Yeah, sorry, daydreaming. What did you say?"

"I asked you if you told Tim you were coming."

"No, I didn't. I talked to him to find out what he was doing this week but wanted to surprise him."

"That's exciting. I hope he has a girlfriend with him." That seemed a weird thing to say. What would I say if he had a woman with him? I wondered if she'd see me as old and if she'd already know my name.

Chapter 77

Standing on the tarmac, Alfredo handed me a phone number. "Here's my number if you need anything." It struck me as a little odd, but then it also offered a wisp of comfort as I jumped into a taxi. Three blocks away from Tim's address, I pulled out his last letter:

Dad,

Been thinking about you and wanted to tell you how much I appreciate you're sticking by me. I got a little crazy for a while, but now I'm finding out who I want to be. I hope one day Mom will forgive me.

Tim

The driver stopped in front of a warehouse idled by Sunday, a single light bulb burning over the back door. Clutching Alfredo's hotel number helped me nose open the heavy metal door left slightly ajar. There, four cars posed in varying stages of repair, hoods up, wheels dangling like skeletons in a closed museum.

The click of a wall clock timed my creeping toward an opening at the back of the shop where scraping noise from an unhappy machine echoed down a hallway. Then a beaded doorway, small bed and milk crates used as furniture unveiled a simple life where a man wearing safety glasses hunched over a piece of metal. His back to me, sparks flew off the spinning grinder. I froze, but the man turned.

"What the—?" he said. I smiled but said nothing. "Holy crap, Dad. I thought I was being robbed." Holding out his arms, Tim embraced me, the sound of back slaps bouncing off the cinder block walls.

"Came to have a drink with my son." I offered him a pint of bourbon I'd stashed in my bag. "You got two glasses?"

"Yeah, sure." It didn't take two minutes until we were yammering about grandma and his mom, why I was there, and how'd I gotten through the locked outer door. Tim touched every thought as if none other existed.

"My girlfriend went to get Chinese food. She'll be back in a while but had to run home first to feed her cat. She always leaves that dang door open. Florida would have a fit if he knew; he worries about the cars.

"I closed it all the way, so she's locked out now," I said.

"She has a key but won't use the dang thing. Stubborn." I now got a better look at his project on the table.

"What are you working on?"

"Wall art for Cheryl, sheet metal. She's crazy about fish. See, here's one big fish in the middle. Around his fat body and big tail, I'm cutting out other small fish following the big guy. These starfish will connect the little fish to the big boy swimming in a parade together."

"I like it. Your granddad used to do stuff like this."

"I remember seeing a couple of his things at granny's." Tim looked uncomfortable but deftly changed the subject. "See how I'm making the body a little convex, so it makes the fish look more three dimensional."

"You're getting pretty good with your hands."

"For sure. Florida is teaching me how sheet metal is a kind of skin that can be brought to life; he thinks I got a knack. I'm saving money, too. He pays me a little more as I get better. Says that keeps me motivated."

"Smart man. He around?" I asked.

"He's over in Spokane but will be back tonight."

"Good. I'd like to thank him for helping you along."

"I'm straightened out now, Dad. No drugs. I drink a few beers but not much else. Cheryl is religious, so she keeps me straight, but really, I just want to learn. Heck, Florida is a genius with a torch and a hammer."

I had another drink, then we settled into loopy chatter. Leaving

Mississippi had been the right move for Tim, and I wondered what would have become of me if I'd done the same, if I'd left when life blew up.

"Who's your drinking buddy?" a sassy voice called out, then Cheryl shook my hand. A petite redhead with green eyes and spunk, she balanced that insouciance Tim wore like a favorite T-shirt. Seeing the two of them made me think of Janine and how happy this match would make her, but I wasn't about to open that box of spiders. Nope. So, the three of us ate shrimp curry while Janine stayed locked on the other side of that shop door lit by one lightbulb.

A couple of hours later, they dropped me at my hotel only half a mile away. The plan was for Tim to pick me up at six for breakfast, then I'd knock around town sightseeing as I didn't have to be at the workshop until Tuesday. Cheryl hugged my neck like she'd known me forever, and I wondered what tales about me she'd heard as she did already know my name. The two hundred dollars I wasn't able to lend Tim for that speeding ticket rumbled like indigestion, but he seemed to have forgotten I wasn't there when he needed my help. Before leaving town, I planned to slip a little greenery under his pillow. But first I had a fish to give away.

Lumbering out of Cheryl's car at the Green Country Inn, I noticed Tim a little distracted. I was certain he was thinking about his metal art.

"Son, before you leave, I got a little something for you in my suitcase. Let me dig it out right quick."

"Oh Dad, I wish you hadn't done that. I don't need a thing, and I know how tough things have been."

"Didn't say it was necessary—it's a gift. And you know what? I think my timing is perfect."

"Yeah?"

"I met this guy in New Orleans who does all kinds of metal and glasswork, a real craftsman. Anyway, he did this mobile of a school of fish and it was about the most impressive thing I've ever seen."

"A school of fish, huh? I like it."

"Made a bunch of standalone pieces, too." I unwrapped the fish. "Here's one I picked out for you."

"Oh my God." The hotel sign flashed alternating white neon and green, each time changing the glass inside the fish to a different hue.

"Would you look at this?" Tim said. "See how he tucked in this little brace to hold the glass steady, and these glass slabs fit exactly in this cage. . ." Tim jabbered at ten thousand words a minute holding the fish up to the light, inspecting the bottom and sides like a kid with a new super toy. Cheryl and I studied his near boil of enthusiasm.

Handing the treasure to Cheryl, he hugged me so hard my back hurt.

"Thanks, Dad. You knew, didn't you?"

"Knew what?"

"That I was starting to create stuff on my own. This fish is a message, right?"

Chapter 78

The night crept with fish climbing steel cages. A stiff neck and a cup of instant coffee before daylight pushed me out the door on an impromptu walk to Tim's place. As I reached his parking lot, he pushed open the shop door, then snickered: "You like surprises, don't you?" We both knew words didn't matter.

Two blocks away, a neon *Coffee* sign reminded me of Flo's cafe. She would love Tim. The place was packed with working people, guys in plaid flannel shirts, CAT hats, and heavy boots. We looked like any two men headed to the job site together, making a living and trying to sort out the grind of necessity. No suits here.

"I'll knock around town today," I said. "Maybe go over to the fish market and watch them chunk a few salmon. Think we could grab dinner tonight? Like to take you and Cheryl out. Florida, too, if he's around."

"Sounds good. There's a little seafood joint up the road, good fresh stuff that's not too expensive."

"Works for me. They got a bar?"

"Yep. But why don't you let me treat?" Tim said. "This trip must've cost you a bundle already."

"Nope. Hitched a ride on a private jet." His scrunched face waited for more detail, but I enjoyed creating a little mystery. "Besides," I said, "we have so much to catch up on that I might have to pay you to listen. Heck, I got a whole story about this writer's workshop."

"So, my old man is a Hemingway?"

"Yeah, if you mean I like liquor and fishing, but my book is more like

Orwell." Then the moment relaxed, like the old days having pancakes before going squirrel hunting. I couldn't decide how much to discuss the divorce or Emma, but I figured a drink at dinner would help smooth over the past.

As the strong coffee took hold, we chatted about the plane ride, but just as quickly Tim was off extoling all the skills he'd been learning. Florida rebuilt the back steps on Cheryl's mom's house, and Tim had helped out, so he got a feel for working with wood and liked it. Dad could have taught him these things if Tim and I had been swapped in time. I squeezed his neck. "Proud of you son. My dad would be, too."

Back at the body shop, dawn arrived on cranberry light. "I usually open up and Florida comes in around seven-thirty. He's letting me get the hang of what it's like to run Slick's. Most days he closes up late. He doesn't socialize much."

"You've found a good mentor. It's important to see how successful people behave." Tim's flashing green eyes reminded me I was exactly his age when Dad never made it home that Saturday.

Shop lights soon glared, and a pot of coffee filled the concrete cold with a homey aroma. Tim busied himself turning on compressors and opening cabinets. I settled into a newspaper hijacked from the café. Before long, voices echoed, but I was reading about some charlatan they'd arrested for real estate fraud. A few minutes later, off to my left, a man came through the outside metal door stopping short as if he didn't realize anyone else would be there. His stare made me uncomfortable.

"Hey, Florida, this here is my dad. Dropped in on me unexpected." Fidgeting as if irritated, the man put his hands in his jacket pocket.

"Yeah, well, hey there," he said. "I better get to work." Not the warmest greeting, but the bushy beard, tinted aviator glasses, and John Deere cap pulled down low painted him as a loner, or maybe a Unabomber.

"Excuse me there, Mr. Jones, but I wanted to thank you for helping out my boy here."

"No need," Florida said, then pulled up his collar and walked back toward the outside door. But the way he walked caught my attention, a slight stoop from years of crouching, neck stiff. Tim futzed with a headlight assembly as he talked to me over his shoulder.

"Don't mind Florida," Tim said. "He's not used to strangers. It's not you, Dad. It's him." And the familiar connection from breakfast softened the edges of this grumpy shop owner.

"Guess you're right," I said. But the way this fellow kept staring at the floor left me anxious. This guy could be some kind of pervert or con artist. Florida hurried outside.

"Hey, Florida, hang on a sec. Need to ask you something," I said. He stopped but continued facing his truck.

"I got to go," he said.

"Just need a minute." I suspected as long as he couldn't see me, he'd stay frozen, but off to our left a compressor kicked on, and as he turned his head to look, I slipped in front of him from the other side. He shifted away from me, but I tracked in lockstep with his rotation until we stood face-to-face. His eyes searched for something on the ground.

"There's something familiar about you," I said. "You ever been to Mississippi?"

"Long time ago," he said.

"I see." His detachment pinged a nerve in my neck. Those hunched-up shoulders suggested shyness, but some irresistible force pulled my hand over to touch his bushy red beard threaded with gray. I didn't even realize I'd moved. He recoiled as if I'd punched him.

"Don't say nothing." The Canadian accent didn't fit, then his red beard jerked me back to the Leaf River, that weekend when I was twelve camping with Dad for three days, the first time I ever noticed the color of his facial hair.

"Is it you?" I asked, then my dad's southern accent drawled from behind the beard.

"Tim don't know nothing." My ankles collapsed me backward onto a large barrel of unopened solvent. This stranger stared me down.

"Look," he said, "I know this ain't right, but I can explain. Let me tell Tim I'm taking you over to Pike's market. Wait by the truck."

The driver's side door to his old red pickup slammed, breaking my trance. "Get in." His brusque voice shook loose the realization that for twenty years this was the moment I'd dreamed of, and yet now I wanted to run away.

Staring ahead, he never looked at me, those sharp features I remembered now sagged from a life I hadn't seen. I tried to remember days when those blue eyes weren't angry.

"Where we going?"

"My house. Don't want to be in public yapping about all this." Manicured lawns turned into unkempt patches of dirt around small frame houses until the lazy ears of a hound dog perked up from the concrete steps of a shoebox house clad with asbestos siding.

"Sit down. I'll make coffee." A little wood carving hung above the maildrop on the porch. "F. Jones." It occurred to me the sign meant "Fake Jones."

I pulled up a chair, and the place closed in on me like a cave, a single person's home with barely two of each kind of dish, but clean. He puttered with the coffee pot before turning to me. "You done spilled the worms in the river now. What you doing out here?"

"That should be my question," I said. "But I came for a writing workshop and decided to surprise Tim." My words bounced off his vacant stare. "Looks like I'm the one who got surprised."

"Look," he said, "I know this jolts you, but give me a listen before you start preaching. I been wrong. Ain't saying different." He walked to the refrigerator for milk. "Dang, son. I panicked, that's all." His hesitation sparked my anger.

"Do you know what you've put Mom through?" I asked. "How she's spent her whole life waiting for you to come home, even throwing a birthday party for you every year?" Dad held a finger to his lips, telling me not so loud.

"Yeah, I know. Tim told me his grandma never gave up hope." His neck stood the tallest part of him.

"Got caught in a money bind. A friend fleeced me, then I lost more on the dogs. Your mom and I was desperate even before the IRS crawled up my butt. I had to save the house for Ina."

"Oh really, you saved the house, did you? And here I was thinking Mom and I had to pay off the IRS, sell most everything we owned, even that GTO you built for me. And I guess all that money from the rest of the family and the church, I must have dreamed that up, too?" The screech hurt my ears.

"No, I know. But I had it figured that the numbers worked if I was dead."

"If you were dead? What kind of lame-brain logic is that?"

"You know, my life insurance."

"Mom never cashed the policy. We scraped together everything we could after the government took all your tools and stuff. If Ira Goodman hadn't helped us out, they would have taken everything, but he's a good lawyer and the bloodsuckers were satisfied when we didn't have a penny left." I felt an urge to grab the butcher knife on the counter.

"I didn't know about the life insurance," he said. "Figured she'd cashed it."

"There was no body, no death. That means you have to wait seven years. And even then, Mom wouldn't do it." I slammed the table with my fist. "You don't know squat about money, do you?" He turned his back to me, and a shadow of humiliation fell across the room.

"I sent money as soon as I could," he said. "Never stopped."

"Mom only told me about that a month ago."

"I got to tell you something else. A few times, I slipped into Ina's house to look at her mail. Needed to know she was okay. I went on Sundays when she was at church, looking for collection notices."

"She had a feeling someone messed with her stuff. You go in my house, too?"

"Couple times. Needed Tim's email."

"Damn, Dad. You broke into my house?"

"I wanted to help. Did what I could for Ina, even put some extra savings aside here in case she ever needed it, but there was no way I could contact you or her directly, too risky. And I didn't want to put you in jeopardy by knowing I was alive." He scrubbed his hands at the sink.

"A few years ago, when I was snooping, I found a letter from Tim apologizing for embarrassing the family over that marijuana mess. That gave me an idea, but I needed his email address. Figured he was in a bad spot and needing a fresh start, so I sent out junk mail to him, saying I was a master craftsman looking for apprentices. I had to send it a dozen times, but finally caught him frustrated enough and he answered. That's how Tim ended up in Seattle. He has no idea who I am."

Some fuel line in my brain severed. I couldn't speak.

"I know I tricked Tim, but I had to. Figured he was the only family I could reach out to without getting caught."

"You know, I was having a pretty tough time back then myself," I said.

"I know, son. That's why I wanted to help Tim, to pull some load off you. I saw them bills on your desk but figured Ina's money could help out if you got too hard up."

"Were you ever going to tell any of us you were still alive?"

"No. Thought I'd be arrested for insurance fraud; then I couldn't help nobody."

"I hate you." Rotted hope ignited. "All those years, and you were only thinking about money."

"That ain't so," he said. Hiking up his shoulders, he reminded me of that creepy Ichabod Crane book I read as a child.

"I need air," I said. Through the backdoor I saw a little trail leading off into some woods. With no sense of touching the ground, I walked, trying to reframe that two decades of uncertainty was nothing but deception. I came to a small creek nestled on both sides in bright green moss, then sat on a flat rock the size of a refrigerator.

"I call this Broccoli Creek," Dad said. I didn't even turn my head as the light falling through the trees wiggled like glow worms.

"You're right to be mad. I deserve it. But I done the only thing I knew. Figured you two was better off with the insurance money than with me."

"Please don't talk anymore," I said. "I need to figure out what to do now."

"Son, let's leave things be. I'm trying to pay off my shop, and I'll give it to Tim when he's ready."

"Good idea. Let him be your son." I began walking up the creek.

"He's not my son. You are. You're the person I knew could best handle things when I left. Didn't see no other way."

"Me handle things? For twenty years, I've bounced back and forth between fractured and clueless because I blamed myself for your leaving."

"That's plum crazy. It was my own doing. You was always the smartest kid around; I knew you'd be all right."

"When you disappeared, it gutted me, left me lost. Mom was the strong one. She kept me from losing my mind." I sat down on the deer moss.

"Would you tell me one thing?" he asked. "You said you was here for a writing thing. What's that about?"

"Like you give a crap. You're just changing the subject."

"No. I want to know." He paused as I reloaded my resentment. "All I ever do is work, but I never stopped thinking about how you always used words. Never seen nobody spin things like you did as a kid. All them long days, in my heart, I hoped you'd do something big."

Either he was a great actor, or the vitality of those strong arms had simply evaporated, and there he sat, elbows on his knees stranded on a hillside of gray and green.

"A writer's workshop. I wrote a draft of a novel."

"Why don't you go on to your class, then? Do what you come here for. We can sort this after you're done." His idea rushed at me like Thelma and Louise learning to fly.

"No. We're going to start cleaning up this mess by telling Tim you're a fraud."

"That ain't a good idea. He's in a good place now, no need confusing the boy."

"Tim has been lied to enough; he deserves the truth. We all do."

Chapter 79

Dad went back to the shop to meet with the man who'd sold him the business, Mr. Ladrone. I stayed at the house to make the phone call I dreaded.

"I know, Mr. Pippen, it's unfortunate. I'm in Seattle now but have a family emergency I can't ignore. I'm not asking for a refund, but if I could apply the tuition to a future workshop. . ."

Getting that worry out of my head helped even as I doubted I'd ever return for another seminar. But I had to think about Mom and Tim. I puffed around his house trying to burn off antsy irritation, until I noticed the details of Dad's life captured in the little things. There wasn't one picture anywhere, no family mementos, no traces of what he'd abandoned. Even his closet contained not a thread of the old life, and Mississippi became a fictional land even for me.

Mom and Dad had each purified the past by ejecting any artifact containing a voltage of intimacy. They had shifted into an exaggerated present, me into lopsided obsession with the past. Walking through Dad's empty house, I plundered his loneliness, his own disruption of time that left his life so sparse. Mom and I had each other; he had no one, then an old muffler groaned from the driveway.

"Get your business done?" I asked.

"Kind of. Regular monthly payment to Ladrone. I always pay in cash."

"So how much longer before you're all paid off?"

"That's the thing. It was a ten-year agreement and I'm about halfway through. I asked if it could pay off the balance early, but Ladrone won't do it. Wants his payments steady."

"Nice of him. Don't know if that's even legal," I said. "Can I take a look at your contract of sale?"

"Don't have one. Verbal understanding. Afraid to put anything in writing." He turned to look at the hummingbird feeder outside the kitchen window while I sipped on my anger.

"No contract? How do you know he'll honor the sale?" I asked.

"Don't know. Plus, he told me this morning the overall price has to be raised by another ten percent. Seems the business is worth more now than when I first bought it."

"No more, please. I can't take this Misery News Network anymore." I walked outside toward the rocky trail up to a boulder next to a small waterfall. Dad followed ten feet behind. "Let's start from the beginning," I said. "Tell me what happened after you left Hattiesburg."

"Went to Georgia first," he said. "No family there. Figured I could disappear. Worked in a little body shop in Atlanta for cash, kept my mouth shut. Spent five years letting the dust settle. Then I moved to Pensacola doing bodywork, carpentry, whatever I could."

"Did you ever get married again?"

"That's insulting, Larry. I faked my death, but I never abandoned Ina. I may not be smart, but I've always been loyal. Never thought about another woman. Figured that was part of my punishment. Quit drinking, even took some correspondence business courses while I moved around the south, till I met a guy from Houston who knew somebody in Seattle, so here I am."

The words vibrated inside me, my emotions oscillating between pity and anger. He tried asking about Janine, and Mom, even my book, but I dredged his past until he sighed with exhaustion. I didn't want to believe him; I wanted him to be a liar, but Ladrone had been diagnosed with some disease called sarcoidosis and his panic about dying lungs had turned into a quick sale of his shop to Dad.

"Look," I said, "we have to meet Tim in a couple hours and tell him the truth. But first I got to ask you something." I picked up a rock and skipped it across a calm pool eddied by a fallen tree. "What kind of kid was I? Lately, I can't remember."

"Son, you was my hope. I looked at you like a piece of me that never got born. I knew I was a poor role model, couldn't teach you things about money and learning, the stuff your brain understood. All I knew was work and fishing." He paced, stooping more with each lap around the flat-topped boulder.

"You taught me about creativity," I said.

"Me? You can't mean that old junk I used to make—flowers and sundials, all that crude stuff?"

"Yeah, Dad, those things you brought to life made Mom happy."

"I was only messing around. Never thought serious about it, kind of like fishing, something I enjoyed but knew couldn't support a family."

"Really? You never thought about how your job kept you from becoming an artist?" His craggy face froze as if understanding language for the first time.

"See, that's what I'm talking about," he said. "That kind of thinking never entered my skull. I was simple labor. Life for me was fixing things. That's what made me a man." He walked to the far edge of the path to glance up the hill.

"Seeing you and your mother get new clothes or a birthday present, I found pride in that. I didn't care about myself or dreamy stuff like my creativity. When I got into money trouble, I knew I'd failed Ina and had to fix things."

The only real closeness I'd ever known with Dad was on a riverbank or at his fishing shack, but these minutes next to Broccoli Creek had taken us beyond the mutual admiration of catching a nice bass or making a long kill shot. We were finding a new current of honesty in a stream of time we'd lost. He might have become an artist, but instead he chained his creative will to a life of labor. No one in his childhood had ever called him special, never activated his artistic soul the way he'd once done for me, the way Maya did for me. And so, he flew along, a common rock in space, not knowing why, not knowing who.

I wrapped my arms around shoulders now a little less like granite. "Listen to me, Pop. You've been wrong, dead wrong, but you didn't know it. You were always an artist, a good one, and you still are. I'm sorry I never told you that." For once, then. . .

Chapter 80

We agreed to give Tim the news at dinner, and I imagined my son listening, measuring a response, then exploding with anger the way I had. I wanted to pick up the phone and call Mom and Vi, Emma and Leon, look for all the scattered pieces of my life now needing to be wedged back together.

"New Washington" had disappeared into unlit territory, and I wondered if Raja's world would survive, but it was time to put myself into dad's world, to understand all those years he'd wandered in a self-imposed servitude. My cell phone interrupted.

"Anthony, this is Maya. Are you all right?"

"Yes."

"Pip called Lily saying you had a family emergency and wouldn't attend the workshop. What happened?"

"I've had a strange day," I said.

"What does that mean? Do you need help?"

"No. Don't worry."

"I'm coming to you right now. Are you at your hotel?"

"No, I mean, you don't need to come."

"Yes, I do. Tell me what happened."

"I will. But I need to absorb things."

"Is Tim okay? Are you hurt?"

"I'm fine, Tim's fine, everyone is fine—even my dad."

"What?"

"My dad. I've been with him all day. He's alive."

"Anthony, this isn't funny. What's going on?"

"My dad has been living under an assumed identity. He's been mentoring Tim without revealing who he was. I'm on my way to tell Tim the truth."

"Oh, my God. Is this real?" she asked.

"Yes. But what will I say to Mom?"

"Nothing. That's your dad's job."

Chapter 81

Tim and I met at seven for a beer. Cheryl's mom had a rough chemo session, which left dinner to only us guys.

"Had a good day," I said. "Saw things I never thought I'd see again." A long draw of Fat Tire gave me a moment of calm. "But before Florida gets here, let me ask you something."

"Sure, Pop."

"Grandma and I talk about you all the time. You know she hates not having you around to cook for, right? And I've been carrying that load solo." Tim slapped me on the shoulder.

"Right man for the job, Pop."

Laughter gave way to an awkward space. "Son, I want to know if you'd ever consider coming back to live in the south."

A swig of beer, then Tim spoke in a hushed voice without looking my way. "Only came out here because my options sucked. My plan was to get some skills, then slip back into Hattiesburg while Mom wasn't looking."

"Your mom has gone through her own changes. Some of her anger might have been frustration about her own life, not yours." Tim turned, his face building to a reaction when a large hand squeezed my neck.

"You boys got the jump on me, maybe I'll take a Tire myself," Dad said.

I wondered if he remembered he'd stopped drinking. I'd deliberately taken a quiet table away from the bar, hoping for as much privacy as a restaurant could offer us.

"Tim, I got some news I need to share," Dad said. Tim sat up straight as if glad he didn't have to talk personal stuff anymore.

"You giving me a big raise?" Tim's perfect teeth gleamed.

"Maybe. But somebody done led you wrong, and it's time to set a plumb line on the truth." All three of us leaned forward. "Our situation ain't exactly what you think. Fact is, I ain't exactly who you think I am." Dad glanced at me for help, but I enjoyed another taste of beer. "Well, you know how you said your grandpa disappeared a long time ago?" Dad said. "I know something about how that happened."

"Huh?"

"Dang it. Here's the sanded down fact—I was that fool who disappeared twenty years ago. Your grandpa ain't dead, just stupid."

Tim's pale blue eyes blinked back at Dad, but he couldn't seem to organize any words. I expected a lava flow when Tim slapped the table so hard that the bartender twenty feet away jerked a cold stare our way.

"You mean, you're my grandpa, Thomas Winstead?"

My ears still ringing from the slap on the table, I placed my hand on Tim's forearm. "Give him a chance to talk, son," I said.

"What for? Don't need no more words. That's the grandpa there I always wanted to know. Now I know him." Tim jumped to his feet, wrapping his arms around my dad's shoulders, and in that moment my boy reminded me of mom's dead-reckoning commitment to family, a steadiness unconcerned with doubt.

Dad puzzled a look at me as we both stalled on Tim's reaction. This wormhole back through time had become a strange journey indeed, and my beer buzz struggled to keep pace. But soon, oysters and stone crabs began cementing this new family reality for all three of us, a meal among generations we'd never before been able to share.

Tim and Dad sprinted ahead in conversation, each grabbing tidbits of the past two years. Dad had been a skillful liar. He'd fictionalized a new life, scripting himself into Tim's world through the creation of a fictional Florida Jones. Genius, Dad become the dramatist acting in his own play.

Back in my hotel room at midnight, my cell phone brimmed with messages from Maya, but I wasn't ready to talk. I needed a new frame to contain what was happening. Tim was roughly the same age I'd been when my dad left, but where my life had been subtracted from, Tim's life was now being added to, and the harmonic shift of generations struck me as a wholeness we'd all yearned to find.

Staring at the ceiling in the dark, that image of Randy came to me, those last few weeks of his life in that semi-dark room of whispers. Four days before he passed, he'd touched my hand and struggled to speak: "Larry, people don't want the truth. They want reassurance." I wish I'd told him we need both.

Enthusiasm is the reverse of fear. Tim proved that to me with his reaction. He hadn't been afraid, not filled with dread of the unknown, and from a distant land Thea whispered a new name, Astra, the daughter Raja would come to cherish. The child whimpers that same frailty Tim had from that hospital morning when my hands first held him, something perfect that was part of me, and part of Dad, too. And I'm sure Emma was smiling.

Chapter 82

As the plane taxied to the terminal at the Louis Armstrong airport, I left Mom a voicemail saying I'd be home early and to pick me up at the bus station on Wednesday. At baggage claim, Emma met me carrying a handwritten sign with the name, *Anthony*. An hour later, Pete Fountain's clarinet, Emma's chocolate brownies, and windows full of cranberry-colored glass seduced me away from the upheaval of the past few days. Em avoided any prods to unpack my Seattle trip.

A spirited game of Pictionary ended with Nicole caterwauling at my horrible guess about her pizza picture that I'd called an "utter pie." So much depends on a child's laugh.

Over coffee, Em slipped into a serious squeeze of a couch pillow. "I was wondering something," she said. "Perhaps writing a short story about Raja first, you could develop the novel from a focus on Raja's defective humanity." Here was my editor/confidante tinkering at the aesthetic of truth, but this darker tone from her didn't fit.

At midnight, we sipped a dessert wine and sampled white grapes, then she wrapped me with arms hinting desperation. I wondered if she sensed Dad was alive. Around four in the morning, I got up to get a glass of water, returning to a turquoise-colored scarf draped across my pillow.

"A present for Anthony."

Under the delicate fabric, a rough wooden frame and a sky-blue mat. "It's Raja," she said. Lamplight sharpened angular lines, the almost digital appearance of his collar against the portrait of his face framed by hints of gray in his dark hair. Small, ultra-white fingers tried to hide a deformity of spirit. I wanted to absorb the cool blues, the demure texture of linen. Then, behind the first button of his shirt, obscured, a thin chain held an oval setting with a ruby-colored stone, a barely noticeable sealed heart.

"I'll finish Thea next."

"My dad is alive." My words plunged without guidance as if a button on a too-tight garment had popped loose. For seconds, Em merely stared at me.

"In Seattle?" she asked, her right hand beginning to quiver. "News here, too," she said. "In my mailbox Monday, I found a dead moccasin wrapped around a magnolia blossom. A Mississippi message, it seems."

Chapter 83

"Let's go get breakfast," she said. Two hours of talking and a brief sleep had left us ready for a walk.

"How about beignets? I'm a tourist after all." Em took me to a corner coffee shop instead of Café du Monde, but the beignets melted on my tongue. Then a speedy stroll through Jackson Square with its circus atmosphere of street musicians, mimes, and weirdos led us away from Earl-town. Without even noticing how we got there, we stared at Vi's red door but made no effort to go inside. Earl had locked Em behind a new barricade, and as she glared at the door, I zipped back to days as a substitute teacher where a W.H. Auden quotation hung on the classroom wall: *And what looked like a wall turns out to be a world with measurements of its own.* Em needed me to say nothing.

Two hours strolling through antique stores and art studios then parked us at the bus station where from her purse she pulled a bag of healthy goodies for my ride north. "Yum, cauliflower muffins." Her demeanor withdrawn, she didn't even argue that they were kale chips. I wanted to urge us forward, to pull Em away from the shadow of Earl, but she'd retreated.

Maybe the center wouldn't hold between us. Maybe alcohol and a lunatic ex were problems too profound, but I needed to know. "Em, when Earl ruined your paintings, you said he took off, right? Did he ever see Nicole again?"

She only offered a stare.

"Not trying to pry, only understand. I don't like snakes."

"Me neither," she said. "But talking about Earl only creates laws of attraction. I don't want to send that out into the universe. I told you, Roy warned him not to come back, but now he has. This can't end well."

The half-hour oscillated between unresolved pieces of Earl and newly found pieces of Dad, and I almost missed the bus. As soon as I took a seat, I wondered whether Louisiana was the most dangerous place on earth or the safest.

Soon, the city of Hattiesburg presented her familiar images, and the jolting bus ride downtown shook loose an old disquiet, the state fair in Jackson when I was five where I got separated from my parents. The known universe disappeared that day, only a sea of strangers swirling. But I hadn't been alone then, only misplaced, and slumping into the bus seat, I realized I didn't have to be misplaced any longer.

Down the last bus step into a crowd of strangers writhing around the luggage compartment, I rotated my beam in search of Mom. She would be wearing that old green raincoat she'd worn for years, but I couldn't find it, so I busied myself with a museum of suitcases. Weary leather in hand, I turned and almost knocked over a lady standing behind me. But it wasn't Mom; it was Janine.

"Got everything?" she asked, as if we'd only been shopping.

"Yeah, but where's Mom?"

"At her house. I dropped by to give her fresh snap beans and onions from my Mom. Ina told me she was supposed to come get you but was all in a panic because her car battery died. I told her I'd be happy to grab you." I was pretty sure Janine hadn't wasted that phrase.

"Oh. She could have brought my car. It's parked in her driveway."

"She said you'd say that but was afraid to crank it, too complicated. Anyway, I have a belated birthday present for you, so I thought I'd pick you up and let your Mom relax."

"I don't know if we need to keep giving each other gifts, Janine. Connie and Bill might not understand, and frankly, I'm not sure I do either."

"Don't be silly. It's nothing. Connie doesn't even know, and well, Bill—he's not around much anymore. Stupid story. Let's skip it."

When we reached her car, she popped the trunk and handed me a square package, flat and heavy. "Happy Birthday. You're always so practical, so I thought this would be perfect." And the time machine to yester-life hit the starter.

The red wrapping paper revealed a new socket set and a complete family of screwdrivers. Our whole marriage flashed before me as a winding path of misunderstanding. The confident look on her face betrayed that she was clueless about me now, and apparently about her own life.

"Thanks. I've been meaning to pick up a seventy-two-piece ratchet and screwdriver set with slip-proof handles; it will help me with my writing." She slapped me on the arm good-naturedly, but we both knew that any chance of genuine connection had long since fossilized, then an odd glimpse framed Janine as the sister I never had.

The rain started just as we got into the car, and I wanted to tell Janine I loved Emma and how I'd seen Tim and that he soaked up every detail about his mom. But all I could come up with was: "I'm glad it's metric."

Her face hung gaunt and pasty, and with the engine idling, she turned toward me. "It's just me and Connie now. She has a job offer in Houston and wants the two of us to move there next month." She faltered, but her crackling voice couldn't hide the distress of not knowing which direction was up.

"Sometimes you have to move ahead to find your real life," I said. "Maybe that's what we're both doing." An inert eye flash signaled to me how lost she was, and all over again came that year when we were nineteen and neither of us had any idea how to become adults. She'd been innocent and hopeful, and I'd been anxious to prove myself after Dad's disappearance. With the slightest tug of sadness, one of those nameless little drawers I'd stuffed my life into eased itself shut, and I couldn't locate those cravings for Janine anymore.

"Won't your parents be upset?" I asked. Janine faced straight ahead, adjusted the inside mirror, then began backing up.

"At least they care if I leave." And she turned on talk radio. Yes, home again.

After two blocks, I took a risk. "Hey, do you mind stopping by Pete's Corner right quick? Want to pick up a surprise." Janine stared ahead without saying a word. A few minutes later I scooted into the restaurant.

When I returned to the car, she had changed the radio station to an oldies channel, and a few turns later we parked in Mom's driveway. "Want to come inside?"

"No need. Tell your mom bye for me." I closed the car door and started walking away. "Hey, wait, you forgot your surprise." I walked over to the driver's side and placed my arms on the rolled down window so that Janine and I were eye level.

"It's a Boston cream pie for you and Connie. On the plane I remembered it was your favorite."

"You didn't?" A first hint of hope cracked in her voice. I kissed her forehead the way a brother might send a sister off on a trip to somewhere new.

"You're a good person, Janine. We've each made our mistakes. I don't regret our years together, but I'm your friend now. I mean that. So this week, let me take you to lunch. I'd like to understand what's going on with you. And I need to tell you that your son misses you."

Chapter 84

After chicken and dumplings and four biscuits, my brain slowed enough to realize that Dad hadn't called Mom yet and she still didn't know why I'd come home early. If I hadn't been so bloated, I might have overreacted. Reaching for the old survival toolset, I decided misdirection would suffice: "Unfortunately there was a family emergency, and the workshop had to be rescheduled."

"Oh, that's too bad. Hope everyone is okay," Mom said.

"They will be," I said. "But seeing Tim made the trip totally worthwhile. His girlfriend, Cheryl, is gorgeous." Enough decoy, but my old maneuvers were losing potency in new Anthony time. I ducked out early for home. Guitar, worn-out Wranglers, and the seduction of my couch inspired a nap to recover from all that eating.

I missed Em. Plugging in my dead phone, I hoped Maya would call, or someone, maybe even Eleanor, though she hadn't called in a month. My last voicemail was from Vi. "Hey, Larry," she said. "Ran to the drugstore for laryngitis medicine but saw you and some woman outside my door. Didn't have the voice to yell out. You unlost yet?"

I'd already decided not to go to work the next day, so a deep nap sent my dreams sloshing between Broccoli Creek and Lake Pontchartrain, then a flash of silver.

"Don't move, fat boy," a voice said. The smell of sweat and cigarettes reminded me of rotten food while a butcher knife pressed hard against my throat. Then, a mop of greasy hair drooped over my nose. The voice swung round to the end of the couch above my head, and though I still couldn't see a face, the knife never left my chin.

"I know what you done," he said.

Words tried to gurgle, but I froze.

"You done stole Emma from me. Poisoned her with a bucket of lies, ain't you? Well, I'm here to steal something back. I know you rich, so let's get me some of that green cash you got hid." He now pointed a black snub-nosed pistol, and I got a look at how skinny he was.

"Okay. Stay calm. I've got money," I said, then led him to the kitchen where I took four hundred dollars from an empty flour canister in the cabinet.

"Give me everything. Wallet. And this watch. That fine guitar, too." He pushed me through the house, picking up cufflinks, my coin collection, wedding band, and even the jar of loose change on my dresser. His jumpy behavior reminded me of a hungry sparrow. "You got any drugs?"

"Ibuprofen."

The whack to the back of my scalp sent my nose bouncing off the hardwood floor. "Listen up, funny boy. I know where your mama lives, too. I bet she got some jewelry worth pawning. You keep your mouth shut, or I'll pay her a neighborly visit. Maybe get a little sweet love while I'm there." With that, his boot gouged my ribs, and grabbing my ear, he twisted it as if his hand were a screwdriver. "Now, get your fat ass up and give me your guns."

Looping a piece of rope through the door handles on the stove and refrigerator, he tied my hands and feet, and for the next two hours, I wriggled the knot until it finally loosened. First, I called the police, then Em who didn't answer, so I left a message of only three words: "Earl robbed me." When Mom didn't answer, I left a voicemail telling her someone had broken into my house. I hoped I didn't need to worry about her since she ran a Fort Knox-level security check each night before bed at seven o'clock.

Within minutes, the yard erupted in red and blue. Questions, strangers, my quiet world mutated into spectacle. Officer Shelbourn called to have a police car posted at Mom's house, then she took me down to the station for fingerprints that could eliminate my presence from the sweep her team gave the entire house. Downtown, I was asked more questions, then Officer Marion brought me a coffee and said a friend was waiting in the lobby.

"Gus? What are you doing here?" I asked.

"My brother called. He's the dispatcher, recognized your address. Let's get out of here." He drove us to the Two-Acre truck stop where all the big rigs stopped off I-59, then over bacon and eggs, he listened to my *Law and Order* episode.

"Missed you all this time, stranger," he said, sipping his tomato juice. "You know, I never liked Janine. Too bossy." The words insulated me from the violated place I knew my house had become.

"I know," I said. "Missed you and Sissy, too." Neither of us knew what to say next, but the clouds above fresh coffee pulled at us with a familiar gravity.

"Look," he said, "I never got to say stuff to you after Randy died. You drifted pretty far away after that. Hell, that crazy guy should've died a dozen times diving off The Falls like he did." Then, staring at his jellied toast, his words seemed too empty to handle.

"It's okay, Gus. I know. We three were family. But the truth is, I haven't been on stable ground since my dad disappeared a long time ago. These five years since Randy passed only laid out more big cracks for me to fall into."

"Guess that ruckus with Janine didn't help none neither," he said.

"For sure. But it wasn't her. I sort of came apart on her." Gus stared, looking for something, and I knew I needed to talk before he did. "Met a woman in New Orleans I think might understand me."

"They say geniuses are everywhere," Gus said, then stabbed a sausage I hadn't eaten. He grinned like a twelve-year-old.

"Name's Emma. Her ex-husband is the one who robbed me."

Those words set Gus back in the booth as if a bad smell rose from his plate. Then he shrugged his shoulders. "Shelbourn will find him," he said, then bit off a piece of purple toast. Gus paused again, and I expected his next words to be about Earl, but instead he leveled a hard stare.

"You're a dumbass, ain't you?" he said. "You think your dad deserted you, and that Janine did, too. Goober, you got it all wrong. Nobody gave up on you; you gave up on yourself."

Now there was a practical guy, and his bluntness reminded me of good times when the brusqueness between us had been nothing but humor. I thought of those boundaries Em said kids needed. I guess friends build a sanity fence for each other too, even when we don't know we need one.

"Thanks," I said. "Needed some fresh abuse." My chuckle diffused the rising seriousness, but he knew, and I knew. We'd both changed. He sat there a mature adult who'd put together a stable life, while I was still caught in my pinball machine of overreaction. I needed diversion. "So, how's the construction business?"

"Respectable. Landed a new subdivision over in Petal. That place is growing. Also went in halves with my youngest brother, Karl. A body shop in North Forrest. High-end stuff not wrecks. The guy's an artist, so I'm helping him get a start."

"Good. Out in Seattle, Tim has been an apprentice learning bodywork. Got a talent, I think. Guess he's the one taking after Dad."

"Well, tell him if he ever wants to come back home, maybe we can put him to work. But I got one condition," Gus said. "You got to come back to Friday night poker."

Chapter 85

Mom called at seven. "Are you all right?" she asked. "Two people called me about your robbery before I got your voicemail, and there's a police car out front."

"Everything is fine."

"What did they steal? You don't keep anything valuable, do you?"

"No, but Mom, I recognized the guy. Emma's crazy ex-husband. He's a meth-head. But listen to me. He knows where you live; that's why the police car is there."

"What does that mean?"

"It means we're putting your valuables in the safe deposit box. That creep is probably in another state by now but no need to take chances."

"Do you think I should go to Meridian and stay with Dena a while?"

"Not a bad thought. Or you can stay here for a few days. I'm buying another gun today and getting a security system. We're getting you one, too."

"He took your guns? Now I'm scared."

"I'm coming over right now."

"No, I'm going to Teensa's and then I'll come to your house."

My phone rang the instant I replaced it into the cradle. "Don't you worry, Roy has called out the army. The sheriff is on his way to Hattiesburg to meet with your detectives."

"Good, but Earl said he knew where Mom lives."

"Oh my God. He's going to end up dead. Maybe that's what he wants."

"If he messes with Mom, his wish is coming true," I said.

After hanging up, I sat immobile until a red cardinal slammed into the window by the den. Sometimes they see themselves in the mirror-effect and attack. The jolt landed at exactly the moment I realized Earl's intrusion was the misdirection I needed to figure out why Dad had gone silent. *He wouldn't desert us again.* The stale air convinced me to walk down to the old birch tree. Though I felt heavy as a dump truck, I climbed.

As my feet dangled in the cool, the separation from the ground reminded me how disjointed my whole adulthood had been. But for a short beat, I was a boy again with all my confusion left down below and the spirit of my past sitting up high with me.

After an hour, I inched out onto that old elevator limb, then paused while Gus and Randy yammered in my memory, those lost days when the unknown wasn't fear but simple thrill. We'd flirted with disaster too many times to count: The Falls, the high rope swing at Blue Lake, and that time my Honda 50 couldn't make the curve by the gravel pit when that thud into the azalea bushes ripped a whole in my side that took four stitches.

The thinning fog warmed on the day, and maybe it was the oxygen from the trees, or even the exercise of pulling my lard butt up that spiral of limbs, but halfway down I remembered that little boy at the zoo watching his red balloon drift away. Innocent, oblivious to time's seizure of his life, color and a dangle of string leaving him travelling the unnoticed way. So much depends upon a red balloon.

Chapter 86

May began with poker night. Down the stairs to Gus's basement, the merry-go-round of my life spun in reverse. "Lookie here, my favorite donor has arrived. Hope Janine left you a couple dollars to lose," Gus said. Blurting from his chair, he bear-hugged me, and immediately a Budweiser dissolved the space between sympathy and sarcasm.

A few minutes later, Sissy came downstairs, carrying a brown paper bag. "For such a momentous occasion, I bought you a six-pack of that horrible Pabst Blue Ribbon you love. It's cold. You guys don't leave any of it behind." She plopped it on the table, then mussed my hair without another word. The five other guys at the table helped me christen my moment of return to the bubble I'd let slip away.

I stayed until eleven, winning and losing about the same amount, but I wanted to get home and finish my letter to Emma. I only drank two beers, and everyone kidded me that my ex-dominatrix still had me on a ball and chain, but I told them I was taking antibiotics. Some habits make for difficult change.

A month earlier, Emma and I had begun writing serious letters, not emails, and my periodic installments became a form of meditation. After brushing my teeth most nights, I wrote a few paragraphs so that individual mailings to her might reveal days of thought rather than the narrowness from one sitting. There, sticky words flared as a collection of daily detail, the same sensation I had each night as I opened my volume to Proust's river of words.

That poker night clued me to familiarity I'd forgotten, and while Emma and I studied the discipline of snail mail, we tried not to let Earl interfere. His malignant presence needed to be removed, and I wanted a no-Earl world. Dad had been silent for almost a week, and the panic of fresh abandonment flowered like roses in May, but I refused those thorns and instead fed the urge to call Vi, though I never did.

Wednesday after midnight, I tore into writing, afraid to stray too far from the chronic worry of how to tell Mom the truth about Seattle. I immersed Raja in the birth of Astra, my streaming catharsis defending me yet again against the darkness of uncertainty. Once more I tried calling Dad. His voicemail had stopped answering.

Missing my guitar, I wanted to hold Em, and the chill of separation sent me walking onto the front porch. In my mailbox, Janine had left that old kaleidoscope Dad had given me eons ago. Patterns. Chaos as pieces. I was a core of disorder. Maybe I didn't have to be practical or artistic or have all the answers, didn't need the hard edge of words to make myself whole. Maybe life is only worry twisted into a story.

Chapter 87

Emma had a seminar to attend over the weekend, so I planned to barbecue chicken for Mom. I committed to myself that if Dad hadn't called her yet, then I would reveal my secret. Saturday morning opened with bright sunshine.

Around eleven, I finished ironing my shirts for the week, hoping to save a little money on dry cleaning, the weekend ritual helped ready me for the hyper order of Monday. As I walked to the closet to hang up my work, a car crunched the gravel outside. As usual, Mom must have come early, surely with a load of peas to shell, and I braced for her mocking my ironing skills which she found amusing.

Passing through the den, I looked out front but no car. *Must be in the back.* That probably meant she'd brought something heavy like a whole bushel of purple-hulled crowder peas to keep her awake while we watched the Braves on television. Mom believed she must bring more food than she eats, or world equilibrium might tilt out of balance.

Popping open the kitchen door, I expected to see her lugging something up to the porch, but instead I saw only a newish white pickup truck with Louisiana plates. The idea it might be Roy excited me. On the truck bed, a green tarp covered something. I rushed down the steps, but no one was there.

About halfway to the strange vehicle, I heard a voice coming from the front of the house. "There you are. Knocked on the screen door but no answer," a man in khaki-colored coveralls walked toward me.

Under his big floppy hat, an ultra-white face beamed, dad had shaved his beard and trimmed his long hair. "Well, thank you. It's good to see you too," he said, his little jibe jolting me back into realizing I still hadn't spoken.

"I've called you a dozen times," I said. He kept walking while surveying my yard.

"Lost my cell, but you came to see me, so I'm returning the favor. Even brought you a present." He moved toward the truck, chatting about how nice my home looked, but the habit of words failed me, and with a flick of flamboyance, he whipped off the tarpaulin. If it had been a woolly mammoth, I would have been less shocked at what I saw. Dad hiked his foot onto the bumper as if a teenager again.

"It can't make up for them lost years, but I need you to know I never stopped thinking about you and your mom."

In the truck bed lay the *Saturday* sculpture from Iron Arts, the father and son holding between them a stringer of fish. Through the bottom of my soul, a leak ruptured, and poisonous, corrupted misunderstanding raced to escape. Dad stared at the black iron, and the flicker in his eyes hinted of his own movie reeling a lost past.

He touched the metal boy. "I made this piece, and another one, years ago. Never finished them because I couldn't figure out how to show them to you."

"Dad? Are you Max—I mean Mobile Max—from New Orleans?"

He stepped backward in whitewash. "How do you know that name?"

"This sculpture came from Iron Arts, Reid Perder's shop, right?"

He turned to walk away, then looked sideways. "Now I get it. That fish you brought to Tim, Reid made it, right? I thought I recognized his touch. This here was a hunk of crudeness when I left Louisiana. Reid finished it."

"Mr. Perder told me the guy who made this was a real artist." Dad tensed as he crawled back through time, searching for what he'd lost, or simply left behind. "Dad, when I saw this work in New Orleans, I told myself it was something you could have done. I swear I did. Something about the scene reminded me of the Tickfaw."

The screen door to the kitchen screeched as the rusty spring winced a complaint. Mom stood calmly on the porch, and inside my gibberish-filled head, I figured something wasn't right. She didn't seem surprised at all. With a slap, she dusted her skirt, looking sharply at the old door.

"Here you are," she said. "Didn't you hear me pull into the front yard? Good Lord, had to lug those two pies in all by myself."

Dad placed a hand on my shoulder. "She knows," he said. "Started with coffee at her house. You're my second stop." The unfinished project of my life unfolded over the next few hours as days remembered and days that never happened. Both Mom and Dad studied my reactions to see if I caught the little weavings of detail now fraternizing as pieces of a family puzzle being put back together.

"No, Reid said I could have this piece for the back pay I never picked up. Said I could have the other one, too, if I'd come back to work for him. He's getting older and maybe needs a little more help. Wants to get away from the paperwork, too, but that job ain't for me."

"Why don't you sell *Saturday* yourself?" I said. "Maybe it could help pay off the Seattle shop." I even surprised myself with how stupid this sounded. Two hours earlier, he'd given me an incredible gift and my response now was to have him sell it like a prize watermelon. "Sorry, I didn't mean to sound ungrateful, just thought, maybe. . ."

"Slow up, son. This whole situation is a shock—I know—but hear me out because I can't stay around here long." I looked at him and then Mom. She seemed way too comfortable.

"Okay," I said, "but first tell me something. How long has Mom known you were alive?" She stepped between Dad and me.

"You already know that answer; I've always known. But Thomas showed up at daylight this morning. That was my first proof. We talked nonstop until this moment, and I know pretty much all I need to about Seattle and Tim. What I don't know is whether your dad is a fugitive because he ran out on the final IRS paperwork."

"Look," I said. We paid off the settlement back then and you never heard anything else from the government, right? And you never collected the life insurance? We may not even have a problem."

"I'm still paying the premiums, too," Mom said.

"Wish I'd known that a long time ago," Dad said. "But I suspect them IRS buzzards ain't done with me. Don't matter. I'll face it. I'm tired of living like a scared rabbit." His voice lost commitment to what he was saying like maybe he didn't know if he had the will to remake a whole life. I had to fight off the thought that he might run off again.

"Listen, here's what's going to happen," Mom said. "Larry will talk to Ira and find out if there's still trouble with the IRS. We've got to bring that to certainty. If we have to, I'll use the money I saved." She and Dad didn't even look at each other. This deal had already been struck.

"After that mess is figured," Mom said, "if there is any money left, maybe we'll try to pay off the Seattle shop. Thomas already told me the owner is a swindler, but we're invested, so we got to try. But here me now: I don't want Tim staying out there on the other side of the world. They don't even have butter beans and okra out there."

"Woah, woah. Tap the brakes, folks," Dad said. "What if Tim don't want to move back south? He likes this Cheryl girl." Mom and Dad looked at each other, both a little wilted, and then she walked over and cupped both hands onto my face.

"I don't care what it takes, but we're getting this family back together even if we need the governor's help," Mom said. "And, Larry, that's where you come in."

Chapter 88

Monday smudged with disappointment as two contracts fell through and my best salesperson, Doug, resigned. When Ira called at three, I prepared for the bad news. "Look, Larry, he won't have to go to jail, but probably owe a fine."

"You sure?"

"No. That's what my contacts say."

"Okay. Please start the process and find out when Dad needs to appear."

My parents wanted an endpoint and took the news as positive. Dad also said Ladrone would take an early payoff for the business if we paid a twenty percent penalty on the balance.

On Friday, karma came to visit. At four, my office door opened and there stood the VP of HR. Thirty minutes later, I headed to my car with a box of personal items and a two-week severance, Humpty Larry again celebrating the thrill of gravity. Why I had a smile on my face wasn't clear. Maybe Spinoza was right, and I was only a rock confusing freedom with momentum, but the fizz of liberation sure felt like hope.

For two hours, I speed-walked the path at Hattiesburg Zoo, trying to weld together this inappropriate giddy sensation with the dread of Friday night poker. But unpacking the old skill set, at eight I drank beer, laughed, and contributed ten dollars without hinting that I'd soon be collecting unemployment. At midnight, Gus walked me to the car.

"I see you've gotten better at cheating," I said.

"No, better at letting suckers like you beat yourself." He placed a pinch of Copenhagen snuff under his bottom lip.

"Gus, I got fired today. Getting awful good at rejection." He studied my grin.

"It ain't rejection. See, what you put out into the world comes right back to you. Ain't you ever done any yoga and learned what karma is?" He leaned against my car. "But while you're wandering through that idea, tell me something, do you still know how to work a hammer?"

I barely remember leaving, though I'd only had three beers in four hours, so instead of heading home, I picked up a coffee at the Two-Acre and for no sane reason drove north. Going south would have put me at Emma's in two hours, but the night sprawled moonless with white border lines along the highway framing pine trees wandering as shadows who'd lost the sun.

After a few miles, the heater became so hot that I thought I was jogging. The moment sharpened as sweat burned my right eye stretching a tiny rainbow between me and my windshield. And from the scratchy blur, that cool steely darkness from Iron Arts returned me to the aura of mystery that had filled me that first day at Reid's studio. And into the overripe air of my car, an idea leapt into being, a formed thing already too big for the box of me and swollen with a yearn to be spoken.

Chapter 89

Mom left for Meridian to stay with Dena, so I packed extra clothes for my trip to Emma's. At four, I approached the elevated highway over Pontchartrain and studied a freighter passing underneath. Then, up the span I cruised with my windows rolled down and the salty wind slapping my face. Ahead, cranes and barges clumped together on the shoreline of this urban reef alive outside my windshield.

Emma had forgotten to tell me about Flo's birthday party, so I was already an hour late, but I had a stop to make first. A half-hour later, I pushed open the familiar door garnished with roses.

"Hello there, my friend," Reid said. "How about a cup of joe?" A quick scan revealed the open slot next to *Summer*. "What brings you this way? More training?" His casual tone left me a half-beat off sync as I realized Dad hadn't told him anything about his Hattiesburg life.

"Flo's party, sixty-fifth, you know," I said.

"Oh yeah, I'll drop by later. Trying to avoid the devil juice these days," he said.

Reid poured an oil slick into my cup.

"But there's something else I need to talk to you about," I said.

"Well, son, let's have it. You need another fish? I could raise the price if you like?"

"No fish today, but thanks for the offer. But I do have an idea I'd like you to chisel on."

"Okay," he said. "You want a job?" Black hotness sloshed onto my shoes.

"Well, maybe, but that's not exactly why I'm here. Reid, do you know who I am?"

"Well, thought you was Larry Winstead."

"I'm still Larry. But what I mean is do you know my father?"

"Now you got me scrambled. You said he was dead. Right?"

"I did. But his personnel file has been updated. See, my dad is Thomas Winstead." No reaction. "That's the fellow you know as Mobile Max."

Reid's coffee cup shattered in a crude dark lake. "What? I don't understand."

"Come with me," I said, and we walked outside. After opening the trunk, I lifted the blanket covering *Saturday*. Reid turned Wonder-bread white.

"Let's go back inside," I said. "I got an idea for you to ponder."

Chapter 90

Forty-five minutes later, the hive in Flo's Diner buzzed with people swooping in patterns of group chatter. I didn't see Em, so I eased over to the counter.

"Is that my birthday hat?" Flo asked, pulling me into a hug. "Your sweetie went to pick up her friend, Sally. She'll be right back. She about gave up on you."

"Had some business on the way. But Happy Birthday." I handed Flo the gas station hat I bought in Slidell, sequins spelling out the phrase: *Mardi Gras is my birthday party.* Thunder cracked from across the room.

"Mama's boy! Get on over here." Roy's face was splotchy as a bowl of okra and tomatoes. Perhaps the heater was running a bit too hot. Beer and wine flowed, music rattled the windows, and worries hid behind hugs and laughs. When Emma pulled into the parking lot, I went out to meet her.

"There's my prince charming," she said. "Larry, meet Sally Purdy, from over in Waveland. Best dancer you ever saw." The smell of Chanel intoxicated me after Em hugged my neck. The rest of the afternoon saturated with boiled crawfish, fried speckled trout, and enough desserts to populate a diabetic hospital. Not wanting to appear snobbish, I partook of seconds on everything.

Emma and Sally drifted off into old friend stories, so I pulled Flo to the side. "Think I could see *Prism of Friends* one more time? Had myself a little setback this week, but I want to put down a hundred-dollar deposit. Can give you the second half next time I'm in town."

"Maybe you should talk to Emma first? Get a better price."

"Nope. It's for sale, and I'm buying it. Collecting upstart female artists, you see." Flo, of course, had no awareness of Maya's paintings at home, but the idea of artwork binding together people merged with my three-glass wine vision to fill me with hope.

"Your call. Consider it sold," Flo said.

Later that evening back at Emma's, the euphoria of pretend wealth faded into the reality of unemployment. But as always, while I'd lolled, Em cruised. Producing a surprise, she revealed two finished paintings: the exterior of Roy's cafe, and my favorite, a young girl looking up at a red balloon escaping to the clouds.

Em's volcanic creativity had been prescient, as two days before I'd received a letter from Maya informing me Alfredo also wanted Emma to join the February gathering at his Argentine ranch. Em was still fermenting from the call when I gave her the news.

"I'm going to sell these and put the money toward my South American airfare." Her youthful enthusiasm swept me back into breathable atmosphere, and I knew I was going to buy this new balloon painting, too.

"You going to show them at Flo's?"

"Yep. And Reid said I could hang things in his shop, too. I told him about Alfredo's summit."

Her exuberance intoxicated me, but I had to make sure neither Earl nor the disappeared Genies interrupted the night's euphoria.

"And Roy will keep Nicole that month. I'm going to double up on yoga classes, so come February I'm buying souvenirs in Buenos Aires."

"Yes, siree. I'm going to buy me some gaucho gear for sure," I said, remembering the fourteen dollars left in my wallet. For four years, being laid off had nearly snuffed out my confidence as a man, and yet, this time, being fired simply meant I needed to close certain drawers in my life and open new ones. Things would work out, even if I had to hit up Mom for a loan; liberation sometimes comes as debt.

Emma went into the kitchen but spoke through the open door. "Hey, Larry, what were you and Reid talking about so seriously? You had him staring out into space."

The day's movie rewound: "Reid, got a question for you. I met this lady named Viola Veo. Said she'd met you once in the Garden District. You remember her? It was at a Mrs. Tate's house."

"I remember Mrs. Tate. Elegant woman. But not sure about Veo," he said, then scratched his two-day stubble. "But there was a singer years ago called Vi Veo. Not sure if it's the same person."

At that moment, Em's hand had squeezed my neck as she pulled me onto the dance floor to stomp a few toes, and I wondered if Vi had gotten her voice back yet.

Chapter 91

Around three the next afternoon, my phone rang. Reid wanted me to come to his home only a few blocks away. Soon, a wrought iron railing and an iron sculpture of a girl with a watering can reflected an orderly world, even if one a little too museum-like.

"How about a cup of Community?" he asked, then we sat in rocking chairs on the front porch. "That idea you dropped on me yesterday kept me awake all night," Reid said. I rocked faster. "Might be a stretch but having old Max and your son come help in the shop don't sound all bad." A side glance hinted concern. "You don't mind if I call your dad Max, do you?"

"Nope. He's Max to you."

"Anyway, I could use the help. E. C., my best guy, got hurt in some fool car racing mess. Out for a couple of months, maybe for good."

"Sorry to hear," I said.

"But son, I need to tell you I got concerns. Max disappeared like a ghost. Not sure how much trust I got left, though I do admire his skill. Even like him as a friend."

I sipped my coffee without swallowing, The throbbing in my neck sounded like highway traffic. "I understand. Dad let Mom and me down with a ghost move, too. But now I know why. He thought he was helping us."

"Yeah, you told me that, but running off like he did didn't help me none," Reid said. An arched eyebrow spelled his reluctance wasn't a rejection.

"Dad needed to be invisible and knew he couldn't plant roots anywhere back then. Maybe could have explained things better, but to help Mom and me, he had to keep himself free."

"I get that," Reid said. "But I need assurance. I'm too old for guesswork."

We sipped in silence. "If Tim is here, too, that's a real tie-down on Dad. After all this ache he's caused everybody, I can't see him disappointing his family again."

"Could be," Reid said. "But I got a different notion. You said your dad had a little savings, right?"

"Yeah. Not sure how much."

"So, what if Tim came to work with me here in the commercial business like we discussed, but your dad took a different role?"

"You don't want Dad and Tim both to work at Iron Arts?" I asked.

"Kind of. Just listen. I want Max and me to start an art studio together. I got space in Iron Arts. It'll be cheap, a separate business."

"So, Dad would do mainly creative stuff?"

"Eventually. We might need to work towards that transition for a while, especially while we break Tim into the business. But I want to make a showcase where locals can sell their stuff in our studio, like Flo's place but with sculpture and glass, too."

My pacing shifted into warp speed. "I've got the perfect name for the studio," I said. "Reid Thomas Associates."

"I love it," Reid said. "See what you did there, how quick you spotted putting our first names together to capture the whole idea? Larry, you're smart and practical. Maybe I got another idea, too."

"Have a room for authors to do book readings and signings?"

"Hadn't thought of that," Reid said. "Could be? But what I was going to say is that I need a good general manager to oversee both businesses. Somebody to keep things orderly, you know, contracts, advertising, and such. I need a better bookkeeper for starters." His words searched the darkness inside me, and I pictured Leon rocking away on this porch with us.

I hadn't even told Reid about getting fired, but maybe he saw New Orleans clutching me. "You mean me?" I asked. "You want to hire me?"

"Yeah, Larry, you. You weren't too shrewd negotiating that fish I sold you, but I saw you tried to do the right thing. You're a decent fellow, and you don't use your smarts to beat people down. If I was to be the CEO, you could be my general manager."

My shoe-burning pace led me to the realization that what had felt like a negotiation had been something much bigger. Reid held all the leverage over the Winstead clan, but unlike Ladrone, he didn't want to swindle us. "You drive a hard bargain there, Reid. But maybe bringing in a passel of Winstead men might put some fresh verve back into all of us," I said.

"Now before you go thinking you snookered me," Reid said, "I need to add a few details—namely, some Winstead cash. I want to tie all of you in a bundle of ownership responsibility, but I need to figure out some numbers. You understand I'll maintain majority ownership in both businesses as long as I'm alive. This ain't no charity deal, Mr. Winstead."

"Fair enough, Mr. Perder." The calculator in my brain crunched, and I had the weird urge to call Chub. Long-term equity incentives for business performance and growth percolated with a sudden surge of too much energy to sit still, but a coolness settled in as I imagined Tim and Dad reacting, and Mom, too, as she'd have to move to New Orleans. Then the stormy thought zapped me that this arrangement might also starve my writing time. But I couldn't worry about problems yet, I needed to be practical.

"In two weeks, Dad and Tim are coming to Emma's house for Memorial Day," I said. "Let's see if you and I can put a plan together by then. I'll make sure Mom is here, too—she'll have her own vote. In the meanwhile, you figure what kind of stake Dad could maybe buy, and I'll sell a couple of Winstead New York penthouses and figure out what kind of cash we'll have for chipping in. By the way, as general manager, I was hoping to have my own private jet."

Chapter 92

I stayed with Em a few extra days to let my mind fall into the orbit of potentially moving to New Orleans. Walking the river paths at Woldenburg Park became therapy, but I needed more, so on the third afternoon, I stood in front of the New Life church watching people exit the choir room.

"Well, well, my Mississippi trashman?" Leon said. He'd lost weight and looked healthy in his blue sportscoat.

"Had to give the Dalai Lama my news. I'm not a genie anymore." He didn't react. "But I did get to pull one last wish out of the bottle—my dad is alive."

"Tell the truth," Leon said as he glanced up the street toward his house. "Where'd he show up?"

"Seattle. Serendipitous discovery." Leon had to get ready for work, but we sat a moment on an iron bench. "Guess being a district manager was riskier than I figured," I said.

"I'd be willing to take the chance." His words tensed his shoulders. "You got yourself fired, didn't you?" I didn't say anything. "You still writing?"

"Trying to. Lot of confusion these days."

"That so?" He took a pack of Juicy Fruit gum from his pocket and offered me a piece. "How about doing me a favor, would you? Why don't you try and stand up? Go ahead, do it." My face crinkled, but I pushed off the cold bench.

"That ain't what I asked. You stood up. Now this time, just try to stand." After another miscue, I got the point. A minute later, we wandered toward my car.

"You mind if I talk plain to you?" Leon asked. I shrugged. "You got a case of privilege. You thinking life is hard, but you making your own problems."

"But Leon. . ." Then I had nothing to say.

"Your life slants toward options while you mope around studying the past. But the whole time, you got options."

"But. . ." Leon raised his hand as a stop sign.

"Yesterday I ran into an old friend. She told me about her Easter visit up in Hattiesburg with a lady whose son thinks she's a con artist."

"Huh?"

"Now settle down. Vi been knowing all along how you look down on her."

"I never meant to."

"That's your privilege at work, money privilege, life privilege. See, the color of your skin never caused you hardship. Black folks is different. We know people suspicious of us, how they say we got to work our way up where it's okay to give a white boy like you a easy advantage. Now don't get me wrong, black folks make problems for theirselves, too. That's why I'm in this church here today. All I'm saying is we don't all get to start at the same place."

I couldn't immediately process his words. Leon continued: "See, you done got yourself fired, confused your head about your writing, and even went and disrespected about the smartest, kindest woman I know when all she been doing was helping you. You making your own problems." Those white teeth peeked at me, and for the first time in days, I smiled.

"Dang, Leon. You city folks tough on a country boy." He blurted a laugh. "I'm still going to write "War and Peace, Southern Edition," but while I'm running the spell-checker on that project, I came here to talk to you about something different."

"You ain't doing network marketing are you? I don't need no skin lotion." I truly laughed.

"No. I'm not. But I might need a bookkeeper. You still do that on the side?"

"A little. Finished my QuickBooks certification. Even starting part-time at Delgado in a Business program. But the New Life keeps me pretty busy."

"This is all early stage, but a friend of mine owns a business here and wants to lighten up on his workload. My dad used to work with him. We're kicking around the idea of Dad and my son joining the business and me becoming the general manager. The first thing I would need is a good bookkeeper, maybe start as a side hustle until we can see what we got. But Leon, if this works, I see you being an owner just like me."

"Hmmm. Thinking big, are you? But this is more conversation than I got time for right this minute," Leon said. "You around next week?" I nodded. He stared deep into me. "Let's talk then, but one question first."

"What's that?"

"You still drinking?"

"Not so bad."

"Uh-huh. Losing your job, leaving your hometown, finding your daddy, you got a lot going on. Might need to slow up a little." Now that was what practical sounds like.

"I know. But I'm getting ahold of my life."

"Good. But this Saturday, we got a special guest talking to the group here, an old friend of mine who seen some big changes himself. Maybe come give him a listen, as a favor to me."

Chapter 93

The following two mornings after Nicole and Em left for the day, I continued patrolling the Mississippi river walkway. Elderly people idled along, artists captured scenes with color, and rollerblade maniacs darted like flies.

After stopping at a park bench to rest, a gust of wind blew a purple shopping bag sporting a smiley face against my leg, and I blurted a little laugh. My irreverent noise frightened a lady walking past, nudging her into a faster pace. I wondered how many white people skittered away when Leon chuckled to himself at some private little amusement, and this kaleidoscope of new understanding about my life twisted another notch. But before I could ponder the meaning of life, I had to deliver an apology.

"I knew you'd be along," Vi said. "Your mama told me the news about your papa." As always, Mom and Vi had scouted the future.

"I guess you two are planning a little crow-eating party for me?"

"No need. You already gorging yourself."

"Vi, I thought finding Dad would straighten out my life. Not so sure now."

"It'll be okay. Let things happen a little. Don't be rushing so much."

"I've made a mess of everything."

"You found your daddy, didn't you? Did pretty good there. You see, character is a thing to be earned. Our mistakes are little trophies that sit right alongside the good things we do, like how you've always been loyal to your mama." And the stained glass in the window behind Vi burned a buttercup yellow.

"How come you never told me you were an owner at The Jazz Station?"

"You never asked."

"This is one of those character lessons, right?" I asked. "Do you think I would have treated you different if I'd known you had a little money? I'm ashamed to say but it did occur to me you could have been a con artist."

"I knew that."

"Guess listening isn't my best skill."

"Give yourself time. Your daddy ain't lost no more; maybe now you unlost, too."

"Yeah. But I need to say something." She sipped her moringa tea. "I treated you wrong. I'm sorry, Vi."

"We're all ignorant, only on different subjects. That's what Will Rogers said, and I believe it. But that's what living is, swapping out the wrong stuff we did for the right stuff we learn."

That word, unlost, became an adrenalin injection, and an image popped into my head of a new character named Katrika, a selfless nun helping poor people in the bowels of New Washington.

The alarm on Vi's watch reminded her of a doctor's appointment, and after a peck on my forehead and assurance her throat was getting better, Vi buried my face in a hug. "I lost my job." She stepped back and cocked her head.

"You didn't lose nothing. Maybe janitorial work ain't your calling? Maybe it is. But the money, the fancy title, that ain't important. Finding love is the real duty of life."

Chapter 94

Tacos for dinner, then while Em showered, Nicole and I read a little poetry. With such a quick mind, she easily memorized, *I'm Nobody, Who Are You?* Then we took on *Mending Wall*, after which I explained that Emily Dickinson and Robert Frost were superheroes.

The next day, Cummings and Eliot and Frost all rattled lines at me on my walk, and I began to pull toward me an image of Chub painting next to this same river. The slosh of river boat waves spoke to me of Raja dabbling water-colored sunsets from his forty-second story apartment as Astra drills her vocabulary "ma-ma." In the dark city below, a young nun, Katrika, delivers into the world a baby boy, the child fated to marry Raja's daughter yammering at the cat asleep on the forty-second floor.

Even on daily meanderings, I carried my pistol. Earl hadn't shown up again, and Roy heard a rumor he'd been spotted in Pensacola, but crazy doesn't just disappear. My paradox of sympathy and resentment for Earl left me conflicted as I grappled with the idea that he'd only seen me as stealing his family. His response had been to steal Emma's hope. But Earl hadn't succumbed to some unfortunate fate. He'd made choices. I wondered about that old girlfriend, "pedaling cocaine dreams," Em had called it. Why had he bought that motorcycle that so wrecked his body? Earl could have been a storehouse of different people, maybe a shop owner, or a small-town mechanic, maybe an artist venting the rebellion of a discontented life. But he became corrupted potential, the pitiful result of blinded life.

What would have happened without Mom to anchor me after Dad left? That was her Lord Jim moment. Or if the Genies hadn't led me to

New Orleans? I could have jumped from the ship's deck of responsibility into self-annihilation, but I didn't. I discovered a prism of friends who cared. And I dreaded what I'd do the next time Earl stood in front of me.

Emma and I orbited one another in strengthening gravity. Hours with her passed without a timepiece, ticks of time gradually tightening the bond between us as we allowed normal to deepen. Casual life became familiarity without binary swings of emotion. She painted with ferocity; I wrote and walked. That first week of drama-less living I joked that we were in a "post-sauce" phase: I'd decided not to drink alcohol until I could taste South American hospitality, and Em committed to a life-long ban on red pasta sauce.

Along the unnoticed way, I'd lost the conflict about becoming a serious writer; instead, I became a busy writer while still managing part-time hours with Reid. And neither the future nor the past overwhelmed the present.

Chapter 95

Mom called Saturday to say she'd decided to stay at Dena's house another week, so Em and I settled into a routine, one without mention of Earl. Later after parking at New Life, I heard voices in the choir room, then recognized in the dozen gathered people the pregnant girl and the gentleman with the Fedora.

"Let's get started, folks. My name is James Augustine Aloysius Joyce, and I'm an alcoholic. I lived in Shreveport most of my early life where my mother was an English teacher, hence the famous Irish writer's name she assigned me, but my friends call me, Jimmy." Already I liked this Filipino of about fifty. "My saxophone is how I met, Leon. But he asked me to speak to you today about self-talk rather than music." Leon interrupted with a raised hand.

"I should have mentioned Jimmy and I played gigs back in the nineties. . ." Leon almost missed his chair he sat down so abruptly.

"I had a perfect childhood. Mom taught high school; Dad was in construction. We didn't much go to church, and my parents often had friends over to the house. I was bookish with no siblings, no real friends." Jimmy paused for a sip of water, his face the color of a new basketball.

That all changed one November day when I came home from band practice and found my parents unconscious on the couch, a candle knocked over had caught the curtains on fire. I panicked, not knowing whether to put out the fire, drag my parents outside, or run for help, so I stood paralyzed with a broke mind." He paused to let us all build this image. "Until a neighbor yelled through the front door. I don't remember what happened next, but I never saw my Mom or Dad alive again."

"They died?" an elderly white woman in the second row blurted. Leon tamped his hand toward her as if asking for patience.

"Overdosed on heroin cut with rat poison. At the time, I believed the smoke from the fire killed them, but a few years later my Aunt Vickie told me the truth. After that, I became a different person. See, that day when I went into my house, I never even choked on any smoke, and yet everybody let me think my parents had died of smoke inhalation. It was all a big lie to protect me."

His stare touched every face in the room. "I turned fifteen before my aunt told me the truth. She was moving me and her to New Orleans and wanted me to know the danger of drugs in an urban city. I took the news as a chance to go crazy, stealing, drinking, smoking pot, trying to prove the world couldn't trust me just like I couldn't trust it. Does this make sense to anybody?" He paused, then pointed at the old man in the funky hat.

The old man faltered, then spoke: "When I was a teenager, my dad shot my mom in the face, then killed himself. I know what you saying about not trusting things." Group sharing went on for a few more minutes with Jimmy calling on each one of us to speak; several people only nodded that they understood, me being one of them.

"I quit school and became a full-time criminal," Jimmy said. "A few years later, I got caught robbing a woman in Biloxi and spent seven years in Parchment. That proved to me that I was human trash and that my parents were right not to have loved me." He stared at the pregnant girl. "My thinking was all upside down until prison where I met William Fault. He got me to reading books again. I even wrote a thousand-page journal. Got my GED and declared myself to the Lord. I'm here today to pay forward what Bill Fault taught me and to tell you something you need to know—how we talk to ourselves is who we become."

He turned to the pregnant girl. "Tell me something. Is there an idea you believe for certain happened but that might not actually be true, like me believing smoke killed my parents, or maybe like they couldn't have loved me or they wouldn't have done what they did."

"Well, I don't know," the girl said. "Maybe. I feel guilty my baby doesn't have a real home to be born in."

325

"Okay. So, what about the fellow who helped get you into this situation? Do you blame him?"

"Both of us, I guess. I'm stupid. Had a good job but drank it away. Pretty sure I ain't a good person."

"There it is. Most of us think we don't deserve happiness, aren't good enough to be loved because of the mistakes we've made." A murmur passed through the room. "But there's something you need to know. This violence and betrayal we've all known, these traumas are what feeds the belief that we don't deserve to be loved. That's what happened to me. I believed my parents abandoned me, and that idea became the certainty proving to me I was worthless. Every decision I made after that served to bring me misery." Two women in the last row began mumbling to each other.

"Please, let's not have side conversation until Jimmy has finished," Leon said. The room silenced.

"I got more and more angry. Aunt Vickie tried to help, told me she loved me, but I saw her as fake, lying again. I didn't want to feel anything, so I put a wall around me to keep everybody out. But what I didn't realize was how this wall also kept out my love for music, and books, and for any chance I might have for love or friendship. But most of all, this wall kept me in a prison of pain. I sentenced myself to unhappiness, and every day I served my time like I had no power to change anything." Again, he stopped. The room, quiet as a morgue, had its own pulse not quite audible.

"Do you see how we self-medicate with alcohol, or violence, or sex to dull down that pain we always keep alive? How we numb ourselves any way we can? That same numbing that destroys joy, and thankfulness, and creativity, anything that could give us hope?" Another group was scheduled to use the room and someone knocked softly at the locked door, but not an eye left Jimmy.

"Now folks, give me one more listen before we go. You're good enough. You were always good enough. You got to keep telling yourself that because it's the only way you can ever find love again. If you feel guilty about choices you've made, that's okay. Guilt comes from what you've done and it's your signal it's time to make different choices. Guilt is action gone wrong, but being ashamed of who you are, that's different. Shame murders your soul. Feeling ashamed of who you are as a person amplifies that same corrupted voice that's been telling you you're worthless. Right now, today, this minute, that weary habit of shame has to stop. You hear me? Do you hear me? You're good enough, you're good enough, you're good enough to be loved. And you always were."

Chapter 96

When Jimmy stepped back toward his chair, every person in the room exploded to their feet, shaking their fists in the air as if a revolution had sparked and the guillotine of truth had come down on the oppression of broken belief. The group rushed Jimmy to shake his hand, but I needed to be alone. Outside, the clear air skittered through the new growth on those big red oaks, and after plopping down on a steel bench, I let a percolating idea for a poem wander through my head.

"Thought you slipped off," Leon said. But before I could answer, the fedora gentleman whistled for Leon to come over and speak with a young woman seemingly in distress. Jimmy sat down on the bench with me.

"I didn't want to leave before I told you how profound your talk was," I said, "you touched a lot of people in there." Jimmy draped his arm over the back of the bench.

"And what about you? Did you get touched?"

"Yeah. You reminded me what a good liar I've been." He offered a slight nod.

"Leon told me a little about you finding your dad. That's good news, right? You got to prove yourself wrong." I wasn't sure if that was a joke. "Larry, you ever think about letting a higher power help you a little?" I don't know why, but his shift gave me a little comfort as I knew where he was heading.

"Already helping me. Found my dad, right?"

"Guess so. But you're also at an AA meeting."

"Yep. But your talk showed me something new. See, after dad disappeared, I convinced myself he was either dead or had deserted

Mom and me. Never even considered there could be another reality. But the truth I didn't understand was that he'd made a sacrifice. His duty was to his family and that meant he had to fix his money mess the only way he knew how, by disappearing. His plan was broken, but his heart was good. And it was me who became absolutely certain of something uncertain."

"Sounds like you're making progress but could still use a chat with Jesus."

"Maybe, but see, I got a voice in me I need to deal with, and it's getting stronger. It used to call me a failure. Now, that voice is speaking something different."

"You becoming a preacher are you?"

"Nope. But I do want fresh words to help me write about broken people finding other broken people and how together they can find ways to make things whole.

Leon walked up to the bench, and I could tell he'd been listening.

"Sit down, Leo; your friend here is teaching me," Jimmy said.

"Look, I don't know anything; I just know what lost looks like. But I'm going show up here at New Life for a while and try to talk myself into getting unlost." Leon showed me those nice teeth.

"You doing good, white boy. Keep talking."

Chapter 97

Nicole was downstairs with the twins for the night, so back at the duplex, I sat on the couch in the quiet listening to Jimmy's voice on the little tape recorder I'd slipped into the AA session.

At eleven, Em came in from working the cafe. "You okay?" she asked.

"Yep. Listening to something I want you to hear. I made a pot of tea."

After Jimmy's thunderous finale, Em wrapped her warmth around me.

"I love you, Em. I used to think I didn't deserve you, but now I know I do." I picked up the pad of paper I'd scribbled on all night, then handed it to her.

"No, You read it to me," she said.

"It still needs work." She didn't even blink.

The Crossing

Skies color
After you, and
A city reveals
With tofu and tea,
Sunshine glass drops,
And soft-bended steel.

A prism in the shade
Is truth with no voice
Railing at the dream
Of all that should have been.

Man-child to man in
A city finding strength,
Artists and lovers,
Climbers of the Sun,
Fleeing what happened
On handholds of one.

Fate flies as a rock
Mindless in the air,
Not knowing when,
Not knowing where, so
We Chop, we Carry,
We entangle the news
Of me becoming me
And you becoming you.

"And know:

That the shining behind my eyes
Comes from a life divine."

L.W. & LS

Chapter 98

The end of May brought us to Memorial Day repurposed as a Thanksgiving family reunion. After reading Proust until two, I woke up on Em's couch at daylight replaying my previous nine months, that belated gestation of my adulthood.

Thoreau once climbed Mount Katahdin in Maine, and when he pushed through the cloud layer near the summit, he experienced contact with something, a power, "not bound to be kind to man." As he peered into the rawness of nature, into the face of indifferent forces, he realized that man's quest of the flesh is a search for spirit, the awareness of a realm into which consciousness cannot roam though we sense its impalpable kinship with mind. My moment didn't offer such a window into an austere universe or leave me trembling before nature's unremitting indifference to man but rather left me with an image of the dormancy I'd locked myself in for two decades.

The sweet smell of Emma's coffee drifted over me while her cranberry aperitif collection flirted with the early sun to share a wine-dark red above me. But before the rich dark color sent me drifting off into the idea of blood recognition, that family root now beginning to thrive again, my cell phone cracked the tinted light.

"Hello, son."

"Hey, Mom. Where are you?"

"Crossing Lake Pontchartrain. Should be at the bus station in half an hour. Vi is picking me up. Her sister has asked to meet me out at the cemetery. Can we pick up anything on our way to Emma's?"

"No, we're good. Roy's boiling fifty pounds of crawfish and smoking a ham and Emma is seasoning Big Bird for the oven. Says she knows Dad and Tim haven't had a real turkey day for a while, so she's calling this weekend Memorial Day Thanksgiving. She's a lunatic. You girls go have fun with the dead folks."

"Before I forget," Mom said, "tell Emma I love that painting she sent. It looks just like you, so important and handsome."

"Yeah, okay. We'll see you and Vi later."

Our conversation rattled an idea out of hiding—this extended family group of ours was becoming a societal swirl, the kind of human gravity that becomes the foundation of pioneer cities or maybe new religions. Familiar is what family is. But my deep thought thinned as I imagined Mom's face thinking about her boy, unwavering in focus, that same loyalty that kept Dad's existence alive, even as foolish mouths tossed ridicule. Her tenacity was family gravity, but I hadn't understood the science of loyalty back then.

Shards of light from the beveled shelf splayed on the far wall, each a fine true spectrum of color. The wholeness of the light made sense to me, the paradox of one versus many, and I wondered if all people must split apart before they can form the entirety of self. Maybe not. But I did.

Years of blind caroming had felt like balance, normal almost; and the firmness of the heavy couch beneath me reminded me of Plateau Rock. I was still unsure what this shaky voice within me wanted to say, but as I studied the rainbows on the wall, I realized the prism doesn't judge the light. I needed to remember that.

One day I might leave books behind for others to read, books that might help someone. Mom's fingerprints would be all over those volumes, and Dad's, too. Thank God for that. But maybe out there, a soul needed to hear my voice the same way I'd needed Maya telling me I was an artist and Jimmy testifying that I mattered. Sometimes simple words make profound impact, good and bad. But absorbing Mom's unflinching faith and Emma's belief in me had reframed my structure of self, and I no longer worried so much about what might happen tomorrow. The world didn't seem so dense, and I wasn't so complex I couldn't understand myself; but like Raja, I was still repairing damage. Those twenty years of stumbling had left unfinished maturing I'd tried to ignore, but a little chopping and carrying would fix that. There's only one story to be told about life: a person is born, then dies. The real importance is the thing in between, the commitments we refuse to abandon. It took both Mom and Dad to teach me that.

As I looked back on things, I knew I'd be all right. We all would be. Yeah, we still had plans to work out with Reid, and on Sunday, Leon and I were having coffee at Iron Arts, but a new gravity had touched us all, and we just needed to let it take us home. Dad still needed footing to find his lost life. I would help him with that. The journey of living reinvents itself with no real stopping or starting, only the illusion of those shifts. And from where we now sat, maybe, just maybe, the window to normal would stay open so all of us could lean in and see the future. I was pretty sure that with Emma by my side, we were climbing through that window together, going to the other side of normal to find that unspoken language that informs the soul and paints truth with color and words.

"Larry, quick, come in here. You have to see what Reid brought," Emma said.

With fantasies of a gigantic chocolate dessert from old sweet-toothed Perder, I stuck my head into the living room. Reid was chatting with Nicole, and there in the pastels of muted emotion, his stormy-blue eyes danced, a father's mournful remembrance of his own lost child, I figured. Something timeless surrounded that image of the gray, old father smiling at the young girl, a moment grasping in time for an image never to be lost, or discovered again. I ached in sympathetic intercept for all that missed life. Nicole laughed at his magic trick with a quarter, no notice of time or void.

"Well, hello there, Reid." Reaching over to shake his hand, I noticed his smile not on me but directed toward the table behind me holding one of the most beautiful things I'd ever seen—an inlaid mother-of-pearl guitar with polished burl so luxurious it would make a Rolls-Royce envious. My lungs struggled to function.

"Wanted to say thanks for all your good work and to offer a little welcome to the city of New Orleans." As I lifted the gorgeous instrument, the color swirled in blending lights, and I became dizzy. Words wouldn't form. Reid cracked my stupor.

"No, son, you play it, not drool on it." He took the guitar and magic flowed in a song I'd never heard, sounds I imagined were a lost daughter whispering in his head, echoes of loss and abandonment that unlike Reid, no longer rattled in my ear. "It's yours now, son."

"I don't. . . It's too much. Thank you."

Nicole accidentally knocked a glass of milk on the coffee table, so I placed the guitar on top of a bookcase and reached for the paper towels. Em whispered in my ear: "See. Anthony has lots of friends."

Her beautiful eyes lit up the room, and I knew that this day was one of Vi's lighted handholds leading out of the abyss falling away behind me now. Reid may not have felt this same holistic connection, not yet anyway, but he too had begun to understand that healing is more profound than regret. As he slipped quietly to the back of the room, I remembered all the beauty he'd made, and all the sadness he'd known. His was a life of fullness, not perfection, and a tasted bitterness most of us never want to sample. But still, I recognized that vintage humility, the kindness of a good heart undiluted by pain. I could help Reid; I simply knew it. Dad already had. The hole in Reid's life couldn't be filled, but it could be improved, and I would get him to help me write a character pursuing exactly that project. Reid didn't realize it, but he was going to collaborate as an author.

It was almost time to go pick up Tim and Dad at the airport, but I already felt their distant touch. It had always been that way, but I had to be baptized by a fall into the rapids of life before I could sense the gravity of love that all along had been reaching across time to buoy me against darkness.

As the front door opened, Mom popped her head through, cornucopia hat first. And then I heard Vi's hoarse but familiar voice: "Yoo-hoo. Party helpers reporting for duty. We brought roses for the table." Of course, they did. Seeing Mom happy again was my greatest joy, and the best part was that it was real. We weren't hiding things or tricking ourselves, and the truth was something we no longer needed to dread.

Yep, this was the day I'd wanted for twenty years, one with full hearts, broken hearts, and hearts as generous as rain all gravitating toward one another. I needed this; we all did. I looked at the guitar and realized Reid wanted me to know he appreciated my bringing back his friend, my dad, back to his shop. Seeing this seasoned man settle into laughter with Mom and Vi, with little Nicole by his side, I couldn't help feeling that when we find loneliness in life, we should be reminded that our journey is simply not yet finished. Finding those dark places within us means we must keep on going till we find that lighted place waiting for us, that hidden handhold someone is offering, even if we don't know it yet.

Souls know what minds struggle to find, and perhaps all that churning inside us helps us understand how to contact that same crazy swirling in other people. Now I'd come to realize the blood and bond linking us together is stronger than any yearn to withdraw, that lesson all these people were still teaching me. And I wondered if Leon could hear me thinking as he moved through a quiet building whispering echoes.

Chapter 99

The feast lasted for hours with music and laughter and Roy even dancing The Twist. At seven the next morning, I slipped into the kitchen to make coffee. Em was still asleep. The door to Nicole's room stood open; Mom and Dad had slept there as Nicole stayed downstairs. A rustling at the front door turned out to be Mom who had taken my car to buy donuts. "Coffee, Mom?"

But before she could answer, a howl exploded outside. "Fire! Fire!" Roy shouted.

I jerked open the door and ran onto the landing to see Roy downstairs with a garden hose spraying down the inferno engulfing my car. In his pajamas, bare feet trying to avoid broken glass, Roy looked like a fireman in a Sesame Street farce. "Molotov Cocktail," he said.

"What's happening?" Emma said, running into the living room.

Mom stepped to the railing, holding out in front of her an object I didn't recognize at first—a pistol. Scanning the driveway, she looked like one of Charlie's Angels ready to play hero.

"What's that?" I asked.

"My new Glock. I call her 'Sweet Love.'"

The End

"We are asleep. Our life is a dream. But we wake up sometimes, just enough to know that we are dreaming."

Ludwig Wittgenstein